It's reality TV.
It's survival with a sociopathic "big brother."
It's a killer's playground where
fear

And the

D0836308

Please turn to the back of the book for a special afterword: "*24/7*: Fact and Fiction."

24/7

Jim Brown

BALLANTINE BOOKS • NEW YORK

A Ballantine Book
Published by The Ballantine Publishing Group
Copyright © 2001 by Jim Brown
Afterword copyright © 2002 by Jim Brown

All rights reserved under International and Pan-American Copyright Conventions. Published in the United States by The Ballantine Publishing Group, a division of Random House, Inc., New York, and simultaneously in Canada by Random House of Canada Limited, Toronto.

Ballantine and colophon are registered trademarks of Random House, Inc.

www.ballantinebooks.com

ISBN 0-345-44698-4

Manufactured in the United States of America

First Hardcover Edition: November 2001
First Mass Market Edition: June 2002

OPM   10   9   8   7   6   5   4   3   2   1

To Franklin and JoAnn Brown (Mom and Dad)
who gave me life, love, and laughter

And to Kathryn who makes that life worth living 24/7

ACKNOWLEDGMENTS

This book would not have been possible without the help of many people. I would like to thank Kenneth and Beverly Herr for their unfailing support; my editor, Joe Blades, for his terrific insights and great patience; as well as the members of the Eugene Professional Writers Group (the Wordos), particularly Jerry and Kathy Oltion.

I would be remiss not to thank my amazingly talented son, Jason Brown, who hears my ideas before they strike the page, and my daughter, Jennifer Brown, who is far away but is always near my heart.

And a special thank you to the "Remarkable Mark," my friend and agent, Mark Ryan of the New Brand Agency, one of the rare and genuine good guys.

The only way to really live is to sometimes be on the edge of living and dying, or danger and nondanger.

MARK BURNETT,
Producer of *Survivor*,
talking about reality television
on NBC's *Today Show*

1 CARRIBEAN SEA

The helicopter dropped from the sky, falling like a grace-less bird toward the abiding sea. Dana Kirsten clutched her seat, willing her hands to be talons. The aircraft, which had seemed incredibly small in Jamaica, now felt positively minuscule.

Like a coffin.

The pilot nudged the yoke. The roaring machine re-sponded like a spirited horse. The descent stopped less than a hundred feet from the water. The pilot looked at Dana, a plug of chewing tobacco causing his lower lip to protrude like a goiter. "You look scared. I thought you said you liked flying?"

Dana took a breath just to see if her lungs were working. "Flying, yes. Falling, not so much."

He laughed. The chewing tobacco formed a black teardrop on the corner of his mouth. "Wasn't trying to scare you. Well, I wasn't trying *just* to scare you. Wanted to show you something." He pointed out the right side.

Below her in what had been a seamless sea, a school of bottle-nosed dolphins sliced through the placidity, carving white gashes in the blue-green canvas. Dana counted eight, then spotted another three dorsal fins farther out to the right. One pair swam so close together that, from her vantage point, it looked as if they were touching.

"That's a mama and her baby," the pilot said. "Here, look at this."

He flipped a switch and a monitor that sat between them winked to life. At first she couldn't tell what she was seeing, then as the pilot manipulated a small, pencil-size joystick, the scene changed, revealing a close-up of the sea speeding beneath them.

"I've got a geo-stabilized camera mounted under the bird. I'll be making a regular flyby while you're on the island. Here, you try it. It's easy. Forward is zoom in, back is pull out, left and right are left and right."

Dana maneuvered the joystick. He was right. It was easy. Within seconds she had found and zoomed in on the dolphins. Sure enough, the one on the left, toward the protection of the pod, was significantly smaller than the one on the right. Mama protecting junior from the horrors that emerge from the wild of the sea. "They're incredible."

"Thank you," the pilot said, smiling as if dolphins were his own creation. "Little odd though. Don't usually see them in this area. Got to be at least a dozen miles from the course they usually run."

For a moment Dana wished she had a camera, then realized how silly that was. Once they landed everything she saw, said, or did would be on camera—everything for the next seven weeks.

"You think that's something, watch this." The pilot hit another button. The scene changed to two people gauzed in static. He turned a small knob and the image cleared.

"Television?"

"Not just television." He flipped a switch on the side of the monitor. Voices issued from a tiny speaker. She could hear perfectly but couldn't understand a word.

"Japanese television," he explained.

"That's nice," she said, not sure what response he was looking for.

"And not just Japanese. Chinese, Russian, every movie

station in creation—I can get them all with this. My brother is in the Navy, works in electronics. He fixed me up with a special satellite dish that will pick up signals others can't. I can watch movies or TV shows from almost anywhere."

"You speak Japanese?"

"Nope, but if I ever learn, I'll have something to watch."

The helicopter overshot the dolphins.

"Do you have to go so fast?" she asked, her stomach still fluttering from their earlier drop.

The pilot dabbed away the teardrop of tobacco with a handkerchief. "You're the one running late."

Running late.

She checked her watch. Late, of course. She hated her watch. Not that there was anything wrong with it. It was a good, durable timepiece. But it always seemed to be mocking her, a jeering, digital reminder of just how late she really was—again.

This time, however, she had an excuse.

Six months ago when she first tried out for *24/7*, America's newest reality television show, she made it all the way to the final round only to miss out by one. Then, less than twenty-four hours ago, Nelson Rycroft, the show's creator, had called. A contestant had dropped out because of illness. Dana was the *new* contestant, number twelve.

And now, thanks to that simple phone call, Dana Kirsten had a chance to win a miracle.

She hadn't felt this good, this full of hope since graduating from high school. A time when, thanks to her talents as an athlete, the world seemed hers for the taking. She had just set two high school track records and won a scholarship to the University of Florida when she became pregnant.

"I hear they've got a doctor, a fisherman, even a former nun on the show," the pilot said. "So what do you do?"

"Depends on the day. Monday through Thursday I'm a checker at Save-a-Lot. Friday and alternate Sundays I work at a boutique in the mall. Saturday night I tend bar. But mostly, I'm a mom."

"Damn," the pilot spit into a Dixie cup he pulled from beside his seat. "When do you rest?"

Dana smiled. "Christmas."

"So what's your husband do while you're off working all them jobs?"

"I'm not married."

"Oh."

The child's father had been a junior in college the year Dana graduated from high school. She thought she was in love with him. And he thought she was a nice distraction from his studies. When he learned of the pregnancy, he went crazy, declaring that the child was not his and calling Dana a "whore," even though she had never been with another man. The last thing he said to her was "I never want to see you again." So far he had gotten his wish.

Pregnancy derailed her plans, and the world that had seemed so bright and full of promise became dark and scary. Though devastated by the news, her parents were nonetheless supportive. But they weren't wealthy and the only way Dana could afford to support a child was to take any job she could find.

Since it is difficult to run track when your body is being measured in trimesters, the scholarship disappeared and with it any chance of college. At eighteen, Dana Kirsten was on her own.

Then Jenna was born and it was as if heaven had opened up and their brightest angel had tumbled into her arms.

"How many kids?" the pilot asked.

"Just one. A girl. Jenna. She's ten."

"Got a picture?"

"Does a dolphin have a blowhole?" Dana pulled a three-by-five from her breast pocket, one of the personal items she had elected to bring with her. The pilot looked at the snapshot, shifted uncomfortably in his seat, then handed it back. "Cute, ah, cute kid."

Dana was so accustomed to the leg braces and arm crutches that she sometimes forgot how uncomfortable they made others.

Jenna was two when the doctors diagnosed her with a severe form of muscular dystrophy. It would be a miracle, they said, if she lived to see her sixteenth birthday.

"She, ah, been in an accident?" The pilot may have been ill at ease, but he was still curious.

"Muscular dystrophy."

He nodded as if, in addition to being the creator of dolphins, he was also a medical expert. "The Jerry Lewis disease, right?"

So much for being an expert. "Yeah, the Jerry Lewis disease." It was a common misconception that there was one disease called muscular dystrophy. In reality there were forty separate neuromuscular diseases. Of which, the doctors told Dana, Jenna had one of the worst.

At that moment a clock had begun to tick. An insidious *tick, tick, tick,* running in the back of her mind, counting down the seconds until Jenna was gone and Dana's world came to a crashing end. For ten years she had been consumed by fear and that ticking clock. She imagined an autopsy revealing deep ruts in her brain worn by the repetitions of the same question. *How can I save my daughter?*

And now—she had a chance at a miracle.

An experimental treatment, being tested in Switzerland but still forbidden in the United States, was offering great promise. It would be years before it was okayed by the FDA, ultimately too late for Jenna. But there was hope.

The winner of 24/7 would receive two million dollars and—as the often-televised promo exclaimed—"his or her heart's desire." Dana's *heart's desire* was for Jenna to become part of the Switzerland test group.

The island jutted out of the sea like a mole on the perfect face of the Virgin Mary.

Vassa Island.

Located between Jamaica and Haiti, it was roughly two square miles in size and shaped like a teardrop.

At their low altitude Dana had to look up to see the top of the massive red-and-white tower rising obscenely in the tropical air.

It's like humanity giving the technological finger to God.

She knew the tower was merely the most visible aspect of the most powerful television transmitter ever created—and just the beginning of the mechanical marvels awaiting below. Even so, an odd sense of foreboding settled over her as she gazed out the window.

Sheer, white cliffs ranging from five to forty-five feet ringed the exterior. A small beach and a makeshift dock, both located on the middle part of the teardrop, offered the only ship access to the sea.

The interior was covered in scrub trees, grass, and underbrush, while closer to the beach, the island was mostly exposed rock and erratic cacti. Made of raised coral and limestone, the island was porous. Sinkholes, the contestants were warned, were a very real danger, particularly following a powerful rainstorm.

It was here that they would play the game. Twelve players competing for seven weeks constantly on-camera and being voted off one by one by viewers. But the real problem would be the challenges. Designed to their individual psyches, they promised to push contestants to face their greatest fears. All in the name of entertainment.

The pilot had slowed the helicopter giving Dana a panoramic view of the island below. The juxtaposition of technology and nature was jarring. On its own, Vassa was a foreboding place but with the remains of no less than eight attempts at colonization, it was downright creepy. Like a ghost town in the wild, wild West.

"Hell of a place to play a game," the pilot mumbled.

"Don't tell me you believe the silly myths?" she asked. "It's just network hype. Embellishment to add another dimension to the show."

He huffed.

"What?" Dana pushed. "You think the place is haunted? You believe in the curse of Vassa Island?"

He scrunched his nose as if detecting a particularly offensive odor. "I've been flying tours out of Jamaica and Haiti for more than twenty years. I've heard things. Seen a few things, too. Way before there was talk of doing a TV show here. All I'm saying is, if it was me, I would keep my eyes open and my mind, too."

The chopper swung in an arc and began its descent.

From 1969 to 1972, the United States had tried to operate a military listening post here. It had been the largest and final attempt to colonize Vassa and now those ruins lay around the island like a strange pox of decay. The old military barracks and several of the other buildings had been completely refurbished for the game. Dana knew, from the show producers, that many of the other buildings had been remodeled as well, but in more subtle and frightening ways. They would be part of the challenges she would have to face.

Only one building was completely new, a smaller circular cinder block construction fifty yards from the main beach: the Round House.

It was here the contestants would receive their instructions and ultimately be voted off the island—one every three days—by the viewing public.

Dana left the helicopter, head bent low, the pilot's words fluttering through her mind like a cold wind. *Keep your eyes open and your mind, too.*

A woman in khaki shorts and a yellow-and-red Hawaiian-print shirt with a stopwatch strung around her neck met Dana at the helipad. "Got to hurry," was her only greeting as she led Dana to the renovated barracks now called "the dorm."

"Put your stuff in here," the woman said. "Yours is the last bunk. The others are being briefed at the Round House."

"Hi, I'm Dana Kirsten." She offered her hand.

"Yeah, I know. I read your bio. Sorry, we've got to hustle. We're live in"—she looked at the stopwatch—"twenty-two minutes and fifteen seconds. Holy shit. No time for formalities." She opened a small, well-padded box. "There's a whole big routine that Smiley is supposed to go through when he puts this on you."

"Smiley?"

"The host, Brant Nelson . . . Ah, don't tell him I called him Smiley, okay? Anyway, there's no time for the routine, so here."

She held out a thin metal collar. Less than half an inch thick, it was dominated by what looked like a jewel in the center, suspended in a circle and connected by crosshairs.

"This is your choker-cam. Click it around your neck."

Dana expected the collar to be cold. It wasn't. The inside was covered in a soft material that made it reasonably comfortable. It clasped in place with a loud click.

"There. Once on, it can be removed only with a special electronic key. Testing one, two, three . . . can you read me?"

"Pardon?" Dana asked. Something on the collar moved. Dana yelped in surprise.

The woman with the stopwatch smiled. "I'm talking to the guy operating your choker-cam." She tapped the glistening object in the center of the collar. "This is a small mobile camera. Someone, somewhere will be watching at all times."

Dana tentatively explored the device with her fingers. "I knew we would be wearing cameras but I didn't know they could move."

"That's why the lens is suspended in the crosshairs. It can cover about a 120-degree radius. And for the next seven weeks it will be your constant companion."

Dana heard a slight whine and felt the tiny camera moving again.

"Raymond," the woman snapped, looking at the necklace. "Stop that!"

Dana craned her neck but was unable to see the lens.

"He was trying to look at your boobs," the woman explained. "Bad Raymond, bad."

SEATTLE, WASHINGTON
Warehouse District

Tucker Thorne knew he was in trouble the moment he saw the mouse. Not that seeing a mouse in a warehouse was unusual, or that there was anything extraordinary about this particular mouse.

No, Tucker was alarmed because the mouse was looking at him.

The warehouse was lit by a series of flat fluorescent panels producing a drizzle of anemic yellow light. Shadows grew like milkweeds, filling cracks and crevices, sprouting across dirty, gray concrete, climbing over boxes. A place far more suited for rodents than reporters or, in his case, a reporter wannabe.

The mouse moved toward him, stopped, stood on its hind legs, sniffed the air in a series of quick twitches, and stared. Its grayish brown fur was the color of cemetery dirt, and its eyes as black as the period at the end of a death sentence.

The concrete floor was cold, and the sensation seemed to be working its way up Tucker's feet and legs, chilling each hair. He shifted his weight, adjusting the DVC-Pro digital television camera on his shoulder.

The mouse, perhaps being camera shy, scurried away, disappearing behind a stack of crates marked HEADLY FURNITURE AMERICA'S FAVORITE with a smaller stamp that read: MADE IN CHINA.

With the mouse gone, nothing moved. Nothing breathed. Quiet and cold. Like the dead.

The silence was worse than the cold. More cunning. More deliberate.

A necklace of sweat began to form just beneath the collar of Tucker's shirt. He forced himself to breathe. The air was gelatinous, thick, and dirty.

Elliot Kay Simon was alive.

Never mind that the FBI had found his body near his exploded van—and across the street, and on the roof of the house next door, and on a parked patrol car where it soiled the exterior and caused the officer to soil the interior.

Never mind that Simon had been identified, absolutely and positively, by dental records.

None of that mattered because Tucker Thorne had seen a mouse.

And now he knew with creepy, crawly certainty that the card-carrying crazy man with a propensity for bombs and the grandiose idea that he was God's best buddy, that *that* man was back from the dead.

Given the insufficient information or time for review, reaching this conclusion was something akin to solving the entire *New York Times* crossword puzzle with nothing but the down clues during a two-minute commercial break. But Tucker was good with puzzles, very good, in fact, phenomenally good. And had been since childhood, when he spent two years confined to a bed with little to do but work crosswords, jigsaws, and brainteasers.

Now his mind seemed to make these impossible leaps without provocation. His *puzzle sense*, Gwen called it. Grief suddenly overwhelmed him, a tidal wave that washed away fear, leaving a barren, mental landscape in its wake. In the year and a half since her death, he had tried to come to terms with his loss. But at times he missed her so acutely he feared his heart would break and, instead of blood, it would be his very soul that bled out.

Clank.

The sound of metal on metal reverberated through the building and shook Tucker from his thoughts.

It was followed by the subtle, more frightening sound of a lock being engaged.

Tucker's puzzle sense made another extraordinary leap in logic. Not only was Elliot Kay Simon alive, he was here, in the warehouse, locked inside with Tucker.

VASSA ISLAND
The Beach

"Stand by," the floor director shouted, and even the jungle seemed to quiet at his command.

Dana Kirsten couldn't feel her toes. She knew they were there because she had seen them just this morning.

But now, with lights blazing, cameras rolling, and knowing she would soon be seen by millions of people the world over, she had the overwhelming urge to look down just to be sure.

The twelve contestants stood in a semicircle in front of the Round House. The show's host, the one the production staffer called Smiley, stood in front of them. A beige mike was unobtrusively clipped to his tan safari shirt.

Oh, God, now I can't feel my legs.

Dana pictured herself toppling over, falling face forward in the sand, numb from the waist down. The absurd image made her—snicker.

The host gave her a mean glare, then shook his perfectly combed blond hair once to give it a slightly tousled look.

"We're live in five, four, three, two . . ." The floor director cued the host, who ignited his signature smile.

Dana Kirsten was suddenly mortified at the thought of being on television—*live* twenty-four hours a day, seven days a week for seven weeks.

Brant Nelson's voice went up in volume and down in pitch as he delivered his carefully written preamble as if it had just occurred to him.

". . . With six hundred and thirty-eight cameras, many of them hidden throughout the complex and jungle, and with each contestant wearing his or her own personal camera, plus the world's most powerful television transmitter, as well as a geo-synchronous satellite, this is the biggest television studio ever created. . . ."

Nelson paused for dramatic effect. Dana heard the howl of fear in the back of her mind.

". . . but television is only part of it. We here at the Globe Television Network have gone the extra mile. With this simple upgrade"—he held up a CD-ROM—"available for purchase at participating stores, you can go to any of those six hundred and thirty-eight cameras any time day or night. Giving you, the viewer, unprecedented access to see everything. And since this is cable, I mean everything."

A nervous chuckle came from the group.

I wonder if they can see my toes? Dana thought.

"These twelve contestants are competing for the amazing prize of two million dollars and their heart's desire," Nelson continued. "But to win your heart's desire, you have to face your greatest fears—and in the next seven weeks these brave competitors will do just that and more . . ."

One of the mobile cameramen walked down the line of contestants shooting from his hip for dramatic close-ups.

He's going to be looking up my nose, Dana calculated.

When the camera came to her, she stuck her tongue out. The cameraman snickered. Dana smiled sheepishly, feeling a little silly. In a contest that depended on viewer participation, maybe giving the audience a raspberry wasn't such a good idea?

The man standing next to her laughed. She gave him a sideways glance and tried to read his name tag. JUSTIN was all she could make out.

He winked. Dana felt herself blush.

"Each contestant has been the subject of an intense psychological study, allowing us to design personal challenges and other little surprises to their individual psyches. In other words, we know their nightmares, and on this island nightmares come true."

More nervous laughter but now with just a hint of anxiety.

"And then there is the history of Vassa Island. See for yourself."

A prerecorded story of the mysterious island, emphasis on *mysterious*, began to play on the monitors.

"We're in tape, people," shouted the floor director. "Back live in a minute, fifteen."

Keep your eyes open and your mind, too. The pilot's warning flashed through Dana's mind like lightning on the horizon. Aware that the report was more fiction than fact, she tried to ignore it. But some words and phrases slipped in: ". . . haunted . . . one hundred disappeared . . . lost . . . twenty-two dead . . ."

Dana looked at her feet, but took little solace from the clear impression of her toes in her Nike running shoes. Her choker-cam began to move. She touched it with her fingers. The lens was pointing down. Remembering her escort's earlier admonishment to the camera tech, she whispered, "Quit looking at my boobs."

"Sorry," said the man next to her.

She laughed, which he must have found encouraging. "I'm Justin by the way."

"Hello, Justin by-the-way. My name is Dana."

"Stand by," screamed the floor director. Dana looked out across the beach, half expecting the seagulls to fall silently from the sky in compliance. "We're out of tape and live in five, four, three, two . . ."

"Brrrr . . ." Nelson shuddered dramatically for the camera. "Not a place I would want to spend the night, let alone seven weeks. But for one of these contestants the curse of Vassa Island will be broken as they walk away a multimillionaire."

A seagull unimpressed with network television wheeled in the azure sky. The surf lapped the shoreline.

"So who are these brave, but foolish, souls? Let's find out."

First in line was a short, bulbous man, soft to the point of being spongy. He reminded Dana of a caterpillar standing upright. A horseshoe of brown hair accented a mushy face with large round eyes, framed in expensive round, gold-rimmed glasses.

"Charles, you're a CPA from Toledo, Ohio," Smiley said.

"That's right, I'm a money man, accustomed to dealing in facts and figures, dollars and cents. And I can tell you right now, you're wasting your time talking to these other losers because Charles Penton is going to be your winner."

Several contestants booed, which only made the CPA's smile larger.

"You seem very confident. Care to tell us why?"

"No offense to my fellow contestants, but I'm smarter than they are—pure and simple. The public is going to recognize that. No way they'll vote me off. And even if they try, it won't matter. Like I said, I'm smart. I'm going to find all the *safety stones*."

Nelson nodded. "Now, we should explain that before every vote, contestants are allowed to use one or all of the safety stones they have collected. One stone eliminates ten percent of the vote against them."

"And ten safety stones make me invincible," the CPA said.

"But first you have to find them," Nelson added. "And I assure you they're not just lying around on the beach."

While Nelson continued working his way down the line, Dana shot a glance at Justin, the man standing next to her. Dark hair, good-looking, incredible eyes and . . .

"Stop looking at my crotch," he whispered.

Before she could stop herself, Dana laughed out loud.

". . . well, somebody is certainly in a good mood," Nelson said, stopping in mid-interview.

Oh, crap.

Cameramen scrambled to follow as the host skipped over the next three contestants, going directly to Dana.

"Dana Kirsten." He said her name like a judge pronouncing sentence. "You were the last one to arrive, weren't you?"

Dana leaned forward to speak into his lapel mike. He

shook his head and pointed to her choker-cam. "It's got a built-in mike. Of course, you would have known that if you were on time."

Laughter from the group.

"I was a last-minute—"

"We're just honored that you finally decided to join us."

More laughter. She had been late because she was a substitute contestant, but Brant Nelson was making it sound as if she were careless. In a game where public perception equals victory, interpretation was crucial.

"Actually there was an illness," she began, her voice cracking.

"Glad you're feeling better," the host said, cutting her off and clearly enjoying himself. "Because you were late, you missed some of the briefings. Do you think that puts you at a disadvantage?"

"Well, actually . . ." She stopped just short of addressing him as Smiley. "Actually I'm just glad to be here."

With a dismissive nod, Brant Nelson moved quickly back up the line to the contestants he had skipped.

Justin nudged her with his shoulder and snickered like a schoolboy, making her smile again.

The next few minutes were an anesthetizing blur as each contestant was introduced. The live intros were interspersed with specially prepared videos revealing their lives in the real world. Because she was a last-minute replacement, no such tape existed for Dana.

Preambles completed, Nelson returned to his spot in front of the group. Addressing them like a wise man before the masses, he began to explain how the online voting would work. Then, unaccountably, he stopped in midsentence. A mustache of sweat appeared on his upper lip and his complexion seemed wrong, shifting from tan to pink to red. The island hung in an artificial moment of silence. Shaking his head, Nelson cleared his throat and tried to continue. Dana noticed all the mobile cameras were down. Several of the operators sat on the ground, some fanning themselves, others were rubbing their faces and hands as if trying to remove an invisible stain.

Is the show over? Has something happened to the transmitter?

Nelson rubbed the back of his neck. He blinked and for a second he was back. "Sure is hot out here, folks. These people are certainly in for . . ." The words died in his mouth.

A woman screamed. All of the support personnel were now stumbling from their posts. Some rushed to the sea; others rolled on the sand.

Nelson began to wail in agony.

Dana stared in terror.

What the hell?

His skin was now red, the color of raw meat, and it was *moving*. It rippled like skim atop a bowl of pudding and began to *bubble*.

Nelson fell backward in the sand. His blistered face continued to undulate. One of the contestants, an elderly black man with thin gray hair and a timeworn face, rushed to his side.

Dana Kirsten was grounded in place, watching in disbelief as the host, the cameramen, and all the support staff fell where they had stood. Their faces were alive— inflamed, burbling, seething. Then . . . rupturing.

2 JACKSONVILLE, FLORIDA

Jenna Kirsten drew back from the television as if snapped at by a snake. She had been watching the show with keen interest, listening intently as the host talked to her mother. *My mom on TV—how cool is that?* Then everything changed.

Now she didn't know what she was watching. In all her years as a TV viewer, she had never seen anything like it.

Is it real?

It couldn't be! It looked like something from a monster movie, the kind that came on late at night and Jenna was forbidden to watch but did anyway. People were running and crying and screaming. And that horrible close-up of the host as his face . . . *exploded.*

Can't be real. Can't be real.

The screen went blank.

Then a slate appeared: TECHNICAL DIFFICULTIES—PLEASE STAND BY. After three months of intense publicity, the network had just pulled the plug on the debut episode of the most expensive television show ever made.

That was when Jenna Kirsten knew it was real.

The world froze, becoming a perfect tableau of that moment, fossilized in her mind forever by a single, chilling thought.

Momma.

VASSA ISLAND

For a moment, Justin Rourke flashed on Desert Storm, back to the sand, back to the hell of combat. Then reality asserted itself and he was jerked into the present. This wasn't Iraq. This wasn't war. It was something worse.

The gruesome screams of men and women dying in pain reverberated through the tropical air like the baneful wail of the last dinosaur. Then nothing. Silence. A moment of absolute stillness.

The older black man standing on Justin's left had been the first to move, rushing to the body of the host. "Dead," he announced to no one in particular before he dashed to another body, then another. Justin forced himself to act as well, counting on battle-hardened nerves to get him through.

The bodies were all the same—dreadful, disfigured, and lifeless.

A seagull cawed, a strangely tormented sound as if the bird were mourning the dead and forewarning the living.

Justin searched his memory for the old man's name. Efrem—Dr. Efrem Dutetre.

"Dr. Dutetre? What the hell is this?" he asked. Half question, half plea.

The old man shook his head. The creases in his face seemed deeper than just a moment ago. "I don't know. I've never seen anything like it. Never. It—it seemed to have hit everyone at once, killing within minutes. Yet . . ."

Other gulls now joined the chorus, the beach echoing with their haunted cries.

Dr. Dutetre looked back at the other contestants and frowned. Thin, white hair clung to his head like fog.

"What is it, Doc?"

More gulls. Crisscrossing the beach in brilliant flashes

of white, swirling in the air like diminutive, somber angels gathering the souls of the dead.

"Twelve. We're all here, all the contestants. Why hasn't it affected us yet?"

The others remained where they were, pivoting from side to side, uncertain and nakedly terrified.

Charles, the CPA, reacted to the doctor's words. "Yet? What do you mean *yet*? Oh, God, the birds." His hand went to his mouth.

A gull had landed on a body and was picking at the face.

Justin grabbed a piece of driftwood and hurled it at the bird. It took to the air in a flutter of white wings.

"*Yet*, Doc?" Justin prompted.

The doctor pursed his lips in thought. There was a meditation in his quiet eyes. "If this has a biological origin, then it may very well be contagious. And even if it's not . . ."

"We're still in danger," Justin said.

More gulls landed and began plucking at the corpses. Seagulls were not carrion eaters, but neither were they finicky, and the still warm bodies had assumed neither the attitude nor smell of the dead. "No way this is an accident."

"Then whoever did this may still be here?" the CPA cried, his voice shriveling in fear. "We're going to die. Sweet Mother of God, we're all going to die."

Panic surged through the group like fire through straw.

An alarm, the sound of Gabriel's horn calling the faithful home, jarred the island. A sense of doom, of dread, an unholy certainty that things were about to get worse settled over Justin's mind.

"It's coming from the Round House," said Dana. They followed her into the building.

*   *   *

Situated in the center of the compound, the Round House was just what its name implied, a perfectly round building that was approximately thirty feet across. There were two doorways, one opening toward the beach, the other toward the jungle. Inside, the walls were bare except for four evenly spaced cameras and two speakers. A three-foot, four-sided reader board hung from the center with another camera hanging beneath.

Dana Kirsten was the first to enter the chamber, her footsteps sounding like gunshots. In the center of the room was a round five-foot metal structure with twelve indentations, each with a thumbprint scanner, a small receptacle for safety stones, and a sealed, six- by five-inch box in which instructions were to be presented.

The alarm stopped as the last contestant entered the room.

It knows we're all here, Dana noted.

The speakers sputtered with the pop-hiss of an open microphone. The voice was electronically distorted, the sound of Satan on acid.

"I am Control. And this has just become the ultimate reality show. Welcome to 24/7. Welcome to the end of your life."

The voice, deep and deformed, shook the very air. Dana imagined she could feel every word resonate in her bones.

"Each of you has been exposed to a designer virus, a derivative of Ebola . . ."

"Ebola," the CPA whimpered, burying his pudgy face in his hands.

". . . And as you have just witnessed, it is painful and fatal. But the virus can be held in check with a simple injection—a vaccine that must be administered once every twenty-four hours . . ."

The CPA continued to cry. Others studied their hands

as if the virus were a visible entity that, if spotted, could be plucked off like a fat tick.

". . . At twelve noon, your clue-boxes will open. Inside is a simple, bee-sting injector. Use the vaccine and live for another day . . ."

The sound of crying filled the room like a swarm of cicadas.

". . . There are twelve contestants. At noon tomorrow I will provide eleven injections . . ."

The CPA wailed as if physically pierced by the words.

". . . But here is the really *fun* part . . ."—the voice sneered—"Since America and the rest of this fetid world are so fascinated with this repulsive form of voyeurism, I think it only fair that they participate by way of online voting."

The air seemed to cool. The tropical heat replaced with the icy wind of fear.

". . . The person receiving the most votes will *not* receive the vaccine. In other words, the viewers will decide who lives and who dies. . . ."

3 WASHINGTON, D.C.

The sun bore down on Washington, D.C. with skin-shriveling intensity. A breeze that anywhere else would have been refreshing did little more than stir the dust and move hot, stale air from one place to another. It was particularly oppressive at Dulles International Airport where Dr. Sherman Lorrik had just retrieved his luggage from the baggage carousel. He rolled his shoulders and rubbed the back of his neck. The flight from the Middle East had been exhausting and his right leg throbbed, forcing him to rely on the cane more than usual.

"Dr. Lorrik? Dr. Sherman Lorrik?" An impeccably dressed young man stepped around the side of a white limousine. He had short, neatly cut brown hair that spoke of military or law enforcement employment. "I'm here to pick you up."

Not military, Lorrik amended himself. A military man would have added a sir at the end of that sentence. Law enforcement then. "I didn't order a car."

"I know." The driver opened the limousine door. "It was sent for you."

"By whom?" Lorrik asked.

"Please Dr. Lorrik, there's not much time."

Too tired to argue, Lorrik climbed into the back as the chauffeur loaded his suitcase into the trunk. The supple leather seats caressed his body, a welcome change from the rear-numbing airplane seat he had been strapped to for the past twelve hours. The car was designed for function as well as luxury. In addition to a television and minibar there were two telephones, a fax machine, and a computer terminal.

"So which government agency do you work for?" Lorrik asked. "One of the alphabet agencies? FBI? DEA? ATF? Please don't tell me you're with the IRS."

The engine purred to life. "What makes you think—"

"I'm a psychiatrist and a sociologist, as well as a busybody. It's my job to think." Lorrik adjusted his bad leg, groaning at the effort.

"You okay?" asked the driver.

"Secret Service." It wasn't a question.

"What? Ah, yes, as a matter of fact, I am with the Secret Service. How did you—"

"Know?" Lorrik finished. "Your lapel pin. I know

you each have different designs, but honestly, no one wears lapel pins anymore. Except the Secret Service."

"You're very observant."

Lorrik shrugged off the compliment. "Should have figured it out the second I saw you. Must be more tired than I thought. Nothing a hot bath, a shot of brandy, and a good night's sleep won't cure. My address is 1214 Welshire Gardens."

"I'm sorry Dr. Lorrik. I know you're tired, but my orders are to take you elsewhere."

"Elsewhere? Where the hell is *elsewhere*?" Lorrik demanded.

"The White House."

VASSA ISLAND
Round House

A brassy shaft of sunlight lay across the Round House floor, pointing at the Vault like an accusatory celestial finger. Soft plaintive sobs, the sound of faraway bells in a forgotten monastery, tolled faintly in a pronouncement of grief.

Dana Kirsten didn't cry. She felt as if God had reached down and touched her brain thereby overloading her senses. The tears were there, just waiting to be shed, but instinct told her that giving in to her emotions amounted to giving up life.

Click-whirrrl.

An electric motor whined as the robotic camera hanging beneath the four-sided reader board panned to the left and then down, pointing toward Charles, the CPA. The man no longer looked like a caterpillar standing up but like a series of deflated balls stacked against the white stucco wall. Tears covered his face as if tears alone could wash away the insatiable virus.

Whirrrl.

The lens turned, focusing on the crying man.

Who's watching us? Dana wondered. After what had happened, she couldn't imagine they were still on the air. But how quickly had they pulled the plug? Jenna would have been watching. The thought of her daughter seeing the horror Dana had just witnessed, even filtered through a television screen, left a stain on her heart.

Click-whirrrl.

The camera lens turned again, drawing up on the short shaft. Wide shot, Dana reasoned. She stared at the cold, black lens. It stared back, unblinking.

"Any suggestion, Doc?" Justin asked. Dana recognized him as the man who had made her laugh just before the world tilted and they all slid down a rabbit hole the likes of which even Alice had never seen.

"We have to stay calm," the doctor said. "Stay calm and figure out how to fight this."

"It's a virus," the CPA cried. "It's in our blood. Our blood. We're going to die just like they did." His voice faded into a whimper.

"You ain't dead until you're dead," said a man whose thick lips were circled by a close-clipped Vandyke beard and a mustache that could have been drawn on with a black marker. His name tag identified him as: BURTON/ WELDER—NORTH PLATTE, NEBRASKA.

"Oh, that's good. Really helpful. Let me write that down in my little book of collected wisdom." The acid comment emanated from a woman whose bobbed, dirty blond hair had healthy black roots. She wasn't wearing makeup and didn't appear to be contemplating its application anytime soon. "We need answers not fortune cookie quotes."

Burton rolled his massive shoulders and huffed. "I'm open to suggestions, lady."

"Brenda. My name's Brenda Segar, and I ain't no lady."

"That's the fuckin' truth," Burton agreed.

Brenda straightened and glared. Her profession was listed as *butcher*. Dana had no trouble picturing this woman hacking slabs of beef into manageable proportions with a meat cleaver the size of a dinner plate—and enjoying it.

Justin stepped between them. "Now is not the time."

Dana took the opportunity to read his name tag: JUSTIN/PILOT—DALLAS, TEXAS. *Pilot?* Interesting. Their eyes met. She looked away.

"Any ideas what this virus is, Doc?" Justin asked. "What we can expect?"

The doctor shook his head. "No. I've never seen anything like it."

Justin gestured toward the speakers on the wall. "That electronic voice said something about Ebola."

The doctor pinched his lips between his thumb and forefinger. White eyebrows hovered over amazingly clear brown eyes like thick summer clouds held aloft by an invisible wind. "This isn't my field. I am—I *was* a general practitioner. Retired now. We didn't get a lot of flesh-eating diseases in Groves Cove." He paused, taking a labored breath.

"It's certainly possible," he continued. "Although, this acts far faster than any case of Ebola I've ever heard of."

"Ebola? The flesh-eating disease?" The CPA stood up, back still against the wall. His round, ruddy face was tracked with tears, the whites of his eyes marbled with veins of red. "Jesus. Jesus."

"What about the vaccine the voice mentioned?" Justin asked. "Do you think there is one?"

"No way to know for sure. But it's certainly possible."

"Possible?" The CPA squealed. "What do you mean, possible? There's got to be a vaccine, got to be."

Click-whirrrl.

One of the four wall cameras turned, found the CPA, and stopped.

Justin held up his hands. "Let's all try to stay calm. That's the important thing."

The CPA laughed; it was a strained sound. "No. The important thing is we're all going to die."

A woman in her late forties with short, straight black hair went to his side and put an arm around his shoulders. Dana remembered her from the interviews—Nora, a schoolteacher from Idaho and a former nun.

The CPA shrugged her off. His eyes were wide behind his gold-rimmed glasses, the panicked look of a man seeing the fires of hell as he falls from grace. "I don't want to die. I don't want to die."

"Shut the fuck up," Burton, the welder, snapped. His hands were knotted into fists, veins throbbed on thick, muscular arms. "One more whiny-ass word and I will personally pull the injector from your bony hand and laugh in your face as your skin burns off."

The CPA was silent.

A hot, dry wind soughed through the open door stirring the smell of sweat and fear.

Click-whirrrl.

A second wall camera turned, attracted to the raised voices like a bug to a light.

The audience is watching, always remember the audience is watching, the producers had emphasized. Only now, when Dana thought of the audience, she thought of a multi-eyed monster with a voice like an electric guitar and the power to kill with a glance.

Justin raised his hands. "I suggest we concentrate on finding a solution instead of fighting."

"I have an idea," Dana blurted, sounding more composed than she felt. "They chose us, in part, based on our occupations."

Justin nodded, warming to her logic. "That's right. In fact, they insisted we condense our lives into one-word descriptions for the name tags."

"Exactly," Dana said, oddly pleased by the smile Justin offered. "Let's find out what each of us can do. We can use our expertise and special skills to get us out of this. Doctor, isn't there an infirmary on this island?"

The doctor's eyes brightened. "Yes. Yes, I believe there is. We saw it on the tour. Maybe there's enough equipment to run some tests, see just how serious this is."

The CPA began to mutter, but when he looked at Burton, he swallowed whatever complaint he'd been formulating. Instead, he merely shuddered.

Dana shuddered, too. Something in Burton's eyes. No—something *not* in his eyes. They were lifeless, as if the virus had already claimed a crucial part of his humanity.

The camera turned; the lens twisted.

Dana tried to ignore it. "Does anyone else have medical experience? Anyone who may be able to help the doctor?"

A woman with shoulder-length red hair and an ivory, freckle-dappled face raised her hand. "I don't know how much it helps, but I'm a veterinarian." She crossed her arms across her chest and laughed nervously. "My name's Nerine—Nerine Keleman."

The doctor smiled for the first time since the crisis began. "Any help would be greatly appreciated, my dear. The biggest difference between your patients and mine is yours are generally nicer."

"Great. What else?" Dana looked at the pilot. "What do you think our priorities should be?"

"Staying alive," a woman interrupted. Even dressed in khaki shorts and a tank top, her desert-island ensemble no doubt, Renee looked more like a fashion model taking a break between shoots than the real estate agent her name tag declared her to be. "Here's the thing. If we want to live, we've got to get off this damn island."

"I'm with her," said a man with thin black hair and the leathered face of someone who spent days in the glare of an unfiltered sun. "Name's Foster and I've been a fisherman for eighteen years. If there's anything on this island that floats, I can get us out of here. There are several islands in the area—hell, Jamaica's not that far away. Depending on the speed, I can have us there before dinnertime."

An excited murmur rippled through the crowd.

The doctor shook his head. Tufts of white hair, thin as cotton candy, gamboled in the ocean breeze. "No, no, no, no. We can't leave."

"What do you mean we can't leave?" demanded the CPA.

The old man took a slow, deliberate breath. "We've all been contaminated, with a virus we know nothing about. Is it contagious? How is it transmitted? Is it an airborne pathogen, like the flu, or passed through the exchange of body fluids? We don't know. And until we do, we can't leave."

"No offense, Doc, but shouldn't we be in a hospital to answer those very questions?" Justin asked.

"Yes. Of course. But what if the virus is highly contagious? What if it's spread with every breath we take? We could contaminate an entire country in a matter of hours."

"Couldn't we make masks like they wear in hospitals?" Renee suggested.

The doctor rubbed his forehead. A fresh breeze wafted into the room, bringing with it the smell of the sea and the slight musk of fish. He looked up. "I'm afraid you are not understanding the gravity of our situation. The virus can only be held in check by a vaccine and even then only for twenty-four hours. That means a hospital would have less than a day to discover a cure for a man-made pathogen no one has ever seen. Hundreds, perhaps thousands, would die before an answer was found. And the first of those victims would be us."

"This can't be happening, this can't be happening," muttered the CPA hugging himself, rocking back and forth on the balls of his feet. Burton gave him a glance, then shook his head in an it's-not-worth-it gesture.

Click-whirrrl.

The audience is watching.

"Oh, crap," Dana said, the truth suddenly occurring to her. "We're on television."

"And you're surprised by this?" Renee said, making no effort to hide the annoyance in her voice. "Hell-o. It's a television show."

Dana shook her head. "You don't understand. We're on television now. I mean, after what happened, I just assumed the network pulled the plug."

"Yeah, they would pretty much have to, what with the dying and all." Renee sighed.

"But Control said the viewers will decide who lives and who dies. How do they do that without watching the show?"

Renee paused, a flaxen wave of hair falling over one perfect lapis lazuli eye. "But it's too violent, too graphic. It's mass murder, for Christ's sake. No way the network could let it continue."

"They may not have a choice." The speaker was a thin angular man, in his twenties. "Sorry to interrupt. It's just, well, I think Dana's right. We are still on the air."

"How? How could we be?" Renee demanded, brushing back the errant hair with her manicured fingers.

The young man flinched at her sharp tone and his oblong face grew even longer. "My name's Cory—Cory Nestor. I'm a systems manager. Basically I'm the guy who keeps all the computers running at the company I work for. Computer geek," he added, smiling shyly. "So I'm pretty interested in the setup here."

He shook his head, his blond, spiky hair cutting swatches in the tropical air. "It's quite amazing, really. State-of-the-art everything. Krest Technologies software and Shard 315 computers that aren't even on the market yet. And the transmitter, holy cow!"

"And that means?" Justin prompted.

"The island is self-sustaining. Independent power supplies. That's plural because there's more than one. I counted at least four. Computer programs monitor everything from the lights to the locks. You know all those little surprises they were talking about, the personal challenges we're supposed to face? Computer-controlled, every one of them. It's incredible."

"Are you going to reach a point anytime soon?" Renee asked.

"My point is, the same thing is true about the transmitter. Computer-controlled. Even if the network tried to shut it down, they couldn't without physically being here."

"So they have to air it?" Dana asked.

"No."

"But you just said . . ."

As he talked, his gestures became grander, his voice trilled with excitement. "Certainly the network can choose whether or not to put the signal on their channel. But they can't stop the signal from being broadcast over the open air. I mean, that's one heck of a television transmitter."

"Biggest ever built," someone added, as if you couldn't say one without the other.

"Meaning anyone with a satellite dish can pick up the signal. But the big thing is the Internet. They've got more than twenty-two direct links to the Web. And I'm sure people are already creating mirror sites. There's no way to shut them all down. We have to assume that somebody is watching at all times. All times."

Dana thought of her daughter.

Click-whirrrl.

The center camera moved as if to confirm Cory's scenario.

Justin tapped his fingers against his lips. "If a signal can get out then one can get in. If we can get the doc talking to the authorities, maybe they can figure out what we're dealing with."

"I'm on it," Cory said, his voice filled with boyish excitement. "The television building is our best bet."

"I thought that was off-limits," Dana said. "Production crew only. Locked up tight. The television building is where the on-island crew is based."

"Is or was? But odds are good no one had a chance to lock it before"—he frowned—"you know . . ."

Justin sighed. Not the sound of a man defeated but the sound of someone steeling himself for a difficult task. "There's something else we have to do. We've got to remove the bodies. Or once they start decaying, we'll have more than just the virus to worry about."

Dana looked at her watch. Less than twelve hours before one of them died.

4 SEATTLE

Tucker Thorne had eight minutes and ten seconds to live.

He woke in stages: confusion, pain, and then, with the return of his memory, panic. Through blurred vision he could make out wooden crates and boxes and something lying beside him. A blanket? A duffel bag?

A body.

Tucker's vision snapped into focus. His source, the man who had guided him here, was dead; a two-inch hole where his left eye should have been.

Tucker screamed.

He tried to stand, but his feet were bound with duct tape.

And his hands? Something was wrong with his hands. He was holding something. He looked down and the smiling face of Donald Duck looked back. He was holding a clock, a child's clock—and, taped to it, three sticks of dynamite.

He yelled, slinging his hands like a man trying to fling off a spider, but the clock remained. He couldn't open his hands, couldn't let go.

"SuperGlue," said a voice from the shadows. Elliot Kay Simon stepped into the anemic light. His face was now covered in a dirty-blond beard and his hair hung heavy and unwashed on all sides.

"I glued a bomb to your hands," Simon elaborated,

his voice oddly thin and shrill for his six-foot burlap bag–shaped body. "Are you the one who killed God?"

Simon's huge brown eyes bulged slightly as if under great pressure from something cold and dark growing inside his oblong head. Beneath a nose that looked like a ball of dirty socks was a lopsided smile. A viscous string of drool teetered at the corner of his mouth.

Drool?

"I think . . . I think maybe you are." Simon lifted his head and stared at Tucker from the bottom of his eyes as if looking at one of those Magic Eye paintings, the kind that reveal a hidden picture if you stare at them long enough.

Two and half days ago, sitting at the counter of the Krispy Kreme this had all seemed like a good idea, a brilliant idea. Never mind that the reporter Tucker was working with had dismissed it with a wave. Or that the source was a self-proclaimed anarchist who, paradoxically, was proficient with computers. At the time all Tucker could see was an opportunity for promotion from photographer to reporter.

The anarchist, who called himself Freedom, had dirt-molded dreadlocks and eyes that were a patriotic red, white, and blue. His uniform was a tie-dyed shirt and torn jeans—and he used the word *man* as if it were a comma.

"It's the same dude, man. It's Simon, man—I swear it," he had told Tucker.

Just over a month ago, a mental patient named Elliot Kay Simon had planted a briefcase full of explosives inside the Krest Technologies Research Center in Seattle, reducing the building to ruins and killing one hundred and thirteen people.

No one knew why.

Not only did Krest Technologies employ Simon's brother, who by all accounts he loved dearly, but the enigmatic company founder, Harlan Krest, had personally paid for much of Simon's mental care.

For two days Elliot Kay Simon was the focus of the largest manhunt since Timothy McVeigh. Until he finally surrendered, then committed suicide by blowing up his van just as a SWAT team approached. Another fourteen people were killed, bringing the grand total to one hundred and twenty-seven fatalities. Not counting Simon.

"They found a body, or what was left of it. Identified him with dental records," Tucker had reminded his source.

The anarchist slid a file across the counter. *Pretty organized for an anarchist,* Tucker noted. Inside was a copy of a police report on Simon. Listed under education was three years at the University of Washington and one year at the Oregon Educational Dental School.

"A dentist?" Tucker asked in disbelief. "He studied to be a dentist?"

The anarchist smiled. "Never finished, man. But you can bet your ass he learned enough to fake his own dental records."

Tucker strained trying to pull his hands from the bomb.

"I wouldn't do that if I were you," Simon warned. "Might set it off prematurely."

"Look, I think there has been some kind of a mistake. My name's Tucker Thorne. I'm a photographer for the Globe Newschannel. I, we"—he nodded toward the body—"we're doing a story on warehouse fraud."

Simon turned his head to one side then another. The string of drool touched the top of his black T-shirt.

"I don't know who you are and I promise I could never pick you out of a lineup," Tucker lied. "So how about I get out of here and forget I ever saw you?"

Simon's bulging eyes shifted to the side. For a moment he was mentally gone, transported to a world where black was white, up was down, and blowing a hundred-plus people to bits was considered a swell idea. Then he was back.

He wiped the drool on his arm and appeared coldly coherent. "Nice try. How did you find me?"

"I told you, I don't know who you are."

"*Shut up!*" Simon screamed, logic replaced with a raging fire of insanity. "*You shut up!* Don't you lie to me; don't you lie to me."

Tucker was quiet.

"How did you find me?"

"Venus Rising," Tucker said.

Shortly before the bombing, the anarchist named Freedom claimed to have met a guy in an antigovernment chat room who called himself *Venus Rising*. The guy was freaky, even by anarchist standards, talking about a new God with whom he was in personal contact and how this new God wanted Krest Technologies destroyed.

The very next day the Krest building in downtown Seattle was turned to rubble. In the aftermath, it was revealed that Simon, released from a mental institution just two months before, had been living on his brother's boat: *Venus Rising*.

Then, three days ago, Freedom saw a new message in the same chat room.

<THE NEW GOD IS DEAD. THEY KILLED HIM. KILLED HIM.>

It was signed: <VENUS RISING>.

Freedom was convinced the entire rampage, including Simon's paranoid delusions, was part of a vast government conspiracy, the whole thing a setup to cover some insidious evil plan that would ultimately bring an end to personal freedom and life as we know it.

Tucker didn't buy into the conspiracy theory. But if he

could prove that Elliot Kay Simon was alive it would be the biggest story of the year. Sure to get him promoted.

Freedom had asked for a meeting and Venus Rising told him to go to a warehouse down by the docks. The anarchist and Tucker arrived early with Tucker planning to hide and secretly record the entire meeting. They split up after entering the warehouse. It was the last time Tucker saw Freedom alive.

"Venus Rising?" Simon said. "You knew I was alive because of the chat room?"

"That—and I saw a mouse," Tucker added.

A look of puzzlement painted Simon's volatile face.

"A bank camera across the street got video of you leaving the Krest Building," Tucker explained. "Instead of a briefcase you were carrying a cage. A rat cage."

"I couldn't let them die." Simon's voice was suddenly younger. "They had done nothing wrong. But there they were, being probed and prodded and used like, like . . ."

"Lab rats?"

Simon nodded, missing the sarcasm. His protruding eyes wobbled in their sockets. "So I saved them. Let 'em go here."

"And I saw one," Tucker said. "When it didn't run from me, I knew it wasn't wild. It was used to people. That's when I put it all together. Then the doors locked. I tried to run and I don't remember after that."

"I slugged you in the back of the head with a two-by-four," Simon said, then, his voice changing from youthful to despondent, added, "God's dead. And when the clock strikes three, you will be, too."

Tucker checked the clock in the center of Donald's tummy.

Tucker Thorne had three minutes and twenty-one seconds to live.

5 WASHINGTON, D.C.

Those he didn't know by face he recognized by name or title. Twenty-two of the most powerful men and women in the country, ranging from the director of the FBI, to the surgeon general.

So why the hell am I here? Lorrik wondered.

Sure, he was well known in his field, worked with the FBI a few times, had even been published in several scientific journals read only by people published in scientific journals, but basically he was a teacher. There were certainly others with more impressive credentials.

Dr. Sherman Lorrik was escorted to the only empty seat at the table. A briefing paper, similar to the one he had been given in the limousine, lay in front of him. He thumbed through it, noticing several additional pages, then set it aside for later review. His immediate interest was this group and the debate he had walked in on.

An admiral, who looked as old as the sea, rapped the table with his knuckles to emphasize his point. ". . . and I'm telling you, I can have a naval group in there and get those people off the island within two hours."

"We can't do that, Admiral," countered the surgeon general. She was a small woman with short gray hair and small square glasses and, despite the disparity in size, was not the least bit intimidated by the admiral. "We cannot risk further exposure until we know exactly what type of virus we are dealing with."

"We've got containment suits," the admiral puffed.

"It's still too risky, Admiral."

The director of the FBI agreed. "We have to see this for what it is, a biological terrorist attack on American citizens. Exposing the rest of the nation may be exactly what they want."

Biological terrorism.

Lorrik and others had warned of just such a thing. The warning signs went all the way back to 1993 when Canadian officials stopped a man with a bag of white powder later identified as *ricin*, enough to kill thirty-two thousand people. Then, in 1995, a man in Lancaster, Ohio, was arrested for buying bubonic plague bacteria through the mail.

Terrorism by biology was inevitable.

The president sat back in his chair. With his coat off, collar open, and hair slightly mussed, he looked more like an accountant than Commander in Chief. "What sort of virus kills like this?"

The surgeon general leaned forward, her elbows resting on the polished teakwood. "It doesn't match anything we have on record. The voice, this Control, referenced the Ebola virus and so far that is the closest resemblance. But Ebola doesn't act this fast."

Three carafes of ice water were practically empty and at least two people were visibly chewing on ice. *Dry mouth,* Lorrik noted, a common symptom of stress.

The president looked at the only man in the room Lorrik had met before, the director of the FBI. "Do we know *who* we are dealing with, Norman?"

The director cleared his throat. "Not conclusively, sir. We've received calls from several organizations claiming responsibility but nothing that can be substantiated. Candidly, I don't think we've heard from the actual terrorist yet."

The president rubbed his face with his hand. "Why do something this dramatic, obviously designed to gain maximum attention, and not take credit? Does that make any sense?"

No one answered. The room reeked of frustration and confusion. The distorted image on the highly polished conference table seemed to reflect the emotional state of the moment.

Perhaps it was because he was too tired to be intimidated or because he had gotten so captured in the drama (just like watching television) Lorrik raised his hand to speak.

The president looked over as if seeing him for the first time. "Ah, Dr. Lorrik. Thank you for joining us."

The president knows my name? Lorrik was temporarily rattled. *Why does the president know my name?*

"For those of you who have not yet met him, this is Dr. Sherman Lorrik, the eminent sociologist."

"The guy who was kidnapped and tortured?" someone whispered, though audibly enough.

Lorrik unconsciously rubbed his still painful right leg.

"The very same," the president continued. "Since that incident almost three years ago, the doctor has specialized in terrorist and hostage situations." The president took a sip of water, perhaps giving Lorrik a moment to regain his composure, then asked, "So, what do you think, Doctor? Why haven't we heard from those responsible?"

Lorrik took a breath to focus his thoughts. "They are waiting for a better time."

"A better time?" the president asked. "Hell, they've got half the world watching. What could possibly be a better time than that?"

Lorrik cleared his throat. "When the *whole* world is watching. And, if I'm right, things are about to get a lot worse."

SEATTLE

Tucker Thorne had three minutes and twenty seconds to live.

Elliot Kay Simon rocked his head from side to side. His distended, yellow eyes reflected the fluorescent light like fun house mirrors. "New God quiet now. Quiet. Maybe all the stars will die—maybe."

Tucker could feel sweat tickling his upper lip. His kidneys felt full and ready to release. *Never saw Bruce Willis or Arnold Schwarzenegger peeing in their pants.* The good news was, when the bomb went off there wouldn't be enough left for anyone to know whether he soiled himself or not.

He moaned. What did it say when the good news was being blown up?

"Earth, air, fire, and water," Simon mumbled. "Show me the way, show me the way."

"Peter Frampton."

Simon frowned. "Lao-tzu."

"Okay, whatever, but I'm pretty sure it's Frampton."

"Ann Frances Robbins knows the truth." Simon's head bobbed back and forth like a man keeping beat with a silent drum. ". . . through the glorious dozen shines, the secrets of the new . . . the extant of knowledge serpentine, property of the few . . ."

Tucker was quiet. The fear that covered him like a cold sweat was now hot and acidic, consuming his flesh, chewing through muscle and tissue, supping on his bones. Simon was a man only in appearances as if insanity were a living, breathing creature wearing a suit of meat.

"I am His sword. I am not dead."

Tucker's heart trembled in his chest. Logic, his friend and companion, his co-conspirator, was gone, deserting him. Leaving a deep, empty hole in his mind that yawned like an open grave.

"Scream if you want." Simon's voice was only slightly louder than a whisper. "Scream and scream. But there's no one to hear you. On this world or any other."

Simon muttered, vanishing into the shadows. The powerful scent of his aftershave remained.

Tucker Thorne had three minutes and fifteen seconds to live.

VASSA ISLAND
The Dorm

Thirty-two feet long and fifteen feet wide, with twelve army cots and crates upon crates of canned goods, the dorm was disturbingly cramped. A counter with a sink and running water and an airplane-size bathroom added to the claustrophobic atmosphere.

With the exception of a can opener, two pots, and a ladle, there were no kitchen utensils. Some of the contestants used leaves as makeshift plates, sticks and stems for forks and spoons. The majority ate directly from the can, pouring food into their mouths rather than going to the trouble of creating utensils.

Justin Rourke *drank* a can of pears and washed it down with bottled water. He ate mechanically, mandated by logic not hunger. The bodies had been stored in a shed down by the marina. At best it was a temporary reprieve. Already the smell was stifling and it would only get worse.

Especially if more of us die.

It wasn't the first time he had worked with casualties. As a chopper pilot during Operation Desert Storm, he had ferried the dead and dying from the battlefield to the makeshift hospitals. Soldiers. Men with the faces of boys. Kids who would have looked more natural in a fast-food uniform than a military one.

It had been the most difficult thing he had ever done—until now.

These were not men in uniform, people prepared to pay the ultimate sacrifice in the service of God and country. These were just people. Regular people. Men and women in shorts and loud T-shirts, their biggest worry being sunburned, all expecting to go home when the job was done.

And now they were dead.

No. Not just dead, murdered. This virus was a monster. A hideous beast that sucked the blood from your skin and boiled away your face and extremities. The dead were mutilated.

Slaughtered.

The food had no taste. Justin ate without conscious thought.

The twelve of them were alive, for now. They were also alone, cut off from the States and neighboring islands by a sophisticated scrambling device that allowed signals out but let nothing in.

Justin thought of his charter business, of his money problems, of his buddies and beer. Each year, he and four of his best buds would take two weeks off to fly around the country hitting all the great and not-so-great golf courses. It was a chance to blow off steam, drink too much beer, and meet women, lots and lots of women.

It was sophomoric, irresponsible, and a hell of a lot of fun.

Now, looking at what may very well be the end of his life, Justin was surprised that *he didn't regret a moment of it.*

There were other regrets. Not taking care of his business. His failed marriage, a dozen failed relationships. No kids, he loved kids. No one who would miss him—truly miss him.

Then, inexplicably, he thought of Dana Kirsten. *Where had that come from?*

He choked down the pears. He had to keep up his strength.

There would be more dead tomorrow.

SEATTLE

Tucker Thorne had two minutes and two seconds to live.

Elliot Kay Simon had worn a powerful cologne and his scent remained in the air as if to mark his turf.

Tucker ignored it. He searched the warehouse with his eyes. If he could find something sturdy, something he could put between himself and the bomb, then maybe he could survive.

Yeah, but your hands will be blown off.

There had to be another way. Had to be. He was out of options and out of time.

"Here lies Tucker Thorne," they would say at his funeral. "A wannabe reporter who died a photographer. Killed by a plastic statue of Donald Duck. May he rest in *pieces*."

A lifetime of careful living, of always covering his ass, choosing to be smart rather than brave, and now he was going to die like the coyote in a Road Runner cartoon.

There had to be a way out. Something he was missing. Something he had overlooked. But he could see nothing that offered hope. Freedom, the anarchist, lay on the floor, his body already taking on an offensive odor. Crates of American furniture made in China stood by waiting. Nothing else.

A puzzle lover since childhood, Tucker couldn't help but note the irony of being scattered like a jigsaw.

Then he remembered Donald Duck.

Tucker Thorne had one minute and five seconds to live.

6 WASHINGTON, D.C.
The White House

"Dr. Lorrik, a moment please."

"Of course, Mr. President." Dr. Sherman Lorrik sat back down.

The meeting of what was now being called the Vassa Island Task Force had lasted for over two hours, ending with a tentative plan of action that Lorrik still wasn't comfortable with.

The president waited until they were completely alone before talking. "Dr. Lorrik, do you know why you are here?"

"I've been trying to figure that out. Certainly this is within my area of expertise, but there are others with far more practical experience."

The president traced his reflection with his finger on the highly polished conference table. "Perhaps. What did you think of the meeting?"

"Interesting. Tell you the truth, I enjoyed watching the group dynamics of such a diverse gathering. A lot of strong-willed individuals."

The president rubbed his temples. "Lot of egos. Bottom line, it was bullshit. A lot of political posturing and ass covering."

Lorrik was surprised by the president's frankness.

"Don't get me wrong, we need a task force—a place to debate, agree, and solidify our options. But there is more to this than the public or even the task force understands."

Lorrik waited for the president to continue.

"This isn't just biological terrorism is it, Doctor?"

Lorrik shifted in his chair. His bad leg was throbbing. He ignored it, curious to see if this detail-oriented president had actually made the same leap in logic he had.

The president rubbed his palm across the table as if trying to wipe away his reflection. "I think we're looking at a tangent scenario. I believe you wrote a paper on that very topic. Published it in the *Journal of Psychological Theory*."

There it was. Lorrik smiled without meaning to. "That was more than a year ago, shortly after my kidnapping."

The president looked up from his ghostly reflection. "A particularly bright aide pointed it out to me. It stuck in the back of my mind until today."

"I'm impressed."

"Don't be. I'm a repository of worthless information. Sometimes it's useful, mostly it's just clutter." The president shifted forward. "So you don't believe the twelve contestants are the intended targets of this attack?"

Lorrik tapped his fingers on the table. "No, sir. I don't."

The president nodded and sat back in his chair. "This is a *psychological* terrorist attack then."

"Yes, sir."

"And the intended victims?"

"The American public."

Hands flat on the table as if holding it down should the laws of gravity suddenly cease, the president sighed. "You can understand why I didn't bring it up in front of the others."

He did. The tangent scenario was a theory even many of his colleagues failed to grasp. How could the actions of a few affect the many? Not only affect, but disrupt, destabilize, and possibly destroy? Lorrik knew the answer, as apparently did the president.

"So how do we fight it?" he asked, then smiled. "As memory serves, your article didn't offer a solution."

Lorrik shifted his weight hoping to stimulate the blood flow to his bad leg and ease the pain. He waited for the throbbing to subside before replying. "By launching our own attack."

"On the island?"

"On the public. We meet manipulation with manipulation."

The president exhaled through his nose. "Sweet Jesus."

He sat back in his chair, body sagging with exhaustion. After a moment he took a slip of paper from his breast pocket. "One more thing, and this is personal, just between you and me."

"Of course."

He passed the paper to Lorrik. It contained a single name, in the president's handwriting. "No matter what, this person must not die."

VASSA ISLAND

The surf lashed the beach like a Roman flogging a Christian. With a little imagination one could hear an agonizing moan in the cacophonous crash of sea meeting shore. The seagulls were fewer now, their lonely cries made all the more haunting by their lesser numbers.

Dana Kirsten stood on the beach, bare feet sinking into the wet sand, and stared out toward horizon, toward home, toward Jenna. The Atlantic Ocean was less than twenty minutes from their home in Jacksonville, Florida. In the summer, on Dana's alternate Sundays off, Jenna would pack a picnic lunch: peanut butter and jelly sandwiches, baloney sandwiches, anything-that-would-fit-between-two-slices-of-bread sandwiches. Add an apple, candy bars, two bottles of water, and they were good to go.

Despite her condition, or because of it, Jenna prided herself on being self-sufficient, and she took great pleasure from making the lunch. "You've worked hard all week, Mama. Today, I'll take care of you," she would say, then smile, ivory teeth suspended between pink cheeks.

The beach was not user-friendly for the physically challenged. Feet weighed down by metal leg braces would sink to the ankles. Crutches the same. Each step was a test, its completion a success. Faces would turn, other children would point fingers, and Jenna would smile as if it were just the two of them, as if being together was all that mattered.

And it was.

But this was not *their* beach. And although Vassa Island was aesthetically more pleasing than the gray waters of Jacksonville Beach, it lacked the heart and soul of her native coast. This shoreline did not represent success and love, but failure and captivity.

She would get out of here, she would survive. She had to. For Jenna.

Dana wiped away a single tear that had escaped the confines of her willpower. Then she turned and walked away as the sea lashed the island for sins unimaginable.

SEATTLE

Tucker Thorne had thirty-eight seconds to live.

Using his legs to pull himself forward, he inched his way across the concrete floor. It was slow and undignified—but so was being blown into a thousand fleshy bits. Reaching the nearest crate, he lined the clock up with the wooden edge. Then, turning his head and gritting his teeth, he banged Donald Duck's butt against the corner of the box—again and again and again—expecting the dynamite to ignite at any moment.

On the eighth try he was rewarded by the sound of cracking plastic. He shook the bomb. Shards of plastic littered the floor. He shook it again—harder. Two AA batteries bounced on the concrete.

The clock in the center of Donald's tummy went black with four seconds remaining.

VASSA ISLAND

Dana watched as the baby blue sky became pink, then red, then all the colors in between, melting slowly from day to night. The glory of the sunset endured in stark contrast to the repellent island.

Confessing that she didn't want to sleep next to a window looking out on the jungle, Nerine, the veterinarian, asked Dana to switch beds. But as darkness fell and the jungle woke, Dana began to regret the change.

The insect hum was disquieting and put her in mind of a dozen, spinning blades in a distant sawmill.

Something wailed. A banshee? A dying beast? The dead come back to scream for justice?

She pulled the blanket up around her neck and tried to go to sleep but her eyes vigilantly opened at each new, unexplainable sound. The night air moved like a stalking beast. Palm fronds rustled and bushes quaked menacingly.

She thought of Jenna, concentrating on the image of her daughter: her face, her eyes, her bashful smile. Then, as exhaustion slowly pulled her into sleep, Dana got the vague impression of someone, something, outside—stalking.

7 SEATTLE
Globe News Headquarters

The Globe Television Network was centered in a black glass and brick high-rise two blocks from downtown Seattle. The first fifteen floors housed the entertainment division, the top six, the news.

Following the lead of NBC and Fox, Globe had created its own cable channel for news. The Globe Newschannel was young and edgy. The newscasts were personality-driven, anchored by recognizable talent stolen from other networks, fraught with moving graphics, dramatic music, and edited in a style more akin to MTV than broadcast journalism.

And now Tucker Thorne was about to become their newest reporter.

Though exhausted, he was also elated. After the bomb squad successfully defused the dynamite still glued to his hands, he had been rushed to the hospital where doctors removed the remainder of the clock and bomb. His palms, sore and raw, were slathered in gel and covered by two white gloves giving the appearance of oversized cartoon hands.

He didn't care. Even without video proof that Elliot Kay Simon was alive, he had a hell of a story that was sure to garner a promotion to reporter.

He had been a reporter before, but that was in a small market television station where he had to shoot his own stories. When the network offered him a job as a photographer at three times the salary, he took it, figuring it would give him the inside track on his ultimate goal of reporting on a national level.

That was four years, seven months, and two weeks ago.

And he was still a photographer—but not for long.

Having called the story in from the hospital, Tucker had expected to be interviewed in the emergency room. When that didn't happen, he assumed they were focusing on the hunt for Simon. But he fully expected to be on the air soon, as the only living witness to the miraculous return of Elliot Kay Simon.

No one looked up as he entered the newsroom. No one said hi or asked how he was doing or patted him on the back. The only acknowledgment came from a graphics operator who looked at his gloves and snickered.

A rundown of the next news hour was taped to the assignment board. Tucker's story was not the lead. In fact, it didn't even appear until the fifth segment and then only as a twenty-five second reader.

What the hell was going on?

One of the most notorious killers in the country had returned from the dead and no one seemed to care.

The news director was chewing on a submarine sandwich and grunting into the phone when Tucker arrived at his office. He waved Tucker in and motioned for him to sit.

With a wide face, bald head, long mouth, and pencil-point eyes, Rubin Hearth bore an amazingly strong resemblance to a shark. It was a look he tried to diminish with a skinny beard that clung to his chin like a remora. In reality, Hearth wasn't nearly nice enough to be a shark.

"What the hell were you thinking?" he shouted as soon as he hung up the phone. "That's a twenty-five-thousand-dollar camera you jeopardized."

"A man died," Tucker said.

"Don't get me started on that. The liability, the civil action. It will be a miracle if his family doesn't sue the network and you."

Tucker was dizzy with confusion. "But Elliot Kay Simon—"

"Is dead. That was the FBI on the phone. And they assure me that Simon is unequivocally dead."

"But I saw—"

"Unless you went to hell, you didn't see Simon. If you saw anyone at all."

"What do you mean?"

"I mean, you're a suspect in a murder investigation. And, effective as of now, you're suspended without pay."

Shock came first, followed quickly by a wave of anger. "The police don't consider me a suspect."

Hearth shook his head. It was easy to imagine a hapless swimmer dangling from his jaws. "They haven't officially cleared you either. Now get out of here before I quit being a softie and just fire you."

Tucker had no memory of leaving the office and returning to the newsroom. Less than two minutes ago he had been on top of the world. And now?

"Tuck? You okay, man?" Clarence Bickman was a six-foot-three-inch-tall African American with a shaved head and a thick mustache who, despite his intimidating appearance, never lost his temper—unless you called him Clarence instead of "Brick," a nickname that had stuck since high school. A fellow photographer, he was also Tucker's best friend at the station. "I heard about the bomb."

Tucker looked around the newsroom, suddenly wondering if he would ever see it again. "I can't believe it, Brick. Shark-face just suspended me."

"Say what?"

Tucker recounted his conversation with the news director. When he finished, Brick was fuming. "Spineless bastard. If it's any consolation, his balls are in the vise over this Vassa Island crisis."

Tucker looked at the wall monitors. Each displayed a different television network, all showing scenes from a tropical island. "What is this? And why is it on every channel?"

"Man, you have been out of it."

It was Tucker's turn to listen with disbelief. Like everyone, he had been exposed to the hype for 24/7, the most expensive reality show ever produced and the pride and joy of the Global Television Network, the news department's parent company. But he was completely unaware of the most recent developments.

"Network pulled the show, but can't stop the signal. And the Internet is wide open. It's a nightmare for the company. And as news director, Hearth is in the middle of it."

Tucker suddenly understood. How do you cover the biggest story of the century when it means bashing the people who pay your salary? Particularly when you're a butt-kisser like Hearth?

"The asshole made a logistical mistake. He tried to downplay the story. Big, big mistake. Made it look like a cover-up, like the whole news department was caving to corporate pressure."

"Dumb ass."

"Yeah, well, now he's scrambling to catch up." Brick shook his head. "It's our network. We've got more access than anyone else—and we're still behind the curve."

SEATTLE
Tucker Thorne's Apartment

Tucker Thorne entered his apartment, closed the door behind him, and locked it. A single bag of groceries was cradled in his left arm, a fresh loaf of garlic bread stuck out of the sack, tempting him with its aroma.

The apartment, a small two-bedroom, single-bath, was dominated by cardboard boxes, stacked three high in places and scattered about the living room, kitchen, and bedroom. Only one bedroom, which doubled as an office, and the bathroom were completely assembled.

The boxes called to him, teased him, nagged him. He would empty them—eventually. But not now. Not this soon.

It's been eight months, his higher brain reminded him. Soon. He would do it soon. Just—not yet.

His old place was larger and better with a clear view of the cool Puget Sound. But after a year of restless nights and half-remembered nightmares, he had finally conceded. The place was haunted. Haunted by her memory.

He sat the groceries on the kitchen bar that doubled as his table and ripped off a chunk of garlic bread. He closed his eyes, savoring the flavor.

The scent of fresh bread brought a hint of warmth to the somber apartment.

Gwen.

The name came with a lightning bolt of memory. Olive complexion, soft winsome face, eyes large and expectant. His hands clenched, mouth tightened. No. Not now. He was improving. He could go almost an entire day without thinking of her—almost. He had to gain control. This was no way to live.

Concentrate on your career. You're going to be a reporter. A television journalist. You can do it. You will do it. She would want you to.

Gwen.

Again the name. Again the jagged strike of memory and pain.

Tucker lay his head back staring at the textured ceiling. A spider had built a web between the oval light fixture and the ceiling, the threads of which undulated softly in the push of central air. A moth, long dead, hung between the silken latticework. Dead. Suspended between heaven and hell. Just like Tucker.

By the time the can of spaghetti was heated and ready, he had lost his appetite. The garlic bread no longer held any magical appeal. He ate anyway, washing down his food and driving back memories with beer. Once finished, he put the dishes in the sink, then returned to the couch, his second beer growing warm in his hands. On the coffee table the Seattle Times crossword puzzle lay half-finished in ink. Next to it was a nearly completed jigsaw puzzle of The Seven Wonders of the World.

Gwen.

Sometimes, late at night when he closed his eyes, he could sense her, smell her, feel her weight in bed beside him. It was those times when he ached the most, when his soul wept like an open sore. They would have been married by now. But instead of celebrating their first wedding anniversary, Tucker had been left alone to remember the anniversary of her death.

Returning to the kitchen, he picked up a bag of potato chips. His shirt was tight, the fabric strained at the buttons, a reminder of the weight he had gained in the last two years. Chips—they wouldn't even have been in the house if she were here. He closed the bag and put it back in the cabinet.

"The best way to say no to junk food is not to see it," she would say.

The memories were warm and soothing. She had never doubted him, never stopped believing. "You were a terrific reporter and you will be again—soon."

He hoped she was right, but after today he wasn't so sure. Simon had been his best and possibly last chance.

Too tired to nap, he went to the computer in his bedroom. It took less than a minute to find a discussion on 24/7 and less than ten minutes to download a bootleg copy of the program that allowed users to access the island cameras.

He watched with disdain, clicking from camera shot to camera shot, seeing nothing but sand, surf, and people talking.

Borrinng!

Two women—half running, half stumbling—hurried out of a plain beige building, slapping their arms and legs, shouting and screaming. Tucker turned up the volume and was immediately greeted by a string of curse words.

What the heck is going on?

One of the men fell to the ground rolling in the sand as if his body were on fire. A striking blonde with shoulder-length hair and a fashion model face began ripping her clothes off.

The camera zoomed in.

Damn! This was getting good.

VASSA ISLAND

Justin Rourke woke with a start, gasping for air like a man running a marathon. It was still dark, morning little more than a vermilion line drawn across the black horizon. Despite the cool, moist air, he was covered in sweat.

The nightmare again. The one he could never remember, identified only by the sense of terror it left in his mind. He closed his eyes, trying to control his breathing, then his pounding heart.

A delayed stress-related condition caused by exposure to severe circumstances during the Persian Gulf War—that was the diagnosis of his government assigned shrink.

Bullshit!

Justin had seen a lot of horrible things during Operation Desert Storm, took part in many of them, but there was nothing that could account for the cold certainty, the feeling of utter shame, left by what he thought of as the *invisible nightmare*.

He dressed, opened a can of peaches, then headed out to explore the island.

After the war Justin opened his own charter air service out of Honolulu. The weather was great, the flying a hoot, and the fringe benefits—attractive female vacationers looking for a spot of island romance—very beneficial. Low stress, high fun. But the nightmare continued.

Of course there was the problem of finances, namely the lack thereof. He had used up all his seed money and what profits he made went into keeping his aircraft in the air. Good as he was as a pilot he was equally bad as a businessman. But Justin had never been the type to obsess over money. Something would present itself, it always did.

This *24/7* was to have been that something. The money would make him as free on the ground as he was in the air. For his heart's desire, Justin had his eye on a vintage World War II–era Lockheed P-38 *Lightning*; a hell of an airplane, a stallion in the sky.

His mind continued to wander as he cruised the island. Three hours later, thirsty and tired from his effort, he headed back to the dorm. He had just rounded a bend and had the dormitory in sight when he heard the screaming. That was followed quickly by people running, falling, and in some cases, stripping.

Dana jumped up on the cot. The fisherman screamed in pain and ran out the door followed closely by Burton and Renee.

Across the floor—back pressed against the wall, eyes saucers, body trembling in fear—was the veterinarian, Nerine Keleman. Dana had never seen such fear—not when the television crew had died in horrible pain, not when the voice in the Round House had told them of their own fate—never like this.

This was different. A primal terror. A child's fear, manifested in an adult.

There had only been five of them in the dorm when the voice of Control shook the room. Dana was still in bed and Nerine had just come over to thank her for switching beds the night before.

"Nerine Keleman, your personal challenge is to retrieve the five safety stones by confronting the dark things that live beneath your bed. You have fifteen minutes. Your time starts now."

"Your greatest fear is something under your bed?" Renee laughed.

Nerine ignored her and returned to her bunk, where she squatted and looked at the darkness beneath it. "I don't see anything." Her hand, elbow, and then her entire arm disappeared beneath the cot as she explored the darkness in search of the lifesaving safety stones. She came up empty. "Nothing."

"He said *your* bed," Dana remembered. "We switched bunks. Maybe he means this one."

"Good point." Nerine returned and repeated the process under the bed where Dana lay. "Nope." She started to remove her hand, then stopped.

"What is it?" Dana asked.

"I . . . I'm not sure." Her voice was suddenly brittle and shrill. "Feels like—"

She screamed, jerking her hand out, clutching it to her bosom as she stood, quickly backing across the room.

"Nerine?"

A scorpion, eight inches long with a segmented tail curled over its back concluding in a venomous stinger, scuttered from under the bed.

"Spider," Nerine chirped, voice pinched thin by fear.

"Not a spider, something worse," Burton said. He marched down the aisle between the beds in long, quick strides. He looked at Dana and grinned. Something dark shifted behind his brown eyes. "Dead scorpion," he said, stomping the insect flat beneath his size fourteen work boots.

He looked at Nerine, who had climbed onto the bed across from Dana. "You going to reach under there for the stones?" he asked. He didn't wait for an answer. "Didn't think so."

A quick peek to make sure the squashed arachnid had no waiting friends, then his arm disappeared beneath the bed. Everyone watched and waited.

"I can feel something," Burton said. "Just at the tip of my fingers. Can't quite reach it."

He pulled his arm back, looked at Dana, winked, then crawled beneath the bed. A fog of anxiety as thick as anything old London was capable of settled over the room. This was the first of the personal challenges and as such, an indicator of what the rest of them could expect.

No one knew if the safety stones would work under this new, deadlier game but it was worth a shot.

"Got something," Burton said, his voice muffled by the mattress. "A box. Can't move it."

The room held a collective breath. Nerine whimpered.

"Hey, it's opening it's, it's . . . oh, my God! Oh, my God, get me out, get me out!" Burton screamed, his legs thrashing, head banging against the undercarriage.

Foster, the fisherman, grabbed him by the ankles and pulled.

The welder slid from beneath the bed, his screams growing louder. His head, neck, arms, and back were covered in scorpions.

Burton stood. Scorpions scrambled to his face. He knocked them away as Foster brushed the insects from his back. Then Foster began to scream as the eight-legged creatures hustled to his hand down his arm.

Then there were more. Dozens upon dozens pouring from under the bed in a great wave of undulating brown. Aggressive and angry, lobsterlike claws snapping, curled tails and stingers ready.

And still they kept coming.

Dozens turned to hundreds. Carpeting the floor. Charging down the aisle. Moving faster than Dana thought possible in numbers too large to count, adding Renee and Brenda to their attack even as the pair turned to leave.

The scorpions, swarming at the foot of Nerine's bed, began to climb. Her skin was a color Dana had never seen. Her eyes swelled with a child's horror. Her back against the wall, she pushed against the side of the building as if hoping to break through and tumble to safety outside. Dana had the definite impression that if the scorpions reached Nerine, if they climbed her body as they were climbing her bed, she would die of fear.

Dressed in nothing but boxer shorts, T-shirt, and a short sleeved blouse, Dana studied the squirming mass. Her shoes lay somewhere beneath the undulating horde.

Scorpions.

Individually they were usually not fatal. But in multiple numbers they could bring down the largest man.

"Nerine, Nerine, get out of here." Next to Nerine's bed was one of the eight large supply crates scattered around the dorm. "The crate, Nerine—climb onto the crate."

But the young woman didn't move. Her eyes expanded, an expression of consternation and panic.

Grabbing her blanket, Dana threw it midway between the beds, then jumped. She felt the crunch and heard the abhorrent gnash of flattened scorpions beneath the cloth. As if seeking to avenge their now pastelike brethren, the swarm began climbing Dana's bare feet and legs.

The pain was instantaneous. A fierce biting sting multiplied by ten and they climbed her body like dozens of tiny grain thrashers attempting to harvest her flesh.

Jumping up on the bed with Nerine, Dana grabbed the blanket from that bed and flung it across the floor as well, removing the most immediate threat. For just a millisecond she considered jumping back on the blanket crushing as many of the little bastards as possible, but the look of undiluted terror on Nerine's face told her there wasn't time.

"Nerine, we've got to go."

No response. Her eyes rolled alarmingly in their orbits.

Dana pushed her toward the crate, urging her to climb. She did, though her movements were slumberous. Dana followed her up onto the crate.

The scorpions charged with renewed force, quickly

covering the bed. Nerine moaned. They were safe for the moment. But only a moment.

Screams and shouts came from outside the dorm, then a new voice under control and in command—Justin. He would know what to do.

"Oh, no," Nerine mewled.

The scorpions were climbing the crate.

Justin Rourke moved swiftly, snatching the fire extinguisher from its holder, pulling the pin and firing in one smooth gesture. The white foam struck the doorway with a tremendous whoosh, effectively ending the charge of the scorpions.

Renee Bellacort, wearing nothing but her bra and panties, shrieked in pain. Red welts covered her legs and arms.

"Get in the water," he ordered. "All of you."

The group charged for the surf. He turned back to the dorm. The white foam was doing the trick, cutting the swarm in half.

What the hell was going on?

"Hey, anybody?" someone cried. "We're trapped in here."

Dana.

He fired the extinguisher, forcing a part in the curtain of insects, clearing a path into the room. "Dana?"

"Up here." She was atop a crate with Nerine. The veterinarian lay with her back against the wall, her mouth was open, her body jerking. "She's having some sort of a seizure. She must be allergic. Another sting could kill her."

Justin stepped up his pace, the powerful extinguisher whooshing a snowy passage through the crawling creatures. "Stay where you are, I'm coming."

"So are the scorpions," Dana shouted. She had taken off her blouse and was using it to swat the scorpions as they climbed the crate. "Hurry!"

She was right. The insects were making a diligent effort and would soon reach the top.

Justin was less than six feet from the crate when the fire extinguisher sputtered, spat, and quit. "Shit!"

The invaders rushed in like a tide. He could survive long enough to reach Nerine and get her out of the building, but he couldn't carry both Nerine and Dana. As if reading his mind, Dana shouted, "Don't worry about me. Just get Nerine out of here."

Justin dashed forward. Scorpions crushed beneath his hiking boots. He reached the crate before feeling the first sting. Once started, the stinging intensified as more and more piled on. *Damn, they're fast and angry.*

No time to brush them away. Dana pushed Nerine toward him. He draped her over his shoulder, turned, and ran.

The doctor had arrived in response to the shouts and was tending those who had sought safety at the water's edge. One seemed particularly bad; Justin recognized him as the welder but couldn't recall his name.

He lay Nerine on the sand and yelled for the doctor. Her eyes rolled back in her head, revealing egg-white globes that seemed impossibly large.

Scorpions, still clinging to him, raced up his legs. He brushed off as many as he could. "I've got to go back," he shouted to the doctor, swatting at his pants and groin.

"No. You've suffered too many stings," the doctor said.

But Justin was already sprinting for the building, his mind desperately seeking a solution.

Dana anxiously whisked the scorpions with her blouse. It wasn't enough. There were just too many.

Something pinched the back of her feet. She turned. The scorpions had climbed the opposite side of the crate and were advancing like a raging fire.

"Dana."

Justin.

"Don't come in," she warned. "There are too many."

He was studying the floor, his face a composite of concern. "Just hang on. I'll get you out of there."

"Too late. It's too late." She was preparing to jump, run for the door, and take her chances. She moved to the edge of the crate, bracing herself to leap as far as possible. "Just like high school," she muttered.

Skrrenchh.

The sound was faint but odd enough to catch her attention. The sound of something mechanical—opening.

"Dana, the wall, the wall!" Justin shouted.

A ten-inch section of baseboard next to her bed had opened up. Hundreds of new scorpions flooded the room.

Too many, too many. She would never make it.

She looked at the ceiling, searching for an answer. The dorm was a no-nonsense affair constructed for function, not beauty. The crossbeams on the ceiling were exposed. Without taking the time to think, Dana jumped for an I-beam, grabbing it with her fingers.

She rocked like a human pendulum over the current of claws and stingers. Her arms aching, she began slowly making her way across the dorm. *The door, how far to the door?* Her muscles burned. Her arms felt as if they were being pulled from their sockets.

Keep going, keep going.

She didn't look to see where she was. She couldn't think about how much farther she had to go.

Just keep moving.

Her hand slipped.

Dana fell.

It was only a few feet, but it felt like forever. She tensed, anticipating hard contact with the floor followed by an overwhelming surge of scorpions. Instead, she felt the strength of Justin's arms. She looked at his face and then at the floor. He had ripped the mattress off the first two beds, creating a foam pontoon over the sea of bugs.

 SEATTLE

Tucker woke with a start. His right foot kicked the coffee table. Pieces of a nearly completed, five-thousand-piece jigsaw puzzle flew like chunky confetti. He didn't remember falling asleep and, for a blink of an eye, thought he was back in the warehouse, the strong scent of glue in his nostrils, the weight of the bomb in his hands.

Gasping for air, he looked around, confirming his location and the absence of any bug-eyed maniacs. He leaned forward, resting his arms on his legs, his face in his hands, and he groaned softly. Somewhere in the apartment complex a door slammed. A child cried. He could hear laughter. All the sounds of life permeated the gossamer-thin walls.

Tucker lifted his head and looked at the puzzle. Only the left-hand corner remained intact. The tip of the Sphinx against a blue sky backdrop.

"Damn." He wiped his face and tried to pull the sleep from his eyes. But images of Elliot Kay Simon were tattooed to his retinas. His source named Freedom was dead; Simon was alive; and nobody in his news department seemed to care. All because of *24/7*.

"We interrupt life to bring you a TV show," he muttered.

To make matters worse, two hours before, he had received a phone call from the shop steward threatening to expel Tucker from the union for violating occupational guidelines. "You're a photographer. Photographer. You are not authorized to function as a reporter. Do you understand?"

"I had a hell of a story," was Tucker's feeble and ultimately futile defense.

"I don't care if it was the second coming. Violate union rules again and you will be kicked out. And I don't have to remind you that being out of the union means being out of a job. Understand?"

"Yeah, yeah, yeah."

Tucker pulled himself from the couch and half stumbled into the kitchen looking for something to eat. The cabinets burgeoned with canned goods; the freezer was a shrine to frozen dinners. Too much trouble. He grabbed the bag of chips and crunched noisily.

Any chance of advancement was gone. Even keeping his job was in question and, although he knew he wouldn't be charged with murder, the stigma of being a suspect would hardly enhance his résumé. Maybe he should have let the bomb go off?

Without Gwen, what did it really matter anyway?

He took a deep breath and was overcome with a sudden sense of apprehension.

He looked around the room, trying to identify the source. The kitchen window was open. Dappled sunlight, straining through the Seattle haze, cast Rorschach shadows across the living room wall. An open book called *Mensa Logic Brainteasers* straddled the arm of the easy chair. A *TV Guide* from the week before lay on the floor turned to the movie section. And an empty cereal box sat on the end table next to a ceramic lamp with a white shade that had gone brown with age. Except for the puzzle pieces now scattered across the grayish brown carpet, nothing had changed.

The uneasiness remained. He closed his eyes and tried to qualify it, a feeling like—*like someone's in the room.*

He opened his eyes. His heart paused between beats.

Again he surveyed the room. Again he found nothing. Events of the last two days had made him jumpy, that was all. He exhaled, releasing some of the apprehension with his breath.

You're just being silly, he told himself. *There is no one in this room.*

Not *this* room, but what about the others? Aware that he wouldn't be able to rest until he proved himself a fool, Tucker got up to check. It took several seconds to will his legs to move, and then, he only took baby steps.

The bathroom was first. Small, cluttered, brown mold growing between the shower tiles, it was otherwise empty. His bedroom was next to the bath. The door was open. He looked around the doorframe. The sheets were off the bed, the dresser drawers open, their contents a jumbled mess. Clothes lay on the floor while empty hangers hung in the open closet.

He sighed. Just like he left it.

The phone rang, causing Tucker to jump. It rang again. He hesitated, catching his breath, then picked up the receiver without saying anything.

"Hello. Hello, Tucker?" The voice, soft and mildly accented, belonged to the last man in the world he expected to hear from. His mind raced over a dozen possibilities for the call, none of them good.

"I'm here. What do you want?" he asked.

A sigh leaked across the phone line. "I want to help you."

"You want to help me?" Tucker stiffened. "The last time we talked, you said, and I quote, 'I hope you die a painful and ugly death and I hope it is soon.' " Tucker stared at his reflection in the polished wood of the coffee table. The image was twisted and distorted, looking the way he felt. "You said I killed your daughter—my fiancée."

The line was quiet, both men lost in memories.

"Have you changed your mind?" Tucker asked.

"No," the caller admitted. "No, I haven't. But I'm going to help you anyway. Out of respect for my daughter. Because I believe she truly did love you."

Tucker absently rubbed the palm of his left hand against his pant leg as if trying to scrub off some unseen stain. "How? How can you help me?"

Another pause. This one elongated. The phone line hissed, then Dr. Sherman Lorrik said, "By giving you the inside story on *24/7*."

VASSA ISLAND

Dana walked along the edge of the surf. Her legs, pocked with red splotches, were now covered in a greasy salve. Her skin itched all the way to the bone, but the doctor had forbidden her from scratching. Burton Rudyard had gotten the worst of it, his face was discolored and swollen. But thanks to the doctor's treatment, he would live. Everyone would live, at least until the vote.

The sea reached for her. The froth of oxygenated water tickled her toes. The breeze off the water was the perfect counterbalance to the day's heat. An island paradise. But Dana knew it was an illusion. There was a monster on this island and it was living beneath her skin, swimming in her blood.

Something other than pain had come from the scorpion attack: information. "The game's in play." Justin had summed it up as the doctor applied salve to their injuries.

The game is in play.

What does that mean? Dana wondered.

To win your heart's desire, you must face your greatest fear—that was the show's slogan. Not only did contestants have to keep from being voted off by viewers; they had to survive all the physical and psychological challenges, many of which were tailored specifically for each contestant.

The producers knew Nerine Keleman had an unnatural fear of spiders. She had prepared herself to deal with some sort of challenge centered around that fear. But the reality, the sheer number of insects was like nothing anyone anticipated. And under no circumstances should scorpions have been used.

The game was indeed in play, and the danger factor had been ramped up to a lethal level.

The producers had boasted that the entire island was booby-trapped, engineered with computer-controlled obstacles. Nothing was as it seemed. Old buildings that looked like ruins may actually be highly sophisticated traps filled with inventive and terrifying tests. Everything was automated, run by a series of state-of-the-art computer programs.

The game is in play.

Did that mean the safety stones worked as well? Could she save her life by beating the test and using the stones?

Tick, tick, tick.

Dana's old Timex, battery-powered with a digital readout, hummed softly. The ticking came from a different source, a sealed chamber in the back of her mind where unpleasant memories were locked away from conscious thought. Most of the time.

Tick, tick, tick.

When Dana was five, she had accompanied her parents

to see her grandmother. Nana-Mom, as they called her, was sick. Cancer, someone said—a word Dana didn't know, but didn't like just the same.

Dana loved going to see Nana-Mom and associated the visits with holidays, cousins, and homemade cookies— lots and lots of cookies: gingersnaps, thumbprint, oatmeal, chocolate chip, and marshmallow-covered cornflakes made into Christmas wreaths.

But on that last visit something was wrong. The house was filled with cousins and aunts and uncles, and there was food—casserole this and casserole that, apple pie, pumpkin pie, two kinds of chocolate cake—but no cookies.

Nana-Mom's had become a cookie-free house. And that just wasn't right.

In fact, nothing was right. First Dana's mother had said Nana-Mom was sick. Then later, she said Nana-Mom was going to see Jesus.

If she was sick, why was she going on a trip?

And if she was going on a trip, why wasn't everybody happy?

Dana wasn't real sure who Jesus was but she guessed he was important, a celebrity like Santa Claus or Elvis. So why wasn't Nana-Mom excited?

The answer came from Dana's ten-year-old cousin. "Nana-Mom is dying."

"Uh-uh," Dana challenged. "She going to see Jesus Presley."

"You're just a dumb little baby. Any minute now, Nana-Mom is going to be dead. You do know what dead is don't you?"

Dana shook her head.

Her cousin rolled his eyes. A spider was crawling across the bottom step. He stomped it flat. Then, lifting the dead insect by one of its legs, he waved it in front of her. "This is dead, stupid. This is gonna be Nana-Mom when the big clock says it's time."

It was an experience Dana never forgot. And even now the thought of that dead spider swinging between her cousin's fingers made her arms break out in gooseflesh.

In the family room of her grandmother's house an old grandfather clock marked the seconds with a flamboyant *tick*, and the hour with chimes that could drown out the horn of Gabriel. The kids called it the *big clock*. Dana had spent the rest of that day and much of the night watching that clock, waiting for it to come to life and squish Nana-Mom dead like a spider.

Tick, tick, tick.

As day went into night, as the crying grew heavier, the big clock grew louder.

Tick, Tick, Tick!

Each second was louder than the one before it. Dana fell asleep in front of that arrogant, insidious clock only to be awakened later by wails of anguish. Nana-Mom was dead. Stomped flat like a spider.

Tick, tick, tick.

For thirteen years the memory of that clock had been silent—until the day doctors told Dana her daughter would never live past her teens. That was when the clock, now living in her head, began to count the seconds again. And now, here on the island it was growing louder, each tick more brazen than the one before it. Dana Kirsten took a deep soul-cleansing breath, holding the warm, moist, tropical air in her lungs, savoring it for a moment before exhaling.

Tick, tick, tick.

The big clock continued keeping time with pernicious accuracy, marking the moments left before Dana Kirsten and everyone else on this island was smashed flat like a spider.

*   *   *

The first aid station was in a small building a football field away from the dormitory. Justin Rourke grimaced as Dr. Efrem Dutetre applied more salve to his multitude of bites.

"How is the pain?" the doctor inquired.

"It stings and I'm a little nauseated, but I'll live. I'm more worried about falling down. With all this grease on me I'm likely to slide right off the island."

The doctor snorted. "You must have a hell of a constitution."

"My older brother used to say I was just too stupid to get sick," Justin confessed.

"Used to?"

"He was a cop. Got killed on the job."

"I'm sorry." The doctor looked around the building. They were alone for the moment. "I want you to take it easy for a few days. There's no way of knowing how the scorpion venom will react with the virus already in your blood system."

It was a thought Justin had not considered. "Recommendation noted," he said.

The dorm was the only luxury on the island. The cots provided a reasonably comfortable place to sleep and the canned food assured that the contestants had plenty to eat. The idea was for the players to be free to concentrate on solving the puzzles and entertaining the viewers.

Now the dorm belonged to the scorpions.

Justin bit his lower lip in thought. Scorpions? Nerine? The baseboard? What did it all mean? Each personal challenge was accompanied with an answer. Figuring it out would not only allow them to reclaim the dorm and their food supply, but it was also worth five safety stones.

The trick was to look at the problem from different angles. Everything was relative. Find the right perspective and you would find the answer. It was a lesson taught over and over by history, one of Justin's passions. Repeatedly the victors were the ones who viewed the challenge correctly.

So what was the proper way to view a scorpion attack?

Justin changed his perspective by starting with the answer. Obviously, that would be pesticide. It would have to come with some sort of delivery system, most likely a pressurized tank. So the answer would involve a hiding place large enough to accommodate that tank. Which could be almost anywhere.

All right, another angle.

Where had the scorpions come from?

The small trapdoor on the baseboard. One under the bed and one beside it. But how had they gotten there? Obviously they had been put in place before the show began. Which explained their aggression.

Maybe the answer was there, too?

Dana Kirsten walked the shoreline until she came to a large log. She sat drawing circles in the sand with a stick and imagining she could feel the virus moving, *scheming*, as it waited in her bloodstream.

She didn't see the fisherman until he sat down beside her. He held a cigarette in his right hand as if it were a precious jewel. They each had been allowed to bring one personal item. Dana had brought a picture of Jenna; Brenda, the butcher, had brought a wicked looking knife; and Foster had brought a carton of cigarettes.

"We're getting off this island. You with us?" He took a deep long pull on the cigarette. The tip turned bright at the increase in oxygen.

"What do you mean, leave?"

He held the smoke in his lungs, giving the carcinogen plenty of time to do its job, then he slowly blew smoke out of the corner of his mouth. "There's a boat over at the dock. Couple of 'em in fact. Couple of jet skis, too. I reckon it's what the host and support crew were going to use to go back to their plush accommodations on one of the other islands. I checked out the biggest boat. Diesel engine, plenty of fuel. Piece of cake. I can get us out of here."

"I thought the doctor said we couldn't leave?"

He looked at her for a moment. His brown eyes seemed uncommonly dull, as if constant exposure to the sun had scored the corneas. "I'll tell you a secret."

A seagull cawed, then dived for the water.

The fisherman grinned. "I'm the guy that's gonna win this thing."

"Win?" Dana frowned. "What do you mean win? You're going to survive to the end?"

The fisherman laughed, a phlegmy sound not far removed from a cough. "Don't you get it? There is no virus. No Control. It's all part of the game."

Dana held the thought for a moment. Could he be right? Sweet God, she wanted him to be right. "What about everyone dying in front of us? And the bodies Justin and the others moved?"

He took another drag on the cigarette, then exhaled slowly. A smile was buried deep in that patchy brown beard. "No, they said they moved the bodies. And as for the dying? Hell, you ever heard of special effects?"

The seagull was back. No fish.

Foster looked over his shoulders as if they were in downtown Manhattan instead of a lonely beach in the Caribbean Sea. "I shouldn't be telling you this. Shouldn't tell anybody." He paused, letting his eyes lick her body.

Dana drew her legs up and wrapped her arms around them, making herself into a human ball.

The fisherman was unfazed. "Fact is I like you. A lot. You and a couple of the others are okay. I've decided to let you be in the final four."

"Final four?" For a moment, Dana wondered if the virus could affect your mental processes.

He laughed, which turned into a hacking cough. "It's all an act—makeup, special effects. That's it. The others, the ones who claimed to have stored the bodies—they're in on it. It's a television show, for Christ's sake. They aren't going to let people die on TV." Foster sucked his cigarette. "Think about it."

Down the beach someone began to yell.

Four people stood by the waterline pointing toward the sea.

"What is it?" Dana asked, then noticed a shape. "A ship?"

"Ships, plural," said a woman with dyed red hair and a necklace displaying all the signs of the zodiac.

"Are they coming for us?" Brenda Segar asked.

"No. They've just been sitting there."

"So what are they waiting for?" the CPA asked.

Dana was pleased to see that he was no longer crying. *Wonder if he just ran out of tears?*

"They ain't here to get us off. They're here to keep us on," said the woman with the zodiac necklace.

"Keep us on? What does that mean?" The whine was building in the CPA's voice.

"It means they don't want us to leave," Dana answered. "Not yet anyway." The words felt like barbed wire cutting her throat. "The doctor was right. They can't chance us exposing the rest of the population to the virus."

The CPA began to cry.

Batten down the hatches, it's going to be a—typhoon, Dana thought, then chastised herself for being so callous. Still, the sight of the whimpering man was just grating. They were all scared; they all wanted to go home.

But, for the most part, they were all holding up except for Mr. Money.

The woman with the red hair turned and introduced herself. "The name's Pheodora—Pheodora Cuvier."

"She's a psychic," Brenda added.

"Nice to meet you. I'm Dana Kirsten. A psychic, huh?"

"Yeah, and she's real good, too," Brenda answered. "She knew that I'm a butcher, that I had just broken up with my boyfriend, and that there was this guy, this other guy who sort of likes me and I sort of like him but neither of us want to make the first move and . . ."

Brenda talked in a rapid fire up-speak that reminded Dana of a kid banging on a toy piano. For her part, Pheodora just shrugged as if to say, *What can you do?* Obviously she didn't take herself nearly as seriously as Brenda did.

Dana liked that.

"So what do you think is going to happen, Pheodora? Some are saying people won't vote. What happens then?"

The psychic chewed on a piece of bubble gum. *Her personal item?* "I think they're wrong. People are going to vote. Bet your sweet ass on that. They're going to vote a lot." She leaned over so her face was only inches from the camera around Dana's neck. "But they shouldn't. You shouldn't be part of this," she told the audience. She straightened up. "But they will."

"If Pheodora says they will vote, they will vote," Brenda said. "She knows things. This one time—"

Dana interrupted. "Why are you so sure?"

Pheodora shrugged, then blew a bubble the size of a softball. She let it live for a minute in the warm morning sun, then popped it and pulled it back into her mouth. " 'Cause I know people. It's sort of what I do."

Dana nodded. The psychic was echoing Dana's own

thoughts. People will vote. They will certainly vote. And then? One of them would die.

Unless?

The fisherman's words sounded in her head.

This *is* the game.

The alarm sounded. The summons to the Round House.

It was time.

They walked in funereal procession.

As the last person entered the room, the alarm stopped.

How does it know? Dana wondered.

Each alcove was marked with a name. For a terrifying moment Dana feared that, because she was a last-minute alternate, they had forgotten to reprogram her alcove; but she found her name on the opposite side of the room. Pheodora was to her right. A woman identified by her badge as a teacher, to Dana's left.

"Showtime," Pheodora said.

Suddenly the four-sided reader board that hung dominantly from the center of the ceiling came to life. Their names were on the left, an empty space marked VOTES on the right.

At the top, a clock presented the time: 11:59:22.

They waited quietly. The sound of breathing echoing in the round building created a bizarre cacophony of wheezing background music for the horror movie that was now their lives.

The clock changed to: 12:00:00.

Nothing happened. Then the right side of the board came to life. The votes were being counted.

Dana tried vainly to keep track of who had what, who was leading, who was safe. But her eyes seemed tethered to her own name, her own column: fifty-eight votes . . . fifty-nine . . . sixty-three . . . eighty-eight . . .

They were voting for her, people were voting for her to die.

Ninety-one votes.

Suddenly Dana prayed her family had organized to save her. But that meant choosing someone else to die.

One hundred and fourteen.

The thought was too barbaric to contemplate, but there it was.

She forced herself to look at the others' votes to compare her total numbers with theirs. The whimpering CPA led the count with more than twelve hundred voting for him to die.

Twelve hundred?

My God, how many people were voting? How sick was the world? But truthfully that was her second thought. Her first was relief. Shameful, self-interested relief.

The CPA began to cry louder.

One thousand, two hundred and ninety-eight votes.

No one else was even close.

A second alarm sounded. A combination buzz and bell.

The room was quiet save for the sound of the crying CPA. Then, Control spoke.

"The votes are in. Charles Penton, you have been exiled from the island. The rest of you, place your right thumbs on the scanners at your alcoves."

They all obeyed. Dana saw that a red bar ran under her finger, then a box popped open. Inside was a device that looked like an inhaler.

"This is a bee-sting injector. Apply it to your arm or leg and press the trigger. You will be inoculated. You will live to see another day."

"No. No!" The CPA shouted. "No!" He beat on the box in front of him. It hadn't opened. "It's not fair. It's a mistake. I need my shot. I need the medication."

The room rang with the sound of his fist hitting the box.

At first Dana thought it was a hot breeze, a blast of tropical air, then she realized it wasn't coming from outside but inside. Her skin was getting warmer. She was uncomfortable. It was difficult to breathe.

The virus.

It's real. It's real. This is not a game.

Her hands were shaking as she placed the injector against her left arm and pulled the trigger. As the name implied, a sting, little more than the prick of a bee, struck her arm. The relief was almost instantaneous. She closed her eyes forcing herself to breathe deeply, to enjoy the cooling sensation that ran through her body.

"No!" the CPA screamed. Blood covered his hands as he beat them raw pounding on the box. "No, no, it's not fair, not fair!"

Dana was surprised to see he was no longer alone.

Justin. The pilot pushed the man away from the alcove, then attacked the box with a crowbar. A *crowbar*—he had come prepared. Dana watched in amazement as Justin forced the bar under the lip of the box. He pressed down with all his might, his face taut and red with strain. The doctor joined him.

The CPA backed up until he struck the wall. His tears were unstoppable. His skin was now an unhealthy red.

The box popped open, the sound echoing in the room like a shot.

They did it.

Pushing himself away from the wall, the CPA ran to the alcove. Justin and the doctor stepped aside, their heads hung low.

The CPA stood before the ruined box just looking at it. This time he didn't scream. He didn't cry. Something behind his eyes whispered to Dana that he was already dead.

"Empty," he muttered. "It's empty."

His face began to move. The skin rippling like a body underneath a bedsheet. Then, incredibly, the skin began to bubble, to brew. The CPA screamed in pain. This one was different from all the others—a primal scream of defeat and agony. His skin began to burst. Blood gushed forward, running down his face, hands, arms, and legs. His wail was impossibly long, impossibly anguished. Dana knew it was a sound she would hear for the rest of her life.

The CPA collapsed to the floor, no longer resembling a person but rather a silhouette of a man painted in blood.

Dana forced herself to look away. She looked at the central camera that hung beneath the reader board. It was turned toward the CPA. She heard the lens move as the camera zoomed in.

The CPA died in agony.

And the world watched.

The other contestants were crying now, tears ignited by heartbreak and horror.

The electronically distorted voice of the one who called himself Control spoke. **"Eleven contestants, ten days."**

9 SEATTLE

The epiphany came at 10:17 A.M. Pacific Standard Time, one hour and fifteen minutes after the horrifying death of the CPA on Vassa Island. Nelson Rycroft had been sitting alone at his desk, more depressed than at any other time in his life.

His career, his remarkable career, was over.

At thirty-two, Rycroft had been the network's wonder kid, the man with the golden nose. "I can smell a hit like others smell farts," he joked. The upper echelons laughed—because it was true.

Rycroft had started at Globe as a page and received a promotion of some sort every two months thereafter, moving from gofer to mail clerk to assistant to the assistant of production and on up the line until he reached deputy assistant to the director of network production.

Then, for a time, the promotions stopped.

The problem was not in Rycroft's work but in his superior, the man tying up the next rung on the ladder. A man with a reputation far greater than Rycroft's.

That was the first time that fate asserted itself on Rycroft's behalf, proving, at least to Nelson Rycroft, that he was a golden child, his rise to greatness predetermined and unstoppable.

His mentor had been the creator and driving force behind, what was then, the most popular and successful reality show in television history: *True Life.*

The premise was simple and elegant. Forget a handful of people in a stressful situation living under the public microscope; *True Life* put an entire society in the spotlight. A former movie studio was purchased and doubled in size. Then a makeshift community, complete with roads, shops, homes, schools, and even a church—everything needed for a normal life—was built under a sky of studio lights.

The number of cameras was extraordinary. The magnitude of scrutiny amazing.

The contestants were carefully selected, in some cases entire families, from as many different walks of life as possible, all chosen specifically to create maximum turmoil. Then they were forced to live in a human terrarium.

The public loved it. Until its premature end.

From the beginning one participant stood out—a young woman who understood the concept and knew how to work it. Her name was Sherine Beauvant, a sexy blonde with haunting cobra-black eyes. Prior to the show she worked as a laborer at a medical supply factory. Two weeks into the program, she was one of the most recognizable stars in the country.

It wasn't racial, religious, or political conflict that brought viewers to the show in record numbers; it was something much simpler, more basic: *sex*.

With her innate ability to understand what the public wanted, Sherine set out to become a star whether she won the contest or not. She immediately stirred things up with a string of torrid affairs. Because the Globe Network was a cable channel, many of the encounters were shown uncensored, with the camera discreetly moving away at the appropriate time to prevent the charge of pornography.

The show quickly went from two nights a week to six, each program live, interspersed with taped highlights. On most nights Sherine's breasts were the star. Men loved her, women hated her, but everyone watched her.

The public couldn't get enough, intoxicated with the rampant destruction, watching with disbelief as Sherine moved from the single to the married men. The more challenging the catch, the greater the interest.

The only man considered unattainable was a forty-two-year-old minister, a father of three, married twenty-one years. He had never gotten so much as a traffic ticket or returned a video tape without rewinding it.

The minister was the moral center of the program. As Sherine went through other men like an allergy sufferer goes through tissues, the minister offered her nothing more than spiritual counseling.

Then two and half months into the three-month-long show, Sherine whispered something in the minister's ear, just loud enough for the microphone to pick up. "I've found a blind spot. The one place in all the world where we can be alone and no one can see."

Later that evening, in a restricted area, closed off for construction, Sherine waited. And to America's surprise, the minister came. The sex was fast and passionate. Afterward, as she dressed slowly and he looked at her, breathing heavily, he asked when they could meet again.

Sherine had laughed. "Never," she said. Her smile became a sneer.

He blinked with disbelief. "Please. Don't tease me. When can I see you?"

Her sneer became a giggle. "You're such a silly man. I've gotten what I wanted."

She then pointed with one long, evilly perfect finger, to a dark corner of the ceiling, a spot the minister had failed to see.

A camera.

"Smile, you're on television."

His world ended before her sentence did.

"Live," she continued, clapping her hands together like a child opening the perfect Christmas gift. "*Live*, for all the world to see."

His heart seemed to die between beats. His life destroyed in the name of entertainment.

She giggled at his screams, laughed at his threats.

His hatred became a wildfire, quick and devastating. She was evil incarnate. A beast. A creature.

"What are you going to do, preacher man? What are you going to do?" She waved at the camera, her perfect fingers swirling. "After all, you agreed to this, agreed to be on reality television."

He snatched a screwdriver from a nearby workbench. Then screaming, "How's this for reality?" he plunged the shaft deep into his chest.

And the world watched.

It was the last blow. The show was pulled from the air. Reality television was over.

At the time Rycroft knew he should have been upset, worried for his mentor, but as soon as the numbing shock wore off enough for other thoughts to be born, he realized what it meant. His mentor was finished. The way was clear for Nelson Rycroft.

That was five years ago and now Rycroft was the network's number one guy. Two years ago he had single-handedly brought reality television back to the small screen. And now, *24/7* was to have been his crowning glory.

Then this.

The police, the fucking FBI had kept him tied up for ten hours—ten hours—like he was somehow responsible for what was happening. Hell, no. *Why would I slit my own throat?* Rycroft had asked. He was many things, but suicidal was not one of them.

But the real problem was the network.

He knew he was in trouble when the high-level meetings began and, for the first time in five years, he was left out. The irony of being brought down by the same sort of scandal (albeit a lot worse) that brought down his mentor was not lost on him.

But, unlike his mentor, he refused to give up.

Nelson Rycroft was not a quitter. He was a winner. He would turn this around; he would make this work in his favor. And his old accomplice, fate, would help. Although at first, he couldn't imagine how.

He watched helplessly as the network pulled the show and denounced what was happening. But the signal from the island couldn't be stopped. Even without Globe running the program, people with satellites were picking it up. Other networks were airing excerpts. Everyone seemed to be making money and getting monster ratings. Everyone but Globe.

Then there was the Internet. Anyone with a computer could still access any of the six hundred and thirty-eight cameras.

It was the worst-case scenario. The network was being clobbered with its own club.

Nelson Rycroft had not left the building since returning from the police station. He had spent the night in his office, alternately wondering how long it would be his office and watching the Internet feeds.

That morning he had watched with the rest of the country as an accountant from Ohio melted to death. It just kept getting worse.

But a short time later he had his epiphany.

He asked for and received an emergency meeting with the president of the network. Any hope that the response was prompt because of the high regard he was held in quickly evaporated when the head man said, "So, I assume you are here to tender your resignation."

That took Rycroft back a bit. But only for a moment. Looking around the office—at the incredible view of Seattle, the awards on the walls, the photos taken with the rich and famous—Nelson Rycroft made himself a promise. By this time next year, this office would be his.

Then, with fate sitting on his shoulder, he made his pitch and watched with amusement as the color drained from the old man's face.

VASSA ISLAND

They left the Round House stunned and silent, the walking dead, as if they all had just glimpsed the future and witnessed their demise. The others, the crew, had been strangers. The CPA was different. They knew him, even if they didn't like him. And now he was dead. And soon they would be too, unless—

Unless what? A miracle?

The ground was porous and yielded easily to the board Justin Rourke was using as a shovel. Within half an hour he had dug down four feet. He was beginning to doubt himself when he struck something hard and metallic.

He scraped away the dirt revealing a large, four- by six-foot box with a small latch handle. It turned easily. Inside he found twenty to thirty dead scorpions, a large pressurized pesticide tank and a small knit bag containing five vermilion glass balls—safety stones.

The trapdoor indicated where he should look. Finding its approximate location on the outside of the dorm, he had begun to dig, reasoning that there had to be a place to store the scorpions, and that place would most likely also hold the answer.

The pesticide was sealed so as not to kill the bugs prematurely. He lifted the tank out of the box. It was just over ten pounds, but at an awkward angle. His muscles ached and for a moment he thought he was going to throw up. The doctor's warning flashed across his thoughts.

We don't know how the scorpion venom may react with the virus already in your system.

Then the tank was free. He undid the plastic covering on the nozzle, unlocked the handle, and primed the pump. A wide arc of sour smelling, yellow-white liquid spewed out.

The scorpions would be dead, the dormitory livable, by dinnertime. But more important, Justin now had five safety stones, meaning he could negate up to fifty percent of the vote.

* * *

Returning to the dorm, Dana was debating what to do next when Renee Bellacort, the beautiful real estate agent, said she had an announcement to make. Then, affecting a voice that seemed unnaturally girlish, she turned to one of the wall cameras and said: "Actually it's a confession."

Confession.

The word was like the banging of a gong. Everyone was paying attention.

Wringing her hands, her brown eyes veiled in tears, Renee licked her collagen-perfect lips, paused for a breath and then, in a voice just above a whisper, said, "I . . . I'm pregnant."

"Bullshit!" Pheodora Cuvier muttered as she sat on the bed next to Dana. "If she's pregnant, then I'm a virgin." Then, turning to look Dana in the eyes, she added, "And believe me, honey, I ain't no virgin."

"It's too convenient," Dana agreed, somewhat surprised by the intensity of her own disbelief.

"Right. And what about the physical they gave us before we came here. Damned if those doctors didn't poke and prod me in every pokeable and prodable spot on my body. Including some that weren't but are now. You telling me she got pregnant in the last three days?"

Pheodora shook her head. Moon-shaped earrings swayed with the gesture. "I ain't buying it. Not for one minute. Look at her."

Renee was holding court at the far end of the dorm. Several women and several more men were gathered around her, ostensibly offering support. The tears were gone, replaced by a dazzling smile. Whenever one of the men said anything remotely funny, she would throw back her head and laugh, exposing her neck and offering an unrestricted glimpse of her breasts. Sometimes she would reach out and touch one of the men on the arm or shoulder, producing a grin so wide it cleaved the recipient's face.

"She's a bitch, that's what," Pheodora said. "And she's playing us all for fools. She knows if people think she's pregnant, they won't vote her off."

Dana shook her head. "She may be a bitch, but she's a smart bitch. I don't know about you, but I'd thought of that."

As Dana watched Renee, someone else was watching her. Burton Rudyard shifted his position, putting the support post between him and the two women. The redhead with the flashy wardrobe held little interest, but the other . . . He sucked in a sharp, invigorating breath. Something hot and beastly moved in the back of his mind and he imagined a creature with black claws and a breath of fire shucking off timeworn chains. A creature yearning to be free.

He had noticed her the first day. Others were prettier but there was something different about Dana—her tight body, the way she held herself with confidence and determination. Yeah, she appealed to him on a deeper level than he imagined possible.

Something about her spoke to him, sang to the dark side he worked so hard to hold in check. But he knew, just by looking at her, that she wanted it, needed it. He could tell she would fight and scream and cry, all the time secretly loving every minute of it.

Control yourself.

The scorpion stings had left him sick and swollen and remarkably free. The venom had not only reminded him of his own mortality, but had freed him from the shackles of convention.

For thirty years Burton had maintained control, successfully keeping his dark side in check. He made a good living as a welder. And even though his two marriages ended in divorce, one after less than three months, he was not some desperate loser who could only get a woman by force.

No. He knew he was attractive, knew he appealed to women, at least until they got to know him. Still, that dark side wanted more, wanted control, power, and complete domination.

He touched his forehead. It was hot and clammy. His hand came away moist with sweat. It was getting harder to constrain himself. But, if death were truly imminent, why bother? Why not die happy?

No. Compose yourself; don't lose control.

But as he sat on the bunk in the island dormitory, feeling himself grow hard at the thought of dominating and destroying Dana Kirsten, he knew something had changed. Something wicked and wonderful had broken loose.

The psychology books that he plowed through looking for ways to control his darker impulses called it a *stressor*, a triggering event that caused deviant behavior to escalate. Yeah, well, being contaminated with a lethal virus, knowing you are going to die sometime in the next twelve days was certainly a *stressor*.

Across the room Dana laughed. Her eyes brightened like lightbulbs in that moment when the lightning hits the house, that fragment of time before the fuse blows or the building goes up in flames. He wondered if they would flare as brightly in fear?

He bit his lower lip until he broke the skin. The hot, salty taste of blood was invigorating. It made him think of her.   ·

10 SEATTLE

The downside to the Globe Newschannel's continuing success was that true journalism was often sacrificed for sexier stories. The upside was Tucker Thorne now had the inside scoop on the sexiest story of them all.

"You what?" asked the news director incredulously. They were in the office of the network vice president, on the top floor of the Globe building. What would have been a commanding view of downtown Seattle was marred by a steady, gray rain. Silver trails ran down the glass distorting the ambient light, making it difficult to discern the sky from the horizon.

The vice president sat behind a large mahogany desk with walnut veneer and a hand-rubbed catalyzed finish. He had been quiet while Tucker made his pitch. And remained so, as Rubin Hearth, the news director, reacted. "This is bullshit."

"I think it's very logical. You make me a reporter. I give you the scoop on the biggest story of the year and Globe beats all the other networks. Simple."

"Give us the story, and maybe, just maybe, we'll talk."

Tucker shook his head. "I can't believe you're asking that. Right now I'm a photographer, not a reporter."

The news director growled, turning his sharklike head from side to side, as if looking for a lonely swimmer to chomp on. "You can't do this. You can't blackmail us into promoting you."

Tucker shifted in the black leather club chair, which he suspected cost more than his car, and directed his comments to the vice president. "And I'm not. I'm just negotiating the terms. This is a unique opportunity. A win-win. You get the inside scoop, I get the promotion, union's happy, you're happy, I'm happy. See? Lots of happy all the way around."

"As an employee of this company, you are obligated to share any information you obtain while on the job. Any information."

"I didn't *obtain* this information on the job. As far as obligation, I'm obliged to take video for you and that's it. A fact that the shop steward has already called and reminded me of. And I know you don't want to go against the union, now do you?"

The vice president snickered. The news director was not amused.

"Forget it, we will not be blackmailed by some over-zealous camera jockey too stupid to remember his place, just because he stumbles across a piece of useful information for the first and probably the only time in his life!" The news director's jowls shook as he yelled, his forehead furrowed into an imposing V.

The vice president held up his hands for silence. He sat forward, the expensive leather of his executive chair popping softly as it reconfigured to support his new position.

Tucker's mouth was dry. His hands and feet were numb. He was taking a gamble—a big gamble. And the news director was right; he was trying to blackmail the company. But it was a gamble worth taking. Having a bomb glued to his hands had given him a new perspective. What was the worst that could happen? They would fire him? So? He would still have all of his appendages, still be alive.

"Okay, son," said the vice president. "Provided the information you have is legit, go ahead. You're a reporter."

"What?" the news director spat. His bald head was framed in a horseshoe of freshly dyed hair. Even his scalp seemed flushed. "This is ridiculous."

A reporter.

Tucker held the moment for one full breath savoring the victory. *If only Gwen were here to see it.* "Thank you, sir. You won't regret it."

The news director crossed his arms and huffed. Tucker offered him a smile and continued. "First of all, this will not be my only tip. My source is at the highest level and assures me he will keep me posted."

"Who's your source?" the news director demanded.

"I would tell you if I could, but I can't. My source is very adamant about that. I'm to be the only one who knows."

"Bullshit!"

"So you've said," the vice president observed, then turned back to Tucker. "What have you got?"

Tucker nodded. "A United States Naval group has been dispatched to quarantine the island."

"Ha, that's your tip?" the news director jeered. "Hell, I've known that for hours."

Tucker smiled then continued. "And, in approximately forty-five minutes a Special Forces Strike Team will launch an assault on Vassa Island."

COVINGTON, GEORGIA

Godzilla roared.

Fifteen-year-old Bobby Vance rushed to the computer. Godzilla was the sound effect that indicated he had an instant message. An alternately red and yellow banner flashed across the bottom of his screen.

<GO TO CAMERA 159>

The boy's fingers moved like a concert pianist's as he quickly typed in the proper commands to access the camera he wanted.

He was taking a sick day from school. In fact, almost everyone he knew was taking a sick day. Some of the teachers, too.

His bedroom had been transformed into *24/7* headquarters. Maps of the island had replaced pictures of Britney Spears and Christina Aguilera. His television, tuned to CNN, was left on with the volume low, but with the remote handy so he could turn it up when he heard Vassa Island.

In a way, *24/7* was the best thing that had ever happened to him. Bobby Vance was a ninja at the computer. Within hours of the crisis, he had designed and executed a program that cycled through one hundred of the main island cameras, staying on each for five seconds then moving to the next. Tapping Enter would stop it on whichever shot was being displayed at the time. He had already sent out twelve copies of the program to friends and friends of friends. Some of them were even cute girls.

Puberty had been slow to come to Bobby. He could use any edge he could get.

Although he had noticed something odd. Sometimes one or two of the cameras, even the choker-cams worn by the contestants, would stop working, anywhere from one minute to an hour. No big deal, he could still follow the action on the other six hundred–plus cameras. Still, the glitch was odd.

Bobby and his friends had developed an alert system that would make Paul Revere proud. Whenever anyone saw anything of interest, usually involving nudity, they would flash-alert the group. The current flash-alert sent Bobby to camera one hundred and fifty-nine.

The computer screen flickered once, then Bobby's

breath caught in his chest. Nerine Keleman was taking off her shirt. Bobby glanced to the side of the screen where he had taped a legend identifying the location of each camera. Nerine was in a small storage room of what had been the supply shed back when Vassa Island was used as a military listening post. For the most part, the contestants had been changing in the tiny bathroom or under blankets. Obviously, Nerine had found what she thought was a safe spot.

But camera number one hundred and fifty-nine was a stealth camera, one of many hidden on the island. The contestants had been warned of this but it was easy to forget.

Nerine began to unbutton her shirt.

Although she was thirty-two, ancient by teenage standards, she was nonetheless appealing. With shoulder-length auburn hair, subtler than the vibrant red of the psychic, and with small features and rose-soft cheeks she reminded him of old photographs he had seen of Ann-Margret, the actress.

Her shirt came off. He dry swallowed. She was wearing a white lace bra, the top half was see-through. She reached behind her back and undid the clasp.

At that very moment Bobby Vance felt as if he were rocketing through puberty.

SEATTLE

"You're crazy." Under normal circumstances the chairman of the board calling an underling crazy would have been a bad thing. But these were not normal circumstances. And Nelson Rycroft was no ordinary underling. In fact, this was the response he was counting on.

"Just let it sink in a minute," he advised.

"I don't have to let it sink in," the chairman pro-claimed. "It's crazy. Do you know how much this will cost us? How much this already has cost us? Hell, our stock has fallen thirty-two percent from yesterday to today . . ."

Rycroft made a mental note: *buy more stock*.

". . . we're struggling to avoid bankruptcy here. And even if we do somehow survive, the company is left com-pletely open for a hostile takeover. You've effectively killed this network."

Rycroft smiled, which only seemed to make the chair-man's already red face grow darker.

"So you're saying this network is dead?"

"All but," the chairman spat.

"Good. Then we have nothing to lose and everything to gain."

The chairman opened his mouth to speak, but paused, allowing the logic of Rycroft's plan to sink in.

The younger man took advantage of the opening. "Think of it. Everyone is making a profit off this. Even if we could somehow prevent our competitors from airing excerpts, it would do nothing to stop anyone with a satellite dish from dialing it up, not to mention the Internet."

Rycroft leaned forward as he spoke. "It's already out there and it's going to stay out there no matter what we do. It's not going away. So stopping it is not an op-tion. And since it can't be stopped anyway, why should everyone profit from this, but us? We're victims here, too. We're the ones who have had the most expensive show in television history stolen from us. It seems only right that we gain some small profit from the result."

The chairman shook his head, still not convinced. "But the public. We're getting hate mail. Did you see those picketers this morning? We are public enemy number one. And now you're suggesting we go back to the original plan and air a nightly program?"

Rycroft shook his head. "No. Not like the original planned. That was just an hour. I'm suggesting two hours. Every night from eight to ten. The best of *24/7*."

"But the sponsors?"

"Will leave, yes, I'm aware of that. I'm also aware that as soon as they see the numbers we get in the ratings, they will come crawling back, begging us for airtime."

"But the public good . . ."

"Screw the public good," Rycroft snapped, the force of his objection causing the chairman to jerk back in surprise.

The younger man took a slow breath, then spoke more softly. "It's out there. It's going to be out there no matter what we do. And we are going to be condemned no matter what we do." He paused, pursing his lips. "So, why not make money."

The old man steepled his fingers, tapping his lower lip.

Got 'im, Rycroft thought. "Give me one show and I guarantee the highest ratings this network has ever seen."

VASSA ISLAND

"Ah, Nerine?"

Nerine Keleman jumped, clutching her half-removed bra to her chest. "Don't come in here," she squealed. "I've got my shirt off. They'll see me on your choker-cam."

Dana chuckled. "Yeah, well about that. Look up at the smoke detector in the right corner. Do you see the cable? That's not a power cord. It's an optical cord. In other words, that's a camera."

"Oh, my Lord." Nerine hurried out of the room as if

confronted by a snake. Her face was burnished red. "I was just about to . . ."

"Make a lot of people very happy—yeah, I know. I almost did the same thing this morning."

"I should have known better. It's just, well, it's almost impossible to get into the bathroom, and when you do there's not enough room to change." She put her shirt on and quickly buttoned up the front. "Why would they hide a camera like that?"

"Better television. Remember, they said there were over six hundred cameras here and that many of them were covert. Come on, I was about to change myself. I'll show you a place in the jungle. I'm reasonably sure it's safe."

He waited for thirty seconds, then followed as quietly as a shadow. He found them quickly, alerted by Dana's laughter. Burton smiled. He loved her voice.

I wonder how her screams will sound?

"Stop it, stop it now," he mumbled to himself. What was happening to him? What in God's name was happening to him?

Somewhere, deep inside, hidden in the farthest recesses of his mind, something dark and wicked laughed. He stopped in his tracks and put his hands over his ears. "Stop it, stop it, stop it," he repeated.

The pounding of his heart was now in rhythm with the laughter.

Think of something else. Think of work. Welding. When was his last job? Last week? It seemed longer, infinitely longer. He was repairing stanchions at an auto shop. Good work. Good money. He thought of the torch, the blinding sparks viewed through his protective visor, the hiss of pressurized fire on stern metal. The sound, the sound. The cry of a thousand women screaming at his feverish touch.

* * *

A warm wind slipped through the trees and caressed her erect nipples. Dana took a deep breath, tasting the wet salt air, letting it invigorate and refresh her inside and out. She stretched out her arms and sighed, then casting an eye to her new friend she teased, "Sure you don't want to try it? Kind of refreshing."

Nerine offered a nervous laugh, then developed an incredible interest in her shoes. She had changed first and quickly.

Dana laughed. "I'm embarrassing you."

"No. No. I'm fine." Nerine shrugged. "It's just that if I look up then you'll be on camera, remember the choker-cams?"

"Oh, God, I can't believe I forgot about that already." She slipped the short red top over her head. It was a crop top, leaving the midriff exposed to the elements, far cooler than the safari shirt she had been wearing. "There, I'm dressed. You can look now."

Nerine raised her head tentatively. "You sure? I feel like I should stick a dollar in your panties."

"A dollar? That's all? This is prime real estate. People would pay big bucks to see these puppies live and in person," Dana joked. She usually wasn't this bawdy, but she felt a special closeness with the women on the island.

Dana heard something in the woods.

"What?" Nerine asked, picking up on the other woman's sudden distraction.

Dana held up a finger for quiet and studied the jungle behind them. Nothing moved, nothing rustled, then a bird cawed taking to the air in frenzied flight. Dana shrugged, suddenly feeling very foolish. "Guess I'm just a bit jumpy."

Twenty yards away, behind a thicket of briars, the man remained perfectly still. He waited till the conversation resumed, then slowly, very slowly Burton moved forward.

11 VASSA ISLAND

Justin was one step away from death. One strong north wind and he would go hurtling fifty feet to the rocks below. Even this far up, the surf sounded with fierce authority as it flogged house-size boulders.

He held out his arms and let the sea breeze cool him down. He had followed the jagged trail two-thirds of the way around the island and was sweating profusely. But it was worth it. As a pilot, he appreciated seeing the big picture and took comfort in having the entire island laid out at his feet.

His lap around the island served three purposes: first, to familiarize himself with the physical layout; second, to note areas not covered by a camera; and third, to find out what he wasn't supposed to know.

From his cliffside vantage point, Justin saw five buildings that did not appear on the map. He noted the location of each.

The buildings, the majority of which were left from when Vassa was a military base, were in various stages of ruin. Or appeared to be. Engineers had gone to great effort to ensure that all additions blended in with the rest of the island. But Justin had discovered a flaw. Most of the structures were marked with small, white wooden signs: EISENHOWER BUILDING, PHRIXUS PAVILION, GANYMEDE

HALL, PATTON BUILDING. The signs all appeared to be hand-painted and in some cases were so faded and peeled they were hardly readable. But closer inspection revealed that several were actually vinyl prints applied to wood and digitally altered to appear old.

It was a subtle thing, nothing anyone would notice unless they tried to flick away nonexistent paint chips. To Justin it signaled that these buildings had been severely altered and so were most likely to house the coveted safety stones.

He stepped back from the cliff and looked at the island interior. It was covered in scrub trees, brush, and porous rocks, the latter making the whole island prone to sinkholes after a stiff rain.

A history buff, Justin reviewed what he knew about Vassa Island. Both Vassa and its sister island, Navassa, had been discovered in the early 1500s by Christopher Columbus. They were ignored for three hundred years as settlements grew on other, more hospitable parcels of land. But in 1857 Vassa was discovered again—this time by an American named Peter Duncan who claimed it in the name of the United States of America, despite serious protest from Haiti.

Justin picked up a stone and hurled it into the interior of the island. A startled bird with long black and blue feathers took to the air. The thing that had transformed Vassa from obscurity to choice property was guano— birdshit.

The year before Duncan came to Vassa, Congress passed the Guano Act, which allowed the United States to claim any unclaimed, uninhabited property that had guano. In the mid-1800s guano was used as a powerful organic fertilizer and more than a million tons of the bird droppings were mined from Vassa over the next fifty years. Haiti took the question of ownership all the way to the Supreme Court and lost, though it could be argued that the court, based in America and functioning under U.S. law, was less than impartial.

No matter the ownership, Vassa never enjoyed a peaceful existence. Seven separate colonies were decimated or completely wiped out, sometimes by storms, sometimes by fire, sometimes by no discernible reason at all. The death toll associated with this two-mile parcel of land was proportionately one hundred times higher than any island of comparable size.

When other, cheaper fertilizers were discovered, Vassa was again abandoned. In 1929 the United States returned, this time to build a lighthouse on the high point of the island. Vassa was located in an increasingly popular shipping lane. But again the curse of the island exerted itself. Three separate light keepers died on duty and one disappeared completely, never to be seen again. The lighthouse fell into ruins within fifteen years.

In the 1960s the United States again returned, this time to set up a scientific base reportedly to study hundreds of indigenous plants and insects, many of which had never been seen before. But rumor and innuendo suggested it was really a military listening post, which was later confirmed thanks to the Freedom of Information Act.

Soon satellites made listening posts unnecessary and once more, Vassa became a ghost island. Occasionally, during the fishing season, fishermen would camp on the beach, but even these temporary establishments were haunted with tales of unexplained death and tragedy.

And now, here we are, Justin thought. Once more Vassa was the home of unwanted guests and once more it seemed that the wrath of the island was being felt.

He looked out at the sea. From the cliff he had a good view of the ships on the horizon. A new ship had arrived, this one dwarfing all the others.

"Sweet Jesus," he whispered recognizing the profile. "That's a carrier. They've brought in a fucking aircraft carrier."

He advanced like a python, slow and methodical, crawling, pulling himself forward with his elbows, guided by his ears more than his eyes. Dana and the other woman were yammering, going on and on about the stupid things women liked to go on and on about. Occasionally, Dana would laugh. The other would, too, but Burton could only hear Dana.

Twice he had been forced to come to a complete stop when his forward motion was impeded by his painful, throbbing erection.

What are you doing, the voice that represented his higher self cried, but the cry was diminishing, growing ever fainter. After thirty years of dominance, the roles had been reversed. His darker side, his truer side was now running the show.

Stop it, it's not too late.

But it was. He was going to die. They all were.

He had tried to fit into society, tried all his life. He'd come close but never close enough. Two failed marriages and more jobs than he could count were proof of that. Becoming a contestant on 24/7 had been his last and best chance.

Now that chance was gone.

Death was a certainty.

He was surprised with the ease with which he accepted his fate. Maybe too easily?

Was he suicidal?

Perhaps.

Or just practical?

More likely.

Regardless, the realization of death was surprisingly freeing. Death meant no repercussions, no moral judgments, nothing to stop him from finally feeding the hunger.

He reached behind him to the small of his back and carefully pulled the knife from his belt. It belonged to the butcher, Brenda. He had taken it in the middle of the night. It was the biggest, meanest knife he had ever seen. The knife was important. The bigger the blade, the greater the fear. The greater the fear, the more the fun.

A part of him thought he should wait, hold off until he got Dana somewhere alone. He shook off the idea. This was perfect. Dana had chosen the spot herself.

Bringing his knees under him he slowly rose to a squatting position. He shifted to the right peering around a shrub bush. He could see them both. The veterinarian had her back to him. Dana was looking forward.

Good.

He would take the veterinarian first. Putting the knife to her throat to assure Dana did as he asked. Then, when he was sure she was incapacitated, he would kill the vet, pushing the blade deep into her throat, pushing to the bone while Dana watched.

That should amp up the fear factor.

He would take Dana to a spot he had chosen earlier, then rape her while the whole world watched. Somehow that made it all the more erotic.

He laughed out loud.

The girls stopped talking. Damn, his control was completely gone.

Burton Rudyard stood up.

The pier's aging gray wood creaked and popped beneath their feet as they walked. Twice Brenda stopped, afraid of plunging through the boards into the sea. Each time, Foster took the butcher by the hand and pulled her forward. "Come on, ain't nothing to worry about."

The twenty-one-foot fiberglass boat rocked slowly,

tapping the pier, sending subtle vibrations through the wood. Brenda shook her head. "I don't know. That's a pretty small boat for a very big sea."

Foster, a fisherman by trade, scratched his shaggy beard and grinned. "She'll do just fine. Besides, I've put to sea in smaller than this. Trust me. I grew up on the water. If it can float, I can sail it."

Brenda tossed a wild berry she had picked earlier into the water and watched as it slowly sank. "Didn't you say you were from California?"

A wave lifted the boat and pressed it against the dock. The whole wooden structure shuddered.

"Yeah, so?"

"So, that's the Pacific Ocean. This is the Caribbean Sea. Big difference."

Something popped. It sounded like a board. They both stood still.

"Shit, if we don't get off this thing, we're all going to be in the water," Brenda warned.

Foster ignored her. "The sea is the sea. Salt water, waves, and wind. That's it. Besides, the Pacific is a hell of a lot meaner than this little stretch of water."

Another pop. "I ain't kidding, man. Stay if you like, but I'm getting off this damn dock." Brenda ran toward the shore. Foster stayed a heartbeat longer, then followed.

She picked up the argument. "I'm a city girl. I don't know shit about the water. And a trip on the fucking S.S. *Minnow* doesn't appeal to me."

"Then stay," Foster said, changing tactics. "Stay and be duped. Fine by me. Hell, I'm a fool for even talking to you. Should just let you go on thinking this is real, while I finish the game and claim the money."

"Hey, I didn't say I wasn't going. I just said I wasn't comfortable with it. You know?"

Foster grunted.

"Damned if it don't look real," Brenda continued. "When that accountant guy died, I about peed my pants. And I don't scare easy. How the hell did they fake that?"

Foster laughed. "Ever go to the movies? You see Arnold Fucking Schwarzenegger get shot to hell and turn into a robot? It's called special effects. They can do anything. Besides, the trick wouldn't work if you could tell it was a trick."

He pulled out a pack of cigarettes and tapped the pack against his leg. "What did you say you did for a living?"

"Butcher," Brenda said. "I cut meat. I cut the hell out of meat. Nobody is better with a cleaver. Nobody."

Foster ripped the cellophane from the cigarette pack and tore off the top, dropping the trash on the ground. "You ever seen a man die?"

Brenda shook her head. "Well, my grandpa. But he was in a hospital. They just, like, pulled the plug and a few minutes later he was gone."

"Well, I've seen plenty of men die," Foster lied. He pulled a cigarette from the pack and put it in his mouth. It balanced on his lower lip as he talked. "Plenty. And let me tell you, if you had ever seen the real thing you wouldn't be fooled by the special effects. It's all just part of the game. And the people smart enough to figure that out and get off the island move on to the next round."

He put away the pack and pulled out a disposable lighter. It was white and red and extolled the virtues of drinking Budweiser. "Remember what that producer fellow, what's his name, told us?"

"Rycroft," Brenda said. "Nelson Rycroft. Slippery dude. Didn't much care for him."

"Yeah, Rycroft. Remember he said this wasn't going to be like anything we've ever seen before? Well, I don't know about you"—he motioned toward the island with the lighter—"but I ain't ever seen nothing like this before. Never."

Brenda nodded solemnly. Foster could tell she wanted to believe. But the truth was, he wasn't so sure himself. Despite what he was saying, when the CPA died it had looked real, damn real. Smelled real, too. He lit the cigarette and took a deep draw. It didn't matter. He was thirty-three years old, had been making his own living since he was thirteen and he would be damned if he was going to sit on his hairy ass and let a bunch of goddamn strangers decide whether he lived or died.

Hell, if they were sick they belonged in a hospital. Regardless, Foster Merrick was getting off this island.

"Holy shit!" Brenda said, pointing to the horizon. "What kind of ship is that?"

Foster sucked his cigarette. "A big fucking ship, that's what it is. One of the cruise ships. Maybe that's where we're supposed to go."

"Don't look like a cruise ship to me."

Me either, Foster thought but remained silent.

The doctor was standing on the beach, shielding his eyes with his hand and looking out at the sea as Justin came running down the trail.

"Is that what I think it is?" the old man asked.

"If you think it's an aircraft carrier, it is." He looked at the doctor curiously. "How did you recognize it?"

The doctor grunted. "I've got a son who served on the *Carl Vinson*. Why would they send a carrier?"

It was the same question Justin had been asking himself. That was a lot of muscle for a simple blockade. He could think of only one reason for such an obvious precaution: the virus. It had to be worse than anyone realized.

Any thoughts of being rescued were quickly evaporating.

"Still no luck with the radio?" Justin asked.

The doctor locked his hands behind his back, standing

at parade rest. "Cory Nestor, the computer guy, is working on it. Says the signals go out but nothing comes in." He nodded toward the island interior. "I tried the phones, the radio, I even tried old Morse code. Nothing. They hear us, they see us, but we can't hear them."

"Some kind of scrambler?"

The doctor shrugged. "Some kind."

Something moved on the horizon. Justin shielded his eyes. "Ah shit!" he spat as cold recognition grabbed him.

"What?"

"Get everyone inside—now."

WASHINGTON, D.C.
The Situation Room

It was called the Situation Room, but it looked more like NASA's mission control. In a way it was. Over forty-two monitors made up a massive video wall, with dozens of others scattered around the room all displaying different scenes live from Vassa Island. Next to the video wall was a massive screen where the area of highest interest played. Twelve cubicles, each manned by a technician watching one specific player, all equipped with three monitors and a VCR, covered the far wall. An eight- by ten-foot topographical map with a complete mock-up of the island, buildings, and blockade ships occupied the center of the room.

Since Dr. Lorrik had last been here a new piece had been added.

"What's that?" he asked a man in a naval uniform.

The man, who was easily ten years Lorrik's junior, spoke in a well-trained, respectful cadence. "That's the *Kennedy*, sir. She moved into place less than an hour ago."

Lorrik felt the sharp bite of fear. "The *John F. Kennedy*? The aircraft carrier?"

"Yes sir, per Admiral Dougherty's orders."

Lorrik had been given his own station with eight monitors, allowing him to gather as much information as possible from which he would develop a profile not only of Control but of the contestants as well.

He saw the admiral across the room and hurried over to confront him.

Dougherty was a stout man with large shoulders and a neck that looked to be the size of Lorrik's waist. In his youth, he had no doubt been an impressive figure. But age had rounded off the edges and fat had replaced muscle.

"I thought we agreed—just a strike team assault. One unit, in biowarfare gear in and out."

The admiral looked at Lorrik as if he had just been addressed by a talking animal. "The jets are a precaution. Proof that we mean business. It's time we show these terrorists you don't screw around with the United States and especially not the United States Navy. We know what we're doing, Mister—"

"Doctor. Dr. Sherman Lorrik. And I'm not sure you do. The people behind this are well organized and more than capable of advance strategy. I can assure you they are ready to counter anything they perceive as a serious threat. Even sending the helicopter in is a risk but this—war planes, that's asking for it."

The admiral's brow wrinkled. His mouth drew into a sneer. "And just how the hell are they going to do that? No weapons, no troops—how in bloody hell are they going to stop us?"

Lorrik could feel people watching the exchange. "I . . . I don't know," he confessed.

The admiral huffed. A look of self-assurance flickered

in his eyes. "That's right you don't. Now I suggest you sit back and learn from the big boys."

VASSA ISLAND

Lips pursed, jaw clenched, Burton rose from the kelly green foliage like the Great Pumpkin rising from the pumpkin patch. Nerine turned at the sound of laughter. "How long have you been there?" she demanded, hands on her hips like a scolding mother.

Dana recognized him as the welder who had given her the creeps earlier.

Burton's smile twisted into a leer.

"So much for privacy," Nerine said, turning to Dana and offering a whatcha-gonna-do? shrug. "If our peeping pervert was watching the whole time, then everybody got an eyeful."

Dana tried to relax, to laugh it off, but the muscles in the back of her neck remained tense. *You're being paranoid.*

Burton took a step forward. Dana's heart accelerated. An alarm shook the island. The Round House—they were all being summoned to the Round House.

Justin watched from the dormitory doorway as the Navy fighters screamed overhead. These were serious aircraft: F/A-18 Hornets built for war and armed to the teeth. Two of them. The jets cut through the sky side by side, then split, one peeling off to the east, the other to the west.

"What do they want?" someone asked. Several people were crying. The Navy was supposed to be the good guys, their saviors. So why were they sending fighters?

Three people came running out of the jungle. Justin recognized Dana and felt one of the five fingers that was fisting his heart, loosen its grip. She's all right. He watched as the trio ran into the Round House.

The jets shot by streaking out to sea, arced, lined up, and headed back to the island.

A strafing run, Justin realized. No need for the missiles. Just open up with the Vulcan 20mm cannon, reduce every structure on this island to string cheese and the contestants along with it.

Several people approached the doorway. He urged them back inside but held his own position. *What the hell were they thinking?*

WASHINGTON, D.C.

"Oh, shit!" one of the civilian employees cursed. He took off his headset and hit a button transferring the image from one of the seven network monitors to the big screen. "The Globe Newschannel knows about the assault."

Dr. Sherman Lorrik looked up at the screen and smiled without realizing it. Tucker Thorne would never be pretty enough to be in a boy band or to model underwear in a catalogue, but there was a certain edgy handsomeness about him that came across well on television. The volume was turned up. Tucker's voice filled the Situation Room.

". . . the assault will be launched using the latest chemical warfare accoutrements and the most advanced helicopter in the world . . ."

"How the hell does he know that?" Admiral Dougherty yelled to no one and everyone. No one answered. The president of the United States looked up and for just a moment his vision touched Lorrik's.

The anchor asked Tucker for specifics on the helicopter. He answered without looking at his notes.

". . . The MH-53J Pave Low III is designed for special operations: specifically for infiltration, resupply, and extraction in enemy territory. You may recall the dramatic helicopter rescue of a downed pilot during Operation Desert Storm. That was an MH-53J. It has tremendous long-range and low-level capabilities and can fly in any weather, day or night. It carries thirty-eight troops and has an external cargo hook that will lift up to twenty thousand pounds."

Lorrik was impressed. He had mentioned the aircraft only briefly and offered no details. Obviously, Tucker had done his homework.

"What about weapons?" the anchor asked.

"Armed to the teeth," Tucker answered smoothly. "With three .50 caliber machine guns."

"Why the guns?" the anchor questioned. "Are they expecting trouble?"

Tucker shook his head. He was standing somewhere under a small shelter, the ocean framed behind him. Lorrik smiled, knowing it was the wrong ocean. Tucker was still on the West Coast.

"Not expecting trouble, but preparing nonetheless," Tucker answered. "I'm told by a high level source that the Presidential Task Force, which authorized this action, is demanding maximum caution."

"High level source?" the admiral roared. "Who the hell is his high level source?"

Again the president looked at Lorrik. The doctor shifted his gaze lest anyone note the exchange.

On the screen Tucker continued his report. ". . . As the events of the last two days have indicated, anything is possible. Again, the mission is essentially to land on the island, collect a blood sample, and leave. The participants will be wearing the latest bioprotection suits, and a special quarantine chamber has been added to the aircraft. Once they leave the island, Special Forces will remain in quarantine until the Centers for Disease Control and Prevention give the all clear. . . ."

The report went on for another five minutes. When it finished, the war room was quiet, save for the hum of computer hard drives and the soft mumble of communications between the fleet and command. "Visual contact," someone said.

"Main screen," came the response. A different image of Vassa Island appeared on the screen, shot from a camera beneath the F/A-18.

VASSA ISLAND

Dana Kirsten watched as the incredible aircraft did a barrel roll, then soared straight up. Under different circumstances it would have been fun. But in her present situation each new event had to be viewed with fear and a healthy dose of skepticism.

Is that why I'm so unnerved by that Burton guy?

Maybe? But that explanation didn't feel right. Twice she had caught him looking at her. No, looking was the wrong word—ogling was more like it, molesting her with his eyes.

Okay, now you're just plain crazy.

Why would anybody bother with her when they could look at women like Nerine, with her dimpled cheeks, or Renee, with boobs so perky they could put an eye out?

"You all right?" Justin asked from the doorway.

She almost turned to see who he was talking to, then felt herself blush. "Yeah, fine." She pointed toward the sky. "You're the pilot. Any idea what this is all about?"

The jets were now the size of nickels—speeding, deadly nickels with bombs and missiles and all sorts of nasty things.

Justin looked up at the sky. "They're just looking."

She studied him suspiciously. "You're lying."

This time he was the one who blushed. "Maybe a little bit. Those earlier flybys were strafing runs."

"Strafing? You mean where they fly low to the ground and shoot everything in sight?"

"Something like that. But no need to panic. They're not shooting."

Dana looked up at the sky. "Not yet anyway."

The jets were coming back.

12 CARIBBEAN SEA

The MH-53J Pave Low III rose from the deck of the *John F. Kennedy* like a magnificent prehistoric beast taking to a Jurassic sky. The downdraft from the seventy-two-foot rotor kicked up plumes of gossamer-white mist, flattening the ship's wake from diagonal slashes to concentric circles. The pilot checked the readouts then nodded to his copilot and two flight engineers. At three hundred feet the nose dipped toward the sea and the helicopter began moving forward to Vassa Island.

Painted a bluish dark gray, the color of Windex on a wet cinder block, the helicopter was ninety-two feet long and twenty-five feet high and could fly at more than one hundred and sixty-five miles per hour. With forward-looking infrared sensors, terrain-following and avoidance radar, and a map projection display, the Pave Low could fly in almost any weather.

Along with the crew of two pilots, two flight engineers,

and two aerial gunners were four special operatives. The latter wore the latest mobile biological protection gear. Although normally capable of seating thirty-eight, this helicopter had been modified and now carried a complete biological containment unit where the four operatives would remain in quarantine until the CDC examined the blood sample and determined how the virus spread.

WASHINGTON, D.C.

Dr. Sherman Lorrik rolled his cane between his palms as he watched the helicopter approach the island. The plan was sound and necessary. They had to have a sample of the virus to know what they were dealing with. But Lorrik was worried. So far, Control's moves had been like those of a chess grand master. So why leave the island vulnerable to the military? It didn't make sense.

Then again, what could anyone do to stop the United States Navy?

Lorrik shook his head, the thought still unformed. Sitting back in his padded chair, he browsed the room. Most were glued to the main monitor while service personnel continued to work quietly at their assigned tasks. The air conditioner wheezed and a paper on the long central table moved, rising up for a quick peek then settling back on the table.

Dressed in his impeccable uniform with five silver stars on his collar, one two-inch gold strip and four half-inch stripes on his sleeves, Admiral Dougherty watched with quiet intensity. His egg-shaped face was dominated by a thick, shaggy mustache that hung over his mouth like black and gray icicles that he chewed when nervous.

At the moment, he appeared to be grazing.

The view from the helicopter changed, zooming in to

reveal the full beachline. No one was visible, but Lorrik knew from watching the other monitors that the contestants were freaked by the jets and were now looking from the doorways and windows.

The pilot's voice was gnarled by the radio relay, but the important information was transmitted: "Four minutes till contact . . ."

Lorrik continued to roll his cane between his hands. What was he missing?

CARIBBEAN SEA

Behind them the U.S.S. *John F. Kennedy* cut a frothy trail through the blue-gray sea, maintaining its place in the blockade and awaiting their return. Vassa Island lay directly ahead. The pilot, who had flown a Pave Low in Turkey, Saudi Arabia, and Kuwait, knew this helicopter as well as any man alive. He'd flown one of the first aircraft into Iraq during the Persian Gulf War, leading the way for the army AH-64 Apaches. Knocking out Iraq's early air defense system and opening the skies for the aerial bombardment had proved successful in achieving a quick victory in Operation Desert Storm.

Despite his expertise, when the dime-size warning light began to blink, he was momentarily baffled. Then he realized why. It was the fuel cap–lock, an alarm that could never sound in the air because if the fuel cap was improperly sealed the helicopter wouldn't lift off. And once sealed, it was impossible for the fuel cap to be opened while the two General Electric T64-GE-100 engines were engaged.

His copilot reached up and tapped the light. "Has to be a malfunction."

The light continued to blink.

"Write it up. Make sure it's addressed first thing when

we return." The pilot shifted in his seat, checked the other systems, then settled back. A tear of perspiration trembled down his forehead.

The light winked.

Nerves, hardened by countless combat missions, inexplicably quavered. He had faced live fire, antiaircraft missiles, even survived a helicopter being shot out from under him. But still, the little light had found a chink in his armor. He ran the wiring schematics in his head. It didn't make sense. Even with a malfunction, he couldn't figure out how the light could be tripped once the engines were running.

He checked the projected map display. The island was coming up quickly. The mission was proceeding right on schedule.

The light blinked.

As a second droplet broke from the pilot's hairline and tumbled across his frown lines, all hell broke loose.

Every alarm on the twenty-five-million-dollar aircraft sounded at once. Digital readouts, status lights, stall alerts, collision warnings; one siren indicated that the engines had stopped, another that they were working dangerously above capacity. Contradictory, illogical alarms. A heart-squeezing, bowel-loosening cacophony of frightening lights and harrowing sounds.

As the pilot and copilot frantically checked the equipment and the two flight engineers scrambled from their seats looking for answers, the truly impossible happened.

Every system in the world's most sophisticated helicopter shut down.

VASSA ISLAND

"Oh, my God." Justin stepped out onto the sand, hooding his face with his palm. He was no longer concerned with the other aircraft, his entire focus was on the approaching helicopter.

He felt Dana beside him. "What is it? What's wrong?"

He couldn't speak. His vision locked on the aircraft. The magnificent machine began to wobble. Justin felt his internal organs spasm.

Though still approaching, the helicopter was losing altitude fast. The blades continued to turn, but slower. In the event of a total power loss, helicopter rotors were designed to be turned by air pressure, spinning as the craft dropped, allowing the pilot to make a dead-stick landing, jarring but survivable.

The MH-53J shook violently. Something sparked near the rear of the helicopter; the engine caught fire. Then the massive machine exploded in midair, hurling chunks of metal across the beach.

WASHINGTON, D.C.

Sherman Lorrik watched from the secure room deep inside the White House, as the helicopter exploded into a rain of hot debris.

What happened?

His stomach was sour. Maybe the others were accustomed to this sort of thing, but he certainly wasn't. A quick look around told him otherwise. Expressions of disbelief and horror marked the faces of all who watched. Several turned away from the screens; others stood transfixed as if hypnotized.

Admiral Desmond Dougherty's face was slack as if cast of wax then left too long in the sun. His eyes met Lorrik's, then jerked away. Now was not the time to assess blame. Americans had just been murdered in front of the world.

"The jets!" Surprisingly it was the president who responded first. "Get those jets out of there—now!"

Feeling usurped, the admiral snapped back into character. He looked down at his hand where he held a direct line to the *Kennedy*. "Recall those jets—now!" His voice was strained, more shriek than shout.

The main view screen switched to a panorama of the beach.

"What happened?" the president demanded. "Were they shot down? I didn't see a missile trail."

The admiral shook his head. "I don't know, Mr. President. I don't know."

Guilt was the first emotion to escape the blanketing shock. Lorrik had known, had sensed, something wasn't right. The person or persons responsible were too well organized, too forward-thinking to leave such a vulnerable opening. Control had been ready.

But this? Never had he expected such an impossible show of force.

"Oh, dear God," the admiral moaned.

All the air left the room.

VASSA ISLAND

Justin watched as the two U. S. Navy jets streaked overhead, racing for the aircraft carrier. Though capable of reaching speeds up to Mach 1.8, the F/A-18s had been traveling much slower on their strafing runs. The pilots hit the afterburners. The power turbofan engines flared half a second, then shut down.

Justin calculated the rate of speed against the degree drop.

They're not going to make it.

The pilots and the radar control officer ejected from the first plane seconds before impact. The men in the second were still in the cockpit when the multimillion-dollar aircraft slammed into the sea.

13 AIRBORNE
United Airlines Flight 2219

The plane hit an air pocket jarring Tucker in his seat. He was too tired to care. They would land at Dulles International Airport around midnight; he would be at his hotel by one-thirty, asleep by two, then up at 6:00 A.M. to join the horde of other reporters demanding answers from the president of the United States.

Tucker lay his head back on the seat. He had seen the video of the helicopter exploding and the jets slamming into the sea a dozen times and still it made no sense. In interviews the word *impossible* was being batted around by all the military types consulted. Yet, it had happened. He had seen it. The whole world had seen it.

And now the world wanted to know why.

Tucker could feel the soft vibrations as the 747 whistled through the air at thirty thousand feet. Air travel was a part of everyday life for millions of Americans, the technology that allowed them to be shoved into pressurized cans and shot through the sky was taken for granted. But if something on Vassa Island could down sophisticated military aircraft, what chance would a commercial airline have?

Tucker closed his eyes and tried to force the question and all of its cousins from his mind. He had to rest, had to.

In the past twenty-four hours he had gone from obscure

television photographer to on-air journalist doing more than fourteen live shots in his first six hours. He had asked for it and had gotten it—in spades. Blackmailing the company had been his first and, hopefully, last foray into the shark-infested, blood-filled waters of corporate politics.

Still, his overnight ascension had rubbed many the wrong way, setting off warning Klaxons as seasoned reporters, who would have otherwise been front and center, were suddenly relegated to sidebar stories. While the freshly promoted Tucker Thorne was given first crack at any story aspect he wished to pursue.

They hated him. He didn't blame them.

Those same reporters, anchors, and even producers had watched with unmasked anticipation for him to screw up when he did his first live report. That was less than thirty minutes after his showdown with the powers-that-be.

"Talk about a pressure situation," he overheard a field producer say to a photographer. "This is a real ball clincher. I can't imagine more pressure."

In the moment between the field producer shouting "Stand by" and the cue that he was live, the world had dimmed into a surrealist tableau of the truth. Tucker's heart beat against his chest with the fury of an outraged orangutan. And for just a moment he thought he was going to throw up.

In television, it's the live shots that separate the pros from the hopefuls. A nonnegotiable deadline, when everything you say or do is seen and judged by hundreds, thousands, even millions—instantaneously. Everyone makes mistakes, but for a television journalist those mistakes are made in front of the world. And no matter who you are, or what you do, you are only as good as your last broadcast.

It was that pressure, that intensity that chewed talent up like a weed-eater, caused many to run screaming for the safer, easier world of public relations or even law school, and others to become hooked, forever.

Luckily, in that paralyzing moment between "Stand by" and the cue, Tucker realized he was in the latter group—hooked on an adrenaline rush far greater than any drug could ever give.

"I can't imagine more pressure," the producer had said.

Tucker's mind flashed back to the cold, vacuous warehouse. Freedom dead on the floor and Tucker's own life measured in seconds. In that blink before going live, he looked at the microphone with its Globe Newschannel mike flag and realized it was a hell of a lot better than having a bomb glued to his hands.

And then he was on. His detractors were disappointed.

Still, although he knew in his heart he had the talent to make it, it wasn't talent that had gotten him here. Everything was predicated on his ability to get the inside story. And that meant he had to know what brought those aircraft down. And he had to know first.

The crash had been like a spark to gunpowder. Suddenly the events on Vassa Island had taken on international importance. Was this a terrorist act? Had a foreign nation just declared war on the United States?

It was now a matter of national security.

At his request, Tucker would be working out of the Washington bureau for the remainder of the story. And better yet, his friend Brick Bickman would join him tomorrow as his photographer.

Tucker's coat began to play the *William Tell* overture. In his exhausted state it took a second to realize it was his cell phone. Cell phone use in flight was forbidden. But he noticed many restrictions were conveniently overlooked when you flew first class.

"Tucker?" It was Lorrik. The doctor's voice sounded tired and strained.

"I'm on my way to Washington," Tucker told him.

Another air pocket. The service cart clanged.

"Washington. Good. We have to talk."

"Whatcha got?" Exhausted or not, Tucker was suddenly energized and awake.

"No. Not over the phone. Not this. Where are you staying?"

"Hang on." Another air pocket. The plane took a dip, a bad one. Tucker's stomach churned. Or was that just the deepening tension flooding from the digital line? He found his travel information in the left inside pocket of his sports coat. "The downtown Madison Inn."

Tucker waited for a response, listening intensely. He could hear the wind. Was Lorrik outside? No. Not the wind. Heavy breathing. The doctor was gasping. *Like a man running for his life.*

Then, something else. A second voice? One word muttered. Or was he imagining that?

"Doctor, are you all right?" Tucker asked, looking around the cabin, alert to eavesdroppers. The paranoia was contagious.

"When will you get to the hotel?" the doctor whispered.

"Three hours," he whispered back. "Is this about the crash?"

"The bar at the Madison Inn. Three hours."

The line went dead. The plane bounced again. Over the PA, the captain's voice could be heard: the turbulence and a small storm front would be over in a few minutes. But Tucker wasn't listening. His mind was still on the phone call. The conversation, and the voice in the background. His mind filtered through the clutter and congealed the sound into a probable word: "Soon."

JACKSONVILLE, FLORIDA

Her grandparents were just trying to look out for her. She understood that but it still made her mad.

"You can't watch this, sweetie," her grandfather said, his voice rich with pain and worry.

"But it's my momma." Jenna had heard others call her grandfather tough and mean, but she considered him soft and squishy and powerless to say no.

That left Grandmama to be the stern one. "I know she's your mother, but I also know she would not want you to see this. I think you had better go to your room."

There was no television in Jenna's room, but there was a computer. She had brought it with her when she came to stay at her grandparents while her mother was on the island. For school, she said. But it wasn't just for school.

There were no crutches on the Internet, no rigid braces keeping deformed legs straight. Travel from Jacksonville to Los Angeles to Sydney, Australia, to the Library of Congress—or the Barbie Dream Page—was a click away. No awkward shuffling involved.

Jenna loved to surf the Web. Surf implied action, fluidity—all things alien to a ten-year-old with a severe neuromuscular disease. Online she was just like everybody else. In chat rooms she could talk about movies and books and which member of 'N Sync was the cutest, all without stares or whispers or, worse, people feeling sorry for her.

Online Jenna was a ballerina dancing from site to site with an elegant electronic grace.

Her grandparents had taken away the computer up-grade disc that allowed access to the Vassa Island cameras—not understanding that once installed the disc was no longer needed. But as she watched the nightmare unfolding—the dead CPA, the crashing planes, as she watched her mom in the middle of it all—the pain in her young heart was worse than anything associated with her feeble legs and spine.

After a while, she began to think her grandparents were right. She shouldn't watch this.

But she couldn't stop either.

WASHINGTON, D.C.
Madison Inn

Tucker checked in, threw his luggage on the bed, and hurried down to the hotel bar. The room was a quarter full. Busy enough so they wouldn't stand out, but not so busy as to make it difficult to find each other.

Dr. Sherman Lorrik was seated at a small booth near the back. His white hair was thinner than Tucker remembered and he had put on at least fifteen to twenty pounds. His jowls now hung like saddlebags. His normally ruddy complexion was a waxy, unhealthy hue.

He didn't respond to Tucker's outstretched hand, instead he searched the room with his bloodshot eyes.

"What happened to the planes?" Tucker asked as he sat down. The anxiety that had started with the call on his cell phone had continued to grow and was now approaching the level of full-fledged paranoia.

The waiter appeared. Lorrik shooed him away before Tucker could order.

"Doctor?" the reporter repeated.

A candle in a red beveled-glass sconce intended for intimacy, instead cast the table in a haze of scarlet uncertainty.

Lorrik looked at Tucker for the first time. Dark circles cupped his lower lids. "It wasn't just equipment failure," he said.

Equipment failure was the only explanation the Navy

had offered, coming in a terse one-page press release faxed to news departments all over the country. But even the government wasn't foolish enough to think that the American public would buy it.

"What is the working theory?" Lorrik asked. "What's the scuttlebutt around the bullpen? Do you have a bullpen?"

"No. But I can tell you what you're going to see in the morning papers and on the news—terrorists. Possibly a stinger missile or multiple missiles. Shoulder launch."

Lorrik dropped his head and exhaled heavily through his nose. "Jesus."

"The whole thing is a terrorist act," Tucker continued. "Now it's taken on a military angle. Heaven help us if Iraq or Libya is connected."

Lorrik's drink had come containing a lime skewered with a small, plastic sword. He removed the sword and tapped it against the rim of his glass. "Hogwash." He looked up. Some of his usual firmness seemed to return to his face. "How do they explain the lack of a contrail or any other visible evidence of a missile attack? It's ridiculous."

"We've got an entire island held hostage. I would say pretty much anything is possible," Tucker countered. "Other theories include a new, laser-based weapon, microwave burst cannon—James Bond stuff, but all of it revolves around some group or some nation that is powerful enough to create the weapons."

Lorrik slammed his fist on the table. The candle and his drink bounced. "No. No. No! It's stupid and it's irresponsible. Christ, don't you people have any scruples? You go out there with talk of missiles and terrorist nations and you're going to incite a war. Do you understand that? I'm telling you right now as a sociologist with some acclaim, that those allegations will ignite this situation. Right or wrong. And that's exactly what Control wants."

Someone across the room laughed, a loud, I've-had-too-much-to-drink cackle, which, coming after Lorrik's ominous statement, put Tucker in mind of a witch and a bubbling cauldron.

Lorrik's head dropped again. His shoulders were hunched, the look of a man bearing the weight of the world.

"So why doesn't the military tell us what really happened?" Tucker asked.

"Because they're fools, swaddled in their own internal politics. They want all the pieces together before they speak." Lorrik stabbed his lime. Pulp floated freely in clear alcohol that Tucker guessed was vodka. "Maybe they're right to some degree? Maybe speaking out will jeopardize their investigation, cause them to lose the only lead they have? I don't know. But I can't let it go on like this.

"This way lies madness," Lorrik muttered.

They were quiet. A breeze flicked the candle in the red sconce causing crimson shadows to dance a nervous jig.

Again Lorrik looked around the room. His hands held the cocktail like a drowning man held on to a lifeline. "It wasn't a missile. It was sabotage."

VASSA ISLAND

The clouds came shortly after the crash. Deep and powerful, a ceiling of gun barrel gray webbed with intense, blue-white bolts of lightning. As the sun took refuge below the horizon, the rain advanced—thick, fat droplets that bombarded the island, drumming on the large tropical leaves, producing a tuneless concert of disharmony. Encouraged by the clouds, darkness came early. It grew from shadows swelling in the corners and flooding across the room in a viscous current of cold black.

The computer-controlled lights winked out on schedule and the dark celebrated. No longer growing, but rising, fully formed in the flick of a second. Thunder rumbled, not warning, but joyous, celebratory, like boastful cries of victory. The military in all its grandeur had come with ships, with jets, a helicopter—and the island had won.

More dead. More victory. More dark.

Dana sat on her cot, hugging her knees, engulfed in a coarse army blanket and staring out the window at the blackness. The usual noises of the jungle were replaced by a steadily growing hiss. Rain on foliage, her mind said. Dark black things, snakes and monsters hissing at technology, her emotions suggested.

Lightning flashed, etching the jungle in electric-white.

Dana thought of her daughter and prayed she hadn't witnessed the crash, the dying, the hell; but she knew better. She had bought Jenna a secondhand computer, priced right when her boss at the grocery store had upgraded a few months before. And the girl had taken to it at once, quickly mastering the idiosyncrasies that caused Dana's head to ache. (*Why was there a button called Alt? And what did it mean anyway?*) In no time Jenna was proclaiming herself Queen of the Internet. At least, in the Kirsten household.

If not at home, Jenna would easily gain access to a computer someplace else—at school, the library, friends' homes. Somewhere. The girl was smart and resourceful.

And, if she were watching right now, she was seeing her mother on the verge of falling apart in front of the whole world.

Dana closed her eyes and willed away the defeatist attitude. But images of that helicopter sputtering in the sky, then bursting into a thousand, burning shards flashed full behind her eyelids. All too real, too close.

The human mind could only handle so much.

When Dana had become pregnant as a high school senior, she thought it was the end of the world. Abortion had been considered, but she had begun to love what was growing inside her the moment she learned of its existence, realizing it was an innocent and not responsible for the circumstances of its conception. It was difficult, at times near impossible, but she had persevered. She had survived.

We do what we have to do, her father had told her. The disappointment in his eyes would remain forever in her mind, but so, too, would the acceptance, the love, and support. A factory worker, on his own since the age of fourteen, he was a man accustomed to hard work and hard times.

But he always survived, no matter the odds.

We do what we have to do was the unofficial Kirsten family motto.

And so she did, surviving the birth, surviving the loss of college, slowly beginning to claw out a life for herself and her child.

Then, when Jenna was two, her pediatrician began to notice several developmental anomalies. He ordered tests, then recommended a specialist. Then came the verdict. Jenna had a severe form of muscular dystrophy. Always fatal. The world almost ended that day. But Dana had a child to care for, a life that depended on her.

We do what we have to do.

So be it. Dana vowed to do everything in her power to make her daughter's life as good and as long as possible. The Muscular Dystrophy Association had been a tremendous help, with doctors and specialists, braces and wheelchairs, as well as an invaluable support network of parents with children suffering from the same thing.

Each year the kids went to MDA camp. For one week a year Jenna and other children facing the same challenges came together like a great extended family. Swimming, wheelchair racing, crafts, and friends. In many ways it was better than Christmas.

They had survived.

And, although the doctors said it was impossible, Dana refused to give up. It was through the MDA she learned of the test being conducted in Switzerland. A test with tremendous promise. But by the time the data was collected, the process proven, then retested, and finally approved in the United States, it would be too late for Jenna.

When Dana heard about the new reality show *24/7*, and the grand prize of two million dollars and what they called *your heart's desire*, she knew she had to try. Because Dana's heart's desire was for her daughter to become part of the Swiss test.

She had auditioned despite a strong anxiety of being on television.

We do what we have to do.

Her first application was rejected. Her second made it to the third stage. Then finally, applying for a third time, in blatant disregard of the rules, she was accepted as a first alternate—making it on the program at the last possible second when someone dropped out.

At the time, it had been her greatest victory. Now it was once more the end of the world. She had seen grown men cry, people with more money and education than she would ever have screaming in panic. How much could one person take? How much was too much?

What do you do when your situation is unsurvivable?

Dana ran her finger between the metal collar and her

neck. Lightning flashed again, revealing her face reflected in the windowpane.

"We do what we have to do," she said aloud.

WASHINGTON, D.C.

"Sabotage?" Tucker asked with disbelief. He had researched the aircraft and knew the MH-53J was an incredible piece of machinery. "Someone in the military? But that's impossible. There are too many people involved. No way one person could do that much damage without someone catching on."

Lorrik rolled his empty glass between his hands. The ice clanked like tiny bones. "It's the only theory that works. Shortly before we lost contact with the helicopter, the MH-53J reported an alarm that couldn't go off in flight. Then all the alarms went off. Everything. That could not have happened without someone sabotaging the system."

Tucker was quiet, letting this new information settle in his mind. *Sabotage?* Someone in the government was responsible at least in part. But why? Why all this effort over what was essentially a game show? It didn't add up. His puzzle sense was in hyperdrive. The pieces just didn't fit. What was really going on?

Lorrik again looked around the bar then back to his empty glass. "The good news is there is a limited number of people with access to all three aircraft."

"So you know who it is?"

"Not yet. But we have definite suspects."

"You said the good news. What's the bad news?"

"Three of those suspects were in the helicopter."

Tucker sat back in his seat. "A suicide mission?"

Lorrik held out his hands, palms up, and shrugged. "It's possible. And if that's the case then—"

"Then there's no one left alive to question."

Lorrik nodded. As he sat back in the booth, he grimaced. He shifted his weight forward like a man with a sore back, a sore everything.

"And I can go with this?" Tucker asked.

"Yes, but with the agreement as before, you can't use my name. I hope you appreciate what I'm doing here. Eventually someone will put it all together and I will most likely be revealed as the leak."

"I do appreciate it. You don't know what this means for me."

Lorrik's face hardened. "I'm not doing it for you. I'm doing it to stop a war. I'll be in touch."

The doctor got up quickly, fast for a guy with back trouble, and hurried out of the bar, looking over his shoulder as he went. Tucker stood and took out his wallet to pay the bill.

His puzzle sense was singing. Something was wrong. Something wasn't right. He threw a five on the table as a tip. The bill caught a breeze and flipped off onto the vinyl seat on Lorrik's side of the booth. Tucker picked it up, then noticing something, ran his hand along the back of the seat. He took the globe off the candle and held the flame next to the seat. The vinyl was slowly returning to its original shape but there was enough of an indication for Tucker to make out a small, rectangular indentation.

His thoughts returned to the conversation. Lorrik had been more than nervous; he had been uncomfortable. Each time he tried to sit back he would wince and promptly lean forward again. At the time Tucker had ascribed it to a back problem. But now the fading indentation told another story. To most people the shape would mean nothing, but to a broadcast journalist the shape and the body language made perfect sense, seemed logical even.

Dr. Sherman Lorrik was wearing a microphone. Tucker knew from experience that the mike would be fastened to a box generally worn on the back of the belt or pants. That was why Lorrik couldn't sit back comfortably and what had caused the rectangular depression.

Someone had been listening to their entire conversation.

14 VASSA ISLAND

Dana woke screaming. Terrible images of the helicopter exploding into a shower of burning refuse were blazing in her mind. She couldn't breathe, couldn't think. What was too much? What was unsurvivable?

Her breath came in jagged gulps and her hands shook like the last leaves of autumn at the prospect of winter.

"Shhhh. It's all right. Everything is all right." Justin materialized from the darkness, suddenly beside her on the bed.

Strong arms surrounded her. She folded into his embrace, burying her face in his wide chest, crying softly in the security of his touch.

He held her, stroking her hair with his fingers, whispering soft, soothing sounds. They stayed that way for a long time—until the tears subsided and control had returned, until the dark evil of her dreams had fled.

"I'm sorry," she muttered, pulling back just enough to look at his face. The clouds had left during the night and the dark had lost some of its foothold to a full moon. Anemic moonlight peered through the window, out-

lining Justin's face. His granite jaw and strong cheek-
bones were evident, but his eyes remained veiled in mystery and shadow. "It's all right. We all need to let loose
sometimes, to vent. It's what keeps us sane."

She laughed. "Considering our current circumstances,
sanity seems like such a bizarre concept."

The lines of his jaw tightened. He took her face in his
hands. The shadows of his eyes took on a life of their
own, reaching out like mooring lines holding her gaze.
"We are going to get out of this. Do you hear me? We're
going to get out of this. I promise."

Words, just words designed to assuage her fear, but
they warmed her, temporarily driving back the numbing
cold of fear. It was just for a moment, but the relief was
real and invigorating.

We're going to get out of here.

She moved before logic or timidity could stop her,
leaning forward till she found his lips with hers. They
kissed softly.

Dana drew back, perhaps more surprised than he
was. An awful silence, a moment that stretched like eter-
nity. Then—he took her face in his hands and kissed her
back. Softly at first. The brush of a butterfly's wing. Then
again harder, stronger, more passionately.

They kissed and touched, and somewhere in the ghostly
moonlight Dana Kirsten fell asleep in Justin's arms.

He watched from the shadows, alerted by her screams,
her delicious, terrified screams. Others had awakened, too,
stirred, then returned to where their minds rested. But
Burton Rudyard was awake, alive perhaps for the first
time in his life. He was a man fighting a losing battle with
his darker self and finding that the extent of his sexual
excitement was so intense, so powerful, he didn't care.

The moon provided just enough light for him to see
Justin Rourke rush to her side, hold her, touch her hair.

Burton watched—quiet like the shadows he slept in.

He saw them kiss, watched them touch, images lost to darkness filled in by his imagination. In the silence he could hear the faint wet sounds of their kisses. But it was another sound that tantalized Burton: the echoing memory of Dana Kirsten's screams.

Dana woke with the sun. This time it wasn't a nightmare, but an idea that pulled her from slumber. She lay awake for a moment enjoying the warmth of Justin's arms around her, the smell of his hair. For an instant she imagined there was no island, no game, no virus, just a daydream as fleeting as a warm kiss on a cold night. She wondered what her family and friends were thinking? *Stupid girl, they're thinking you finally wised up and found someone. Too bad you're both about to die.* More irony.

They had done nothing more than kiss and embrace. But, in its own way, it had been more erotic than anything she had ever done with any other man. Extreme stress is an accelerant. Hadn't she read that somewhere?

Then reality reasserted itself, sharp and hard and abrasive.

Guilt momentarily replaced the fear that had become her constant companion, guilt that she could allow herself even an instant of happiness in the midst of such death and crisis.

She had to live. If not for herself, for Jenna. Hadn't God been cruel enough to the little girl already? Would He take away her mother as well?

She knew what her father would say. "Lord helps those who help themselves. Quit wallowing and start walking."

She lifted Justin's arm off of her. He grunted and rolled onto his other side. His hair was mussed, offering her a glimpse of what he must have looked like as a child. She took her clothes and went to the safe spot in the jungle to dress.

Justin woke and immediately sensed something missing. Then he realized it was Dana. He had watched her struggle with her emotions throughout the evening, watched her toss and turn in her sleep. When she cried out, he had been unable to stop himself. He wanted to comfort her, protect her—a woman determined and independent by nature and circumstance. But she had allowed him to hold her, had cried softly on his shoulder. And then—they had kissed.

"Dana?" he called out tentatively.

Several others were up and busy, but he didn't see Dana.

The fact that he missed her bothered him. He loved women, adored women, but had never had much success with relationships. Emotionally detached, one girlfriend had told him. Yet here he was trapped on an island in a life and death situation and all he could think about was a woman.

"You up?" She stood in the doorway, silhouetted by a rising sun.

"Dana." He stood and rushed to her. He started to kiss her. She offered her cheek.

"Is everything all right?" Had he overstepped his boundaries last night? Had he taken advantage of this fiercely independent woman in a rare moment of vulnerability?

"I've been up for about an hour," she said, her voice strangely distant.

He had pushed too hard, threatened their friendship.

"Come on," she said, motioning for him to follow as she headed across the sand.

He took a step before realizing he was wearing just a T-shirt and boxers. He grabbed his jeans, then hobbled into his pants as he tried to catch up with her. "Where are we going?"

Her strides were firm and brisk. "The Round House."

Justin buttoned his fly. His Rockports were back in the dorm. Mercifully the beach sand had not heated up yet. "The Round House? Why?"

She stopped and turned to look at him. But it wasn't anger he saw in her face, rather determination. "I'm going to confront Control."

They had taken to calling it the clear zone—a clearing a short walk from the dormitory that appeared to be free of cameras. The women used it to change without fear of being seen. Oddly, they never went alone—meaning they had to be careful with their choker-cams.

At forty-eight, Nora Tibits had been a schoolteacher twice as long as she had been a nun. Still, her simple dress, her no-nonsense haircut, and her lack of makeup appeared more suited for a nunnery than a classroom. A third grade teacher from Idaho Falls, she enjoyed her job, enjoyed working with kids old enough to understand instruction but young enough to mold and shape. It was a good, honorable profession.

But not her calling, guilt reminded her. Once she had been more, a nun, a loyal servant of God. It was a challenging, rewarding profession. She treasured every moment of it. Until she fell. Until she let Him down.

From living in a monastery to stripping in the woods, Nora couldn't help but marvel at the transitions her life had made. Trying out for the game show had been a long shot at best, a chance to win millions for a worthy cause. If it were God's will the money she won would go to the church. And as for her heart's desire, Saint Matthew's Home for Children was desperate for a new building.

Worthy cause, worthy cause, she reminded herself.

Truthfully, she had not expected to be selected. She wasn't the "television type." Her once black hair was now one-third gray and her face was plain. Still, the Lord had blessed her with an athletic body, and she remained in good health by adhering to a strict regimen of exercise and diet.

Diversity had been the answer when she had questioned the producers about her selection. Diversity and her heart's desire. Some viewers would be inspired by her goal.

Renee had gone with Nora to the clear zone. Miss Bellacort, as Nora referred to her, was a child of God and so a worthy soul. But she could be trying.

"Getting naked in the jungle—and Tarzan nowhere around," Renee said as she pulled her nightshirt up over her head. "Seems like a waste."

Nora had to turn quickly to prevent the entire display from being shown on her choker-cam. It had been twenty years since the convent, but as her reaction to Renee underscored, she had still led a reclusive and sheltered life.

The world was far more colorful than Nora ever imagined.

Renee was a striking woman, with a firm, full body and a face like porcelain art. Her hair was golden in the truest sense and her eyes were a deep brown.

Nora brushed her own graying hair from her face and kept her head turned. "How did you sleep?" she asked attempting polite conversation.

"Like a rock. Can you believe that?"

Nora was surprised. It had taken her over an hour of prayer before she had finally been able to rest. And even then her dreams were plagued with the burning faces of those who had died. "That's wonderful. I mean, it's great that you can put this out of your mind enough to rest."

Renee laughed. It was the type of laugh Nora had heard once in an art gallery in New York, a laugh that said more about sophistication and social status than mirth. "To tell you the truth, I'm not really worried about all this. You can turn around now."

Nora did. "Oh, my." She quickly turned back.

"What?"

"Your . . ." She cleared her throat. "Your undergarment. You haven't put it on."

"My bra?" Renee laughed again. This time with genuine humor. "Yeah, it's too hot. I'm not going to wear it. Geez, you can turn around. I promise not to flash you."

Nora turned slowly, her face a deeper red than the sunrise.

"You certainly are a dowdy little thing, aren't you?"

Nora checked the buttons on her plain white blouse for the second time. "You said you aren't worried. Why?"

Renee smiled, a swatch of white teeth cut across a perfectly made-up face. A face that belonged on a billboard or a magazine cover, not in the jungle.

"Men aren't going to vote to exile me because I'm"— she gestured to her body with both hands—"Well, let's face it. I'm a hottie. And women aren't going to exile me because of my condition. My pregnancy," she said rubbing her perfectly flat, well-muscled stomach.

"Yes. A baby. A true blessing. You and your husband must be very proud."

"Oh, I'm not married," Renee corrected. "Does that shock you?"

"No. I mean, I come from a small town with a simple background."

The Round House alarm sounded. They headed back toward the camp. "I guess I'm rather conservative. But I understand that people don't always wait for marriage before they—procreate."

Renee stopped Nora at the doorway to the Round House. She put her arm around Nora's shoulder. "Just a word of advice. You might want to loosen up, give the viewers a reason to like you."

Nora could smell perfume. Perfume in the midst of all that was happening? Odd.

"Have a little a fun. Hell, have a lot of fun. There are a few cute guys around here. Loosen up and see what happens."

"Oh, my."

"You'll feel better and I guarantee the viewers will, too," Renee said.

"Aren't you worried about . . ." Nora wasn't sure how to put her thoughts into words. After all, who was she to judge? But just the same if she saw someone in peril, wasn't it her responsibility to warn them? Shouldn't this apply when it was a person's immortal soul that was in jeopardy? "Just be careful. Remember, the Lord sees everything."

Laughing, Renee turned to the nearest camera, squeezed her spectacular breasts together and said, "So do the viewers. So do the viewers."

An alarm cut through the morning air.

Nora checked her plain-faced Timex wristwatch: 10:30 A.M. Too early for the vote. So why were they being called to the Round House?

COVINGTON, GEORGIA

Fifteen-year-old Bobby Vance sounded his own alarm, sending messages instantly to everyone on his call list. The list had started with just Bobby and his friends. But when word of their system reached the chat rooms, Bobby was inundated with requests.

The current call list was up from fourteen to ninety-one with people as far away as Alaska, Canada, and Mexico. Bobby was determined not to let them down. Monitoring the six hundred–plus cameras on Vassa Island had become more than a hobby. It was now a mission.

Ordinarily an A student, Bobby knew he was letting his school work slip. He hadn't started the English paper due on Friday, and he hadn't even looked at his math homework. It was out of character and that was part of the charm. He had always been a model student. But this—how many times did you get to see a life and death situation played out on your television and computer right in your own bedroom? Except it wasn't play, was it? It was real. The CPA from Ohio was dead. The host, the cameramen, field personnel all dead—really dead. Sometimes that was hard to remember. After all, thousands of people had died on his television screen, but that was fiction.

This was *real*.

School would always be there, but there were only eleven people left on Vassa Island. And one of those would be dead by midafternoon. It would all be over in less than ten days.

WASHINGTON, D.C.

If someone had told him that one day he would be president of the United States, he would have politely disagreed but secretly known they were right. If someone had told him his administration would be mired by scandal—well, truthfully, although not happy about it, he would have believed that, too. But if someone had told him that, as president, he would be pulled from a meeting with the heads of state of three European nations, rushed into a small room to watch a grocery store clerk square off against a Darth Vader soundalike, he would have thought them crazy.

Now, watching the television and sipping coffee that was too hot, sitting in a chair that was too cold, he wondered exactly who was crazy.

"Dana Kirsten—she's the mother, right?" he asked. Eight senior members of his Crisis Task Force were waiting. The rest remained in the Situation Room.

"Yes, sir." The director of the FBI handed him a specially prepared copy of the woman's biography. "She has a ten-year-old daughter with a severe form of muscular dystrophy. Works at a grocery store, an outlet store, and as a bartender. Became pregnant in high school. No father listed on the birth certificate. A churchgoer, off and on; currently active in the PTA; a frequent school volunteer but never headed a committee or chaired any campaigns. No evidence of a leadership role. Certainly nothing that would point to her challenging a terrorist."

The president grunted as he flipped through her bio. "Theory?"

"Has to be related to her daughter. I think she's going to beg for her life and probably piss off whoever is responsible for this. It is an unfortunately foolish move."

The president scanned the papers until he reached the section prepared by Dr. Sherman Lorrik. In his comments about Dana Kirsten, Lorrik wrote:

> . . . *apt to be underestimated and overlooked. Something she is no doubt used to and will use to her advantage. Her personal life is a constant surmounting of challenges. She's a fighter, particularly strong if cornered. One to watch.*

In the margin, written by hand, was: *Think mother tiger protecting her young.*

The president closed the folder and smiled. "Well gentlemen, it seems Dr. Lorrik disagrees with you. Turn up the sound and let's see who's right."

VASSA ISLAND

Inside the Round House the alarm was almost unbearable. Several people put their hands over their ears, but no one left. When the last contestants, Renee and Nora, entered the room, the alarm ceased, leaving a silence that was disconcerting in its own right.

Dana stood, hands resting lightly on top of the Vault and stared into the camera that hung just beneath the reader board. Justin stood beside her. He chewed on his lower lip. His dark brown eyes shifted between Dana and the camera.

"Control? Control? You there? Wake up you bastard; I know your secret. I know what you are hiding."

The statement echoed in the hollow room.

Then—**"What do you think you know?"** the deep, electronically altered voice rumbled. Several people gasped. She had spoken to the devil and the devil spoke back.

"The truth," Dana said. She looked around the room making eye contact with each contestant, holding it a second then moving to the next. "The truth about one of us."

"One of us?" Justin asked. "Dana, what are you talking about?"

She held his gaze a moment longer than the others, looking for something in the black void of his pupils. She turned to the group. "Remember how I was late, a last-minute replacement? The rest of you were already here, but I had to be flown in by helicopter? Something about that ride has been bothering me. Then early this morning I remembered."

No one spoke. No one blinked. The world watched . . . and listened.

"During that flight the pilot kept going on and on about this special satellite dish that his brother, who is in naval electronics, had installed on the chopper. He said he could watch movies and television shows from almost anywhere in the world because it could pick up signals other units couldn't."

An excited murmur rippled through the group. If this were true, then they could finally hear from the outside world. "So I checked it this morning and found the system has been destroyed."

"Destroyed?" Justin asked.

"Physically broken."

"Maybe . . . maybe we can repair it," Cory said.

Dana shook her head. "I don't think so. You would have to use a vacuum cleaner just to pick it up. It's smashed into a hundred pieces."

The momentary excitement was gone. Dana waited and watched. A new shock registered in the faces of Justin, Nerine, and Dr. Dutetre. The others still hadn't gotten it.

"The radio was smashed by someone on the island. In other words"—she turned and looked at the camera—"Control isn't acting alone. One of us is his accomplice."

The gasp of disbelief and confusion expressed in the Round House was echoed around the world.

15 VIEWERS

<THIS CHANGES EVERYTHING> was the message flashing across computer screens around the world.

No longer were they looking at eleven victims. Now it was ten victims and one accomplice. An accomplice who was a killer, in league with a monster. Finally the evil that had infected Vassa Island and spread to television sets and computer monitors the world over had a face.

One of the eleven.

But which one?

With only an hour and a half until the next vote, there was little time to decide.

WASHINGTON, D.C.

Tucker clipped the clear plastic tube to the back of his shirt, then put his coat on. The curled tubing was connected to a flesh-colored earpiece that had been created by an audiologist who had used a special foam to make a cast of his ear. The result was a perfect fit.

"Cutting it a little close," the floor director said. Putting his hand over his headset microphone, he added, "The Seattle producer is having a cow. Better get in place."

Tucker nodded as a cameraman adjusted the shot. Though not as large as the Seattle studios, the Washington studios were actually fuller. Half a dozen politically based news–talk shows originated from there.

Tucker shifted on his stool, trying to look at his notes as the floor director adjusted his mike. The butterflies that had been flying formation throughout his gastrointestinal tract were dead, replaced by large angry pterodactyls, with razor-sharp beaks and wings tipped in barbed wire.

There was a difference between going live in the field and going live from a studio. Despite the obvious distractions of field work, Tucker found it infinitely easier, more natural. Something about the formality of the studio turned up the pressure by twenty percent.

"Three minutes," the floor director called. He reached out and took off the white paper makeup bib still around Tucker's neck.

Too much. The stress. The lack of sleep. The live shots. Too much. He could not remember being this nervous. The formality of it all was nerve-racking.

"Tucker, can you hear me?" a woman asked in his earpiece.

"Yes, yes I can," he answered giving the camera a thumbs-up. Whether it was the producer or director, he wasn't sure.

"The anchors will intro a short package on the accomplice theory, then it's out to you for a little Q and A. We've got you high because it's an exclusive. Also the two theories play well together. Okay?"

Tucker nodded. For a painfully long second, his mind was blank. He couldn't remember what his story was, couldn't remember how to talk.

"Two minutes," the floor director announced.

Tucker glanced at his notes. Sabotage. That was his story. Someone had sabotaged the American jets and helicopter. And now there were allegations that one of the contestants on the island was also in league with those responsible. What did it mean? Was there a connection? And if so, what was it? How far did this conspiracy go?

The questions appeared in his mind like jagged pieces of a jigsaw, brightly colored bits indecipherable by themselves that would form a picture if assembled in the correct order.

The image of Sherman Lorrik wincing whenever he leaned back in the booth flashed through his mind. *Was he wearing a microphone?* And if so, *why?*

"One minute," the floor director said.

Through his IFB (for Interruptible Feedback) earpiece, Tucker could hear the story that was running, but the words slid off his mind like marbles on ice.

The puzzle pieces called to him. Something he wasn't seeing.

"You okay?" the floor director asked.

"What? Oh yeah, yeah."

"You were making a funny face." He paused, listened, then added, "Thirty seconds. Looked a little constipated."

Tucker laughed, loosening his facial features, no doubt exactly as the floor director had intended.

His puzzle sense screamed.

"Stand by," the floor director shouted.

VASSA ISLAND

The thought came to Nerine like the scent of rain on a subtle breeze, but it chilled her far more than any force of nature ever could. Like everyone, the veterinarian had been stunned by Dana's announcement. Suddenly the question of who to trust was tantamount to staying alive.

Working in crisis, the group had already developed strong bonds. The idea that one of these people was responsible was terrorizing.

Several contestants wandered the beach; others found a place to sit. Everyone was alone. *They don't trust each other,* she realized.

Nerine went looking for the doctor. The elderly black man was the only one she believed in without hesitation. Working hand in hand with Dr. Dutetre, she had developed a profound affection and deep respect for the elderly physician. It was his fast action that had prevented them from dying following the scorpion attack. And his expertise promised to be their best hope for understanding and beating the virus that lived in their bodies. But not soon enough. The vote was less than an hour away, at which time one of them would die.

If only the accomplice would be voted off. When the virus failed to kill him, he would be exposed.

She tried to think like the audience. Debate would be fast and furious, opinions varied. Talk radio and television shows would be in overload. But there wasn't enough time for discussions of any depth. Leaving only vague impressions with which to make the decision.

That was when it came to her, a new fear different from any she had experienced before. Giving up her search for the doctor, Nerine rushed back to the Round House. A camera. She needed to find a camera.

Who was Control's accomplice?

They were being killed with a virus. Efrem Dutetre was a doctor. How many misguided fools would wrongly assume that the doctor was the accomplice?

WASHINGTON, D.C.

It was a war council in everything but name. The president's top military advisors—part of a new, secret subcommittee formed from the Vassa Island Task Force.

This was their third meeting. "How bad is it?" the president asked, his voice rasping from stress or allergies or maybe both.

"We can't know for sure," began the director of the Central Intelligence Agency.

"Rat's ass," Admiral Dougherty interrupted. "They took down three aircraft. Murdered American servicemen. Make no mistake, this is an act of war."

A glance passed between the president and Dr. Lorrik.

"I say we blow the fucking island out of the sea," Dougherty spat.

The exchange continued for several minutes. Heated words, posing as ideas. Lorrik tried to detach himself to watch with a professional eye.

The president silenced the debate. "Not going to happen," he told the admiral. "At least, not yet. I will do everything in my power to keep us from killing innocent civilians especially on television. Besides, we need to know what the hell we're dealing with."

He turned to a man representing the research arm of the military. "I thought we were months away from a functional weapon of this sort?"

"We are, Mr. President, but obviously someone else is not."

The president chewed his lower lip, his head bent in thought. The false story Lorrik had planted with the reporter had bought them time, shifting the attention away from the chilling truth. He lifted his eyes and scanned the room. He stopped at Lorrik. "Doctor, how long do we have?"

Lorrik sat forward on the edge of his seat. His bad leg throbbed. "Not long, Mr. President, not long at all. The steps we've taken will buy us time and give us a certain degree of control."

"How much time?"

"A day, two at the most. Tucker Thorne is green. As long as we keep him at the head of the parade, we keep everyone off guard. But sooner or later someone is going to figure it out."

The president nodded. "Jesus H. Christ, how could this happen? It's a TV show for God's sake."

No one answered.

The president sat back in his chair. "If the world realizes there is a weapon on that island capable of knocking U.S. planes out of the sky, there's going to be a feeding frenzy. Terrorists, China, Iraq—screw the virus! They'll descend on that island like vultures. Gentlemen, this is bigger than the lives of eleven people on an island. The very security of the United States is in the balance."

Admiral Dougherty spoke up. "That's why I say we blast 'em. We've got the fire power. Let's use it. Reduce that island to a smoldering rock. We use the virus as an excuse, say the island had to be sterilized before the entire world was infected. Who's to know better?"

The president shook his head. "We hold that as a final option. And set a deadline." He checked his watch. "We've got seventy-two hours to end this. After which, we send Vassa Island to the bottom of the sea."

"Sabotage?" the anchor, based in Seattle, asked. "Involving how many people?"

On the screen Tucker appeared in a two-box-split. As the name implied, there were two boxes; the anchor in one with SEATTLE fonted beneath, Tucker in the other with WASHINGTON, D.C. superimposed beneath it. A larger graphic at the top of the screen proclaimed CRISIS ON VASSA ISLAND.

The nervousness that had threatened to consume him vanished as soon as he went on the air, washed away in an explosion of adrenaline.

"No way of knowing. It could be one or a hundred."

Tucker mentally chastised himself for using such an inflammatory high number. But the producer would love it. Fear made must-watch TV. "However, investigators see this as good news."

The anchorman expressed his doubt. Tucker continued. "Sabotage means those responsible had to have access. Access to both the jets and the helicopter."

"Correct me if I'm wrong, but doesn't that mean we have an entire aircraft carrier of suspects?"

Something pinged in the back of Tucker's mind. Something? There was no time to pursue it. "No. Not at all. Access to aircraft is restricted to need only. Particularly when an operation is under way. Don't get me wrong. It is still a lot of people, and that number increases if one person was responsible for the jets and another for the helicopter. We're talking about a hundred to a hundred and fifty. But that's far fewer than the entire nation. It's good news because it means we now have suspects."

The anchorman nodded, accepting Tucker's theory.

"Good job," the producer said in his IFB.

"Thank you, Tucker," the anchor said. "That's our man, Tucker Thorne, live tonight in Washington with yet another Globe Newschannel exclusive, concerning what may very well be the first break investigators have had in this case. That being the . . ."

Now all Tucker had to do was smile and accept the praise.

Except he didn't believe it. The idea that had been pinging at the back of his mind suddenly broke to the surface and bubbled from his mouth without the benefit of conscious inspection.

"It's not sabotage," Tucker mumbled.

"Excuse me?" the anchor asked.

"It's not sabotage," Tucker repeated more sure this time.

The anchor was baffled. Tucker's segment was over.

He shouldn't be talking, let alone disagreeing with his own report. "If not sabotage, then what?"

"I don't know, but I'm going to find out."

VASSA ISLAND

For a second time in less than three hours, the Round House alarm screamed across Vassa Island. The contestants assembled like lambs to a slaughter, which, for at least one of them, it was. Nerine, her eyes goggled in tears, was already there. She had spent the last forty minutes pleading to the camera, trying to assure viewers that the doctor was not Control's accomplice.

Several contestants saw Dana and looked away. No one, other than Justin, would look her in the face. A vile, toxic guilt frothed in the back of her throat. Should she have remained quiet? Had she managed to make a bad situation even worse?

As if to answer, Justin took her hand. "Don't worry," he said.

"But what did I accomplish? If I'm wrong, then all I've done is pour gasoline on the fire. And if I'm right, so what? I don't have a clue who's responsible. So what good is it? I should have kept the information to myself. It's just, I—" She wiped away tears before they could fully form in her eyes. "I just wanted to strike back, to let Control know that he is not in control. I wanted to shake him up. Instead, I shook us up."

"You're being too hard on yourself. Besides, I think you did upset him. But I don't expect him to show it."

He looked around the room. The air was flat and lifeless.

"We may not know who's responsible, but others might," Justin continued. "Remember, the public sees everything. All the time. Someone must have seen something. Besides, the FBI's got those—what do you call them?—profilers. I bet they've already figured out who it is."

Dana offered him a small smile. She didn't believe him but she was warmed by his attempts to lighten her load.

The pilot wasn't finished. He shifted his weight from foot to foot, his eyes drifting up and to the left. He was lost in thought. "So what happens if the accomplice is voted off?" he asked. "Will they die? Will they be revealed because they don't die? This could be the break we need."

The digital clock read: 11:59:02.

"You had better go to your alcove," Dana told him.

Justin moved slightly closer. For a moment, she thought he was going to kiss her right then, right there. And she wasn't sure how she felt about it. Even though they had kissed the night before it was easy to forget that the world was watching, seeing all through the night-vision cameras in the dormitory. Here, in front of her fellow players it was a different story.

Again, his sense of her was surprising.

He kissed her forehead. "It's going to be all right. I promise."

Cory Nestor, the computer systems administrator, had the alcove directly across from Dana and next to Justin. "You're the only one with safety stones," he said to Justin. "If you're going to use them, it had better be fast."

Justin held up one of the red glass objects. "Just one to see if it works." He dropped the stone in the opening immediately to the right of his alcove. If they were playing by the rules of the game, then ten percent of votes against him would be removed.

The clock hit noon; the right side of the board began

to fill with numbers. The voting tabulation was under way.

Dana watched the numbers to the right of her name. The votes were considerably higher than last time, pushing her quickly into the hundreds. Her heart caught in her throat until she checked the rest of the board and saw everyone was getting votes, lot of votes.

They're trying to figure out who the accomplice is, she realized.

There was no obvious suspect. The numbers continued to climb.

Someone gasped. Nerine was two alcoves to Dana's right. Hand to her mouth, tears in her eyes, she began to cry softly. But Nerine's numbers were lower than Dana's. Why was she crying?

The numbers began to change more slowly.

Dana noted at least four people with more votes than her. She took a breath for the first time since the process had begun. Then she realized that one of those with more votes was Justin. The others were Dr. Dutetre, Foster Merrick, and Burton Rudyard.

Dana realized why Nerine was crying. Dr. Dutetre was leading the voting.

The counting stopped. Dana heard the *pop* of an open mike, then the electronic voice of Control.

"Justin Rourke, you have used one safety stone. Ten percent of the vote against you will be removed." The numbers by Justin's name fell.

It worked. The safety stones worked.

"The votes are in. Dr. Efrem Dutetre, you have been exiled from the island. The rest of you, place your right thumbs on the scanners at your alcoves."

"No," Nerine screamed. The doctor went to her, putting his arms around her shoulder, comforting her.

"It's all right. It's all right."

"It's not fair."

"Shhh . . . I'll be fine. I'm right with God. I'll be fine. Use the vaccine."

Dana found it hard to breathe. A lump of pure emotion formed in her throat. Here was a man using his last breath to comfort another. How could the American public sentence this man to death?

Dana moved as if underwater, freeing the injector and taking her medication.

"It's all right," Dr. Dutetre repeated. Nerine had opened her alcove, but had not taken the vaccine. The doctor removed the simple bee-sting injector from its holder and injected the veterinarian who had acted as his nurse.

His skin was red and began to move. He closed his eyes, swallowing the pain.

"Doctor?" Nerine said, touching his arm.

He pushed her away. "No. Not here. I don't want you to see me die." Moving under what must have been extraordinary pain, the doctor stumbled out of the Round House.

Several people were crying now, their sobs a chorus of anxiety and depression.

Then a scream—raw, electric, and terrified—ripped through the tropical air as somewhere in the jungle Dr. Efrem Dutetre died.

The room grew quiet.

The reader board remained lit, but still.

Control was silent. No countdown was given.

The silence stretched into minutes. Muttered conversation began. Questions arose. Was Dr. Dutetre really behind Control? Behind it all? Had his death ended 24/7?

It started as a faint sound, then grew louder, a mechanized voice, laughing. And then—**"Ten contestants, nine days."**

Control continued to laugh.

16 WASHINGTON, D.C.

A hush settled over the enormous room. Even the soft hum of multiple computer hard drives seemed to diminish in deference to the latest victim on Vassa Island. The pause was short-lived, followed quickly by the somber resumption of duties.

Dr. Lorrik stood up slowly, relying on his cane for support. He was tired—too tired, his body protesting the abuse of continued activity.

His body needed rest. A short nap was in order. As he hobbled toward the exit one of the aides began to clap. Then another, and another. More joined in. Several rose to their feet. The entire room shook with applause.

Odd.

Lorrik noted it in the back of his mind where he kept his personal files on the uniqueness of human nature. A man had just died—been murdered. The American public had been an accomplice. And now Dr. Lorrik was receiving a standing ovation.

He nodded by way of acceptance. His face remained somber and serious. Once out of the room and away from watchful eyes, he smiled. Analyzing his own emotions, he found a strange blend of satisfaction and guilt.

Though politically inappropriate, there was reason to celebrate. Forty-five minutes before the votes were tallied, Dr. Lorrik had successfully predicted the outcome.

* * *

He had taken a room at a Washington hotel rather than endure the long drive to and from home. As he rode the elevator to his floor, he decided to allow himself a rare, celebratory drink from the minibar. Not that he was pleased by the doctor's death, far from it. The situation had just become infinitely bleaker for those trapped on Vassa. But his successful prediction meant his logic was working.

He had succeeded in profiling an entire nation.

The elevator door opened, but Lorrik remained inside. Two men wearing black suits, sunglasses, and telltale lapel pins stood on either side of his hotel room door. One opened the door while the other ushered him inside.

Using his cane for support, Lorrik cautiously hobbled forward. Two steps into the room, he again froze. "You?" he gasped. The composure he so masterfully exhibited earlier was gone.

Sitting in a Queen Anne chair, flanked by two more men in dark suits, the visitor turned a videotape slowly in his hands.

Lorrik heard the door close behind him but remained transfixed.

"We have a problem," said the president of the United States.

VASSA ISLAND

Foster Merrick shoved the boat away from the dock, jumped on board, and let it drift away from the pier before starting the engine. The sun was hot and intense, but the spray that kicked up as the boat leaped forward was refreshing.

Foster smiled and looked back at his only passenger. Brenda Segar smiled, too.

Less than twenty feet from the dock and already he felt

a hundred percent better. He was off the island. By God, he was getting away. He still wasn't totally convinced that this island incident was real, but neither was he sure it was not.

However, if it was real, if he did have the virus, he belonged in a hospital not on some goddamn island. Brenda let out a yelp as the boat bounced in the choppy surf. "Either hold on to something or get away from the rail. You fall off, I ain't wasting time coming back for you. And put on your damn lifejacket."

Brenda glared at him. "I thought you said this boat was safe?"

"It is."

"Then why do I need a lifejacket?" Brenda challenged.

Foster shook his head. "*It's* safe, you're not."

Shielding his eyes with his hand, he looked to the horizon. After he adjusted their course, he opened up the engine and headed for the blockade.

WASHINGTON, D.C.

He replayed the end of the videocassette, listening intently as Tucker Thorne broke protocol, interrupting the anchor and declaring that sabotage was not the cause of the aircraft crashing—effectively rendering his scoop and earlier statements invalid and destroying Lorrik's specially crafted scenario in the process.

"So?" the president of the United States asked.

Lorrik looked at him, still startled to see the most powerful man in the world sitting in this hotel room. How had he gotten out of the White House? Why hadn't he just called? He knew this president was a stickler for details. That much was obvious when he made Lorrik wear a microphone for his meeting with Tucker. But to leave the White House? Lorrik began to alter his mental evaluation of the Commander in Chief.

"I'm supposed to be on my way to a briefing at the Pentagon," the president said by way of explanation. "Does that help? Now about Thorne."

Lorrik apologized for being distracted and dropped into the stuffed chair across from the president.

"I thought you said we could control him," the president stated bluntly.

Lorrik nodded. "And we can. He's a reporter because of us and has no national experience. As a result, he should be as pliable as children's putty."

The president sat forward in his chair. He pointed toward the videotape. "That sure as hell doesn't look pliable to me. The son of a bitch just shot our cover story in the ass. And if someone guesses the truth—"

Lorrik rested his hands on the knob of his cane. "Doesn't matter. The sabotage concept is out there, and frankly it is the most likely explanation. Thorne's concerns are little more than hyperbole. There is nothing to back it up and no alternative explanation that is nearly as good."

The president wasn't convinced. "Maybe we aren't the only ones feeding him information," he snapped.

Having recovered from his initial surprise, Lorrik reestablished his personal control. "No. Look at the tape. The idea is definitely an afterthought. As if he thought it and said it at the same time. He's not being fed information. I'm still his best and only source."

The president huffed. "I don't have to tell you how important this is."

Lorrik offered no reply.

The president suddenly leaped to his feet. "Control him or we will have to take other steps. Do you understand?"

Lorrik got up as well. He remained standing until the

president and his entourage were gone. Taking a deep breath he made his way to the bed and collapsed.

Tucker Thorne.

He had never cared for the man. Oh, he didn't hate him. Thorne was an okay person, just not right for his daughter. When Lorrik learned of their engagement, he had been livid. Simply put, Tucker Thorne was beneath them. He came from a working-class family and attended a state school. His breeding was undistinguished.

But Gwen had loved him. "You just don't understand. You're typecasting him, Daddy. Tucker is sweet and funny and caring. He's also smart, very smart. Maybe not book smart like you, but street smart. He's"—she paused in thought, then added—"He's amazing. He's got these incredible instincts. He just looks at things and knows the answer. Like *Rain Man* or something."

"Great, he's an idiot savant."

"No. It's just . . . You should see him work a puzzle, any kind of puzzle. We don't go to suspense movies anymore because he always knows how they end. It's like he looks at the pieces and sees the totality. He really is amazing."

And a con man, Lorrik suspected. Alarmed that his poor sweet daughter could be caught up in the man's scheme, whatever that scheme was, he silently vowed to destroy their relationship. "And there is a big market for puzzle solvers?"

"No. But. He's going to be a national correspondent. You watch. He's going to be famous."

Lorrik huffed at the memory. Tucker Thorne had become a reporter, but only because Lorrik had put him there. Except he wasn't staying put.

How had he known Lorrik was lying about the sabotage?

It's like he looks at the pieces and sees the totality.

Could his daughter have been right?

For Lorrik's sake and the sake of the country, he hoped not.

U.S.S. *JOHN F. KENNEDY*

"He's still coming, sir. He refuses to turn around," the OOD reported. The captain stood with his hands behind his back and looked around the bridge. The helmsman, lee helmsman, boatswain's mate, and quartermaster were all watching him.

"I don't think he's going to stop," the OOD added. An officer of the deck was on the bridge at all times when the ship was at sea. Responsible for everything from the operation of the ship to communications to routine tests, inspections, and reports, each OOD stood only a four-hour watch. Still, at the end of the watch exhaustion and fatigue were evident. Since this OOD was just starting his watch, the captain felt comfortable with his observations.

Peering through binoculars, the captain could see the small boat with its two passengers jolting across the water. "Jesus Christ! Give me the microphone."

"This is Captain Wesley Stroud of the U.S.S. *John F. Kennedy*, United States Navy. Be advised you have entered a restricted area. If you do not return to the island you will be fired upon by order of the president of the United States . . ."

The radio filled with a shower of static.

"Still coming, sir," the quartermaster reported.

"I repeat, change course or be fired upon. Do you copy?"

The radio buzzed.

"Hello? Captain Stroud? This is Foster Merrick of the U. S. S. I-don't-give-a-damn. Get my two million dollars ready 'cause I'm about to win the whole damn game."

"Win? What the devil is he talking about?" the captain barked.

"He thinks it's part of the game?" the OOD said in disbelief. "He thinks it's all part of the game."

The radio crackled; Foster's voice filled the communications room. "I gotta tell ya, everything's been pretty good so far, very realistic except you, Mr. Captain Wesley Stroud. What are you? Twenty-one, twenty-two. Couldn't the producers afford an older actor?"

Several of the bridge crew snickered. The captain withered their smiles with a glance. He keyed the microphone. ". . . Merrick, listen up. You are approaching a United States blockade. Look at us. Do you think these are fake ships? Now I'm telling you, this is the United States Navy and you will turn around and return to the island or you will be shot."

No immediate response then, "Yeah, yeah, those are real ships all right. How the hell did they get the Navy to be a part of this? Must be paying a pretty penny. Maybe that's why they couldn't afford a better actor . . ."

The OOD bit back a smile.

The captain turned to him. "Get Command on the line. And order all ships to artillery alert." The captain brought the binoculars back up. He found the ship and focused on the fisherman. Foster Merrick was waving.

"God help us."

CARIBBEAN SEA

Foster laughed out loud. His passenger, Brenda Segar, didn't share his amusement. "Those look like real ships to me," she said.

"Of course they're real. It wouldn't fool us otherwise."

Brenda scrunched her nose as if catching a whiff of

something foul. "Real ships have real guns. Maybe we should do what they say, you know, head back to the island."

Foster's eyes had been locked on the blockade. Now he turned and looked at her. "Are you crazy? We're almost there. It's almost over."

"But what if it's real? They could—"

"What? They could what? Shoot us?" Foster shook his head. "You think the United States Navy is going to open fire and murder two unarmed American citizens?" He touched the choker-cam around his neck. "On live TV?"

Brenda crossed her arms and thought for a moment. "Yeah, you're probably right."

"Of course I'm right. I'm number-one fucking right." Foster laughed again, a loud and hearty sound, a free sound, laughing on the sea where only God and the fish could hear him.

U.S.S. *JOHN F. KENNEDY*

Captain Wesley Stroud expected to talk to his commanding officer. Instead, he found himself speaking with the most powerful man in the Navy, Admiral Desmond Dougherty. "Subjects are not responding to command, sir. There must be another way."

"Now you listen to me. You are a ship in a naval blockade and nothing, and I mean nothing, is to get by, you understand?" The admiral's voice was somewhere between a shout and a scream.

"Yes, sir, but . . ."

"No buts. Nothing gets by you." His voice was so loud it was distorted by the ship's small speakers. "Nothing. Now are you ready?"

The captain dry-swallowed. "Yes sir, all ships are armed

and ready. We've been tracking target for the last ten minutes."

"Good, good. Do your job, Captain."

Captain Stroud held the microphone for a moment. Around him, his men watched with fearful curiosity. No one wanted to do this. But it was their job. *Ours is not to question why.* The captain keyed the mike again. "Permission to speak freely, sir?"

"Make it quick," snapped the admiral.

"Sir, this boat, these people—they are not armed. We could put them in the hold, lock them away."

"No, Captain. We don't know shit about that virus—how it works, how it's transmitted. I'm told that it may be an aerial pathogen. If that's the case, simply stepping on the deck could be enough to contaminate the whole ship. They are not unarmed. Their bodies are the weapons. So stop them before they jeopardize the lives of your crew and maybe the entire country."

VASSA ISLAND

Dana took another step, then stopped. The room bore the scent of mildew mixed with a sweet and sour tropical fungus. It was neither pleasant nor offensive, just different—adding one more layer of creepiness to this already creepy experience. They were deep inside a long, rectangular building. This was the third room they had walked through.

Both Dana and Pheodora Cuvier held long, black flashlights, revealing the chamber in slow brush strokes of yellow light. Like the rooms before it, this one was empty, stripped to the bone—electrical outlets, wall switches, and light sockets gone. Spiderweb cracks climbed the walls and paint chips were scattered across the floor, crunching like dead bugs beneath their feet.

Real insects didn't wait to be trampled, but scurried away in an annoyed gait, disappearing into crevices or fluttering away in an agitated rush. Something popped and crashed to the floor. Both lights swung to the far corner. A plume of dust rose from a fallen board. A rat, roughly the size of a Saint Bernard puppy disappeared into a hole in the floor.

Both women were gasping for breath. "You okay?" Dana asked shining her light on her friend.

Pheodora had her hand on her chest and was breathing rapidly. "God. That's the third one. You'd think I would get used to it."

The beam of Dana's flashlight returned to the corner. "I don't think I'll ever get used to it. Have you noticed the rats seem to be getting bigger the farther we go?"

"Why did you have to say that?"

"Sorry." After a moment she added, "You want to go on?"

"No, but I will," Pheodora confessed. "Tell me how we got roped into this again?"

"We said we weren't afraid."

"Oh, yeah. We're idiots. I forgot."

"I'm starting to believe you're right." They continued walking toward the next door.

"Of course, everyone sitting at home watching this on TV is thinking we're just a couple of fraidycat girls."

Dust curled in the beam of Dana's light. "Hey, we're the ones in here, right? We're the ones looking. The fraidycats are the ones who stayed back in the dorm."

Play the game, Justin had said. And now that he had proven the safety stones worked, she knew he was right. Each safety stone negated ten percent of the vote. Ten safety stones made you invincible for one round. The producers had said the stones were hidden throughout the island, usually associated with a challenge or something frightening. In addition, each contestant had a personal challenge, built around his or her greatest fear. Personal challenges offered the extra incentive of five safety stones.

Nerine's greatest fear was spiders, but she hadn't been able to see past her terror to find the stones. Justin had, and with the four remaining stones could negate forty percent of the vote against him. And he still had five safety stones associated with his own personal challenge out there waiting somewhere. As did the others.

So Dana and Pheodora were out looking to be scared. And maybe come across their personal challenges.

Something hard crunched beneath Dana's boot. She turned the light on to the floor, hoping she wasn't standing on the remains of one of those giant island beetles they had seen earlier. It was a plastic fork, the tines now broken off. "Damn. Could have used that."

"After it's been lying around in here? Some rat probably picking its teeth with it?"

The door separating this room from the next was closed. The knob, rusted and corroded, cracked like an ancient bone as Dana turned it. The wood had warped and the door was wedged tightly against the floor. Using her shoulder, she forced it open.

Twin beams peered into the darkness. This room was smaller than the others, crammed full of crates and boxes and other associated junk. "Looks like my room in college," Pheodora said.

"College?"

Pheodora shone her light into her face so Dana could see the withering look she was giving her. "Yes, college. I can read and write, too."

"I'm sorry—I didn't mean anything. It's just . . ."

"Just didn't think a psychic would have a college degree," Pheodora finished. "That's okay. I didn't think a pilot could have an ass as cute as Justin Rourke's, what with him sitting on it all the time."

Dana laughed out loud and Pheodora joined her, their voices hitting the far wall and returning slightly distorted and strained. If there were ghosts, goblins, haunts, or spirits hiding among the trash, they now knew the women were there.

Unlike the previous room, this one smelled faintly of machine oil and something familiar Dana couldn't quite place.

"What's the deal between you two anyway?" Pheodora asked as they moved forward into the dark room.

"Why are you afraid of the cold?" Dana asked.

"Uh-uh. You're not going to turn this around on me. I asked you first. Come on 'fess up. Hell, girlfriend, anybody with a TV already knows. So what harm's it going to do to tell little Pheodora?"

Something grabbed her shirt. Dana yelped and pulled. The cloth ripped and she was free. The flashlight revealed a jagged piece of wood from a broken bookshelf that now held a four-inch swatch of Dana's shirt.

"Damn." Dana rubbed her side where the wood had left a red scratch. "Scared me worse than it hurt. That should be worth a safety stone," she yelled to the room. The room didn't respond.

They moved forward.

"I'm waiting," Pheodora said, having not lost the thread of their conversation. "You and Justin. Are you getting a little sump'n, sump'n?"

"No," Dana replied. "Well, maybe. Okay, a little."

"Do tell."

Dana carefully stepped over a fallen shelf. "Watch out for the wood."

"Don't worry about me, girl. I'm part mountain goat. So what's a little?"

"We kissed. That's all."

"That's all?"

"We cuddled a little, too, but that was it."

Pheodora laughed out loud. "You go, girl. Gettin' a little island love."

"I'm glad you approve." Dana stopped, used the light to find a path around what looked to be a legless desk, then continued. "Okay. Your turn. What was your major?"

"Psychology. Graduated, too."

"So . . ."

"Why do I tell fortunes for a living? I knew you were going to ask that."

"You're abilities are amazing. Look out for the pole," Dana warned. "So why do you do the psychic thing?"

Pheodora stepped over the pole. "Money, for one thing. My eight-hundred number stays busy all the time. Plus, I honestly think I help people more as a psychic than as a shrink."

Something scurried in the dark. They stopped. Two poles of yellow light crawled across different sections of the room. They waited a moment before advancing.

"So why aren't you worried about the fear thing?" Pheodora asked. Dana and Pheodora had agreed to go searching together after they realized they had something in common. Neither really expected to face her greatest fear.

Something rumbled. They stopped again. "Did you hear that?" Pheodora asked.

"Thunder maybe."

"Maybe." Pheodora turned her head to the right. Whatever it was, it had stopped. "Maybe, but I used to live in California. That sort of felt like, I don't know, an aftershock."

"Aftershock? I didn't feel the floor shake."

"Sometimes you just feel it in your bones, like a vibration or something."

"Oh, I know," Dana imitated the theme from *The*

X-Files. "This is one of your psychic predictions. If you're Mulder, I must be Scully."

"Very funny." They started walking again. "I forgot. You're not afraid."

"I didn't say I wasn't afraid. I just don't expect to face my greatest fear, that's all. Nothing could frighten me more than something happening to my daughter Jenna, and she is safe thousands of miles away with her grandparents. How about you?"

"I thought about that when they were screening us for the show. It's part of the reason I was excited to come on—because I realized they couldn't truly scare me. The only things that chill me to the core are my father—and the actual cold. So unless they can make it snow in the tropics or bring dear old dad back from the dead, I'll be just fine."

A scratching sound in the dark. This one louder. Closer. The two women stopped. All the talk of fear seemed to make the dark darker. Again the lights revealed nothing. They continued, stepping high to get over broken chairs, a table, and random bits of lumber.

"Are you really afraid of the cold?" Dana asked, finding comfort in the sound of conversation.

"Honey, why do you think I live in California? Hate the cold. Detest it."

"Huh?"

"What do you mean *huh*?"

"It's just a little odd, that's all. What's it called, freeze-my-butt-a-phobia?"

Pheodora cackled and the dark seemed to draw back a smidgen.

"This room's not that big, so why is it taking so long?" Dana asked. They came up on a pair of file cabinets lying diagonally in their path. "We have to go back a step and walk around."

"You just want me in the lead, that's all."

"If I detect a cold front moving in, I promise I'll jump in front of you."

They retraced their steps. Pheodora found a new path and began leading the way. "Wasn't always afraid of cold. I grew up in Wyoming. Snow up to boobs every winter. Mama died when we were little. I was six. My sister was five. After she died, Daddy came to get us. We didn't see Dad much before that, which was fine, preferable in fact. See, Dad was crazy. And not in a fun, you-so-crazy way. I'm talking certifiable."

They stopped. Pheodora searched for the best way around a pair of crates. "Dad was a schizophrenic. I know that now, but then I just knew he was *bothered*. That's what my mama called it. 'Your Daddy's just a little *bothered* that's all.' Man couldn't hold a job, never gave us a dime, was always in and out of mental hospitals. She never said a bad word about him. Just *bothered*, that's all.

"Anyway, Mom dies and Dad shows up and before anybody realizes it, he's got me and my sister in his old Rambler station wagon and we're on our way to God knows where."

They were no longer walking. Dana remained quiet.

"Must of been two, three hours, us driving and him crying and carrying on about God taking his heart. He loved her. He may have been crazy, but he did love her. We were deep into the mountains when the Rambler ran out of gas."

Something scurried in the dark. Neither noticed.

"Dad was in the front seat, me and sis in the back. At least she was looking away when it happened, I'm grateful for that—grateful and a little bitter. Me, I was looking at him. Listening to him talk when he did it. In hindsight I figure the gun came out from under the seat, but at the time it just seemed to materialize in his hand.

Big and black, cold looking, colder than the snow, colder than the ice pushing against the window.

"He looked me in the eyes. I'll never forget it. He looked sad and happy at the same time. How can you do that? I don't know, but he did. His eyes locked on mine. He put the gun in his mouth and pulled the trigger."

Dana gasped in the dark. The moment held and in her mind Dana could hear that horrible shot. She reached out for Pheodora's shoulder, found it and pulled her close. The woman cried softly against her chest.

"It's okay. You're all right now. I'm sorry. I didn't know . . ."

Pheodora sniffled then raised up, embarrassed. "That wasn't the bad part. The bad part was we were stuck, trapped in that car for two days. I lost two toes on my right foot and still have only partial dexterity in my right hand. Two days, alone and cold and in that car with— him. Or what was left of him."

Once more something scratched in the dark. Perhaps looking for a distraction, something to pull her from the memories of that long ago car, Pheodora shone her light out and screamed. A dead man lay in the corner, his unblinking eyes watching them.

"Holy shit!" Dana screamed. They turned the lights away both gasping for air. "I thought we got all the bodies."

"Well, obviously nobody looked in here. Wonder what the poor guy was doing?"

Dana sniffed the air again. The familiar, yet unidentified scent she had detected earlier was stronger now— almost recognizable.

"That's it, I've had enough," Pheodora said. "Let's get out of here."

"Why doesn't the body smell?" Dana's light returned to the corpse.

"Smell? I don't know. Maybe he used deodorant. I'm going. Are you coming or not?"

The light played over the body. Dark hair, wide, fearful eyes, mouth open in an inaudible scream. Pheodora brushed past her. Only the man's head and torso were visible. His lower half was blocked by a broken desk and crates.

"Dana?" Pheodora said, her voice questioning. "Dana?"

"I'm coming, I'm coming. It's just odd that's all." She turned. Her light found Pheodora's back. Her friend wasn't moving, but her light was, slashing across the room in quick jerks. Dana blinked as the light flashed past her in a full sweep. "I thought we were leaving."

She could hear Pheodora breathing in the dark. More rumbling now, somehow deeper. Dana could feel the vibration in her bones.

"Dana? Where's the door. Where's the fucking door?" Pheodora gasped.

"What are you talking about? It's right—" Dana stopped, her light shining on the bare wall. "I thought . . ."

Pheodora's light swept past her again. "Yeah, you and me both."

"But how—"

"Where's the other door? The one we were heading toward?"

Dana repeated the sweep just conducted by her friend. Crates, junk, debris, and wall—nothing but wall. No way in, no way out. But that was impossible.

"Dana?" Pheodora's light had stopped.

Dana moved her light to the same spot. She inhaled sharply. "Where's the dead guy?"

The body that had been there only seconds before was gone.

"Oh, shit!" The beam of Pheodora's flashlight grew

increasingly yellow. She slapped it repeatedly against the palm of her hand. The shrinking doughnut image jerked violently on the wall, then winked out. "Dead. Mine's dead. Thank God we've got two."

"Uh-oh." Dana's light began to fade.

17 WASHINGTON, D.C.

Twenty minutes after being told that hell would freeze over before he would be given another live shot, Tucker was back on the air. The news director had been livid that after breaking the story of sabotage, Tucker had then contradicted his own report.

"That's it—you've proven you're not ready to be a reporter," the news director had yelled over the phone line from Seattle. "Frankly, I doubt you ever will be."

Then the United States Navy blew a small boat out of the water, and Tucker was the first to have details.

Lorrik's call not only got Tucker back on the air; it kept him in the lead with exclusive details of what was happening.

" ... Globe Newschannel has learned that Brenda Segar, a thirty-one-year-old butcher from Cincinnati, Ohio, was killed in a confrontation with naval ships making up the blockade around Vassa Island ...," Tucker reported.

A photograph of the victim filled the screen. The scene changed to a video of Brenda on the island as Tucker continued to reel off the stats of her life. Files for all the contestants had been constantly updated, allowing for the information to be quickly plugged in as needed.

" . . . We've also learned that thirty-three-year-old Foster Merrick, a fisherman by trade, has survived. In this exclusive video from a blockade vessel . . ." The image changed from a photograph of Foster Merrick to grainy video taken from a naval ship. ". . . you can see that Merrick was supplied with an inflated raft and ordered to return to the island."

Tucker was able to report on the exact procedure the Navy followed, what weapons were used and what would happen next. ". . . Experts from USAMRIID, the military's version of the CDC, are on board the U.S.S. *John F. Kennedy* and are supervising efforts to recover the body of Brenda Segar. Every precaution is being taken to prevent further contamination from this still unidentified virus."

The Seattle-based anchor was a sharp brunette noted for asking real questions and expecting real answers. She didn't disappoint him. "What exactly is the USAMRIID? And will they usurp the CDC, essentially take over the investigation?"

"It's the United States Army Medical Research Institute of Infectious Diseases based at Fort Detrick in Frederick, Maryland, not far from here," Tucker explained. "Their job is to develop defense strategies and products against the threat of biological warfare. So they know the latest procedures and have the most advanced equipment— because they've created much of it. After the sample is safely collected, the CDC will take over."

After the live shot Tucker ate a candy bar in the break room and watched an amazing mélange of stories concerning the peripheral effect of *24/7*.

In Atlanta, a mother of three was so engrossed in the program she forgot to pick up her daughters from soccer practice, the youngest of whom was struck and killed by a motorist as they tried to cross the interstate to get home.

In Florida, an electronics store recorded its highest customer walk-in rate ever, after turning all the televisions and computer monitors to 24/7. Now the home office had ordered all of the chain's four hundred stores nationwide to do the same.

And at the Oregon State Prison a riot broke out when inmates accused one another of hogging the limited computer time on the library units.

From the large to the small, stories concerning the show were poignant and frightening. What they said about America was something no one wanted to hear.

Tucker's guilt grew with each story he heard. Was it right for the network to profit so tremendously from the misfortune of others? And what about him personally? While people were dying, Tucker was being promoted. A self-described underdog for most of his life, he couldn't help but feel guilty at being on the other side of the equation.

The press was frequently referred to as jackals. That wasn't fair. At times like these jackals were a higher lifeform.

By four o'clock Tucker was numb with exhaustion. He had had only two hours' sleep the night before and as the adrenaline washed out of his system, fatigue rushed in to fill the void. He left the station shortly before five, taking the subway instead of walking the eleven blocks to his hotel. He caught himself looking over his shoulder as he hurried from the subway station. Twice he came to a complete stop and turned to study those behind him, plagued with the sense that he was being followed.

You're getting paranoid.

Though tired, his mind continued to churn, his damnable puzzle sense heckling his thoughts. If the chopper and jets had been sabotaged, why hadn't other aircraft been launched from a different ship? That was the thought that convinced him that Lorrik's story was a lie. If not sabotage, then what? What could be so bad that it made planting a story about espionage a good idea?

The hotel was busy, bustling with conventioneers when Tucker arrived. He considered eating in the restaurant, but decided on room service instead. The mirrored elevator door opened just as he arrived.

He didn't see the man following him.

VASSA ISLAND

The dark was heavy and thick and in control—a living, breathing thing. "What now?" Pheodora asked, whispering as if the dark had ears and curiosity.

Dana listened trying to see with her ears, listening for the sound of footsteps, movement, the bones-on-concrete scrape of approaching death.

What were the odds of both flashlights dying at the same time? Not very likely. Someone, something wanted them in the dark. "We've got to get out of here," Dana whispered back.

"I'm with you, but how? The fucking doors are gone."

Dana felt the dark laughing. "I'm more worried about the dead guy. Maybe he fell over. See if you can feel him behind the desk."

"No fuckin' way!"

Reluctantly, Dana inched forward, creeping slowly over broken wood and twisted metal. Twice she stopped to wipe sweat from her blind eyes. *How much farther?*

She felt a flat surface slanting sharply to the right. The desk in front of the body.

She crawled over the deformed office furniture, her

hands reaching for the floor, searching for the reassuring presence of a dead man.

Her fingers touched the floor. She inched forward. Slowly, slowly. Her hand made contact with something, small and round. Her mind identified it as a human eye. Yelping, she jerked back her arm.

"You okay?" Pheodora whispered less than a foot behind her.

"Yeah. Thanks for following, by the way." Not an eye, not an eye. Again she extended her arm, hand touching floor, fingers finding the cold and round object.

Skreenchhh.

There was a sharp, scraping sound, followed by faint dull thuds.

"What the fuck is that?" Pheodora's voice had grown high-pitched and sharp.

Dana grabbed the round thing and stood up. Her skin was galvanized, a faint electrical current of fear sparked between the pale white hair on her arms. Gooseflesh rippled across her body. "Maybe Control has decided to take a hands-on approach."

"Don't say that, girl. Don't you dare say that."

Scrraaap . . . thump . . . scrap . . .

In the disorienting darkness the sound seemed to come from no place and everyplace at the same time. Dana turned her head trying to pinpoint it, to lock in a direction. But even if she knew where it was coming from, there was no place to run.

The smell, familiar but unidentifiable, was stronger now.

Scrraaap . . . thump . . . scrap . . .

"It's getting closer," Pheodora said.

"How can you tell?"

"Where else would it go?"

"Are you afraid of the dark, by any chance?"

"Not until now," Pheodora said.

"Then this isn't a personal challenge. They're just trying to scare us."

"Well, they're doing a damn fine job."

"We need a light." Dana thought about the cameras. In the pitch-black their choker-cams would be worthless, but night-vision cameras were peppered around the island. She wondered if people watching at home could see what she could not.

For some reason that thought incensed her, and with anger came control, giving her a small but usable advantage over fear.

"Diesel fuel," Dana shouted.

"Say what?"

"Diesel fuel. That's what I've been smelling. I worked with the carnival one summer. All the rides and things are run with diesel fuel."

"Diesel fuel?"

Dana followed the logic. "That explains the rumbling. Diesel engines. The walls may be soundproof, but we can still feel the machinery."

"So what does that mean?" Pheodora asked.

What does it mean? "The walls are fake," Dana said. "But the doors are real. Remember how it was stuck and I had to push through. They must have had a panel slide down over it. If we can find the location, we should be able to bust through. These booby traps are only meant to scare us."

"Yeah, well tell that to Nerine and the scorpions."

"Let's go back the way we came."

"I'm not sure how we came."

"Do the best you can."

They traveled in silence, reacting to each creak and groan of debris.

A new sound rose in the dark. A tapping, scurrying, scraping sound. Followed by a shrill high-pitched squeal.

"A rat."

More scraping, more squealing. "Not rat—rats," Pheodora gasped.

Dana remembered the trapdoor opening beside her bed and all the scorpions spilling out. In her mind's eye she saw a similar door, a bigger door opening somewhere in the dark and freeing hundreds and hundreds of dirty gray, thin-tailed, disease-carrying rats.

"Dana!" Pheodora shouted.

A pair of red eyes appeared near the far wall. Then another and another—blending with the blackness coming from all sides now surrounding them.

A living sea of red-eyed rats in the dark.

SEATTLE

The protestors booed and shouted obscenities as network wunderkind Nelson Rycroft hurried into the Globe building. He purposely kept his face stoic and firm, reflecting a proper image of concern for the cameras while secretly feeling gleeful.

His show was a hit, the biggest hit in television history. Sure, he hadn't planned on terrorist involvement. Fuck lemonade—they had given him lemons, and he had made champagne. The ad revenues were through the roof and even those who protested the show tended to disappear between eight and ten P.M. when 24/7 was on the air.

Like everyone else in the country Rycroft had looked on with keen interest as Dana Kirsten called for a showdown with Control. Rycroft knew the contestant research by heart. Dana Kirsten had a *moderate* likability quotient, not nearly as high as it should be for the mother of a desperately ill child. He was curious if that had changed after the showdown. And if so, in which direction.

At noon, island time, he watched as people around

the world voted to exile whomever they thought was the accomplice. He had been aghast when the doctor was exiled. But he tried to look on the bright side. The old man was liked well enough, but he didn't pull in viewers from the key demographics, ages eighteen to forty-nine.

And now, less than three days after making television history, he was about to do it again. He hurried to his office, instructing his secretary to set up an appointment with the network president.

Less than ten minutes later the head of the network listened intently as Rycroft explained his plan for a new show, a companion piece to air immediately following 24/7.

"And here's the good part," Rycroft said. "To give it that extra twist of legitimacy, we use someone from the news department."

The president had been skeptical. "I'm not sure any of the anchors will go along with the idea of hosting a show produced by the entertainment division."

Rycroft grinned. "Forget the old fogies. Who wants them anyway? I want to use someone young and new. A reporter."

"A reporter?"

"I want Tucker Thorne."

VASSA ISLAND

"My shirt," Dana yelled in the dark, shouting to be heard over the sound of the rats.

"Where are they? Where are they?" Pheodora screamed.

Dana reached out until she found Pheodora's arm. "I tore my shirt."

"Yeah—well I'm about to pee my pants."

"No. A piece of my shirt was torn off on the way in. Remember? If we find the fabric, it will point toward the door."

The scampering of the rats intensified—the sound of tiny claws on concrete.

"Too many, too many," Pheodora mumbled.

Dana shook her arm. "Snap out of it. Feel around. Find that fabric."

"But the rats."

"Find it," Dana shouted, using her mother voice, the one that told Jenna the time for negotiation was over. "Find it!"

Groping in the dark, Dana tried unsuccessfully to vanquish her image of the rats, gray and thin with hungry, sharp teeth stained red with blood. Had they feasted on the bodies? What would the virus do to an animal?

Twice she banged her leg against something. The skin was broken. A thin trail of blood rivered down her calf.

"Yes!" Pheodora shouted. "I found it. I found it."

Dana locked on the sound of her friend's voice and stumbled toward her. Something brushed across her foot. She jumped, barely swallowing the squeal. Her fingers touched Pheodora, then the broken bookcase with the torn fabric.

"That's it. The door is three feet behind it."

"How can you be sure of the direction?" Pheodora asked.

"I ripped my shirt because the boxes forced us through the narrow opening, just one way to go. Take it backwards and we're at the door."

And so are the rats.

Pheodora screamed. "Something brushed my leg."

"Hurry," Dana shouted. Bile rose in her throat as her shoulder hit something hard, a sword-strike of pain numbing her right arm. "Hurry," she repeated.

Pheodora hit the wall. There was a sickening sound of solid wood. "It's not here. It's not here."

Dana pushed her aside. She hammered the wall. *Thump, thump, thump* . . .

. . . *rripped* . . . She toppled forward, falling through the paper wall and spilling into the next room.

She still had her flashlight, which was now beaming brightly.

Pheodora tumbled out behind her. "Shut the door!" she shouted. "Shut the fucking door."

Dana stood up, pointing the light into the room from which they had just escaped. "No, wait." The beam cleaved through the black. She scanned the floor and the wall.

"Shut the—where the hell are the rats?"

Though audible and sounding like an army from hell, there were no rats to be seen. "Look," Dana said, her flashlight spotting and following a piece of fabric being pulled across the floor on a wire. "It was a trick, all a trick."

A new sound, a thump-thud. No doubt the sound of the dead guy returning to his upright position. "Just a trick."

She took the round object from her pocket and shone a light on her open palm. A bright red safety stone flashed in the light.

18 VASSA ISLAND

Although Nerine Keleman was a successful veterinarian with her own practice, it had not been an easy road. Coming from a family of modest means, she made it through school with the help of academic scholarships and odd jobs, even spending a short time in Washington, D.C. and flirting with the idea of a career in politics. In the end it was her love of animals that lured her to veterinary medicine, a decision she never regretted.

One of the multitude of jobs that she had held was restocking vending machines: candy, crackers, chips, gum. Some of the vending machines were in ladies' rest rooms. These were stocked with feminine products. That was why, when she changed places with Renee in the small, video-free bathroom, she was able to tell, with little more than a glance, exactly what she saw.

By the time she finished washing her hands, her anger had grown to unmanageable proportions. The image of sweet Dr. Dutetre would remain forever in her mind. Here was a man who spent his life helping people, murdered by the American public, while someone like Renee lied and manipulated her way to safety.

Several options occurred to her but in the end she chose the simplest and ultimately most powerful. Hurrying to the Round House, she stopped in front of the central camera, cleared her throat and said, "I have an announcement."

She waited. For what she wasn't sure. Had they heard her? Was anyone paying attention? There was no way to know. She had to assume that someone, somewhere, was watching.

Taking a deep breath to steady her nerves and quell her anger, Nerine said, "Renee Bellacort is menstruating."

She paused, imagining her words electronically zipping through the Internet. Then, just in case they didn't understand what she was saying, added, "This means, that Renee is not pregnant. I repeat, she is not pregnant. She is lying to keep you from voting to exile her."

The camera whined as the lens turned by remote control. Someone was watching. The anger that had been born in her when the doctor died suddenly broke free. Anger aimed not only at Renee but at everyone, all the people who had killed Dr. Dutetre.

"How dare you," she screamed at the camera, at the world. "How dare you pass sentence from the comfort of your cozy bedrooms and offices. How dare you kill a man like Dr. Dutetre. No, not kill—murder, that's what you did. Each and every one of you who voted. Everybody who put their finger on the key is guilty of premeditated murder. Do you hear me? You're all murderers!"

She screamed till her voice was raw, till the last word came out more squeal than language. "Murderers . . ."

She collapsed against the wall, fully aware that she had just sentenced herself to death.

Dana felt good, and she wasn't sure why. Certainly it was nice to have a safety stone to deflect ten percent of the vote against her, but that was a long way from being safe. Yet she felt terrific. Why?

As she listened to Pheodora recount their adventure to the others, she realized what it was: a sense of accomplishment. For the first time since coming to this island, since this nightmare began, she had taken matters into her own hands. She had taken action—and she had succeeded.

And the world watched.

She had been surprised at how quickly she had forgotten about the cameras once the horror began. But whenever she did something foolish or something right, the cameras were the first thing she thought of.

I'm setting a positive example for Jenna, she told herself. Which was true as far as it went. But secretly she knew it was more than that. Who was watching? How many? What did they think? Were her ex-boyfriends glued to the set, watching to see if she lived or died? What about Jenna's prodigal father?

She caught herself thinking about teachers and friends and relatives she hadn't seen since she was a child. Were they watching? And if so, did they see Dana win her first safety stone?

She knew the positive feeling was fleeting. But for now she accepted it, reveled in it, drew strength from her simple victory.

That night Justin came to her cot after the lights were out. Were her ex-boyfriends watching this as well? she wondered, just before sleep took all her thoughts away.

Pheodora woke up cold.

Not chilled. Not cool, but cold. Numbed hands, teeth clacking with cold. The tips of her fingers stung and when she stared at them in the dark room they seemed blue. Sitting up in bed, she clutched the blanket beneath her chin. The others were still sleeping, but no one else was shivering. No one else was blue.

She rubbed her arms beneath the blanket. She could feel the ribbed texture of goose bumps. If she had been dreaming, she couldn't remember it. Could dreams make your flesh crawl?

She took a deep breath and exhaled slowly expecting to see condensation. Nothing.

Of course not, girl. You're in the tropics.

Damn if she wasn't starting to act like some of her clients, the crazy ones who came to her for messages from dead loved ones, insight into what their pets were thinking, and tomorrow's winning lottery numbers.

Lottery numbers? If she could predict lottery numbers, she wouldn't be freezing her ass off on this damn island.

Freezing. No. Not freezing. Tropical island, remember?

She rubbed her arms warming them with friction. Talking about her fears with Dana had been a mistake, had brought it all up again and now she was having trouble sleeping. That was all.

She lay back down. Closing her eyes, she conjured up images of a hot sun on tan-white beach sand. A warm ocean breeze. A campfire.

Cold.

This time there was no mistaking it for a dream. No shifting blame to a busy subconscious. She was cold. Biting cold. She sat up in bed, her blanket falling to her lap. She placed her fingers against the side of her cot, then jerked them away.

What in the world?

It stung her. The metal was so frozen it stung her. She glanced around the room in amazement, looking for someone to share her surprise. Snores and deep breathing were her only replies. Outside she could hear the night creatures—frogs, insects, a night bird or two. No wind. No storm front. Nothing to make the temperature drop.

She saw movement from the corner of her eye. Not in the room but outside. A gray silhouette in the window on the south side of the room away from the light of the moon.

The shape of a man. His back to the dorm.

She squinted. Movement. He was turning. Justin? Foster? Turning. Turning.

As the figure moved, an errant beam of moonlight spilling over the top of the dorm lit his face. Brown hair with gray lines. Pasty white skin. Nose a little long and turned up at the end. She saw his eyes. His thin lips, concaved chin—

Cold.

Her breath caught in her chest. Flash frozen.

Turning, turning. He was at the window. Looking in, looking in.

Cold.

Pheodora was too cold to move. To blink. To think. Her heart frozen between beats. The man in the window was revealed fully now—blinking, breathing.

As Pheodora gasped in disbelief, her dead father smiled and waved to her from the window.

WASHINGTON, D.C.

Tucker closed his eyes. His muscles sagged with relief. He yearned for sleep, but his consciousness wouldn't shut down. Worries careened through his mind like carnival bumper cars.

He had always been plagued by sleeplessness, his eyes easily held open by a difficult problem or unanswered question. Ironically, it was often in sleep that the pieces came together. Answers that were invisible in the light of exhaustion, stood revealed in the radiance of rest.

When Tucker was twelve, he visited the Oregon coast with his best friend and his best friend's family. It was February and the floods were bad that year. It always rained in Oregon during the winter but that year, it forgot to stop.

They were on Highway 99 en route to Florence when the road vanished, disappearing in a fierce gray rain. The Ford minivan stopped just short of a gaping gully where a twelve-foot section of highway had been seconds before. Then came a sound Tucker would never forget—a cascading rumble followed immediately by the howl of crushing metal and shattering glass.

It was three months, two weeks, and four days before he came out of the coma and learned what had happened. Half the hillside had fallen on them. The minivan had been mulched. Tucker, who had been sitting in the back on the driver's side, was the only one spared.

The accident left him with two broken legs, a broken arm and collar bone, and several cracked ribs. He spent the rest of the year in bed. But in many ways, the guilt of surviving while his companions died was worse than the injuries.

It was during that confinement, trapped as much by his guilt as by his broken body, that his mother gave him his first jigsaw puzzle. He quickly graduated from jigsaws to crosswords, from crosswords to brainteasers.

He became obsessed with them. His mother began searching stores for more and more advanced, more and more challenging puzzles.

His therapist said it was Tucker's way of seeking answers, part of his subconscious need to understand *why*. Tucker considered that a bunch of malarkey. He just liked puzzles, that's all.

One night, his mother asked him to explain his obsession. He mulled over her question much the same way he mulled over a puzzle. Then he gave her what was still the best answer he had devised to date. "I like the way it makes my brain feel."

And it was true. The more he did, the better he felt. And the better he became.

Now his puzzle sense—his intuition—was screaming.

Someone's in the room.

Tucker snapped up in bed. A poultice of shadows covered the room. He ripped it away with the click of the bed lamp. The room stood revealed as he had left it—cluttered. A candy wrapper lay near the trash can, his coat was draped over a club-foot chair, his tie lay sprawled on the dresser like a sleeping burgundy-and-blue snake.

Tucker was alone. He got up quickly, slipped on his pants, and rushed around the short wall that separated the sink from the bedroom.

Nothing.

Still, his uneasiness persisted. If not in the room now, then someone had been in there earlier. It was the same inexplicable sensation that had gripped him back in Seattle.

Tucker sighed in exasperation. Of course someone had been in the room. Housekeeping had made the bed and cleaned the bathroom. It was a hotel, for God's sake.

Not housekeeping, though. Someone he knew.

Without wanting to, he began to retrace his steps. Earlier he had changed into his sweats, ordered a burger and fries from room service, and entered notes into his laptop. That was when the strange sensation had begun. But he had been too tired to understand it.

He turned on his laptop. Everything was there. Besides, what was there to take? He had been careful not to write down the name of his source.

A new thought occurred to him. He pulled up his word processing program and clicked on FILE. The menu dropped down, listing the last four files opened. The first was his journal, followed by his personal finance file, rough drafts of stories, and e-mail—but nothing he had called up in the last few days. So someone *had* been in the room, in this computer, looking at his files.

Thanks to the three-hour time difference, it was just a

little after ten in Seattle when he called the apartment
complex where he lived. When Doobie, the assistant
manager, answered, Tucker asked him for a favor.

Twenty minutes later the hotel phone rang. It was
Doobie.

"Okay, now I'm in your apartment. Damn, man, are
you ever going to empty these boxes?"

"Never mind that. Is anything missing?"

"Who can tell in all this mess? Hang on. Your TV's
here. So's the microwave and CD player. *Huey Lewis
and The News*? Bro', we've got to do something about
your taste in music."

"Just keep looking. Try the office."

"Hang on." The sound of footsteps and boxes being
moved traveled across country via the phone line. "Here
we go. Yep, computer is still here. So are your books.
*World's Greatest Puzzles, Master Brainteaser 2000,
Brainteaser 2000, Part 2, The Mensa Puzzles*. What, no
Monopoly? How about *Clue*? That's sort of a puzzle."

"When I get back, you can lecture me about my taste
in music and pastimes. Do me a favor."

"I thought that was what I was doing."

"One more. Sit down in front of the computer and
turn it on." Tucker waited to hear that the machine had
booted up.

"It wants a password."

"Pudding."

The manager chuckled. "Did you just call me Pudding?"

"Pudding is the password, you ass."

"I know. It just booted up. What kind of password is
'pudding'?"

"A creamy and delicious one. The computer is programmed with a cascading code. It changes every day.
Since it's not midnight in Seattle yet, the password is still
pudding."

"Yeah, whatever. You got any porn on this?"

"Just click the start menu. And go up to DOCUMENTS."

There was rustling on the line. "Hang on." More noise. "Okay. Here we go. Journal, budget, Ashley Judd—dude, you do so have porn. You horndog!"

Tucker felt his face flush red. "She's a fine actress. What else?"

The manager continued to read—a total of ten items. Tucker wasn't sure of the order, but nothing seemed out of place. Had he been wrong about Seattle?

"Nothing," he muttered. "Thanks, Doobie. That's all I need."

"Wait a sec. Hello, Ashley Judd. Bro', she *is* a fine actress."

"Will you get out of that? It's just a photo I came across. She reminds me of someone, that's all. Shut it back down."

"Yeah, yeah—hang on . . ."

"What are you doing now?"

"Trying to shut it down. It's a little hard doing this backwards."

Backwards?

The alarm in the back of Tucker's mind started ringing. Backwards?

"What do you mean, backwards?" he asked, positive he already knew the answer.

"I mean your mouse is on the wrong side of the computer, dude. I didn't know you were left-handed."

Tucker smiled in the dark. "I'm not."

Alone in his Washington hotel room, Tucker sorted the random bits of information through his head. His paranoia was not unfounded. Someone had broken into his apartment in Seattle. Nothing appeared to have been taken, but someone had accessed his computer. And the same thing had happened in his hotel room. Nothing taken, but his laptop files had been searched.

Nothing was taken, but had something been left behind? Like a bug? Could he trust the phones? The hotel telephone was seal-formed plastic. No way to remove the mouthpiece without breaking it. That didn't mean they couldn't have replaced the handset for one with a bug already built in it. Or simply tapped his line somewhere outside the building.

Likewise his mobile phone. If they knew the frequency, they could monitor all of his cell calls.

But why?

He thought of the impression in the vinyl at the restaurant. The impression that looked like a mike box. Who was listening? And again—why?

Something dangerous was going on, definitely career-threatening, possibly life-threatening. He was being set up—or at least manipulated.

But what had caused him to believe someone was in the room when he woke? He had felt sure of it. Just as he was sure he knew the intruder.

Suddenly he sneezed. Then he sniffed the air. It was faint, but there. The faint scent of an oddly familiar aftershave.

But he didn't know where he had smelled it before.

He was still trying to figure it out when the sun came up. He ordered a light breakfast from room service, showered, and began to dress.

He was putting on his pants when there was a knock at the door. "Just a second." He buttoned his pants and pulled up the zipper. "Be right there." But when he opened the door the hall was empty.

Tucker looked both right and left—nobody.

His bare right foot touched something. He drew back and looked down. A small three-by-five computer disc lay in the doorway. He picked it up and turned it over. There was a simple white label with four words: TUCKER THORNE—READ ME.

19 VASSA ISLAND

Morning broke over the Caribbean. The sea was choppy and darker than usual, and the wind carried the hint of rain.

Justin was up and gone when Dana woke. She ate breakfast with Nora Tibits, the schoolteacher from Idaho who had once been a nun. Then she took a stroll on the beach, where she watched gulls loop in the gray skies and reflected on her situation. What was Jenna doing right now? Could she see Dana?

As if her thoughts were being read, Dana heard the familiar mechanical whine. She scanned the tree line and found a camera halfway up a tree, twenty yards from where she was.

The camera whined again, no doubt zooming in.

Who is watching? she wondered again. Can't they help? Can't anyone help? The doctor had said they couldn't be removed from the island until the virus was isolated and treated. The downed helicopter and jets further reduced the possibility of rescue.

Then there was Foster Merrick.

The fisherman had stumbled from the sea that afternoon, finally convinced that everything was real. The boat he had stolen had been shot out from under him by the United States Navy. Brenda Segar was dead.

Dana shuddered. They were alone. Visible to the entire world, yet utterly alone.

She checked her pants pocket, looking at her one and only safety stone. Just a piece of cut glass colored red. Yet capable of saving her life. Should she use it in the coming vote?

The death of the doctor added a new dimension of fear to their plight. Everyone was susceptible. No one was safe. Down the beach she saw Nerine Keleman walking in the surf, her shoes in her hands. The veterinarian had been quiet since her rant before the camera. Again, Dana looked at the piece of red glass in her hand, the safety stone. No doubt some viewers would be angry, offended by Nerine's rage. The veterinarian could very well be the next one to be exiled—to die.

Dana's safety stone would negate ten percent of the vote against Nerine, maybe even save her life. Should Dana give it to her?

Sunlight flared off the cut glass, glistening as if lit from the inside. Dana thought of Jenna. Her fist closed around the stone. No, she couldn't give it up. No matter what. She had to put her daughter first and that meant living.

Whatever it took, Dana had to live.

RICHMOND, VIRGINIA

The news car squealed into the hospital parking lot seconds ahead of the half-million-dollar satellite truck, parking in an area reserved for medical emergencies. Six minutes later, the nurse in charge of the pediatrics ward was screaming for security.

Using his newfound clout, Tucker had requested and gotten Brick Bickman temporarily assigned to Washington as his cameraman. Together they hurried down the antiseptic tile floor. Behind them, hospital staff screamed. Tucker caught every third word: ". . . can't . . . authorized . . . police . . . jail . . ." He ignored them.

Stopping a candy striper pushing a cart heavy with kids' magazines and games, he demanded, "Where are the Capler twins?"

"Twins? Down the hall—room 315." She squinted. "Hey, you're that guy on TV. What are you doing in the children's ward?"

"Stop them," an orderly screamed.

But Tucker and Brick were already moving.

"If we go to jail, man, you're going to be my bitch," Brick said, effortlessly carrying the thirty-pound camera.

"We're not going to be arrested."

They turned the corner and broke into a trot. "I'm just saying, that's all."

"Noted." Tucker carried the wireless mike as if it were a baton in a relay race. "Here it is."

Room 315 had two beds. In one sat a girl no older than five. Her identical twin sister lay in the other bed. A woman in her late twenties with the strained face of a worried mother sat between them in a vinyl chair. A man, presumably the father, sat in another chair by the window. Bright balloons tethered to the beds with long nylon strings bumped against the ceiling. A coloring book lay open and a bright purple crayon was fisted in the hand of the first girl.

On the television, coverage of Vassa Island played. *Even here*, Tucker thought.

The father stood as they entered. His quizzical look turned to concern as the large man with the camera came in. There was no time for formalities. Tucker identified himself as a reporter from the Globe Newschannel and asked permission to videotape the girls. He was about to explain why, when two orderlies and a charge nurse bounded through the door.

"Get out of here now," the nurse screamed.

The two orderlies stepped forward to escort them out. Camera still on his shoulder, Brick turned his broad chest toward the intruders. Fluorescent light glinted off his shaved head. The orderlies stopped in midmotion.

"Mr. Capler, I'm trying to save your daughters' lives," Tucker said quickly.

"Save? How?" The father's features brightened with hope.

He pointed to the television. "By preventing the death of someone on Vassa Island."

WASHINGTON, D.C.

Too close to call. That was the official word from bookies around the country, where the Vassa Island exile vote was being bet on as if it were a sporting event. Police tried to stop it. Fourteen people were arrested in New Orleans, twelve in Minneapolis, and thirty in Fresno. But the betting continued.

And the twenty-four hour news organizations fed into it. Every story, every expert opinion was monitored—and reflected in the betting. The president of a new group, Baptists Against Betting appeared on Fox News, declaring that anyone who bet on the Vassa Island vote would receive an ". . . all expense paid trip to hell. . . ." Representatives of the Catholic Church fanned out across the country, like volunteer firemen against a five-alarm blaze, urging members and nonmembers alike not to bet, not to vote, to instead pray for the souls of the victims on Vassa Island.

Dr. Sherman Lorrik watched it all from the White House situation room, sitting before a half dozen monitors flipping between the various stations. From a purely intellectual perspective it was a fascinating situation: a sociologist's dream, a microcosm and macrocosm of society, rife with turmoil, guilt, fear, and rampant curiosity.

The president had called twice in the last half hour.

"When?" he had demanded. The second call was tinged with panic.

"Soon," Lorrik had assured him. "Soon."

"This had better work."

At 11:38, twenty-two minutes before the next vote, the Globe Newschannel went live in the field to Tucker Thorne.

RICHMOND, VIRGINIA

The Globe satellite truck was a rolling television studio, complete with editing equipment, cameras, independent power supply, and a switcher capable of changing between up to four field cameras. Microwave trucks, a favorite of local news organizations, were completely dependent on line of sight to the transmitter. Thirty-, forty-, even sixty-foot masts were needed, depending on surrounding topography and buildings, to get a live signal out.

Not so for a sat-truck. Instead of transmitting the signal to a tower, it sent the signal to a communication satellite that could, in turn, beam the signal to a multitude of ground stations for network distribution. This allowed for live shots from almost anywhere in the world.

But even the most advanced equipment still required time to set up. The camera was locked onto a tripod as Tucker and Brick ran from the hospital. A confused father and half a dozen nurses and orderlies made up the rest of the odd parade.

There was no time to edit the tape, no time to test the setup.

The signal was verified, bars and tone successfully beamed to the newsroom control but no picture had been transmitted. Only live—on the air—would they find out if it worked.

Tucker situated the father just out of the shot. "I'll do the setup, run the video, then talk to you."

The father nodded; his face bedsheet white. A sound operator untucked his shirt, clipped a small black box to his belt and instructed him to run the microphone and wire up under his shirt so only the small lapel mike was visible.

"Twenty seconds," the sat-truck cameraman yelled as Tucker picked up the new microphone, this one hard-wired to the truck. Brick disappeared into the mobile studio. They would run his video raw.

Onlookers were often struck by the lack of fanfare associated with a live shot. Other than the preliminary call of "stand-by," there was no indication of exactly when they were on. Tucker, who was wired to the producers, both in the Seattle control room and in the field, simply began talking.

Inside the truck, Brick had just finished cuing the tape as Tucker began his spiel.

"Kate and Kimberly Capler are four-year-old twins from Harrington, Delaware." At the mention of the girls, the field producer looked at Brick.

"Good to go," the photographer said.

The director punched up the video, taken just moments earlier. Both girls had balloon-bright blue eyes and tousled blond hair.

Tucker continued, ". . . They are sweet, precocious, and suffering from a rare disease known as Fanconi's anemia. And tonight, their lives are tied directly to events on Vassa Island . . ."

"Stand by to take island live," the director said into his microphone. Then to Brick he added, "He's pretty good for a rookie."

"Yeah, I know, but don't tell him I said so."

"Take island full," the director said. The familiar image of Vassa Island appeared on the screen. Tucker continued to talk under the video.

". . . Less than twenty-four hours after the crisis on Vassa Island began, a bone marrow match for the Capler twins was made. The donor wished to remain anonymous, but when doctors tried to establish contact they learned the donor was on Vassa Island . . ."

"Stand by to roll two," the director said.

"That donor is thirty-two-year-old veterinarian, Nerine Keleman," Tucker said.

"Take two." Video of Nerine, taken in her clinic, filled the screen. She was hugging a golden retriever puppy and looking nothing like the woman who had launched into a tirade against the public the day before.

The scene returned to Tucker in the field, this time a two shot. Tucker began a powerful interview with the twins' father, an interview in which the father said, "A vote to kill Nerine is a vote to kill my girls."

Brick checked the time: 11:42. The father's comment would certainly change votes, but would it be enough?

20 VASSA ISLAND

Dana Kirsten rolled the safety stone between her hands. What to do? It was now a matter of strategy. Did she use her stone and negate ten percent of the vote, or did she save it for later?

"I'm using all of mine," Justin said, then explained that anyone watching would know he had the most stones and might consider him a safe bet.

Did the same logic apply to Dana?

Justin placed all four of his stones in the designated receptacle. Dana waited, holding the single stone as if it were the most precious jewel in the world, watching as the time clicked on. At the last moment, she reluctantly dropped it in the receptacle.

The four screens hanging over the Vault came to life. The count began.

The numbers were staggering, quickly shooting past the one thousand mark. The votes were increasing each time. Why?

Dana watched as her own numbers topped two thousand.

Two thousand are voting for me to die?

Justin's went up the fastest. He was the first to break ten thousand. Nerine was close behind. A woman moaned at Dana's right. Renee's fake pregnancy was working against her. She was in third place.

The counting continued.

Dana's breath caught in her chest as her own numbers topped five thousand, putting her in fourth place bearing down on third. Now she was grateful she had used her stone. Was Justin right? Had she been targeted because viewers knew she had a safety stone? Or did people dislike her so much they wanted her to die?

Her thoughts raced, tracing the events since coming to the island, looking for something she had said or done that could have angered viewers. Her strategy had been to ignore the cameras, to focus on staying alive. Had that been a mistake? She knew others were playing to the lens, pleading their case. Perhaps viewers found her arrogant for not doing the same?

Maybe it has nothing to do with the island?

By now her past, all of their pasts would have been talked about and dissected by every television network. Was she being denounced as an unwed mother? A sinner? A tramp? Was part-time work as a bartender being used against her? Was this vote an outcry for moral purity?

"No, no . . . ," Renee moaned.

On the reader board, Justin still held the lead. But Nerine's numbers had effectively stopped while Renee's numbers continued to climb.

Eight thousand, four hundred and fifty-nine . . . Eight thousand, seven hundred . . .

Renee took the number two spot. "No," she repeated.

Justin had cracked the five-digit barrier and was continuing to grow. But was it enough to save Renee?

The tally stopped. Justin was number one, Renee second, Nerine third, Dana fourth.

Fourth. Dana exhaled, her body sagging with relief. Then she looked at Justin's number. He had received the most votes.

Control spoke, "Justin Rourke, eleven thousand, two hundred and fifteen votes . . ."

The air was completely still. Nothing moved. No breeze.

". . . minus four safety stones, eliminating forty percent of the vote. . . ." Again there was movement on the reader board as votes were subtracted from his total.

"Final tally, six thousand, seven hundred and twenty-nine votes."

A woman began to cry.

"Renee Bellacort, you have six thousand, seven hundred and thirty-four votes. Renee Bellacort, you are exiled . . ."

Renee screamed, a harsh animal howl of fear and disbelief. Her cries were broken by the *shush* of the thumbprint-activated compartments being opened up.

"You've got to help me," Renee begged. She left her cubicle, rushing to Foster, grabbing him by the arm. "You're a man. You're supposed to protect me. Give me your vaccine."

Foster jerked his arm away, took a step back, and used the injector on himself.

Renee ran her hands through her hair. "No. No." She rushed to Justin, then Cory, begging, pleading for someone to make the sacrifice to save her. For a moment, a hesitating moment, it looked as if Justin would relent.

No! Dana pleaded with her eyes.

He used the injector on himself.

Renee's skin began to quiver. Her complexion flushed red.

In pain or panic or both, Renee collapsed against the wall, falling to the floor, drawing her hands and feet together in a ball.

Dana used her own injector without hesitation. For her daughter if for no one else.

Renee's cries were like daggers cutting through the air. "No . . . This can't be happening to me. Can't be happening to me."

Pfsst.

It was the faint sound of the final injector. Responding to the cold pressure of the needle against her arm, Renee looked up in shock. A shot. Someone had given her an injection. Someone had saved her life. She turned quickly to see which of the men was her savior. Who had come to her rescue?

But it wasn't a man.

Nora Tibits stood up slowly. Her own flesh was now tomato red, the pain obvious, but she remained silent.

"You?" Renee asked in disbelief. "You? But why?"

Nora nodded, her only acknowledgment. "God loves you," she whispered, then grimaced in pain. Her eyes rolled back in her head as she crumpled to the floor.

Renee's own skin cooled and ceased movement, even as Nora's accelerated. "Why?" she repeated, staring as the former nun writhed on the floor.

Dana knew why. Nora had told her how she had left the church that she loved so much, because she felt she was not good enough for God.

But now, by making the ultimate sacrifice, she had proved her worth, as much to herself as to anyone else.

The voice of Control thundered through the room. "Eight contestants, seven days."

21 WASHINGTON, D.C.

Tucker entered the lobby and walked briskly to the elevators, using the mirrored doors to search behind him. He had been on guard since returning to Washington two hours earlier. If someone was following him, they were invisible.

The doors opened. He entered and punched in his floor. His elation at saving Nerine Keleman and, in so doing, saving the Capler girls had ended when he entered Washington. Now he couldn't shake the feeling that he was a mouse in someone's maze.

The disc left in front of his hotel door had contained the confidential medical records of both Nerine and the twins, revealing that Nerine had anonymously taken the bone marrow test shortly before leaving for Vassa Island.

Tucker could understand why someone would want to disseminate that information. But who? Why had they chosen him? How had they known which room he was in?

He left the elevator and hesitated before using his key card. What would he find inside? Had someone been in his room again? And if so, who and for what purpose? This time he had been sure to take his laptop with him, leaving nothing that could be of any use to anyone.

The room had been cleaned again. His bed made. There was no obvious sign that anyone other than hotel personnel had been inside. Of course, without the computer record he would not have known about the earlier break-in. He sniffed the air. No sign of the odd aftershave.

Again, the image of a mouse in a maze came to mind. He loved puzzles, but this one was too big and missing too many pieces.

When his cell phone rang, he jumped. He took a second to catch his breath before answering.

"Interesting story," said Dr. Sherman Lorrik.

"Thanks. You wouldn't have had anything to do with that now would you?"

Lorrik didn't answer. "I gave you a story, an exclusive on the involvement of sabotage in the crash of those aircraft. You denounced it. I want to know why."

If Lorrik had recorded their earlier conversation, Tucker had every reason to believe he was recording this one. He chose his words carefully. "Because it was wrong."

After a long pause, Lorrik asked, "If you're not going to believe me, why should I give you more information?"

Tucker decided on the direct approach. What would a scientist do if the mouse suddenly became aware of the maze? "Because you have to. You're using me. Manipulating me. Because you need me."

Lorrik scoffed. "How do I need you?" the doctor demanded.

"I don't know—yet. The real question is why should I believe anything you say? Why should I trust you?"

"There are plenty of reporters who would kill for the information I've given you."

Tucker felt his chest tightening. He had become a reporter based solely on his connection to this source. Now he was jeopardizing that connection.

"Then go, talk to them," he said. No matter what had gotten him here he knew he was a good reporter. Now he had to prove it. But he wouldn't be an administration lapdog, performing tricks for tips, pretending he didn't see the man behind the curtain.

"Meet me," Lorrik said. "Downstairs in the lounge in thirty minutes."

VASSA ISLAND

"You what?" Dana asked, although she had heard perfectly the first time. Nora's death had left her surprisingly drained and depressed. Maybe it was because they had talked so intimately just that morning or perhaps it was guilt, shame that the little woman from Idaho would make a sacrifice. Whatever the reason, for the moment Dana felt disconnected as if her mind had become detached from reality.

Is this the way it feels to go insane?

Hadn't she read somewhere that the very act of questioning your sanity was proof that you still had it? The insane never thought they were crazy.

Dana had purposely sought out Pheodora after the vote. Their adventure the day before had made them closer. Next to Justin, she was the contestant Dana trusted most. But now, as they stood alone in the clearing they had come to call "the safe spot," Dana felt herself slipping further into the fog of uncertainty.

Pheodora locked her arms against her chest. Bags hung heavily beneath her swollen, red eyes. "I know. I know it's impossible. Maybe I'm crazy."

Dana smiled. "Must be contagious. I was just wondering the same thing about myself."

Pheodora brightened. "Really?"

Dana continued. "Who wouldn't question their sanity on this island? How do we know what's real and what's not? I mean, those scorpions—there was no doubting they were real. And, when we were alone in that dark room, I swear those rats seemed every bit as real. Only they weren't."

"An illusion," Pheodora said. "And me seeing my father at the window last night?"

"Also an illusion. Or exhaustion. Or a dream. We can't completely trust our senses."

Pheodora looked at Dana. Her eyes seemed unfathomably deep and sad. "Or each other," she added.

The words struck deep and true. She was right. After all, it was Dana who had determined that someone on this island—one of the players—was an accomplice to Control.

Yet Dana had already lowered her guard with Pheodora and Justin. What if Pheodora was making up the story of the illusion? A deflective tactic? Then why would she bring up the issue of trust? To further deflect suspicion? And what of Justin? What did she really know about the pilot? Nothing. Certainly he was good-looking and kind and had a keen sense of humor and a quick mind, but that was superficial, easy to fake. Obviously, Control's accomplice would put on his or her best face.

"So what are you saying?" Dana asked. "We shouldn't work together anymore?"

Tears had formed in Pheodora's eyes. "It doesn't take

a psychic to know that ultimately we will all turn on one another."

A blinding burst of high intensity light slashed across the room. Each burst was bright enough to scar a retina; multiple bursts were strong enough to cause permanent blindness. Even viewed through the small, blackened window cut into the door, each flash left a blurring afterimage.

And somewhere in that room inside the motor pool were Justin's five safety stones.

Justin was seven when he took his first flight in a small private plane. He was in the air less than two hours, but when the plane touched down, he knew what he wanted to do for the rest of his life. Later, he would discover he had a natural aptitude for aviation. And he often suspected it was the one, and perhaps only thing, he did really well.

That love of flying had never diminished. Never to fly again was Justin Rourke's greatest fear.

Blind men can't fly airplanes.

"You have fifteen minutes, starting now," said Control.

Justin Rourke had been marked for death in the last vote. He didn't know if people voted for him because they knew he had safety stones or because they didn't like him. His relationship with Dana could be seen as taking advantage of the situation, preying on someone who was vulnerable.

Maybe they were right?

It had taken four safety stones to save his life. Now, less than twenty hours from the next vote, he had none.

The problem was the lack of clues. Under the original concept of the game, contestants were to receive clues at the Vault, then have three days to find the safety stones before the next vote.

But instead of clues, the Vault was now dispensing the

lifesaving vaccine. So far, the only way anyone had gotten a safety stone was to stumble across the challenge. And, as Justin knew from checking off locations on his map, that was a whole lot of stumbling. His plan had been to systematically go through all the buildings, cover as much ground as possible, and hope to trigger a challenge. His plan sucked. There wasn't enough time.

There had to be a unifying theme, he theorized. Something that ties it all together. Something around which the clues were based. It had been Pheodora who had inadvertently given him the clue to the answer.

But now that he had found his personal challenge, he didn't know what in hell to do about it. He had been in the building less than five minutes when Control spoke.

"Your five safety stones are in the next room. When the door is unlocked, you will have fifteen minutes to retrieve them."

"So what's the catch?" Justin had asked.

That was when the light show began. If he used his eyes, he would be blinded. Though empty, the room was half the size of a football field. Much too large for Justin to cover by touch alone.

"If you are not out in fifteen minutes, you will be locked inside. And the lasers will continue."

He checked his watch. Less than thirteen minutes.

Justin Rourke left the building.

ATLANTA, GEORGIA

Headquartered in Atlanta and originally created to battle malaria during World War II, the Centers for Disease Control and Prevention now consisted of nine divisions and often worked hand in hand with local, state, and even international agencies.

It was the CDC that discovered the cause of Legionnaires' disease, as well as the potentially fatal toxic shock syndrome. Currently, the fight against AIDS was the CDC's number one battle. Until the body of Brenda Segar arrived.

Now the most advanced medical research facility in the world was devoting its resources to discovering the secrets of the Vassa Island Virus.

The first step was to determine just what VIV was; the second, to find out how it was transmitted. Essential information to understanding how big a threat it posed to the rest of the world.

As a science, biology functioned on its own timetable. Nature could not be rushed. Even using every known catalyst available, it would still take days to develop, grow, and dissect cultures for study.

Although it was against his scientific nature to speculate, the director of the research division notified the 24/7 task force that VIV did appear to be a designer virus, specifically crafted for a certain purpose. No small feat and not possible to this degree of accuracy without extremely advanced, cutting-edge technology.

Finding out where it was created was the first step in finding out who created it.

VASSA ISLAND

Justin returned to the motor pool with less than nine minutes remaining. After ripping the right sleeve off his shirt, he folded the cloth once, then tied it securely over his eyes. Effectively sightless, he entered the room of blinding lights.

He could feel the laser light lashing his body. Even though his eyes were closed and masked, the flashes of red flared in his vision.

He took a handful of pebbles from his shirt pocket, threw them in a small arc to his right, and listened. The stones clattered on the concrete floor. He repeated the process straight ahead and then to the left.

More clattering. *Klink, klink, klink, klink.*

He took five steps forward, careful not to slip on the pebbles he had already thrown, then repeated the process. When his shirt pocket was empty, he took pebbles from his pants pockets.

Sweat ran down his forehead.

How long before the door closed and he was locked inside?

There was no way of knowing. A dribble of sweat found its way under the mask and into the corners of his eyes.

Klink, klink, klink, klink.

Rocks clattered across the floor.

The plan was to mimic a dolphin's sonar. In theory, when the pebbles struck the glass safety stones, they would produce a different sound than when striking the concrete floor. In theory.

Klink, klink, klink, klink.

Rivulets of sweat saturated the makeshift blind, breaching the security of his closed lids.

Klink, klink, klink, ping.

Justin stopped. He threw the pebbles forward and to the right.

Klink, klink, ping.

A little more to the right.

Ping, ping, ping, ping.

Unsure of the time remaining, but positive he didn't have long, Justin dropped to his hands and knees. Rocks he had scattered across the concrete bit into his flesh. He searched with his hands.

A knit bag. His hand clamped around the prize. The glass stones pinged against one another.

His instinct was to run. Turn back the way he came and race for the open door. He resisted. Turning around was not as simple as it sounded. Too much one way or another and he would miss the door completely; too fast and he would fall, losing all sense of direction.

He turned carefully in his tracks, then, engaging all his self-control, he began walking calmly back toward the door.

Justin wasn't sure he was out until he stumbled over the doorjamb. He fell to his knees as the massive door slammed shut behind him.

WASHINGTON, D.C.

Tucker had gone downstairs early, hoping to see if Lorrik was being followed. Instead he found the doctor already waiting at a back table and not the least bit surprised at Tucker's premature arrival. Lorrik was sitting in an open-back chair. If he wore a mike box, it would be covered by his coat and not press against the back of the seat. Had he chosen that chair for that very reason?

Lorrik was drinking whiskey. A hard drink that looked out of place in the doctor's soft round hands. He seemed to have aged since their last meeting. His crow's-feet were now deep gouges, as if his eyes had been clawed by angry eagles instead of "crows."

"I want to make one thing clear," Lorrik began. "What I'm about to tell you is off the record, understand? You can't use it."

Tucker paused. "That doesn't help me very much."

"Consider it deep background, very deep. Do we have an agreement?"

It was Tucker's turn to pause. Did he want to commit to such a restrictive position? In the end, curiosity won out. "Agreed."

"Electromagnetic pulse. What do you know about it?" Lorrik asked.

"EMP. A side effect of a nuclear explosion. Lethal for computer hard drives rendering them useless," Tucker answered. "Scientists have worked for years to develop a practical way to create and direct an electromagnetic pulse without a nuclear explosion. It's considered to be a dream weapon."

Lorrik nodded.

"Wait a second. You're saying that's what brought those planes down?"

Lorrik lifted his glass to his lips, held it there for a second as if contemplating drinking, then took a deep swallow. He sat the glass down and dabbed his mouth with his napkin.

Tucker had been baffled by the charge of sabotage. Why would Lorrik make such a volatile allegation? Unless the truth were worse. An EMP weapon certainly fit the bill. He chewed his lower lip in thought. "No, it doesn't track. Commercial aircraft, maybe, but military planes are hardened against such a pulse."

Lorrik shook his glass. The sole ice cube rattled like a pebble in a skull.

Tucker realized for the first time just how red the doctor's eyes were, and he wondered how many drinks he had had already.

"I said, military aircraft are hardened against the effects of an electromagnetic pulse."

Lorrik pushed the glass aside. The ice cube made a final *klunk*. He leaned forward across the small table. "I know."

Suddenly everything crystallized for Tucker: Lorrik was terrified. And now Tucker knew why. "You're saying someone has developed an EMP weapon that is not only directional, but works against what should be the most protective technology ever developed."

Lorrik sighed. "Those planes are made to fly even in the aftermath of a nuclear explosion. But something on that island swatted them out of the sky like gnats."

The doctor sat back in his chair. Again he looked at the glass.

"But that means—" Tucker began.

"That this is bigger than the contestants, bigger than the virus," Lorrik finished. "If such a weapon exists, then the very survival of the United States is at issue. And you can't say a word about it. Do you understand?"

Tucker assumed his ability to be shocked had reached its maximum. He was wrong. "If the public realizes there's a weapon that can render all military hardware worthless, there will be mass panic."

"More than that," Lorrik added. "This threatens not only the United States, but every technologically advanced country in the world. And it's not restricted to military targets. Can you imagine what would happen if such a device was used in Silicon Valley? Or how about the New York Stock Exchange? Or any airport in the world? What happens if China decides it's in their best interest to wipe the island off the face of the earth? Or worse, if they try to take the island and claim the weapon for themselves?"

VASSA ISLAND

Flush with victory, Justin agreed to help Cory Nestor in his effort to crack the Vault. If his lucky streak held he might get something infinitely more valuable than safety stones: the vaccines.

Cory, as a computer systems manager, was positive that if he could remove the safeguards, he could open the Vault. "The Vault has an independent CPU. But, it's also connected to the main computer system. If we shut down the Vault's computer, I can disconnect it from the central system and reconnect it to a computer I control."

"Meaning . . . ," Justin asked.

"Meaning, I say open sesame and it does," Cory said. His long face was festooned with a boyish grin.

"Great! Let's do it."

The grin faltered. "There's a problem."

"Why did I know you were going to say that?"

"The Vault is protected by a powerful electrical grid, most likely boosted to a fatal setting. Killing the main power source won't be a problem, but if I'm correct, there will be a backup and that will be hard to find."

"How do we do it?" Justin asked.

"We have to find, identify, and test every lead coming into the Round House."

Justin looked up at the four-sided scoreboard, the central camera, the four wall cameras—and then he exhaled. "That's a lot of leads. We had better get started."

". . . Follow the stars and find your heart, the soul is nested in the signs . . . ," Cory said with a return of the shy grin. "Sorry, it's a favorite poem of mine."

Justin smiled. "Have you heard the one about the man from Nantucket?"

As predicted, the work was slow and tedious. Three hours later when Dana arrived with canned food and bottled water, the Round House seemed in various stages of decomposition. Exposed wires in a multitude of colors hung like silly string. Dana made a funny face as she opened a can of baked beans and studied the room. "What happens if you pull the wrong wire and the Vault stops working? Then no one will get the vaccine."

"We're being very careful," Cory explained. "That's why it's taking so long."

Justin pulled out his map and turned it over to the blank side. "You know, if we keep a record of each lead we follow, we won't lose time chasing the same ones."

"Good idea."

He checked his pockets, but didn't find a pencil. "Can I borrow your pen?"

Cory touched the small silver pen in his shirt pocket. "Sorry, it's out of ink."

"So why do you keep it?"

Cory shrugged. "You're going to laugh, but I keep it for luck. I call it my safety pen."

"I hate to tell you this, but so far it's not working too well."

"I know."

Dana put an arm around Cory's shoulder. "Well, I have a feeling this time will be different."

When the two men were alone again, they returned to their work. The more they were together, the more Cory loosened up, and the more he loosened up, the more garrulous he became. His knowledge of computers, in fact of all things electronic, was extraordinary. Equally impressive was his knowledge of reality television.

"It's something of a hobby," he said.

"Hobby?" Justin questioned. Cory had just finished reciting the names and occupations of every contestant ever to compete on the American version of *Survivor*.

"Okay, maybe it's more of an obsession," he confessed.

Justin, by contrast, had watched fewer than a half dozen reality shows before being selected for *24/7*. "Of course it doesn't take an expert to know my number is coming up. I'm going to continue to be exiled until I run out of luck or out of safety stones."

"Not necessarily," Cory said. "In the very first year of the American *Survivor*, Rudy, the ex–Navy SEAL, came within one vote of being kicked out in the first tribal council. But he ultimately made it to the final three."

"But wasn't it the players and not the public who did the voting on that show?"

Cory smiled. "Yes, but the public votes on *Big Brother*. On the first American season, one of the housemates—er, contestants—a young lawyer named Curtis was nominated for banishment in almost every vote. Yet like Rudy, he made it to the final three."

"How do you know all this stuff?" Justin asked.

Cory laughed. "Not to be rude, how do you not? I mean, reality TV is everywhere."

Justin chewed on his lower lip. "I guess you could say it's by choice. I used to watch, like everybody else, until *True Life*."

Cory stopped working. Everyone knew about *True Life*. The reality show that almost destroyed the genre—and a network, Globe. *True Life* involved cramming fifty people into a makeshift community built in an expanded film studio. Despite the number of contestants, the show quickly became about one person: sexy Sherine Beauvant.

"I still remember the minister," Justin said.

Cory's pale face indicated he did, too.

"He was such a nice guy." Justin continued, "Three kids, loved his wife, loved his job. I was sure he was the one man who could stand up to her."

"She was—she was—something," Cory stammered.

"I quit watching after the minister stabbed himself to death," Justin said. "Wonder what ever happened to Sherine?"

"She killed herself, too," Cory said, his voice just above a whisper. "Three months after that show. The public treated her like a murderer. Spat on her. Sent her hate mail. She only did it for them, for their amusement; then they turned on her. They created her and they destroyed her."

They worked until the sun began to sink and the sky began to blush. When they returned to the dormitory, Justin immediately saw that Dana wasn't there.

"She says she wants to be by herself," Pheodora explained. "She's sleeping alone tonight."

Justin's disappointment was quickly overwhelmed by a deep sense of foreboding.

22 WASHINGTON, D.C.

The ultimate weapon.

Tucker chewed on a hamburger the size of his fist. He had opted to use room service again so he could watch that evening's edition of 24/7. Although covering the story, he had little time to watch the live feeds. He therefore depended on short blurbs from the AP and, like millions of other Americans, the nightly edited version. He had requested and received a VCR for his room so he could record the show and play it back at his leisure.

But as the show ran, his mind wandered.

Finding it easier to think when he could physically touch the information, Tucker had set up a bulletin board that was now covered in notes, faxes, biographical information, and news clippings. In the right corner was a detailed map of the island, listing all six hundred and thirty-eight cameras. One of the researchers within the news division had noticed a small anomaly—a rolling back of sorts, involving several of the island cameras. Never more than one or two, never longer than a few minutes. Tucker had marked each location, hoping to discern a pattern.

He added a new sheet to the bulletin board. A printout

of information downloaded from the Internet on an electromagnetic pulse. In this age of information a control-
lable, EMP device would be devastating.

The ultimate weapon.

But how did that fit with events on Vassa Island?

Why create the ultimate weapon to hold less than a
dozen people hostage? It didn't track. He had pressed
Lorrik for information on who could have built such a
weapon. Iran, Iraq, China—the list was enormous. Who
was responsible?

Something on the show caught his attention. Tucker
stopped the tape, rewound, and pressed Play. Two of the
contestants were discussing strategy. There! He stopped
the tape again, rewound it, and listened once more, this
time writing down the words.

He stopped the tape and looked at what he had
written.

VASSA ISLAND

Dana opened her eyes and shifted uncomfortably on the
cot. The television building, designed to house up to
twenty-five people—field crews, producers, and sound
technicians—was off-limits to contestants, and it was
the only building with a lockable door. But death had
claimed the crew before the locks could be engaged. Now
the three-story building was quiet as a casket.

The first floor was designed for storage and mainte-
nance of the gear. Equipment-laden shelves lined the
walls and a warren of head-high cubicles occupied the
center. The second floor was filled with digital editing
equipment, computers, a character generator, and a Grass
Valley switcher. The ceilings and walls were covered in
beige pinhole acoustic tile, with low lighting and a raised

floor to allow easy cable access. In a crisis, the entire show could be run from this room.

It was the third floor that drew Dana to this building. What had been eight small offices had been turned into bedrooms to be used by production workers—two cots per room, four in the big room that also had the only window. The cots were the same as in the dorm, so the comfort level was no greater; but since the building was off-limits to contestants, it was completely booby trap free.

Dana had chosen to sleep in the large room and had drifted off, watching the stars through the window.

Until she heard the voices.

She opened her eyes. The plate glass window that framed the ocean also permitted a soft spill of moonlight. She checked her watch. It was still early. She rolled onto her left side and closed her eyes again.

. . . yes I am . . . doctor . . . teaching children . . .

Voices.

Dana opened her eyes again. More awake now, and pissed about it. Pissed at Justin. Had she really become so dependent on a man she had known for only three days that she couldn't sleep without him holding her? The thought brought a stab of anger, then remorse. She missed him. Damn it all to hell! What was she doing falling for a man at the worst possible time?

. . . numbers . . . numbers . . .

What? She was fully awake this time. She held her breath to hear better.

. . . numbers are my life . . .

Voices. Subtle. Faint. Like the background hiss of a poorly tuned radio.

She sat up, focusing her attention.

. . . for over forty years . . .

. . . I love the kids . . .

. . . numbers are my life . . .

More than one. A male and two females. Dana rose from the cot. The voices were coming from the hall. She slipped into her jeans, then moved quietly across the flat gray carpet. She had left the office door cracked for ventilation. She peered out through the crack. Darkness clotted the hall.

The light switch to the hall was just outside the door. She searched for it with her fingers, still hesitant to open the door farther.

. . . a knife . . .

She stopped. Hand on the switch. Eyes straining in blackness.

. . . or a meat cleaver . . .

A woman's voice. Not imagined. A familiar voice.

. . . good with a knife . . .

The darkness in the hall seemed to thicken. Her muscles were pulled taut by fear.

. . . a knife . . .

Fear muttered in her ear, poisoned her mind with anxiety.

. . . a knife . . .

Where was it coming from? The hall? Dana bit her lower lip, easing forward, head through the door into the gelatinous dark, hand still on the light switch.

. . . a knife . . .

Behind her. Now the voice seemed behind her. In the office. But that was impossible.

. . . a knife . . .

No. The hall. Both. The sound was coming from both locations. She had been breathing in short, quick gasps. She forced herself to inhale deeply. "Who's there?" she shouted.

Silence.

Dana felt her resolve growing. "This is not funny." Still no response. She flipped the light switch. Four panels of double-tubed fluorescent lights winked, once, twice, then held, revealing a simple hall with a plain beige wall and the same industrial gray carpet as the office.

Dana exhaled slowly, relieved to have banished the dark.

"The game's over. Come on out."

Something hissed.

"Justin? Is that you?"

Then a man's voice.

. . . numbers are my life . . . going to win . . .

Another man.

. . . practiced for forty years . . .

A woman.

. . . love the children . . .

The voices. Suddenly Dana knew who they were: Charles Penton, the CPA, the first to die from the vote; and Dr. Dutetre, the second victim; and Nora Tibits, the third. All exiled. All dead.

. . . a knife . . . a knife . . . a knife . . .

That voice belonged to Brenda Segar, the butcher who had been killed by the Navy.

Dana remembered the rats that she and Pheodora had heard in another dark building. Though seemingly real at the time, they had been a trick, an audio-illusion. And so was this.

It was coming through the PA system.

"Hello . . . ," Dana called. "You're wasting your time. I know it's a tape. What was I supposed to think—that they were ghosts?"

She laughed and tried to ignore how forced it sounded. "Hello?"

. . . a knife . . . a knife . . . a knife . . .

Even with the lights on, the trick exposed, the words were still chilling.

"I recognize this. It's excerpts from our interviews," Dana said. "So when do I get my safety stone?"

. . . a knife . . . a knife . . . you do your best . . .

Brenda and Nora. Their words edited together. A deep shudder of revelation rippled across Dana's mind. Who had edited the interviews? Even if the computer had been programed to clip sound bites from exiled contestants, it wouldn't have known about Brenda, who died at sea.

"Who are you?" Dana shouted, forcing herself to sound angry to mask her growing fear. "Who the hell are you?"

The hiss of static, then a phrase, stitched together with different voices.

. . . I am going to . . . kill you . . . with . . . a knife . . .

Four different voices fused together in a Franken-stein's monster of a sentence.

. . . kill you . . .

A fire door separated the hall from the stairwell.

. . . with . . .

The handle was a stainless steel L-shaped lever.

. . . a knife . . .

The lever was turning.

. . . a knife . . .

. . . a knife . . .

The mantra sounded without form in the back of her mind. She couldn't hear the click of the lock disengaging or the squeal of hinges as the door ebbed backward into the still black stairwell. Opening, opening, opening.

Dana could see only darkness and the movement of the door. It stopped half open. The voices stopped, too. A new pall of silence like smoke from a cannon's barrage settled over the hall.

Someone was in the building.

WASHINGTON, D.C.

Awakened too early, Dr. Lorrik now stood unshaven and disheveled in the White House situation room. Despite the early hour, the room hummed with activity.

"Another correct prediction," the young psychologist said, his voice equal parts envy and awe. Lorrik had left a list of red flags—potential developments—with explicit instructions to contact him if any occurred. Now one of his bleakest predictions appeared to be coming true.

"It started several hours ago. We were just curious at first. Then this." He hit Play on one of the VCRs.

Lorrik watched with growing concern. Dread chilled his back like a strong wind.

"Who's in the building?" he asked.

The psychologist typed a quick command on his keyboard. A live feed filled the main screen.

"Jesus," Lorrik said, watching as three thousand miles away, Dana Kirsten stepped out into an empty hallway.

VASSA ISLAND

She paused, racked by indecision. There were stairways at both ends of the hall. The door to the one on her right was partially open. The plan was to slip out through the one to her left, go down three floors, then exit the building. But what if there was more than one person? Or maybe they had opened the one door, scuttled down the stairs, and over to the other door?

The PA system popped.

"... *knife* ... *knife* ... *knife* ..." Dead Brenda was chanting in an endless loop.

Time to go. With the refrain masking her movements Dana hurried to the closed door on her left, hesitated for half a breath, then opened it and rushed inside. Security lights bolted to the walls revealed an empty metal stairway. She raced down the stairs taking them two at a time.

Second floor. She didn't stop. She couldn't hear if dead Brenda was still chanting. Couldn't tell if anyone was following. She slipped, caught herself with the handrail, then continued.

Don't you dare fall and twist your ankle like some silly scream queen in a slasher movie, she scolded.

She hit the landing hard. A stabbing pain jabbed her left leg. She winced, oddly pleased with the sensation. It meant she was still alive.

First floor.

She jerked the door open and rushed out into the darkened room, guided only by memory.

She stopped just short of the wall, alerted more by some internal sense than vision. She reached out and her fingers brushed the light switch. The fluorescent panel in the ceiling awoke.

Let there be light.

The light revealed the way out. She rushed to the door, turned the knob, and pushed. The door didn't move. She tried again. The metal creaked, but held firm. She checked to make sure the lock was disengaged, then noticed something black and silver on the door seam.

She touched it. Welding. The door was welded shut.

Footsteps.

Now for the first time she could hear sound other than the message on the PA. The pounding of footsteps as someone descended the stairwell she had just traversed.

Someone's coming.

Was there a back door? A quick look to get her bearings, then she was running again. There had to be a door at the rear of the building! The light had illuminated exactly half of the large open room. Shadows still huddled in the corners.

EXIT.

She saw the sign before she saw the door. It was the same industrial gray, but crossed with a chrome bar for opening. She hit it running. Pain blasted through her shoulder. She bounced back, stumbling, and fell on the carpet. The same insidious blackness that filled the seam of the other door was here as well.

All the doors had been welded shut.

She heard the stairwell door open then clang shut.

She waited.

Someone, some thing, began to laugh. There was a relaxed timelessness to the sound. No need to hurry. There was no way out.

Dana ran, not sure where she was going—just intent on getting away from her pursuer.

Rushing to the nearest workbench, she began desperately searching for a weapon. All she could see were bits and pieces of cameras, small tools, cap-size blocks that were camera batteries.

Drawer after drawer. Batteries, tape, glue, pliers. There was a long screwdriver. She snatched it up.

The laughter had stopped. The PA was silent.

She had lost track of her pursuer.

The large open area in the center of the room was sectioned by five-foot panels dividing the room into a series of cubicles. Willing her steps to be quiet, not raising her head above the partition, she silently crept forward.

"Come out, come out wherever you are."

Dana froze. A man's voice. This time not on the speaker.

"There's nowhere to go. No way out. Doors all shut, all sealed. Tight as a water drum."

The voice, loud and somewhat shrill, was excited like a spectator at a sporting event. Dana turned her head, trying to get a sense of direction.

"Playing hard-to-get just delays the inevitable, that's all."

The voice was coming from behind her. Closer now than before. Crouching, Dana hurried forward, scurrying around the next bend, expecting to be revealed at any moment, moving through the cubicles like a rat through a maze.

Panic swelled in her heart, climbing up her throat and attempting to choke her. She swallowed it down.

"You are a feisty one. I like that." The voice now came from behind her and to the left. She had managed to put some distance between them. If she could just keep going.

Ka-chung, chung.

The sound of boots on metal. Her pursuer was on a desk. Dana hazarded a glance behind her . . .

"Ah, there you are."

Standing on the desk less than thirty feet away, peering down on her, and smiling with lips that looked like a pair of plump, dead worms was her pursuer: Burton Rudyard.

"Time to play," the welder said. He raised the large knife and turned it in the fluorescent light. "Time to play."

23 WASHINGTON, D.C.

"Rudyard, Burton Daniel. Twenty-eight years old from North Platte, Nebraska, population twenty-three thousand. Two years of community college, one year of technical school. Works for Norplat Construction as a welder." The president was reading the bio out loud. "Criminal record?"

Lorrik pointed a third of the way down the page. "Breaking and entering, indecent exposure, a charge of attempted rape—later dismissed."

"Attempted rape?" The president shook his head. Despite the early hour, he was dressed and groomed. He sat in a plush Victorian wing chair, studying the report with the concentration of a man well rested and alert. "How the hell did someone with his record get on a television show where he's alone with women?"

"He was a juvenile at the time," Lorrik said. "The records were sealed."

"So this is why you red flagged him?"

Lorrik sat down with a grunt. His leg was throbbing and stiff. He had already devoured two painkillers and was hesitant to take more for fear of falling asleep or impairing his judgment.

"This is the first we've heard of Burton Rudyard's criminal record. My assessment was based on transcripts of conversations and observation of how he was responding under pressure."

"Amazing." The president laid the report in his lap. "Simply amazing. I knew I made the right choice by calling on you."

Lorrik grunted. He didn't feel so amazing.

Three years earlier Lorrik had been part of a university exchange program that sent him to Paris. In an effort to separate his daughter and Tucker Thorne, he had insisted that she accompany him. It was a fatal mistake. They had been in France less than two days when their entourage of twenty-four Americans was taken hostage by terrorists. When Lorrik attempted to reason with his captors, they silenced him by breaking his right leg in four places. The six-day standoff ended when French Special Forces stormed the building. Thirteen people, including eight hostages, were killed.

Gwen, his daughter, was the first to die.

Lorrik, who had already received acclaim for his work in social psychology, dedicated the remainder of his career to understanding the criminal mind—with special attention to terrorist mentality.

He tried to appreciate the president's compliment, but he couldn't. His expertise came at a price no father should ever pay. At first he blamed Tucker Thorne for Gwen's death. If he hadn't been pursuing her, Lorrik never would have taken her to Paris. But late at night, in moments between slumber and wakefulness, he knew the truth: the yoke of responsibility belonged around his neck and his alone.

Now he was receiving kudos for predicting the very worst in human nature. "I've been lucky. The contestants are in a pressure cooker. Their personal flaws, phobias, and fantasies are showing up at a considerably faster than normal rate."

The president closed the report. "Still, this man kept up a normal facade for close to thirty years. Now he snaps in less than four days. On live television."

"Pending death is a powerful catalyst," Lorrik said.

The president seemed to chew on that thought for a minute. Like the people on the island, the people in the White House were also under extreme pressure. Though the outcome was not life threatening, it could be career ending.

Lorrik was fascinated by the president. He was what laymen call a control freak, involved with even the simplest details—such as having Lorrik wear a microphone to his meetings with Tucker Thorne. But what was truly remarkable was his ability to juggle many complex issues at the same time with astonishing control.

At this moment, for example, Lorrik was positive the president was thinking not only about the contestants on Vassa Island and the national security issue raised by an

EMP weapon, but also about *his* special interest. The secret project that only Lorrik knew about.

"So we've found our accomplice," the president said.

They were interrupted before Lorrik could respond. "Mr. President, Dr. Lorrik—you may want to see this. It looks like the contestant, Dana Kirsten, is going to fight Rudyard."

As they hurried to the Situation Room, the president whispered, "What are her odds?"

"If he knows what we know, not good, Mr. President. Not good at all."

VASSA ISLAND

Dana stood up. Hiding was no longer an option.

From atop the desk Burton Rudyard smiled. "My my, you are a sweet thing, aren't you?"

"What do you want? I've already used my safety stone if that's what you're after."

"You think this is about the game?" He rubbed his thick lips. "Come on, Dana, you're smarter than that. The game is over. It's been over since we landed on this island, since we were infected with the damn virus. We are dead. Dead! Do you understand?"

Hands behind her back, Dana tightened her grip on the screwdriver and tried to evaluate Burton. He was considerably larger and stronger than she, but he was also overweight and likely to be slow.

"Do you really think that Control will let you off this island? Will let anyone off? No fucking way."

She hazarded a look to her left. The door to the stairwell was thirty feet away. Could she make it?

Burton lifted his head and stared at her from the bottom of his eyes. "Funny thing about death—it's rather liberating. Puts life in perspective. Pardon the pun."

He was roughly thirty feet away and would have to go through a maze of cubicles to reach her. One left turn and Dana had a straight shot to the stairwell.

And then what?

One step at a time, she told herself.

"I looked at my life and realized it was a charade. I've never been happy, even for a little bit. And you know why? Hey, bitch!—look at me when I'm talking to you."

Dana turned quickly. Burton's smile was gone and his reddish complexion darkened.

"I've faked it," he continued, "pretended to be happy. Even fooled myself from time to time, but it was always a stupid, stupid lie. I can see that now." His eyes, small and ratlike, seemed lost in the mist of another world. "Know why I've never been happy, Dana?"

The way he said her name, the sound of it coming from those thick, rubbery lips made her shudder.

"Because I've never been true to myself. Never done what I've really wanted to." He smiled. "Until now."

Until now. She had to do something and fast. Time was Burton Rudyard's accomplice. Again she glanced at the stairway door.

"Almost took a girl in high school—almost. It was the closest I've ever come to bliss." He sighed. "Woman was made for man—did you know that? She is, by nature, his to have. That's the truth. That's the way it is with animals, and we are all animals."

"Fuck you," Dana shouted.

She was running before he could respond. A quick left, then straight. She ran not sure her feet were touching the floor, not bothering to look behind her. She registered the sound of his obscenities, then movement, then—she was at the door. Open and up. She climbed, surprised by how quickly the muscles in her legs began to burn with pain, but grateful they didn't falter.

She had made the stairs. Now what?

The doors were welded shut, but there was a window in the room she had been sleeping in.

Second floor. She stopped. Hesitating for half a breath. No good. It was soundproof. No windows.

She was running again. Up, up. From somewhere far below her, somewhere between heaven and hell, she heard him coming, moving up the stairs—slowly, unhurried, confident.

His arrogance made her madder.

Third floor. The lights were still on. She hurried to the window and pressed her face against the glass. The sun was up, peering over the horizon, lighting the sea and the hard ground below.

Three stories. Could she survive the drop? Probably, but not without a cost. She would likely break a leg, and then what?

She looked at the cots. Make a rope with the blankets just like in the movies? But that took time and, despite his arrogantly slow advance, he was still coming.

She hurried back to the hall. What?

There was only one choice. She had to fight him. And she had to win.

It's not just his balls. There are a lot of ways to take a man down.

Claude, a thirty-two-year-old ex-marine was a bouncer at the bar where Dana worked. Stressing that he couldn't be everywhere at once, he had insisted that the women learn basic self-defense. Dana, who had to work three jobs to make ends meet, thought it was a colossal waste of her precious time. But now, she dredged her mind looking for every nugget of golden advice.

"Not just the balls. The eyes, ears, knees, little finger, instep—they're all good targets. A thumb in the eyeball can be devastating. Trouble is most women are too squeamish to use it. Most men, too, for that matter. Don't be."

Not a problem, Dana thought. At that moment she would gladly ram her entire fist through Burton Rudyard's eye.

"The best way to win a fight is to avoid it," Claude had said. Unfortunately that was no longer an option. "But if you have to fight, make it quick and decisive. Most fights are over in less than sixty seconds. Strike hard, fast, and decisively. The first blow will surprise the son of a bitch. Don't give him time to recover."

Surprise. Surprise was her friend and her best weapon.

She picked up a wooden chair and swung it with all her might into the plate glass window. The glass shattered. Shards pricked her arm, drawing blood. She ignored the pain and drew back the chair and hit out again, knocking away most of the remaining glass. Throwing the chair on the floor, she grabbed a blanket off the first cot, tied one end to the metal bed frame, and threw the other end out the window. It hung down less than three feet. But that was enough. She didn't need to go out the window, just make it look like she had.

She hurried into the bathroom, reviewing her plan as she did. Seeing the open bedroom door, Burton would look there first. The broken glass and makeshift rope would cause him to rush to the window and peer out. Then Dana would attack him from behind and—what?

She needed a weapon. She still had the screwdriver, which seemed to be getting smaller by the moment.

Strike hard, fast, and decisively. Claude's advice chimed in her head.

She needed something with heft. Heavy enough to do damage but light enough to swing. The chair? No, it was too cumbersome; he would hear her trying to rush out of the bathroom with it. Then what?

The lid of the toilet tank!

It was a crazy idea, but it could work. She lifted the porcelain top off the back of the tank. The lid weighed about ten pounds. Heavy enough to cause damage, light enough to swing.

If she timed it right, she would either knock him out the window or crack open his skull. Or, God willing, both.

Justin was up early. He had awakened everyone in the middle of the night with his screams. The nightmare again. He couldn't remember it, not a damn moment, but he could feel it, almost taste it.

It was embarrassing, humiliating.

From then on, he had done little more than doze and think of Dana. He had not had the nightmare either night they had slept together. Did that mean something? Was the nightmare about dying alone? Unloved and not missed?

No. That was too simple. The nightmare was vicious and unforgiving and somehow centered around shame. How he could know that without remembering was beyond him, but he did. Now, with the sun just spilling over the horizon, he was anxious to get back to work.

Cory had a serious case of bed head, and his puffy eyes made him look like a schoolkid who had sat up too late watching horror movies. Like the others, he had his sleep ruined by Justin. Neither spoke of it as they ate breakfast from a can and drank bottled water.

"I think I know how to find it," Cory said when they had finished. The Vault was proving to be a difficult challenge. After hours of work, they were still no closer to finding the secondary power supply.

"So how's that?" Justin asked.

"By looking where it shouldn't be."

Where it shouldn't be. For some reason that made Justin think of Dana and wonder where she was and what she was doing at that very moment.

Dana stood behind the bathroom door, peering through a small crack, the porcelain lid from the toilet tank held over her head. How long had it been? Her sense of time was shot.

The only true indication was the ache in her arms from holding the heavy lid.

Where is he?

Something popped and hissed.

Dana jumped, then realized it was the PA system again.

"Dana, Dana, Dana," Burton said. The crackle of the intercom and the emptiness of the building gave his words a haunting, hollow ring. "You are a fireball, aren't you. Good. I like that."

His breath rasped through the intercom. "But you're just not smart enough."

Dana shifted her grip on the porcelain lid, but remained silent.

"But you are imaginative," Burton continued. "I'll give you that. I mean the lid off a toilet? Pretty ingenious. And that blanket out the broken window—marvelous."

Fear marbled her heart. Her mouth was sour. Her arms began to tremble. *He knows. God in heaven, he knows—how?*

"Wonderful thing about this building you picked. Plenty of toys, plenty of toys." His words echoed through the lifeless room. "Plenty of taped interviews for me to make that little blast from the past. Did you like that? How the different voices came together in a single warning, a promise?"

He knows! Pinwheels of light burst and spun in her peripheral vision.

"And then there are all these wonderful televisions. Monitors, I think is the technical term. Once you turn them on—voilà—24/7, my own special edition."

A new sound crawled into the bathroom. An electronic whirr, the purr of tiny motors. She looked out across the bedroom, tracking the sound to the far corner. Then she saw it. A small camera, the lens reaching out, as if trying to touch her.

"I—see—you," he jeered. "Those wonderful television people even bugged their own building. Isn't that nice. Now why don't you be a good girl and give it up?"

Dana dropped the lid. It crashed to the floor, just missing her feet. She didn't care. How do you fight someone who is everywhere? Who sees everything?

24 WASHINGTON, D.C.

"Who?" Tucker asked in disbelief.

The voice on the other end of the line, confident to the point of arrogance, repeated the introduction. "I said, this is Nelson Rycroft, *the* Nelson Rycroft."

"The?"

"Yes. *The* as in *the* creator of *24/7*, *the* savior of the Globe Network, *the* man who is about to launch the next great TV program."

Tucker ran his hand through his hair and tried to get his bearing. "Yeah, I know who you are. I just can't believe you're calling me."

Somehow, Rycroft took that as a compliment. He chuckled into the phone.

"Because I was about to call you," Tucker finished.

Now it was the network wunderkind's turn to be surprised. "Call me? Why?"

"The zodiac—what's with the zodiac?" Tucker Thorne took a step back, studying the bulletin board. He had checked and rechecked. There was no doubt about it: Justin Rourke born August 10, Nerine Keleman, October 25, Dana Kirsten, March 18 . . . they're all here, all twelve.

"Ahhh, you've lost me," Rycroft said. "You into astrology, that it? Need to check your horoscope before accepting a job?"

"Nothing like that," Tucker replied before realizing what Rycroft had just said. "A job? What do you mean a job?"

Rycroft laughed again.

"We seem to be talking at cross-purposes," Tucker said. "You first."

"No, you've got me curious now. What's this about the zodiac?"

Tucker chewed on his lower lip. "That's what I wanted to ask you. Is it part of the packaging? An extra twist? What?"

"I don't have a fucking clue what you're talking about," Rycroft said, humor replaced by exasperation.

"The contestants on the show. I'm looking at their birthdays. Justin Rourke is a Leo, Nerine Keleman a Scorpio, Dana Kirsten a Pisces. Twelve signs of the zodiac, twelve contestants each representing a different sign."

"No way," Rycroft said.

"So I take it you didn't do this on purpose?"

"Fuck, no! This is the first I'm hearing of it." There was a pause. "But you know, I may be able to use it."

"How could you not know? I mean, the odds of this happening accidentally are astronomical. If not you, then someone on your staff. It has to be intentional."

"Nope, couldn't happen," Rycroft said quickly. "No fucking way. I was involved in the selection process from start to finish. We used the most sophisticated technology to pare the group down from ten thousand, to a hundred, to twenty-five, and finally to twelve. Taking into account things like temperament, background, hometowns, religion. We worked hard to get an interesting cross section of America, but more important, I wanted people who could come across strong on camera and, frankly, clash like hell. That's good television."

"Then how could this happen?"

"It couldn't," Rycroft said.

Unless Control had been manipulating events from the very beginning, Tucker realized. Even before the show went on the air. Was that possible? Tucker had to get off the phone, he had to think. What did this mean? Why the zodiac?

"Hey, kid, you still there?" Rycroft asked. Tucker had almost forgotten about him.

"Yeah, I'm here."

"Good, I want you to sit down," Rycroft said. "Then get back up again because you don't have time to sit down. You're the host of *The Truth*, soon to be Globe's newest hit show. It will follow *24/7*, starting tomorrow night."

The air conditioner clicked on with a *whoosh*.

Host? "I'm with the news division. You're with entertainment."

"Already taken care of. I've got a lot of clout with the network these days. You'll still file reports in the daytime, then host our show once a week on Thursday nights."

Papers on the bulletin board billowed as if excited by Rycroft's offer.

"What's the show about? What do you want me to do?"

"It's about the truth. You're going to be live with ten of the best minds in the country. Detectives, psychiatrists, sociologists—all debating a different question each week until you reach a single truth. And we've got a doozy for the first show."

"And that is?"

"Who is Control's accomplice on Vassa Island."

VASSA ISLAND

Burton leaned forward, his face less than half a foot from the ten-inch color monitor, just one of twenty-six that made up a video bank. Using a small joystick built into the switching board, he zoomed in on his target. Dana's tumbling hair circumscribed a face illumined by fear. Her eyes were haunted by shimmering tears. He adjusted the volume so he could hear her breathing—heavy, fast, terrified, like a small animal trapped against the wall.

He trembled with anticipation. Never had he felt such sheer, raw ecstasy.

Burton had followed her to this building last night, then, using a welding kit he found at the marina, he had sealed them in together. The second floor had been a pleasant surprise. Once it was powered up, he could access all the cameras on the island. With a touch of a button he could see into the dormitory; night-vision cameras revealed the world in black and white. Another touch displayed the Round House, the beach, buildings yet to be identified. A black box kept a running time code and camera number at the bottom of the screen.

It had taken him less than twenty minutes to figure out how to edit and less time than that to run the audio through the PA system.

He would die soon. But he would die a god.

A troll doll, with bright pink, Don King hair, holding a sign that read WORLD'S BEST MOM stood next to a digital clock, no doubt a child's gift to a now dead parent. He found the thought strangely exciting. Life and death—this was it, the ultimate.

On the screen Dana had picked up the porcelain lid and was mumbling something, the same phrase over and over again. "How do you fight a man who can see everything?"

As she talked, she was moving toward the camera. "How do you fight a man who can see everything?"

With that, Dana swung the porcelain lid. Camera number 126 spurted and went black. "You put his eyes out," she said, her voice carried by the choker-cam, then that also went black.

Camera number 124 picked her up as she stepped into the hall. Burton could see a green washcloth wrapped around her choker-cam. He could still hear through it, but he couldn't see. She was moving quickly now. Camera number 124 went black, then number 123, number 122 . . .

"Motherfucker!" Burton screamed, as one by one his monitors winked off.

He hurled the troll doll across the room. It struck the far wall and bounced halfway back to him.

She was blinding him.

He keyed the mike. *Stay in control. Don't let her know you're rattled.* "You're wasting your time," he said calmly, then shouted ". . . bitch!" before he could stop himself.

Camera number 118, number 117, number 116 . . .

The third floor was black.

"Bitch!" he shouted to the room. The troll doll lay on the floor, faceup, mocking him. He suddenly wanted to destroy it, rip the head off, smash its potbelly. No, not the doll—the woman, the bitch. He wanted to destroy Dana Kirsten. But first he would have her.

On the monitor bank he saw her enter the west stairwell. She was descending, breaking cameras as she went. Coming to him. Then all the cameras in the stairwell went black at once.

He stared into a black monitor. Thought he saw movement. Then realized she hadn't knocked out the cameras; she had turned off the lights and, unlike the cameras in the dorm room, these were not equipped with night vision. A few minutes later the lights in the east stairwell went out.

"Bitch!" he screamed as he hurried for the stairway door.

It was time. It was time. He stomped the smiling troll as he went.

Mentally she was back in high school. For just a moment, the time it took to sprint the length of the third floor hallway, she was a teenager, a time before motherhood, before the oppressive challenge of just making a living.

After breaking the third floor cameras and turning out the lights in both stairwells, she had gone silent. Waiting, listening. Hoping to hear the creak of an open door. Where was he? What was he doing? She could only guess and hope she had it right.

If he entered the east stairwell, she would hear him. But if she waited too long and he took the west stairs, he would come up behind her. Dana was banking on human nature, gambling that he would rush to the last place he had seen her—the east stairwell—and that was where she had waited. Once she confirmed his location, she would race to and down the opposite stairs.

Creak, squeal.

He was coming.

Dana bolted to the west stairwell in seconds. She was down to the first landing before the door closed, sealing her in the dark. Now she was moving by touch only.

She reached the second floor. She opened the door and rushed inside without pause. The room was alive with images flickering on the monitors, showing still active cameras. She paused, suddenly consumed with an overwhelming urge to look for Justin, to see his face, to send a message to him through the camera—as if he would somehow know she was there and would come to her aid.

But there wasn't time.

Dana hurried to the far side of the room, looking for a spot. She found one and began her task. She was less than halfway through when the stairwell door opened up and Burton Rudyard entered the room.

The time code on the still functioning camera monitors mocked him. He was on a deadline, emphasis on dead. Unless he was at the Round House by noon, the virus swimming in his blood would kill him. Burton was not afraid of dying, but he was afraid of dying without having his prize: Dana Kirsten.

He had only given the top floor a cursory search. She could still be hiding there. But it had occurred to him that he could search the first floor with the remaining cameras.

There was no evidence of her on the first floor. That meant she was hiding. He would have to search the entire building by hand.

Frustrated, he accessed the other cameras. The sun

was up, the day looked bright and hot. He watched as Foster Merrick, the fisherman, hurried into the woods, disappearing for a moment then reappearing on the smaller south beach. *What was he doing?*

He watched as that asshole Justin Rourke and the computer nerd, Cory Nestor, worked on wiring. Could they really get into the Vault? Not very likely. But they might screw it up, make it so no one could get the vaccine. Then everyone would die at noon.

Burton looked around the auxiliary control room, searching for a clue. It couldn't end here, not like this. He had finally embraced the demon within him, and for the first time he was truly alive. He would not die without feeding the beast, at least once.

He saw the answer in a thirty-two ounce can sitting on a shelf near the storage tapes.

He laughed out loud and clapped his hands together. Yeah, that was it. That would work. That would get the bitch out in the open.

Laughing? He was laughing. At what? Had he found her? Figured it out?

Dana wanted to move, wanted to shift her weight, stretch her legs, turn her head—anything. But she couldn't. Burton was less than ten feet away, close enough so that she could take two steps and attack him.

He had come back quicker than she had anticipated. As she settled in, she heard him moving in her direction—or thought he had. Then she heard the volume increase and realized he was back at the monitor bank. Looking for her electronically.

The control room's raised floor had been her answer. Tiles, suspended on metal beams about a foot and a half above the real floor, were designed to allow easy access to the multitude of cables that ran beneath the room. The floor panels lifted just like the acoustic tiles in the ceiling. Dana had barely crawled in when Burton entered the room.

Time was a foreign language, indecipherable to her instincts. Her muscles ached, her legs threatened to cramp. Cables pressed against her chest so hard she imagined long red pressure marks permanently tattooed over her body.

"Hello, bitch!" Burton said, his words echoing through the PA system. "You can hide, but you can't run. And the clock is ticking."

Dana held her breath.

"It's eleven-ten. Fifty minutes until the vote. Fifty minutes until your skin bubbles off the bone." Burton laughed. At what, Dana didn't know. Which made the sound all the more chilling.

He was crazy, beyond mad. Beyond hope.

Through the PA system she could hear something sloshing.

"Hear that? That is an alcohol compound, probably used to clean video heads and such. Let's see. There's a warning here on the can. I'll read it to you: caution, keep away from open flame. Oh, my. Highly flammable it says."

Dana tried to swallow. Her throat was too dry.

A new sound: a flick, hiss. "How about that? Can you hear it? Can you guess what it is? Did you say lighter? Ding, ding, ding, ding, we've got a winner. That is the sound of a butane lighter with a one-inch flame. Flame. Hmmm . . . what did I just read about flame? Oh, yeah, keep away from the alcohol. Warning, warning, danger, Will Robinson."

Again he laughed, a predatory sound akin to the rustle of a rattlesnake's tail.

"Can you guess what will happen when flame and alcohol come together? Poor Dana, burned alive in her hiding place."

Silence. She could hear the faint tick and whirl of machinery.

Her blood supply had been drastically cut. Her left leg throbbed with the pain of uselessness. She didn't know if she could stand, let alone run.

"Fire, they say, is the greatest pain of all," Burton continued. "But, you know what? I like you, so I'm going to give you a choice. You can stay where you are and burn like a lawyer in hell or you can come out, we can talk, maybe play a little. Afterwards, you're free to go. If you're not voted off the island you take your shot and you live to see another day. Choice is yours. You've got thirty seconds before I start the fire."

COVINGTON, GEORGIA

Bobby Vance was in trouble. More trouble than ever before. Serious, life-grounding, perk-removing trouble. As he sat on the end of his bed, head down, studying the print in his simple blue-and-maroon carpet, he could feel the intensity of his father's eyes and hear the disappointment in his voice. His mother, eyes red and tearful, had taken a step back and stood with her arms crossed.

The trouble had been caused by a phone call from his homeroom teacher. In a way it was God's fault. Bobby's mother and teacher were both on the same church committee, and so his teacher knew to call his mom at work, instead of home. She in turn, phoned his father. Now both parents were home, and Bobby was screwed. A word he would never use in front of his parents, but the only word that accurately described his situation.

Mom sad, Dad pissed, and Bobby—well, Bobby was worried.

"What were you thinking?" Dad asked again.

So far Bobby had answered that question with "I don't know," "wasn't thinking," and "other guys were doing it"—none of which had been the answer his father sought.

"Four days. Did you really think you could miss four days of school and no one would notice? We trusted you, son. We trusted you."

Bobby felt something solid in his throat. His eyes teared. Direct hit. Until that point, Bobby's main regret was of being caught but the use of the word *trusted*—past tense—struck deep. They had always trusted him, always. Bobby had been a latchkey kid since fourth grade. He had always eased his parents' guilt about this by acting responsibly. He was a good student, always a B average or better, and he seldom got in trouble.

But that was before *24/7*.

He had only missed three days of school in all of last year. Now he missed four—in just one week.

He couldn't help it. He was hooked, addicted. Forget drugs—this stuff was powerful. Of course, he couldn't tell that to Dad. So Bobby looked at the carpet and bided his time.

Dad was talking, laying out the sentence. Suddenly Bobby caught three words that chilled his bones.

Television? Computer? Remove?

He looked up, his eyes wide with fear.

"That's right," Dad repeated, realizing he had struck a nerve. "No television for a month. None. And . . ."

He looked at the computer screen on the desk across from the bed. Bobby looked, too. His program was working perfectly, flipping through the preselected cameras on Vassa Island, holding on each for just a few seconds.

". . . no computer for . . ."

"But Dad, I need it for school," Bobby interrupted, no longer able to hide the panic in his voice.

"Should have thought of that before. If you need word processing, you can use my laptop. But no more of this—this island-watching all hours of the day and night."

Bobby gasped with disbelief. There was no way to imagine life without the show, without knowing what was happening. The people on that island were his friends, his surrogate family. When his parents were off making a living, Bobby was busy living with Justin and Cory and Dana and even Renee.

"In fact," Dad continued, "I'm taking it right now."

Like a monster in a nightmare, Bobby's father locked his arms around the monitor, intent on removing it at that very moment.

Time jerked like a poorly downloaded picture.

On the screen Bobby saw the island, his friends, his family, saw them for what very well could be the last time—

Bobby screamed and leaped forward.

His mother looked up, gap-mouthed. His father paused in his mission, his arms gripping the monitor.

But Bobby wasn't screaming at his dad or about his punishment or even his predicament. Bobby was screaming at the computer.

He hit the Enter key, his command to stop the sampling program. The image held on one camera.

Bobby pointed, looking to his parents to understand that he could do little more than grunt. His mother tracked his gaze. Her hand went to her throat. Bewildered, his father placed the monitor back on Bobby's desk; then he, too, gasped.

On the screen, on the live feed from Vassa Island, the twenty-eight-year-old mother, Dana Kirsten, was fighting for her life.

25 VASSA ISLAND

To Burton, it appeared that Dana materialized where seconds earlier there had been no one but him.

Strike hard, fast, and decisively.

The bouncer's words were a chant, driving Dana forward, pushing her past her fear, past her pain. Rising up out of the floor, knocking the panel away, she screamed like a crazy person.

Surprise is your friend.

She still had the screwdriver, clutching it like a lifeline.

It's not just the balls. It's also eyes, ears, knees, little finger, instep.

She charged.

Burton reacted at the last possible second. As Dana lunged forward, the silver spike of the screwdriver glinting blue in the weak light, he drew back. Even so, the tool struck his body, plunging deep into his left side just below the collarbone. He grunted in surprise, his right hand lashing out in belated defense.

His hand connected, halting Dana's forward momentum, snapping her head back and hurling her to the floor. The pain, like lightning following thunder's decree, exploded in her chin and face and head.

The moment held; the world suspended.

Then the welder, face contorted into a mask of rage, roared. A degenerative, barbaric wail that she felt as well as heard.

She scrambled to her feet. Unarmed, overmatched, and alone. She turned to run, but he was there. Grabbing her by the shoulder, he spun her around. His face was blood-dark; his eyes were wild and senseless. He was holding her with both hands now. His grip unbreakable, fingers digging into the soft flesh beneath her blouse.

There was a flash behind him, followed by a *whoosh* as flame and alcohol came together.

He smiled—a human expression on an inhuman face.

"You hurt me, bitch!" Each word was a scream.

"Fuck you!" Dana struck out with the palm of her hand, embedding the screwdriver even deeper into his shoulder.

Burton yelped. His grip faltered. With strength born of abject fear, she kicked him in the testicles, breaking his grip. Then she pushed him toward the flames growing behind him.

As she ran, a new cry filled the room along with the growing swirl of cloying gray smoke.

The fire door closed behind her, sealing the beast in his own inferno. How long did she have? The doors would stall the flames, but would it stop them? Instinct drove her upward. The ground floor was still sealed, windowless. Up was her only option.

She checked her watch: 11:32 A.M., twenty-eight minutes to reach the Round House. The blanket was still tied to the bed. Tiny slivers of glass bit into her hands as she pulled it back up out of the window. She quickly snatched blankets from the three remaining beds and tied them together. Her hands were cut and bleeding. Her fingers seemed impossibly thick, devoid of dexterity. She tugged the first two blankets. They held. She began the third.

Trying not to look at her watch, trying to ignore the

open bedroom door, she willed herself to concentrate on the task at hand. She had to do it fast and she had to do it right. Three stories would likely not kill her, but she doubted she would be able to walk, let alone run to the Round House to make it in time for the vote.

Finished. Checked. She tied the fourth and final blanket. It appeared to hold.

She threw the makeshift rope out the window.

Eleven-forty: twenty minutes until the vote.

The rope barely reached the second floor. Too short, too short. She scanned the room. There was nothing else.

The other bedrooms. There were more beds on this floor, two more blankets would at least make it a manageable fall. She hurried to the nearest room. Working quickly she ripped the covers from each bed, then took two more from the next room.

Fourteen minutes until the vote.

She rushed back to the big room. Her mind racing through the next necessary steps, she entered the room and stopped.

Standing in front of the window, her passage to freedom, was Burton Rudyard.

"Bitch!" he spat.

Any feeble hint of humanity had vanished, burned from his face with his singed hair and blistered neck. His shirt was gone, revealing a chest of reddened flesh. His pants were torn and ruined.

Water ran down his forehead, dripping from the tip of his nose, explaining how he had escaped. The sprinkler system must have come on, dousing the fire.

He was burned, no doubt in pain, but still very much alive, standing between Dana and her only source of escape.

Her watch screamed at her.

The beast creature that had been Burton Rudyard read

her mind. "Just minutes until the vote." His words slurred together, as if speaking was a painful task. "Plenty of time for me to have you before you die."

Reality knocked the wind from her, striking harder than ever. How much was too much? How much could one person take? He had challenged her every step of the way and each time she had risen to that challenge. And she would again.

How much was too much? Dana asked herself again.

Her body, mind, and soul acted as one. "You want me, you bastard? Then take me!"

She charged, hurling forward, crashing into him with all the strength she had left. A grunt of surprise, the snap of more breaking glass, and then they were free— tumbling through the air, falling, falling, falling. . . .

26 VASSA ISLAND

Eight times they thought they had found the lead to the secondary power supply. Eight times they were wrong. But Cory refused to give up. Somehow, Justin found it comforting. Cory seemed to know what he was doing, and Justin was happy to assist in any way he could.

That left him plenty of time to think about other things. But the only other thing he wanted to think about or could think about was Dana.

"What are you smiling about?" Cory asked.

"Sorry. I was thinking about . . . something."

"Obviously." A soft grin crawled across Cory's long

thin face. "Something more important than getting off this island alive?"

"Nothing's more important than getting off this island alive. Come on, back to work."

But Cory pressed the issue. "You're thinking of Dana, aren't you?"

Surprise lit Justin's face.

Cory's brown eyes sparked with delight. "You are, aren't you. You're in luuuv."

"What?"

"Justin's got a girlfriend." Cory's good-natured teasing made him sound like a prepubescent fourth grader rather than a brilliant systems administrator. He made an exaggerated kissy-face. "Justin's in love with Daaa-na!"

Justin laughed so hard he began to choke. Cory's banter was so zestful it struck a chord with the child that Justin hadn't realized was still inside him.

Turning back to their task, they worked with increased vigor, both rejuvenated by the welcome distraction.

Four minutes and twenty-eight seconds until the vote.

That God would allow him to meet and fall in love with a woman just days, possibly minutes, before he was to die was very believable to Justin. And if that was the case, he held no grudges.

More than once Justin had benefited from that spiritual sense of ironic satire. Being promoted while those around him who worked much harder were left behind. Being given a second, third, fourth—hell—even a fifth chance to start over. In that respect, he was due for divine payback.

But not Dana. He refused to believe in a vengeful, malicious deity who would sacrifice anyone as loving as Dana.

He could hear Cory and the others calling him, begging him to return to the Round House. He drowned them out with his own yells—beckoning Dana.

When she failed to respond to the summoning alarm, that uneasy feeling in his gut returned. Something was wrong. Something was horribly wrong.

The beach sand was soft and pliable from a short morning rain shower. His feet sank several inches as he ran. The seesawing roar of the ocean conspired to swallow his cries and, in turn, he realized, would muffle her cries for help.

But he would not give up. Couldn't give up. He knew that he would rather die than live without Dana.

That realization was staggering. His vision blurred, masked by hot stinging tears. *Tears.* He hadn't known he could still cry. He fell to his knees, sinking into wet sand, ready to sacrifice his last breath. He could almost hear her voice, almost sense her calling his name, summoning him.

Justin looked up across the beach. It wasn't his imagination. It was real. *She* was real. She was staggering in his direction. He jumped to his feet and dashed toward her.

Justin carried Dana to her alcove.

Nerine rushed to her side. "What happened?" she asked, checking Dana's vital signs.

"I fell down," Dana croaked. Her body was covered with tiny cuts and abrasions. Dried blood stained a swollen lip and the shadow of an incipient bruise was visible on her face.

She had given Justin an abbreviated version of her night, ending with her harrowing, three-story plunge. She had used her adversary as a landing platform, letting him absorb the brunt of the fall. Still, the air was knocked from her lungs and darkness engulfed her for close to a minute. When she came to, Burton wasn't moving. She began stumbling toward the Round House, and she wouldn't have made it if Justin had not been there to meet her halfway.

"Can you stand?" Justin asked, still holding her up.

"Yeah, I'm okay now." When he released her, she staggered and grabbed him again for support. "I'm fine."

"The wounds aren't life-threatening," Nerine said as she hurried to her own cubicle. "I'll clean them after the vote. What happened to her, Justin?"

Justin went to his alcove and deposited his five safety stones a heartbeat before the reader board came to life.

"She was attacked."

The room was soundless.

"Attacked!" Pheodora exclaimed. "Attacked by whom?"

The sunlight streaming through the beachside entrance to the Round House was suddenly blocked.

Dana gasped.

Standing in the doorway—shirtless, bleeding, and burned—was Burton Rudyard.

Hunched over, protecting what must have been several broken ribs, Burton stumbled to his cubicle. The fire had cauterized the wound caused by the screwdriver. A lower front tooth was missing. He seemed not to notice any of this. He wiped blood from his face with the back of his hand. Looking at Dana, his eyes still impossibly wild, he leered. "I'll finish with you later."

Justin left his alcove.

Dana shook her head. "Not now." She pointed to the reader board. The vote was under way.

"Island's not that big," Burton continued. "Not many places to run."

The numbers were meaningless hieroglyphics to her exhausted mind.

"Have you forgotten about the cameras?" Dana asked, surprised at how calm she sounded.

Burton laughed. Blood ran from the gap in his teeth and mixed with saliva that trickled down his chin. "So what? They gonna put me in jail? In case you've forgotten, lady, we're all gonna die on this island. It's just a matter of time. You think I should be afraid of the police?"

Dana smiled, causing her busted lip to twitch with pain. "Not the police," she said. "The public. They've been watching the entire time and, unless I miss my guess"—she nodded as the numbers on the reader board stopped changing—"bye-bye, asshole."

COVINGTON, GEORGIA

Bobby Vance's fingers ached from voting so often, so quickly. His father and mother had each taken multiple turns as well. The scolding was forgotten, the discipline delayed—because removing the computer and ignoring events on Vassa Island was no longer possible.

Sitting back from the computer as the termination bar filled the page announcing the end of the vote, his parents standing behind him, his mother's hand resting lightly on his shoulder, Bobby marveled at the wonder of it all. It was astonishing how things could change in the flash of a computer screen, how events thousands of miles away and happening to complete strangers could so influence his life, could reach into the solitude of his own bedroom.

But mostly, Bobby marveled at how condemning a man to die had become a *family* affair.

VASSA ISLAND

Control spoke. "Burton Rudyard, twenty-one thousand, eight hundred and seventy-one votes. Burton Rudyard, you are exiled."

The madman screamed—the wail of a beast in agony. He charged, pains and injuries forgotten in a frenzied rage. His hands reached for Dana's neck, a murderous intent stamped in his feral eyes.

Justin scrambled across the top of the Vault and jumped, striking the monster just short of his target. Both men fell to the floor in a tangle of arms and legs. Justin was more than able to meet Burton muscle for muscle. But insanity was a powerful accelerant. Burton rolled, reversing their positions, pinning Justin to the floor, his burnt arm pressing into Justin's neck.

As Justin's skin began to bubble, he pushed with inspired strength of his own, knocking Burton aside. He started to scramble back to his alcove and the lifesaving injection. But Burton grabbed him by the legs, pulling him to the floor. Burton's skin was undulating. Burnt flesh burning again. His eyes, wide and churlish, found Dana. "I'm going to hell and I'm taking your boyfriend with me."

Dana's own skin grew hot.

"Use the vaccine," Justin screamed.

The vaccine.

Dana jabbed her thumb into the fingerprint scanner, freed her bee-sting injector, then fell to her knees and injected Justin in the arm.

"Nooooo," he screamed.

Careful to move away from Burton, Dana collapsed on the floor, her back against the Round House wall, remaining perfectly still. "Exertion makes it act faster," she explained.

The skin on the back of her hand became crocodilian. What just micro-moments before had been the cold floor now seemed as blistering as a hotplate. Virus in check, Justin kicked himself free of Burton's grip, hurried to his alcove, freed his own vaccine and returned.

Her face was hot. The bruise throbbed.

She didn't feel the bite as Justin shoved the needle into her arm. She could feel the results at once as a cooling wave blew through her body beneath the skin, stalling the murderous virus for another day.

Burton Rudyard screamed in anguish, not at the maddening pain but with the realization that Dana Kirsten was still alive.

Control spoke. "Six contestants, five days."

27 WASHINGTON, D.C.

"System's check, one, two, one, two. Mike five, this is mike five." The production crew worked like a well-choreographed ballet company. Standing in Studio 2D, clutching a single page rundown, Tucker watched in admiration. Live newscasts—the energy, the raw excitement— were commonplace to him. But this was different. Not necessarily better, just different.

For one thing the entertainment division employed twice as many people as the news department and paid infinitely more attention to small details. A lighting director manipulated gels to create the desired mood, while a woman with a tape measure and no modesty measured Tucker's waist, legs, arms, shoulders, and inseam.

"For wardrobe," she explained.

Wardrobe?

It was common for television anchors and even some reporters to receive a clothing allowance, usually negotiated as part of their contract. But he knew of no one who was actually dressed by wardrobe.

"Do I choose what I'm going to wear?" he asked.

The woman, who looked twenty-five but sounded infinitely older, shook her head. "Now honey, that would defeat the purpose. Trust me. I'm a professional."

She handed him back the brown sports coat he had been wearing. "Dark colors for you. Navy and black. Those are the most flattering for someone with your skin tones."

"Skin tones? I have more than one?"

She shook her head and clucked her tongue. "News people."

Tucker was walked through the process by a man he thought was the producer but who turned out to be the assistant to the assistant producer. He tried to commit everything to memory. On the surface the format was straightforward. Immediately following that night's edited version of *24/7*, Tucker would lead a panel in a discussion on the question of the week: Who is Control's accomplice?

The twelve panelists, up from the original ten, would be divided into two rows of six each. They would sit on a raised platform with Tucker standing before them in front of a massive blue-and-red backdrop emblazoned with the show's name: *The Truth*.

There would also be a studio audience, from which, time permitting, Tucker would take questions.

The panelists arrived at three-thirty, for a run-through. They were an impressive lot and included an inspector from Scotland Yard, a detective from the New

York Police Department, another detective, retired from the Los Angeles Police Department, a former FBI agent, two world renowned criminal profilers, and even an Interpol agent.

But the biggest surprise was a last-minute addition of a member of the Presidential Task Force on the Vassa Island crisis, a man with an international reputation as a psychologist and sociologist and perhaps the greatest cultural profiler in existence, Dr. Sherman Lorrik.

The run-through was rough. Nerves were taut, emotions high, egos higher. Nelson Rycroft, as the show's creator, was beginning to worry. At one point he pulled Tucker aside to explain how he would have to be one part showman, one part ringmaster—and all charisma.

The inclusion of Lorrik on the panel added a new and decidedly uncomfortable twist for Tucker. He became self-conscious to the point of distraction and uncommonly dry-mouthed.

At first he blamed his response on their secret working relationship, the fact that Lorrik was his deep source. He would have to be careful to not reveal that. His powers of concentration were halved. But by the time he had finished bumbling through the first rehearsal, he realized the true source of his discomfort.

Gwen.

Lorrik's daughter, Tucker's fiancée. A woman they both had loved dearly, and presumably the reason Lorrik was helping Tucker.

Gwen, more than anyone else, believed in Tucker's dream of becoming a network reporter. Her support had been unfailing, her encouragement bottomless. And now here he was, accomplishing everything he had ever wanted in less than a week.

And feeling empty.

The truth was, without Gwen, it was a hollow

victory—a fact that was underlined each time he looked at the man who would have been his father-in-law.

Tucker's performance was flat, and the concern in Rycroft's eyes was real.

VASSA ISLAND

The crowbar struck the camera reducing it to scrap with one blow. Foster Merrick moved to the next camera and then the next. When he finished, he stepped back, lit his next to last cigarette, and examined his work. The small south beach was littered with broken plastic frames, shattered lenses, and a crunched circuit board. With a rag tied over his choker-cam Foster was camera free.

He had gotten the idea from Dana's story. It was the final piece in his new plan. And now, working in his self-generated blind spot, he was ready to begin.

As contestants, they had been warned against dismantling or hindering any camera. But as Foster finally and painfully understood, this was no game. They were going to die; the United States Navy was intent on sitting back and watching it happen.

To hell with that. No way he was going to sit here and die on *Gilligan's Island*. If he was sick, infected, he belonged in a hospital.

If the United States fucking Navy didn't want to help him, then to hell with them. He would help himself. He was a fisherman, a man of the sea. No piece of land would ever hold him. And, thanks to a little help from mother nature, neither would the United States fucking Navy.

He finished his cigarette, stomped it into the sand, and started the chainsaw.

*   *   *

You were right.

Pheodora played the statement through her mind again, savoring each word. Justin had whispered that to her two nights ago. But she had been too shaken by the nightmare to follow up on it.

Nightmare, that's what it had to be. Her father was dead. Dead, buried, and feeding the worms. She could remember nothing after seeing the ghost at the window, until the next morning. Further proof that the whole thing, no matter how real it felt, was actually a nightmare.

Unless I passed out in fear.

No. It was a dream. That's why it ended so abruptly.

Just to be safe, she had spent last night in the CPA's bunk, away from the windows. She had slept fitfully, but she had slept, the night tropically warm and mercifully ghost free.

You were right.

"My personal challenge was in the motor pool," Justin told her.

"Exactly what was I right about?" she had asked.

"Remember how you discovered we all represent a different sign of the zodiac? Well, it occurred to me that that might be the unifying theme to our personal challenges, and it was."

"How does the motor pool connect to the zodiac?"

"Outside the motor pool is a glass-covered letter board, containing the names of the different vehicles and aircraft that were being serviced when the base shut down. A couple of letters are missing and the black background is faded, as if the sign hasn't been touched since the military left."

Justin's grin was wide enough to swing in. "One of the items listed was a *Hercules* transport plane. There is *no* way a cargo plane that large could land on Vassa Island. So obviously it was a clue."

"Hercules," Pheodora repeated.

"Exactly. My astrological sign is Leo, the constellation named for the lion that Hercules killed as part of his twelve tasks for Hera. You were right."

It made sense, they both reasoned. Nerine Keleman had an unnatural fear of spiders; her astrological sign was Scorpio; her personal challenge involved an attack by scorpions. Justin's greatest fear was of never being able to fly again; he was a Leo, the strongest of the sun signs; his challenge involved blinding light. Everything tied together.

So what did that mean for Pheodora, an Aquarius? She hadn't figured that out yet.

Of course it didn't help that Renee was driving her crazy.

Nora Tibits's sacrifice had changed Renee for about twenty-four hours. After that, the bitch was back, worse than ever. Acting as if her life depended on it, which it probably did, Renee was relentless in her quest for safety stones. So far, she had recovered two, one hidden among a thousand shells in a clearing not far from the dorm, the second, under six feet of water in the flooded basement of an abandoned building marked Vinson Hall.

Obviously, she had been tipped off by clues, but what those clues were or how she knew where to find them remained a mystery, one Renee wasn't sharing.

Those safety stones were gone now, used in the last vote. And Renee was once again desperate. Desperate enough that she had come to Pheodora for help.

"Why do you think I know?" Pheodora asked again. She was just starting to reclaim her wits after the nightmare. They were in the dorm room, Pheodora eating a can of green beans, Renee yams. Outside, shadows were being lengthened by the sinking sun.

The real estate agent reached over and tapped Pheodora's zodiac necklace. "Because you're psychic. That's why I want your help."

Pheodora shook her head. "It doesn't work that way. If it did I would already have all of the stones. Hell, I wouldn't even be on the island. I would be safe at home."

Renee was not deterred. "I thought about that. What if your powers only work for other people? After all, you did help Dana find a safety stone."

Pheodora puffed and scratched an imagined itch behind her head. That Renee had suddenly developed an interest in the supernatural didn't surprise her. Before starting her psychic hotline, two-thirds of Pheodora's clientele were women like Renee, wealthy enough to pay big bucks for regular visits, arrogant enough to believe the stars came together just for them, and lonely enough to keep coming back for more.

But now, Pheodora had other things to worry about, namely staying alive. And, even if she could point this woman in the right direction, she wouldn't. She didn't wish her harm, but neither would she go out of her way to help her. The entire fake pregnancy and the lack of appreciation for Nora's sacrifice stood as testament to just what type of woman Renee truly was.

"So tune into me. Tell me where to look and what to look for," Renee said.

Frustrated to the breaking point, Pheodora did something she had never done with a potential client. She told the truth. "Look, it doesn't work, okay? Nothing is going to happen if I stand up, wave my hands, and shout abracadabra."

The lights went off.

Dana woke hungry and surprisingly refreshed. The intense pain had subsided. Nerine had given her some aspirin, then cleaned and dressed the larger wounds, and applied medication to the smaller cuts and abrasions. Dana was covered in bright orange splotches, making her look like the world's shortest giraffe.

"You're lucky," Nerine had said. "Nothing broken, just battered. Should be right as rain in a day or two."

Dana had fallen asleep on the small cot in the infirmary, her dreams ripe with images of Burton's leering face. It was evening when she woke, and although still sore, she felt remarkably well and full of hope.

She had looked the devil in the eye and beaten him.

And then there was Justin.

His pure sense of joy and relief when he found her on the beach was revitalizing as was his terror and outrage when she recounted her story. He was miserable and that somehow made her happy. Not for his pain but for his concern.

It had taken extensive coaxing from Nerine to get him to leave her in the infirmary and go back to helping Cory.

As if conjured from her thoughts, Justin appeared at the infirmary door. His eyes sparkling at seeing her, he told her the wonderful news. "I think we've done it—or rather Cory's done it. He's figured out how to break into the Vault."

VIEWERS

In Seattle, Silicon Valley, and at all the high tech and dot.com companies the news spread quickly.

<HE DID IT . . . THE NERD DID IT . . .>

That or a variation thereof was the message that traveled fiber optic cables the world over. At Microsoft, Krest Industries, Apple, and other corporations, workers broke into spontaneous applause at the news.

And in Washington, D.C. less than three hours before his live show debuted, Tucker marveled at it all. Could it really be over? Had Cory Nestor, a self-described computer nerd, saved the day?

Regardless, the question of Control's identity and th

identity of his accomplice remained to be answered. *The Truth* would go on, and Tucker's position as not only a network reporter but a nationally recognized moderator would be cemented.

VASSA ISLAND

"Essentially, we backtracked to the secondary power supply. The leads from the Vault proved too well masked. So I followed the leads to the reader board, assuming they worked on the same feeds."

Dana looked around the room at the motley assembly. They were gathered in the Round House, enthralled as the small man with the big grin talked. All but one, Dana suddenly realized. Where was Foster Merrick? She had forgotten about the fisherman.

"The physical locks are controlled electronically," Cory continued. "By cutting the power and rebooting the system, we should be able to reconfigure the aligning matrix and—"

"Enough babble," Renee said. "We don't understand what you're talking about anyway. We're just glad you did it. Now open it up and let's get that vaccine."

Cory was chagrined that his moment in the spotlight had been cut short, but his smile returned as he pointed to the impressive Vault. Using screwdrivers, pliers, and a monkey wrench, all pilfered from the marina, he and Justin had removed the cover leading to the primary input. Now all that remained was to rewire the system, from the mainframe to the small computer now sitting on top of the Vault. When the power was returned, the system would be rebooted and be under the control of the small machine.

"Justin," Cory said, offering him the honors.

"It's your show. I just handed you things." Everyone laughed.

Justin pointed to a snake's nest of wires on the west side wall. "I'll reconnect the power when you're done."

The work went faster than expected. Standing at the keyboard to the external computer, Cory gave the word. Justin reconnected the secondary power supply. The lights in the Round House winked back to life. The computer chirped and then—nothing.

Cory frowned. The room was quiet. He bent over to peer into the open faceplate. Then his youthful face brightened. "Ahhh, not to worry. I see the problem. Loose lead."

He reached inside the opening.

The sound was short, hard, and impossibly loud. Jagged bolts of blue electricity shot out of the opening. Cory was thrown across the room, where he crashed against the wall and dropped like a rag doll.

Nerine was the first to move. "He's alive. But I can't tell how badly he is injured. We've got to get him to the infirmary."

Justin scooped the young man off the floor. "A third power supply?" he mumbled to Dana as they dashed toward the infirmary.

The air reeked of ozone and burning flesh.

Pheodora closed her eyes and saw the answer clearly. So clear and bright that she marveled at not seeing it before. Fifteen minutes later she stood in front of the building, seeing with her own eyes what she had seen so vividly moments before in her mind.

Touching her zodiac necklace for luck, she took a deep, bracing breath, and stepped into the building marked Ganymede Hall.

When Cory had been hurt in the Round House, Pheodora's hopes had been dashed. Despair as real and tangible as a plague of locusts descended on her.

But then she saw the answer.

It wasn't psychic power that brought her here. She hadn't channeled the spirits of Vassa Island. No ectoplasmic pirate had come to her, severed head in hand, and pointed the way with his peg leg. No, she was brought here by deduction, good old-fashioned, hail-to-Sherlock Holmes logic. If indeed the personal challenges were based on each contestant's astrological sign, then for her the challenge, as an Aquarius, was inside Ganymede Hall.

Ganymede was the name of the golden-haired prince of Troy, whom the great god Zeus kidnapped then took to Mount Olympus to serve wine to the gods. But when Zeus saw how grieved the boy's parents were, he took pity on them and turned Ganymede into a constellation so they could see him each night in the southern sky— Aquarius.

Unlike the building she and Dana had explored earlier, this one had electricity. Light fixtures screwed directly into the ceiling poured a flat, yellow light that splashed the center of the room but left the corners and the walls in shadows. A half dozen long tables standing in military formation occupied the midsection. Empty counters and shelves made up the rest. It looked like a small dining hall. Maybe the officers' mess? Or maybe it wasn't a lunchroom at all; maybe it was just made to look that way by the show's producers.

Pheodora paused. There were three doors leading out of the main room, two to the side and one straight ahead. She took the latter, a swinging door.

This room was much smaller than the first and completely empty. She could hear the restless hum of large machinery and feel the cold radiating from a huge freezer.

The psychic shuddered. No special powers were necessary for her to identify her challenge.

The booming, digitally altered voice of the one called Control filled the barren room. **"Your personal challenge is to retrieve five safety stones from the next room."**

"That's a freezer," Pheodora mumbled.

"The door will remain open for fifteen minutes and fifteen minutes only. Your time starts now."

Something on the door snapped and popped. It opened half an inch. An icy breeze, like a wild mustang, rushed past her, causing the fine white hairs on the back of her arm to stand on end.

No chance to go for help. No time to think it over. She had to do this herself. Pheodora willed her legs to move. Taking the handle in two hands, she pulled the door all the way open. Despite its weight it moved easily, well balanced on its hinges. A stampede of freezing air charged over her, usurping the island warmth with it.

She thought of her father and of the blizzard—the vicious, intense cold. "It's just a freezer, just a freezer," she said aloud, her words coming in puffs of condensation. "Run in, grab the stones, and run out. In, out, in, out. Nothing to it."

The freezer was long and deep. A sheath of white covered the walls and seemed to be exploring the floor with thin, ghostly tentacles. No safety stones. Pheodora stepped inside, desperately looking for the five red globes. A flicker of color in the harsh white room caught her eye. Something behind a block of ice. She hurried forward, her body heat deserting her with each step. She saw the safety stones, not behind but inside the block of ice—suspended perfectly in the center.

Dana stood by the bed where she had spent much of the day recovering. Now she was keeping vigil over

Cory. He was alive, his wounds surprisingly superficial, only a slight burn to his right hand and arm. Dana helped Nerine clean and dress the wound. But it was the bump on the back of his head that concerned them. The young man had awakened, only to fall asleep again moments later, a hard sleep not far removed from a coma.

"If Dr. Dutetre were here—" Nerine began. Her words were absorbed by tears. But everyone knew what she was thinking.

If Dr. Dutetre were here, he would know what to do. As a group, they had far more confidence in Nerine than she had in herself.

"I'm going to stay here with him," Nerine said. Dana and Justin tried to argue with her, saying that she, too, should sleep, but the veterinarian was adamant and refused to leave.

Relenting, Dana gave Cory a peck on the forehead, then left with Justin. The moon guided their way as they followed the trail heading back to the dorm.

A chill ran up Dana's back. She stopped. The dorm was less than twenty feet away.

"You okay?" Justin asked, putting his arm around her shoulders.

A warm breeze, rich with the scent of the sea, arose in the moonlight. The insects and creatures of the jungle that had so troubled Dana the first night now were mere background noise, as comforting as a radio playing low in another room.

"I don't know," she confessed to Justin. "Déjà vu? The heebie-jeebies. Something."

Justin turned the flashlight on his face. "Maybe it's the ghost of Vassa Island." His Bela Lugosi impersonation was more like the Count from *Sesame Street*. "You okay? You look a little pale."

Something?

"I just got this weird feeling." Dana shook her head.

She was being silly. After facing a real monster like
Burton Rudyard, imagined haunts should be a joke. But
the odd feeling persisted.

"Maybe you're becoming a psychic," Justin said, still
trying to make her smile. "You should talk to Pheodora."

Success! She did smile!

"You're right," she said enthusiastically. "I should
talk to Pheodora." And then she hurried to the dorm.

In spite of the cold and her cloying fear, Pheodora had
worked up a sweat. The block of ice, easily weigh-
ing nearly a hundred pounds, was too heavy to lift,
but, pushing with her back and buttocks, and carefully
guarding her exposed flesh, she was able to scoot the
block across the frost-laden floor.

It was slow going. And after several minutes she was
less than halfway to the door. Sweat turned to ice. Frozen
beads of perspiration dotted her forehead. Each breath
of icy air seemed to steal a little more of her strength.

How long had it been? Five minutes? Ten? She looked
over her shoulder at the freezer door, still open and
waiting like the welcoming arms of God.

"One step at a time," she whispered to herself. "Just
concentrate."

But concentration, like her strength, trickled away
with each breath. Memories clawed her mind, shredding
her resolve.

She could feel her sanity leaving with her body heat.
Not for the first time, she wondered if she had inherited
her father's dementia.

She turned to face the door and began pushing the ice
with her bare hands—no longer worried about the flesh
freezing. Concentrating on the waiting door, the blessed
exit, and grounding herself in the physicality of the task,
she lowered her head and inched the ice block forward in
a sudden burst of power. *Not that far, not that far.*

A new sensation cloaked her—the disturbing sense that she was not alone. Not alone? *Dana? Justin?* She looked up, vision sharp with hope.

Her heart froze between beats. Standing by the freezer door was her long-dead father.

WASHINGTON, D.C.

Once the events of the day—the death of Burton Rudyard, the injury to Cory Nestor—were dealt with, *The Truth* settled on the question of the week: Which *24/7* contestant was a traitor?

Fifteen minutes into the show, Tucker saw Nelson Rycroft loosen up and smile. As well he should. Tucker was a natural, keeping a perfect balance between tension and control—instinctively asking the questions viewers wanted answered, challenging responses that were flimsy or evasive, and giving the audience both at home and in the studio a feeling of inclusion.

At eleven o'clock, when the show was supposed to end, the vigorous debate was continuing. Rather than leaving the issue of Control's accomplice unresolved, the network extended the program. The extension added an extra layer of drama. The second hour proved even more riveting than the first.

At five minutes to midnight Tucker announced it was time to reach a conclusion. Each expert was asked his or her learned opinion as to who the accomplice was. In the opening segment of the telecast, Tucker had reminded the audience that Dr. Lorrik had successfully predicted the results of each and every vote, as well as forecasting Burton Rudyard's volatile nature. That, coupled with the fact that he was on the president's appointed task force, meant his was the answer everyone was waiting for.

Tucker saved the doctor's comments for last.

Lorrik had been quiet for most of the evening, often appearing troubled or in deep concentration. Now he spoke with confidence tinged with sadness. "The answer is in the stars. The zodiac. As was first brought to my attention by Mr. Thorne, Control has painstakingly ensured that each of the twelve signs is represented. Why? Because he is a great believer in astrology? No. Rather, it is because he is a great believer in society. And what better way to sum up society, in all its diversity, than the twelve signs of the zodiac. A system of character definition that predates almost every science.

"It's called a tangent scenario, which, in a nutshell, is a plan that makes the victim victimize himself. *We* are the intended victims, not the people on the island. Control is punishing us—our society. A civilization that says naked voyeurism is acceptable, that greed and lust are commendable. By making us choose who lives and who dies he makes us accessories to murder. By accentuating the very worst in us, by pulling it into the light of day and making everyone take a good long look, Control is murdering society as we know it.

"But he's not alone. I have completed an extensive profile. The person most likely to be the accomplice is"—Lorrik took a deep breath—"a male. Moreover, he is someone who is socially adept, a person who is resourceful, but knows how to take orders. He will have at least one sibling who is older and he will have an area of expertise about which he is confident to the point of being arrogant."

The room was hushed. "Only one person fits the profile. Only one person could be Control's accomplice. That person is Justin Rourke."

28 VASSA ISLAND

The odd feeling Dana had experienced on the walk back to the dormitory had really shaken her, an uneasiness accentuated by the discovery that Pheodora was not in the dorm. Perhaps sensing Dana and Justin's desire for intimacy, Renee left to spend the night in the infirmary.

And so they were alone. They moved instantly into each other's arms. Then, without premeditation, they made love. He touched her tenderly and with care, aware of her aches and pains, wincing worse than she when he sensed her discomfort. But each time she urged him on, pulling him to her.

Their lovemaking had been both vigorous and passionate, and afterward Dana had fallen into a deep, warm sleep, marked by a slow, easy rise and fall of her chest. With his lips against her neck, Justin felt the melodic tempo of her pulse.

He knew he should be sleeping, too, saving his strength, but his mind wouldn't shut off. Wild thoughts trampled the quiet parts of his brain. As he reviewed the events of the day, he realized how lucky Cory had been—a slight burn to his hand and arm, a bump on his head from striking the wall. Thank God for small blessings.

But the Vault remained sealed, guarded by a fail-safe they neither expected nor understood. They would not be getting the vaccine that way. And now the plan Justin had formed shortly after this all began was back in play.

He sighed, not relishing the task ahead. He had no choice. He would do what he had to do to survive—no matter what.

He always did.

CARIBBEAN SEA

The air was hot, thick, and vile. He reeked with the stench of the dead animal and the exhaust fumes, so he was forced to stop frequently and vent the bad air and let in the good. Conversely, the water was numbingly cold, sucking the feeling from his feet and lower legs. But Foster Merrick didn't stop.

Despite the number of ships on patrol, it was impossible to monitor every inch of the sea at all times. Still, with frequent helicopter flyby, spotlight, and sonar, any attempt to flee Vassa Island would likely be detected.

But the United States fucking Navy would be looking for a man and a boat—not a whale.

Foster had found the beached mammal the day before. A sweet gift from mother nature. After destroying the cameras on the south beach and working under the cover of darkness, he had quickly gone about the task of skinning the creature, careful to leave the dorsal fin intact. Even with the chainsaw, it was a difficult job and in the end he had to settle for a much smaller portion of the beast than he originally thought. Still, the finished camouflage weighed more than a hundred pounds. The jet ski was from the marina. Lying on it, as flat as possible, draped with the partial whaleskin on top of him, Foster set out into the cold, dark sea, guided by a compass and his innate sense of the sea.

He had anticipated the stench, but not the dangerous gas fumes that forced him to stop periodically for fresh air. Nor had he expected the crushing pain to his neck and back caused by supporting the carcass. He persevered, slipping past the blockade just before sunrise. Then he set course for a small island to the north. With any luck he would be on land and hospitalized before the fatal noon deadline.

WASHINGTON, D.C.
The Good-Nite Motel

The Sword of God stood naked in the center of the room. Outside, traffic bellowed, buses moaned, trucks rumbled, occasionally a horn sounded. People were hurrying about the business of life in blissful ignorance. Alone in a room that stank of cigarette smoke and astringent disinfectant, Elliot Kay Simon prepared himself for the task ahead.

He was both joyous and sad, anxious and fearful. Such was the way of God. Mysterious but wise, seeing into corners where men failed to look, peering beneath the mask of society and staring into the true face of his greatest and most flawed creation—man.

Simon knew pride was a sin, but he was proud just the same.

God was dead, His voice silent for the past four days. The grief had seemed too much to bear. Thoughts of suicide played in Simon's mind like a persistent song. He looked to the stars for answers but without the Almighty Father, there was little solace.

But he hadn't given in, hadn't given up.

Four days ago was also when he met the reporter. And since Simon knew better than to believe in coincidence, that meant the reporter was the key—a suspicion verified by his miraculous survival of the bomb. Tucker Thorne, even his name was portentous.

The Thorn.

Simon had followed The Thorn to his apartment, where he broke in and searched his computer files for clues. He had been following the reporter ever since, from Seattle, to Washington, D.C. Wherever The Thorn went, the Sword of God was not far behind.

And tonight his efforts had paid off. While watching The Thorn on TV, Elliot Kay Simon had once more heard the voice of God.

God was resurrected. And this time he wore a mortal face. Perhaps that was why God was talking to him through the TV instead of directly in his head.

He heard the voice and now he knew what he had to do. He had to save God. And as before, The Thorn would lead the way.

29 NABIA ISLAND

The odor of dead flesh and the acidic bite of gas fuels permeated his skin, embedding itself in his muscle tissue. Fumes poisoned his mind, filling his head with images of poor dead Brenda Segar, her bullet-ridden body rising from the ocean floor to inform him of the proper way to cut a beefsteak.

Foster tried to shake his head, to push the horrid image from his mind. But his head was immobile, bent at the neck and pressing against his chest, held down by something vile. As if all the fish he had ever taken from the sea had come together to form one great beast that was now squeezing the very life from his lungs.

Carbon monoxide.

The notion rose in his mind like a cork from the briny depths. Fear was a good thing, a wonderful thing, a lifesaving thing. Fear brought adrenaline, flushing his system—enough for him to realize that he was hallucinating and to remind him that he was hiding beneath the carcass of a dead whale, inhaling deadly fumes from the jet ski engine.

With terror-induced strength he cast off the whale's corpse.

The pure air was greater than any food or drink. With each breath his thoughts became a little clearer, his goal more defined. If the United States fucking Navy saw him, so be it. He couldn't last another moment under that carcass.

A quick look revealed no ships in pursuit. Blinking, trying to steady and focus his vision, he checked the compass, picked a direction he thought would more or less be toward land, and opened up the jet ski full throttle.

The waves were liquid giants, rising ever higher the closer he came to shore. He was no longer driving the jet ski, just holding on and hoping. Blinking back tears, he saw land—a beach—then a row of shacks and people.

The jet ski ran aground, tossing him into the surf. Swirling blue-green water closed over his face. Salt stung his eyes. He kicked for the surface.

A wave caught him in its frothy fingers, carrying him forward. Sand sank beneath him, offering purchase. He dug in with his fingers.

Land! He had made it. He looked up as another wave lapped his face. He blinked back seawater. A boy, no older than eight, stood less than three feet away. Foster opened his mouth to speak; the words were stolen by a watery fist. He felt the ground beneath him shift, a tug on his legs. The tide was pulling him back to sea. He looked up at the boy. The child didn't move.

"Help," Foster croaked, his throat raw and seared by fumes and seawater. "Get help." The child gave no indication that he understood.

Another wave. The hand of the sea got a better grip this time, pulling Foster under once again. His elbows dug into the sand, anchoring him. He lifted his head from the water, coughing and spitting. Then slowly, inch by painful inch, he crawled forward.

When he looked up again, the boy was gone. Was he gone for help? Foster continued to crawl until his head, then his shoulders, and finally his chest were out of the waves.

He stopped, sucking precious sweet air. The muscles that earlier had burned with the pain and fatigue were now strangely quiet, numbed beyond anguish.

The voices came to him between lapping waves, barely audible above the angry roar of the sea. Voices. He strained to hear, to translate. Words. Definitely words but he couldn't make out what they were saying. A different language? Or was his brain too addled to comprehend? His heart was racing, ears ringing. His skin seemed to itch and burn. No. It was too early for that, too early.

Something hit his back, sharp and hard. Another strike, this one hitting the top of his head. He saw a rock tumble in the sand.

A rock?

His head began to throb, to scream with pain. Gritting his teeth he lifted his eyes. The beach was no longer empty. He could see legs, dozens of tanned, well-muscled legs. The boy was back, with others. Foster raised his head. All males—adults and children.

He tried to speak to explain what he needed. Another rock hit his head, this one larger, sharper. Foster's vision blurred with agony. Something warm began to run down his forehead. He blinked back blood. Another rock, and another, and another.

His right eye was covered in blood and useless. He peered with his left, straining to speak, to understand. "Why?"

As he lay on the beach dying, his head turned toward the village, his good eye focused on the nearest shack. It was made of old boards and looked ready to fall. But there, on the rusted tin roof he saw a flimsy aluminum TV antenna.

Television—fucking television! was his final thought.

30 VASSA ISLAND

The sea was blinking.

At first she thought it was an optical illusion, a sunbeam shattering on a piece of steel or torque of glass on one of the ships. But after five minutes, when the blinking continued and she began to piece together a pattern, Dana realized it was a message.

Someone was trying to signal them from the blockade.

Excitement swelled in her heart but there was no one to share the news with. Nerine and Cory were in the infirmary. Renee was out on a desperate search for safety stones. And she still hadn't seen Pheodora. There had been no sign of the psychic since the day before, and that uneasy feeling Dana had felt earlier was now a howling banshee.

Tick, tick, tick.

Dana checked the time: 6:43 A.M. A minute closer, to home or heaven.

A new day, a new countdown.

Tick, tick, tick.

In less than four hours one of them—she, Nerine, Cory, Pheodora, Renee, or Justin—would be dead.

Tick, tick, tick.

More than twenty years later, the grandfather clock that had marked the last fleeting seconds of her grandmother's life continued to tick. And this time the countdown was for her. Dana brushed her hair back with her hand, pushed the mental image back into its special prison of her mind.

The sea continued to blink.

A signal. She was sure of it. But what did it mean? She knew from watching old war movies with her dad that naval ships sometimes communicated with flashing lights. Justin had been in the military. Perhaps he would know? But where was he?

Working on a plan, he had told Renee.

What plan? The image of Cory being thrown across the room on a man-made bolt of lightning flashed through her mind. Or maybe there was no plan? Last night Justin had reawakened a passion she had not realized still lived within her. And this morning he was gone, without explanation. Why?

No! She couldn't think that way, couldn't worry about things beyond her control.

Her earlier excitement about the blinking light evaporated quickly. Even if they could translate it, what would it say? Hang in there? Be patient? Thinking of you?

Tick, tick, tick. The clock refused to be silenced.

Arcing through the air like lightning made solid, the axe bit deep into the defying block of ice. Splinters of frozen water splattered across the floor. Chips of dried blood flaked off the axe head, leaving a pox of burgundy-brown across the ice. Justin swung the axe again, ignoring the dappled reminder of his morning's task.

It was part of the plan. Unfortunate, unsavory, but necessary.

Swish-chink.

The axe dug deeper into a growing, frozen V, creating an impression of surprise as if the ice were gaping at its attacker.

Swish-chink.

A fragment the size of a fist scurried across the floor. Blood chips from the blade created a grisly confetti. By the time he cracked into the center of the ice block, his shirt was drenched in sweat. Two fresh bruises—one on his left leg, another on his back—ached and burned. A small cut over his right eye cracked and began to bleed anew. He wiped it with the back of his hand.

The freezer door stood ajar, the lock handle demolished by Justin's axe.

"Justin?"

He turned. Dana was in the doorway behind him.

"Dana, don't come in." Suddenly Justin tossed the blade aside. Chopping the ice had purged the axe of most of its gory evidence, but he didn't want her to see just the same. Dana was looking past him, past the ruined freezer door, staring into the cold beyond and a horror more terrifying than dried blood.

"Go back. You don't want to see this."

She ignored him. "Oh, my God. Pheodora?"

"Dana, don't."

"Oh, my God!" She dashed toward the open freezer door.

He jumped between her and the freezer, blocking her passage. "You don't want to go in there."

"Pheodora," she said—a statement not a question.

Justin nodded.

"Oh, God." Dana covered her mouth with her hand.

"It happened sometime last night. I'm sorry. There was nothing I could do."

He hugged her, stroking her hair. "How did you find me? I mean—her?"

Dana pulled back so she could see his face. "The smell."

The smell? The smell of the dead was a scent Justin was all too familiar with, but that didn't apply here. Pheodora's body was frozen.

"Ammonia," Dana clarified. "I remembered smelling ammonia when we first scouted the island. But I didn't put it together until this morning. I worked at an ice-cream plant two summers ago for extra money. There was a strong smell of ammonia there, too. It was used in the freezer. Pheodora was afraid of the cold."

A wave of tears rolled down her cheeks.

"Shhhh," Justin breathed. "It'll be okay. I promise."

"How did it happen?"

He told her about the safety stones frozen in the block of ice, how he had found the ice block in the middle of the freezer where Pheodora had fallen.

"I've got to see her," Dana said.

"No. It's better if—"

"I have to." She pushed him away and entered the freezer before he could stop her. He hurried behind her. She gasped at the sight of Pheodora's body, now veiled in a jagged glaze of frost and ice, a look of total horror indelibly printed on her face. Pheodora had died as much from fear as from cold.

"What could have done this?" Dana asked.

"I'm guessing it was him," Justin said pointing toward the door they had just come through.

This time she did scream, a short bleat of shock and terror. Standing next to the doorway, smiling and waving animatedly, was a man in his mid-twenties, with the same blunt features and red hair as Pheodora. "Her father?"

"Good guess. I was thinking brother."

"No. Her father. He committed suicide when Pheodora was a little girl. Leaving her and a sister stranded in a car during a blizzard, alone with his body."

"Jesus!" Justin shuddered involuntarily.

"How?" Dana began.

"Good question. Interesting answer." Justin pointed to the ceiling. It was made of metal plates held together by rivets the size of walnuts. "If you go to the door and look back you'll see three of the rivets are actually projectors of some kind—blue, green, and red."

"Like a projection TV," Dana said.

"Exactly, only much more sophisticated, a holographic projector. Look at it long enough and you can tell it's a projection, but for someone who was no doubt physically and mentally drained, it would have seemed like the man was back from the dead. I figure this was taken from family videos or something."

"Pheodora told me that she saw her father in the dormitory," Dana said. "At the window."

"If we look, I bet we'll find the same sort of projectors."

"She said her bed was cold, too."

"That would be easy enough. I don't know if you noticed but the dorm, like this building, is a lot bigger on the outside than inside. Chock-full of little surprises. Why didn't she say something?"

"Didn't want anyone to think she was going crazy."

"She was psychic—that ship had sailed," Justin said, then immediately wished he could reclaim his words. Then a new realization hit him. "A night-vision camera wouldn't pick up an image like this."

Dana followed his thought process.

"So if anyone had been watching her that night in the

dorm, they would have seen Pheodora being afraid of nothing."

WASHINGTON, D.C.

Blood.

With less than four hours' sleep, fatigue was a constant companion. But the thought was so compelling, so complete, that Tucker couldn't ignore it.

Jumping out of bed, clad in nothing but his boxers, he turned on the light, rushed to the bulletin board and took down a cluster of papers held together with a large black clip. The word SUPPLIES was scrawled across the first page. He flipped through the list until he came to the section he was thinking about. He rapidly scanned the list of items procured for the island prior to the takeover.

It wasn't until he found what he was looking for, tracked the answer with his finger, and read it twice for assurance that he realized just how much was riding on this hypothesis. From the beginning, the Vassa Island crisis had haunted him like no puzzle had before it. The whispered tips offered by Dr. Lorrik often created more questions than answers.

Why?

Because it didn't add up.

Then last night, hosting *The Truth* and interviewing some of the greatest sociologists and criminologists in the country had been a humbling experience. Suddenly, Tucker realized just how inadequate he really was.

He was a photographer who got lucky and black-mailed his way into a promotion. Certainly he was skilled when it came to crosswords, jigsaws, and brain-teasers. But he had been foolish to think that his so-called puzzle sense could compete with those experts who had more degrees than he had underwear.

He had fallen asleep feeling a fraud and, worse, a fool.

Until he was awakened by a single word: *blood*.

"Sorry to bother you, Doctor," said the voice on the monitor. "I know you were up late last night—great show by the way—but I thought you would want to see this."

Lorrik wasn't listening. On the situation room screen he could just make out a shadow that appeared to be swinging something. "When?"

"Less than two hours ago."

"Location?"

"The marina shed. Not the main building where the tools, supplies, and boat are held, but the smaller one beside it."

"Where the bodies are stored," Lorrik said.

"Yes, sir."

First Foster Merrick and now this. The United States Navy was still red-faced about allowing the fisherman to escape their blockade. Thanks to his choker-cam, they had finally been able to locate him. By then he was dead, stoned to death by a simple people who had watched the show and were trying to protect themselves from the virus. Although how the virus was transmitted was still not known, the CDC had ruled out airborne pathogens. After killing Merrick, the villagers had wisely stayed away from his body. An action that most likely saved their lives.

But this.

He had expected and predicted trouble. Pushed hard enough, everyone would crack—those on the edge like Burton Rudyard first, but eventually everyone. But this, *this* was beyond anticipation.

"Looks like you were right again," the young man said.

The figure in the video remained a shadow. He held a flashlight that provided clear images of what he was looking at, revealing row after row of bodies. But his own image was little more than a silhouette. The marina shed was not equipped with a night-vision camera.

Still the scene was chilling. "Oh, dear Lord," Lorrik gasped. Through the choker-cam he watched as the man reached out in the dark and picked up an object about the size of a cantaloupe.

"Is that?"

"Yep. A human head. Check this out." The young man fast-forwarded the tape. "He worked until first light. He's got a handkerchief around his face, probably for the smell, but just before he left, he passed a window as the sun was coming up."

He stopped the tape. "There."

On the screen was the unmistakable image of Justin Rourke holding the severed head of Burton Rudyard.

"Excuse me, Dr. Lorrik." A man in an impeccable black suit stood waiting. His lapel pin marked him as Secret Service. "I have orders to escort you to the president."

"The president? Ah, yes, certainly." Then to the monitor: "Can I get a copy of that?"

"Just give me a minute."

"I'm sorry, sir. The president wants to see you now."

"Yes, yes. But this will take only a second, and I assure you he will want to see it."

The agent reached out and took him by the arm. There was no mistaking the seriousness of his grip. "My orders are to bring you immediately."

"But the tape."

"I'm sure this young man won't mind running a copy up to the Oval Office when he's finished."

The president of the United States was pacing. He

stopped when Lorrik entered the Oval Office, his face stern and angry.

"Mr. President," Lorrik said, determined to keep control of himself. Never mind that this was arguably the most powerful man in the world; Lorrik would not suffer bullies.

"That will be all," the president said, dismissing the Secret Service agent.

"I gather something has happened," Lorrik ventured.

The president glared.

"I gather something *bad* has happened," Lorrik amended.

"Sit!"

Lorrik did. The Commander in Chief did not.

Keeping the higher ground, Lorrik noted. The fact that the president needed to resort to simple games in order to maintain control actually made Lorrik feel better, flattered even. He never thought of himself as a particularly intimidating person.

Then, to the doctor's astonishment, the president threw a sheet of paper at him. It missed its mark and fell to the blue-gray carpet.

After a moment Lorrik bent to pick up the sheet. Then he made a show of adjusting himself comfortably in his seat before opening the paper and reading what was written on it.

"How? Who wrote this?" he asked, a sick feeling telling him he already knew the answer. For once, he prayed he was wrong. He wasn't.

"Your friend, Tucker Thorne. The son of a bitch thinks he can blackmail the president of the United States."

Lorrik looked again at the note. Despite himself, he was impressed. Maybe Gwen was right. There was a lot more to Tucker than he had ever guessed. "In this case, Mr. President, I think he can."

31 VASSA ISLAND

"So? Can you tell what it says?" Dana asked. They were standing on a dune looking out at the blinking sea. The light she had noticed earlier was still flashing. Justin had asked for a pencil and paper, then spent fifteen minutes jotting notes, plundering his memory for a translation.

"I—yeah, I think so. It's been a while." He rubbed the back of his neck as he talked. The cut above his eyes yawned. Dana watched it closely, worried it would start bleeding again. A slight tentativeness in his gait told her the cut was just one of several injuries he had suffered since this morning. He would say only that his actions were part of a plan, but he refused to elaborate.

"And?" she probed.

"What?" he asked, still looking at the sea.

"The message? Are you okay?"

"Yeah, I'm just—you know, tired."

A lock of hair fell over Dana's eyes. Her father said she hid behind her hair whenever she was insecure. It was the way he and her mother could tell, with unnerving accuracy, when Dana was hiding something. Was she insecure now? They hadn't talked about their lovemaking the night before, and now Justin seemed oddly preoccupied.

Dana brushed her hair back in defiance. For four days she had been fighting for her life, standing up against overwhelming odds and winning. She would be damned if she would let concern over a man distract her.

Justin folded the paper he had been writing on and put it in his pants pocket. "They say for us to hang tough. They're close to a solution."

Worn with fatigue, Cory was nevertheless in good spirits. Nerine had told him she was relatively sure the danger of a concussion had passed.

Now it was Justin who concerned Nerine. She dressed the cut over his eye, then noticed him wince as he removed his shirt to reveal a massive bruise on his back. Justin told her about a nasty fall he had taken, then looked at Dana with eyes pleading for her to remain silent.

Nerine wasn't convinced, but went along anyway.

Renee arrived, carrying bottled water and several cans of food. "I thought doctor and patient could use a little something to eat," she said. She looked at Justin and Dana. "Sorry, I didn't know the lovebirds were here. I only brought enough for three. I can run back for more, if you like."

"No, we're fine," Dana said.

Once they were all settled, Justin and Dana explained what had happened to Pheodora. Renee was particularly interested in Pheodora's zodiac theory. "You think she went there because of her astrological sign?"

"Apparently," Dana said. "She had it all worked out."

"And it worked for me," Justin added. "That was also how I found her body. I knew she was an Aquarius. So I made the same deduction she did."

Dana gave Justin a curious look. She had assumed he had stumbled on her body by accident. Was he trying to win Pheodora's personal safety stones? He had taken Nerine's. Was that his so-called plan—to steal all the stones and stay alive?

"I'm confused," Cory said. "I get how Ganymede Hall related to Pheodora's astrological sign—but the freezer? What does a freezer have to do with Aquarius?"

"The safety stones were frozen in a block of ice that Pheodora appeared to be trying to push out of the freezer."

"And?" Cory urged.

"Oh, I get it," Renee said. The others immediately turned their attention to her. She continued: "I'm sort of into that kind of stuff, you know. Aquarius is the sign of the Water Bearer. Ice is frozen water."

As they were leaving, Dana noticed that the paper Justin had used to decode the naval message had fallen out of his pocket. She picked it up and shoved it in her own pocket while Nerine and Cory were talking.

"I'm going to try to catch some shut-eye before the vote," Nerine said.

"The vote—I had almost forgotten about that," Cory said. Then looking up at the nearest camera, he added: "After Dr. Keleman went to all this trouble to keep me alive, it sure would be a shame if I was exiled." He then winked at the camera.

Gallows humor, Dana thought—though she suspected the statement was not entirely in jest. Desperate times called for desperate measures. And no matter how bleak or outrageous, they had to remember they were on a TV show—dealing with the harshest rating system ever devised.

WASHINGTON, D.C.

"You must have balls the size of watermelons."

"We can discuss my anatomy later," Tucker said into the phone. "Did he approve it?"

"He approved it," Sherman Lorrik said.

"Yes!" Tucker cheered punching the air. It had worked, it had actually worked.

"But there are conditions," Lorrik added.

"What kind of conditions?" Tucker asked warily. He was still in his hotel room, and the remains of breakfast—two candy bars and several snack packs—cluttered the small desk where his laptop sat.

He had been scheduled to appear on three different news programs this morning. He had canceled them all, then took the hotel phone off the hook, only accepting calls to his cell phone. It was a massive gamble, a big gamble, and after his night of insecurity, it seemed downright foolish, even arrogant. But he had to follow his instincts.

All the pieces of the puzzles had finally been collected and were now waiting for someone to put them together.

Puzzles—plural—because he now knew he was dealing with two separate situations, but with a common denominator.

"You and a video crew will be flown to the *John F. Kennedy* and given full access to all aspects of the project, but only if you agree to say nothing about the discovery or destruction of an EMP weapon. . . ."

This was the opportunity of a lifetime—behind-the-scenes entrée to the story of the century. The video alone would be more valuable than gold, not to mention the information—every interview, every shot an exclusive. But, it wasn't enough. "No. I can't agree to that," Tucker said.

The phone line sizzled.

"How about this?" Lorrik proposed. "You agree not to report on anything that is a threat to national security."

Better, but Tucker knew that to the military, everything was a threat to national security. "Who defines threat?"

"Me," Lorrik said.

Tucker smiled. Lorrik was definitely not military. "Agreed."

Lorrik sighed, whether with relief or fatigue Tucker couldn't tell. "There's one more thing, one more condition."

Here it comes. Tucker braced himself.

"I go with you."

VASSA ISLAND

Renee knew she had come to the right place, knew she had a shot at winning her five personal safety stones the instant she heard the speaker click on. And not a moment too soon. The vote was less than an hour away.

She was at the back of the room off one of the oldest buildings on the island. On the wall behind her were two small cubbyholes, each about the size of a mailbox, with a black button between them.

Control spoke. **"In one of the openings are your five safety stones. In the other is a rather unpleasant surprise. You have five minutes to choose."**

It had taken her longer than expected to find the challenge. Renee was a Libra, a sign symbolized by the scales—a sign associated with justice. She had combed the map looking for anything even slightly related to scales or courtrooms or the Justice Department.

No luck.

Frustrated and running out of time, Renee was alternately angry and scared. Then she literally stumbled over the answer: a rusted train track partially hidden by dry grass, down near the marina. There were tracks all over the island left over from when Vassa Island was mined for guano, but these tracks were far away from any of the old mining sights.

Ships. The guano would have been transported by ship. And, since ships could only carry a certain weight, the cargo would have to be measured before being loaded.

Following the tracks away from the dock, she came to a dilapidated building, partially swallowed by grasses and vines. A faded sign identified it as WEIGHT STATION.

Part of the ceiling was missing. Shafts of sunlight, like gleaming columns of dust, lit the interior. The back wall stood out in sharp contrast to the rest of the building—an obvious addition. That was where she found the challenge.

Sweat beaded on her forehead as she studied the two small holes. Which one, which one?

Renee was no fool. She knew her greatest fear involved her appearance. Her challenge would be designed around that. She stared into the holes, both impossibly dark, incredibly deep, wishing she had brought a flashlight. She had quit smoking years ago or she would have had a lighter or a pack of matches with her. As it was, all she had was a tube of lipstick and a compact.

The compact!

She opened the compact and angled the mirror to catch one of the shafts of light. After several attempts she was able to reflect the beam into each hole. The diffused light was weak, though sufficient enough to reveal a small fold of fabric, possibly velvet, that was hanging two feet inside, blocking whatever was behind.

Damn! And she had been so proud of her ingenuity.

"Two minutes," said Control. The booming electronic voice caused her to flinch.

Two minutes? How could she possibly decide in two minutes? The cubbyholes were identical. So which was the right one?

Renee bit her lip in thought.

"One minute."

Time was accelerating at an impossible rate.

Right, left, right, left. *Eeny, meeny, miney, mo—no that was no good. Think, think, think.*

"Thirty seconds."

Shut up, she wanted to scream. *Shut up and let me think.*

Right, left, right, left.

What would others choose? The right hand of God, the right way, the one on the right—forced to choose, the average person would take the one on the right. She was sure of it. And if she was sure, then so was that bastard Control.

"Ten, nine, eight, seven . . ."

Renee shoved her arm into the left cubbyhole, reaching past the cloth, putting her arm in up to the elbow and—nothing.

Had she chosen the wrong one?

She pushed a little farther, extending her arm to its maximum length. Her fingers brushed something—a knit bag perhaps? She grabbed it, feeling the small glass balls, hearing the faint *clink* of the safety stones.

She had done it. She had chosen correctly.

Shkkenk.

A steel cuff snapped in place before she could react, pinching the skin as it locked down on her wrist.

Control spoke. "Now comes the real choice."

Together in the dorm, Dana and Justin had eaten in silence, neither broaching the subject of the night before or of his mysterious plan. Twice she had gotten the impression that he was about to say something and she waited in anticipation—and with a touch of fear. But the moment passed. The words were left unsaid.

Maybe he was waiting for her to speak first?

No, that wasn't right. She wasn't the one keeping the secrets.

She couldn't stop thinking about the note. She could feel it crumpled in her pants pocket, feel its imagined weight, heavy with secrets. Why was she so convinced he had lied to her?

What foolishness! She would read the note and see just how foolish she was being.

When Justin left to use the rest room, she pulled out the note. It was covered in marks and random letters where he was obviously sorting out the code. The finished message appeared at the bottom of the paper.

WARNING: JUSTIN ROURKE IS THE ACCOMPLICE.

Renee wanted to scream, but she couldn't. The part of her mind still capable of reason told her she had to listen, had to hear the rest of her heinous challenge. The steel cuff was tight and unyielding, biting into her flesh. Already the tips of her fingers were becoming numb. Soon she would not be able to feel the bag with the lifesaving stones.

Control spoke. **"A blade is poised above your right wrist. In the center between the openings is a button. Your choice: push the button, dropping the blade and cutting off your own hand, or remain here trapped, missing the next vote and thereby dying from the virus."**

Renee was pale with fear. It all made sense, in a sick, horrid way. Renee was a Libra, her zodiac sign symbolized by scales. And Control had given her an impossible choice.

"Dana!"

Justin was standing in front of her. Staring at her. His eyes—kind, framed in thick lashes, and flecked with concern—had not changed. Nor had his face, the handsome face that had consumed her thoughts.

But now she feared there was something corrupt and depraved behind that face. Could Justin really be in league with Control? Could he even be a killer? And worse—far worse—was she in love with a killer?

He was talking, had been talking for a while, but she hadn't heard a word.

"What?" she asked, blinking like a blind woman suddenly given sight.

"Renee." He looked at his watch. "The vote's in twenty-four minutes, and she's not back. I'm pretty sure I know where she went. I'm going to look for her."

He headed for the door.

Look for her? "Wait," Dana called, hurrying after him.

"It's too dangerous. You stay here."

Why? So you can kill her and take her safety stones?

"I'm coming with you," she said, leaving no more room for debate.

WASHINGTON, D.C.
Dulles International Airport

Cameras, batteries, lights, editing gear. So much to do and absolutely no time to do it. God! He loved this business. Twenty-eight minutes after being advised of the situation, photographer Brick Bickman was packed and ready to go, as were the field producer and the sound technician. Brick had argued for a second photographer, stressing the importance of the shoot.

The network disagreed. Typical corporate decision: spend thousands of dollars chartering a plane, assembling a crew, shattering the budget for food, lodging, and overtime—and then go cheap when it came to manpower. If the story was important enough for all that other stuff, why not a second cameraman?

But his pleas landed on deaf ears, and there was no time to argue.

Bottom line, this was the chance of a lifetime. Brick liked Tucker, always had. But he knew his friend was a little bit odd; he saw the world in a completely different way from everyone else.

Now those quirks were paying off.

The crew was rushed to the airport by helicopter. But as fast as they were moving, Tucker was moving faster, already on his way to the blockade, flying with a member of the president's special task force.

How the hell did he pull that off? Brick wondered. *How the hell did he pull any of it off?*

Ten minutes after reaching Dulles, Brick was in his seat, wondering if they served beverages and peanuts on charter flights? He had missed lunch and, as a big man, he had a big man's appetite.

"Mr. Bickman?"

"Brick," he corrected. He looked up, expecting to see a flight attendant supplying the answer to his peanut question. Instead he saw a nervous white guy in a Globe Newschannel baseball cap, wearing a Yankees jacket, a white T-shirt, and jeans.

"Who are you?" Brick asked.

The stranger smiled, his brown eyes seeming to bulge as he did. "Harvey Kray," the man replied, as if that meant something.

Brick looked past him toward the cockpit, then back again. "You the flight attendant?"

Harvey Kray smiled in an aw-shucks kind of way. "I'm the photographer."

"Say what?"

"I m-mean s-second photographer," Kray stammered. "You're lead. I just do what you say. R-right?"

"Second photog? Those pencil dicks in management said we couldn't have a second photog."

Kray shrugged. "The p-pencil dicks changed their mind."

Brick laughed. "How come I've never seen you before?"

Kray pointed to his jacket. "I'm f-from the New York bureau. The h-home office s-sent me."

"Home office?" Two words that always made Brick nervous—words that were used in sentences like: The home office thinks you're getting too much overtime; or The home office believes cutbacks are in order; or his favorite, The home office wishes you a Merry Christmas. Please accept this twenty-five-dollar gift certificate to Wal-Mart as a token of our appreciation.

"H-home office s-sent me, b-but at Mr. Thorne's request."

Kray's stammer reminded Brick of the 1963 Dodge Dart he had owned back in college. Thing had a bad starter and an almost human dislike for cold mornings. "Tucker? You know Tucker?"

"Yeah."

"You guys worked together before?"

"You could say that. L-last time I saw him I s-sorta s-stuck him with something."

"Yeah? What? Like a check? You have lunch with him and make him pick up the tab."

"Something like that," Kray replied crisply.

Weird cat, Brick thought to himself as he craned his neck in search of a flight attendant. But to his supreme disappointment, there was no food or beverage service on the flight—not even peanuts or a stale cracker. So he finally closed his eyes and tried to sleep.

VASSA ISLAND

Renee's scream reverberated through the building and out the door, causing a flock of gulls to take flight.

Seconds later Justin and Dana arrived at the weigh station to discover Renee's predicament.

Justin tapped his watch. Twenty minutes until the next vote.

Tick, tick, tick.

If she lived to get off this island, Dana vowed she would throw every clock she owned into the ocean.

"Stay here," Justin said to the two women as he dashed back outside.

Renee had a response to that suggestion. "Where the holy fuck do you expect me to go with this goddamn thing around my arm?"

Justin returned immediately, carrying a rusted metal pipe. He compared the width of the pipe to Renee's left hand, then nodded to himself. "Okay. When I say now, press the button."

"What? Are you crazy?" Renee screeched.

"Dana?"

"Eighteen minutes to the next vote," Dana said answering Justin's unasked question.

"All right, all right, just get me out of here. Do it, do it!"

"Now," Justin screamed.

Renee hit the button.

The blade fell.

Dana gasped.

Chinck.

The sound reverberated off the walls. For a moment Dana wasn't sure if it was the sound of blade on bone or blade on metal. Then she heard the click of the restraint releasing Renee's hand and the joyous whoop as she pulled it free.

Justin removed the pipe, offering it to Renee as a souvenir. "I'd rather have the safety stones."

They could hear the blade recede into the ceiling.

"Hey, maybe I can." Renee stuck the pipe back in the hole; the blade came down again. She tried to squeeze her hand past the pipe, but there wasn't enough room. "Damn it!"

"We'd better hurry," Dana said. She stopped at the doorway and looked back. Justin was still standing by the cubbyhole.

"Speaking of safety stones . . ." Then, without hesitation, he shoved his hand and arm deep into the hole.

"Justin!" Dana screamed.

The blade didn't fall. Smiling, Justin removed his hand. He was holding a small knit bag. Inside were five stones. "Ta-da."

Renee stormed back into the room. "How the hell did you—"

"By not being you," Justin interrupted.

"The personal challenges," Dana said. "Only the person they're designed for can trigger them. That's why I couldn't cause the scorpions to come out in the dorm. Only Nerine could, because it was her challenge. But how does the computer know? I mean, Control, whoever or whatever he is, can't monitor us all at the same time."

"Doesn't have to," Justin said, tapping his choker-cam. "He's already belled the cat, so to speak."

"A sensor in the collar?"

"Bingo." He held the stones up to the light. "Beautiful."

"They're *mine*." The change was shocking and instant.

"The bitch is back," Dana whispered.

Renee's beautiful face was skewed by anger and desperation. "Give them to me. Give them to me now." Still holding the pipe, she clutched it like a baseball bat.

"Whoever physically gets the stones keeps the stones," Dana shouted. "It's the rule."

"Fuck the rule," Renee screamed. "This is my life we're talking about—my life, and I want those stones."

Her fingers were turning white from the intensity of her grip.

"Here!" Justin Rourke handed her the bag with the prize.

"No," Dana cried. "They're yours."

Renee didn't hesitate. She snatched the treasure and ran for the door, safety stones in one hand, pipe in the other.

32 VASSA ISLAND

Black clouds gathered in the distance. A brisk, wet wind hissed through the trees as Dana and Justin ran to the Round House, arriving just behind Renee.

Five minutes and twenty-one seconds until the next vote.

Even though they were all there—Cory, Nerine, Renee, and Justin—the Round House felt empty to Dana. The vacant alcoves marked the dead as surely as marble tombstones.

They all went to their assigned locations. Here they were again, for the fifth time, with the executioner's hand on the drop-switch.

Renee's hair, teased by the growing wind, looked like an illustration of St. Elmo's fire sculpted in blond. The pipe that had saved her hand, then been brandished as a weapon, was propped by her side. She emptied the five safety stones from the bag into the appropriate slot, then glared at the reader board as if daring it to condemn her now.

In a flurry of emotions the others watched her. As she did at every vote, Dana thought of Jenna. Was she watching? And if so, how would she react if Dana were exiled? She closed her eyes in silent prayer, willing her parents to keep Jenna away from the TV.

"I've looked everywhere," Dana mumbled, her words piercing the silence. At first, she hadn't realized she'd spoken her thoughts aloud. "Everywhere."

"For your challenge, *your* safety stones?" Justin asked. "You're a Pisces?"

"Yes. And we're on an island, water everywhere. I've looked up and down the beach, in the freshwater pond, along the small beach on the south side. I even looked in what used to be a small library, thinking they may have microfilm and . . ."

"Microfiche," Justin concluded.

"Exactly. Nothing, zip, nada."

"The sea caves?"

"Ah, the Typhoon Sea Caves. I've memorized all the names. Been there, no luck."

Justin frowned. "That was my guess. I was sure your challenge would be in one of them."

"You mean there really are more than one?" Dana asked. "Caves, plural?"

"Yes," said Justin. "There are two, as a matter of fact." He took out his map and looked at it. "Wait—you called it the *Typhoon* Sea Caves."

"That's what it says on the map."

"That's how I read it the first time, too, but that's wrong. It's not *typhoon*. It's *Typhon*. That's it! That's got to be your challenge."

Dana was confused.

Justin explained. "You know the myth of Pisces?"

"No."

"Aphrodite, the goddess of beauty, and her son, Eros, turned themselves into fish to escape a hideous monster. That's why the symbol for Pisces is two fish."

"That sounds right. I don't know all the names."

"The monster chasing Aphrodite and Eros was named Typhon. Your personal challenge is in the second cave."

The second cave! But with less than three minutes until the vote, there was nowhere near enough time to complete—or even begin—her challenge.

Justin left his alcove and walked up to Dana. His face was riddled with anxiety as he pulled out a small knit bag identical to the one Renee had taken from him earlier. Inside were five cut-glass stones. "Dana, these are for you."

Dana gasped. "Justin, where did you—?"

"Pheodora's," he said. "I cut them from the ice."

"But—you?" She suddenly recalled that prior to Burton Rudyard's exile, Justin had received the most votes, only to be saved by the very thing he had just given her.

He looked around at the others, who were trying to interpret his actions. There was no doubting his expression of guilt. Of course, if he were truly allied with Control, he wouldn't need the stones. Then again . . .

Justin pulled a second bag from his pocket. This one, just like the one before it, contained five stones. Nerine and Cory gasped as one. With Justin, Dana, and Renee all having safety stones, this virtually spelled a death sentence for Nerine or Cory.

"I'm sorry," Justin said in their direction. "I'm sorry."

"How?" Dana wondered. "How could you have ten? How?"

A small guilty smile flickered across his face. "Another personal challenge."

"What? Whose?"

"Burton's. I found and triggered his challenge." He touched the cut above his eye. "It's how I was injured."

One minute till the vote.

"But the personal challenges can only be triggered by our choker-cams. And Burton's dead."

"But his choker-cam still works."

Dana struggled to comprehend. The choker-cams were strong, locked electronically. The only way to remove them without damaging the circuitry would be to—Dana gasped.

"Behead him. You—you cut off his head?"

"He was dead," Justin replied softly.

"But still . . ." She tried to deflect the horrifying images. "The axe—you used the axe you chopped the ice block with."

He nodded. "Early this morning, before sunup. That was the plan I was working on."

Did that mean? "And they saw you. The Navy, everybody. That's why they think you're Control's accomplice."

"How do you know about that?" His guilty expression was replaced by one of concern.

"I found the message."

"And you believed it?" His voice was high-pitched and tense.

"I didn't know what to believe."

"You're the accomplice?" Renee shouted. "I knew it! No wonder you gave up my stones without a fight."

The reader board came to life. The vote had begun.

AIRBORNE
Charter Flight 1218

Elliot Kay Simon used his hand to muffle his laughter.
The plan was working. He shouldn't be surprised. After
all, he was the Sword of God on a mission to save the
Almighty. And he was getting a kick out of performing
this new role.

Harvey Kray was indeed a New York–based photographer for the Globe Newschannel. But the real Harvey
Kray was still in New York.

Simon figured that people were always underesti-
mating him, mistaking mental illness for stupidity. *I
might be crazy, but I'm not dumb.* (Snicker.) In reality,
his IQ was higher than eighty-three and a half percent of
the population's, a figure that suggested perhaps he was
sane and everyone else was crazy.

Breaking into Tucker Thorne's apartment had given him
access to network pass codes, making it easy for Simon to
tap into the Globe computer system and learn about the
trip to the blockade. It was also how he discovered
Clarence Bickman's request for a second photographer.

Then it was simply a matter of picking an identity.
Buying a Globe baseball cap and a Yankees jacket easily
completed the illusion.

Simple.

"Folks, we will be landing in Jamaica in approximately five minutes," the pilot said over the intercom.
"Please put your tray tables up and return your seats to
their upright positions. Any laptops or electronic devices
should be turned off."

Elliot Kay Simon lost control and laughed out loud.
He couldn't help it. He was giddy—absolutely giddy. And
why shouldn't he be? He was on his way to save God.

VASSA ISLAND

The numbers flickered across the screen, changing faster than Dana could keep up. With only five people to choose from, the personal votes were higher than ever. Everyone passed the five hundred mark in the first few seconds.

Outside, thunder drummed, a tympanic soundtrack to the life and death drama unfolding in the Round House.

The votes passed the one thousand mark.

One thousand people want me dead. One thousand strangers want to see my life end. Again Dana thought of her daughter. Again she prayed that Jenna was not watching. She heard another clap of thunder in the distance.

The numbers slowed. Several seconds went by without Nerine, Dana, or Cory receiving more than a smattering of votes. The race was clearly between Justin and Renee, each topping the five thousand mark.

But with Dana, Justin, and Renee all having five safety stones, the real contest was between Nerine and Cory.

The numbers continued to climb for Justin and Renee— six thousand, seven thousand, more.

And then it stopped. Although the digital reader board made no sound, when the numbers stopped the silence seemed different: deeper, darker—deadly.

Dana tried to do the calculations in her head but the anxiety of the moment overwhelmed her ability to do high school math. She stared at the board—aware of her own total, one thousand, three hundred and forty-eight votes, and purposely not looking at the tally for the others. The reader board blurred as tears filled her eyes.

Cory and Nerine. She liked them both. They were good people, honest people who deserved better than this.

The voice of Control boomed. **"The vote is over. Dana Kirsten, you have submitted five safety stones. Half the votes against you are removed."**

The reader board changed again. The number by her name dropped to six hundred and seventy-four. She had to look at the others. Cory had received one thousand, seven hundred and eighty-one; Nerine, one thousand, four hundred and three.

Dana was safe. She would live, as would Nerine. But Cory?

"Justin Rourke, you have submitted five safety stones. Half the votes against you are removed."

Next to Justin's name the numbers tumbled backward, growing smaller until they stopped at one thousand, seven hundred and ninety-nine.

Dana gasped. All the blood drained from her upper body. Even with the safety stones, Justin had received eighteen votes more than Cory Nestor.

"Renee Bellacort, you have submitted five safety stones. Half the votes against you are removed."

The numbers fell. Unlike Dana, the drama of the moment had not negated Renee's ability to do math. She was already moving when the total appeared—one thousand, eight hundred and one. Renee had received two votes more than Justin.

"Renee Bellacort, you have been exiled from the island."

There was no time to react to the shock. The counting of the votes and the adjustments for the safety stones had taken much longer than before. All of them had become uncomfortable, the damnable virus waking in their bloodstream.

Dana activated her thumbprint scanner, freed her bee-sting injector, and shot herself in the arm. She could hear the sound of the others doing the same. She looked up to check on Justin, but instead found herself looking at Cory. His cubicle was open, his injector in his hand, but he was not alone.

"Cory, beside you!" At Dana's warning the young man turned, seeing Renee's face just as the large lead pipe came down, swung with desperate strength. The blow crushed his skull, killing him instantly. Renee fell beside the body, stood up with the injector, and rapidly inoculated herself.

Justin was moving, but Renee was ready for him. She swung the lead pipe like a bat, striking his leg and dropping him to the floor.

A thunderous roar shook the room. But this detonation was not nature induced. The sound came from the speakers, not the sky. The booming voice of Control was screaming.

Renee ran out of the Round House.

33 AIRBORNE
Marine Flight, AK9992

Dr. Sherman Lorrik was a fool, an arrogant, pretentious neophyte. That was his self-diagnosis as he flew from the nation's capital to the middle of the Caribbean Sea with Tucker Thorne. That he should reach this conclusion at the same time he was receiving national acclaim seemed fittingly ironic.

Certainly he had been right about events on Vassa Island and had, so far, correctly profiled public reaction. But when it came to his selection of a pawn, a patsy to be used in shaping public response and forwarding the president's secret agenda, he had been dead wrong.

Lorrik had convinced the president that they had to go on the offensive to control the media response. By leaking specific information to one reporter, thus giving that reporter a clear edge, they ensured that the rest of the media would follow suit like hounds on a blood scent. This would, he argued, give them as much control as was possible when dealing with a free press.

The plan was solid, and at the time Thorne seemed to be the perfect pawn: ambitious, indebted, and not too bright—an evaluation substantiated by the man's obsession with games.

Now here he was, flying into the heart of the storm, both figuratively and literally, with the man he had deemed a fool and selected as a stooge—a man who now held the president of the United States by the balls and was ready to squeeze.

And all because Thorne was putting together the pieces of the puzzle.

"Blood? *Blood?* It was as simple as that?" Lorrik had asked Thorne as their plane left Washington.

"Yep. I checked the supply manifest. The infirmary was stocked with several pints of each contestant's blood. Once I realized that Nerine Keleman had the wrong blood type to be a marrow donor for the Capler twins, it was easy to put it together. Nerine was from Virginia, from a good family, and she had worked as a paid intern for the junior senator from that state."

"Yes, but how did you connect that with the president?"

Tucker had smiled, the right side of his lip curling like a wood shaving, a gesture Lorrik noted was often related to his reaching a conclusion or the hint of an idea.

"I looked at a map."

Lorrik frowned. The lip curled more. "A map of the senate. Got it on a tour. It lists the offices of all the senators including—"

"The senator from Texas," Lorrik finished, getting a faint glimmer of what the world must look like through the eyes of Tucker Thorne. "A senator who would go on to become the president of the United States."

The curled lip almost touched itself. "Must have been a heck of an affair. I mean, they must have really loved each other for her to keep it secret after all these years—and for him to use his position to attempt saving her above all others on that island."

And there it was. With one word Thorne had uncovered the president's secret agenda, information he then used to get access to the blockade.

"There is really a marrow donor for the Capler twins, isn't there?" he had asked.

"Absolutely. It wouldn't have worked otherwise. It's actually a White House staffer who agreed to play along."

Lorrik asked Tucker about his career, prior to 24/7, and listened in amazement as Tucker recounted his run-in with Elliot Kay Simon, the Krest Technologies bomber.

Then their conversation returned to the one thing they had in common: Gwen Lorrik.

The doctor confessed that when his daughter was young, he spent hours reading to her. The *Chronicles of Narnia* had been her favorite tale from childhood.

"I know," Thorne had said. "Whenever you and Gwen had a long-distance argument, she'd hang up the phone and go to the bedroom. I'd find her there, reading C. S. Lewis."

"Why?" Lorrik asked.

"Because those books reminded her of you."

"I'd think that would be the last thing she would want after an argument with me."

"Me, too," Tucker said, then added: "No offense."

"None taken."

"I asked her about that. She said it reminded her of the father who took the time out of his infinitely busy schedule to read to his little girl. It reminded her that you loved her and how much she loved you."

In the long stretch of silence following that exchange, Dr. Lorrik began the self-examination that resulted in his ultimate personal estimation: fool.

Lorrik felt he should say something to make amends to Thorne, but despite his expertise in psychology, when it came to his personal life, he was quickly learning just how unqualified he was.

As the plane sped toward Jamaica, he closed his eyes and tried to absorb this new take on the world. Twenty minutes later he was awakened by manic shouting.

VASSA ISLAND

Electric veins of lightning rippled through the clouds as silver nails of rain hammered into the jungle. Dana focused on Justin's back, seeing little else in the gray downpour and hoping they were following the right trail. Wet grasses lashed at her arms and legs, as thunder bellowed like a stoked forge.

The sea caves.

That was where Dana's challenge would be. It was also where they were most likely to find Renee. They had left Nerine in an almost debilitating state of shock, weeping over Cory's body. But there was no time to lose. If Justin was right, Renee had heard the exchange about the sea caves and knew Dana's safety stones were hidden there.

"But she can't trigger the challenge," Dana had pointed out.

"That won't keep her from looking. If she gets lucky, she might even find them without having to go through the challenge. Like I did with hers."

The Typhon Sea Caves, located on the high end of the island, were broken into porous rock long ago and felt as if they could crumble away at any moment. The opening to the second cave, the one Dana had not explored, was smaller than the first and easy to miss.

Night lived inside, sleeping through the day, resting, waiting for the sun to abandon the world.

The roar of the rain was replaced by the fuming sound of storm-teased waves, bashing in fury against cavern walls. The cave opened into a massive cavern lit by klieg lights. The sound of an agitated sea, furious at even momentary confinement, was amplified by the cavern walls.

A computer mounted on a rolling pedestal sat on the ledge that ringed the water. Renee stood in frustration at the keyboard. Whatever she was doing wasn't working. She looked up as Dana and Justin approached, their two flashlights dancing along the cave walls. Then she stepped away from the computer, moving farther down the narrow ledge.

As soon as Dana reached the computer, a new image appeared on the screen. Her breath caught in her throat as if the air in her lungs had been turned into thistle. "Jenna!"

On the screen was a clear digital picture of Dana's daughter, her name and address superimposed across the bottom of the screen. The scene changed. Suddenly, hundreds and hundreds of names began to scroll up the screen.

The sound of the sea was overwhelmed by the electronic voice of Control. **"These are the names of every registered sex offender in the United States. In fifteen** minutes your daughter's picture and address will be sent to every one of them."

Thistles became barbed wire cutting deep into Dana's lungs, while other strands wrapped and constricted her heart.

Control continued: "The only thing that can stop this transmission is a computer disc inserted into this machine."

"Where's the disc?" Dana shouted.

Control was nonplussed. "To the left of your current position, on an outcrop in the sea, is a protective bag containing the disc. To your right, on another outcrop, is a second protective bag containing five safety stones. You have fifteen minutes to get one bag, both—or neither. Your time starts now."

"The disc first, the disc," Dana said, hurrying to the edge.

Justin stopped her, holding her by the arm. He pointed to the churning sea, ten feet below. "Sharks," he said as three gray dorsal fins knifed through the water. "Looks like a metal grate has been lowered at the mouth of the cave. If they've been trapped the whole time, then they are dying of starvation."

AIRBORNE
Marine Flight, AK9992

Tucker's brain was on fire. But a good fire, ablaze with ideas, the flames growing brighter with every leap in logic. He wasn't aware how loud his shout had been until he noticed everyone on the plane staring at him. But there was no time to be self-conscious.

He took out his phone and began to dial. If he was right and not just reacting to a healthy imagination, he was on the verge of figuring it all out: the virus, the game, the EMP, even the identity of Control.

Just before landing, Dr. Lorrik had taken a call of his own. Tucker was pulled from his own thoughts by the change in the man's expression. All color left his face, and the whites of his eyes expanded.

In Jamaica they were escorted to a waiting military helicopter that would ferry them to the *John F. Kennedy*. Somewhere over the Caribbean, after invoking Tucker's promise not to report on anything that threatened national security, Dr. Lorrik explained how things had just gotten infinitely worse.

"The CIA intercepted a transmission an hour ago. The Chinese know about the EMP and appear to be assembling their own strike team to land on Vassa Island."

Tucker was staggered. But Lorrik wasn't finished. "Because of that, the president and the Joint Chiefs of Staff feel we can't wait much longer. The island must be sanitized before noon tomorrow. The Navy will open fire and virtually blow Vassa Island off the map. We have less than twenty-four hours."

"They can't. I mean, the Chinese wouldn't be foolish enough to launch an assault with the whole world watching."

"Who is there to be worried about?" Lorrik asked.

"The United States."

"And if the Chinese get the EMP weapon?"

Who should the Chinese worry about if they get an EMP weapon?

"Me," Tucker said. "Me."

34 VASSA ISLAND

The ledge was less than six feet wide. Below, the sea boiled, waves smashing into the cavern walls, sending plumes of white water airward. A fine mist of sea spray covered everything and everyone adding an unnatural heaviness to the air.

"Fish," Dana mumbled. "I'm a Pisces. Pheodora was right. So how do I recover the disc and stones without being eaten alive?"

It was Renee who answered. "By giving them something else to eat!" she screamed.

The butcher knife that had belonged to Brenda Segar, the same knife that had been stolen by Burton Rudyard, was now in Renee's hand. Justin, the closest to her, jerked back in surprise, the blade missing his chest but finding his leg. The knife bit into the muscle.

He screamed in pain, stumbling backward. Renee jerked the blade from his flesh and drew back for another try. Dana was desperate to help, but the ledge was too small, and Justin stood between her and Renee.

The voice of Control exploded in the cave. **"Renee Bellacort, you have broken the rules. You must be punished."**

Tentacles of blue-white electricity lashed out from Renee's choker-cam, stopping her in mid-swing. The flesh on her neck sizzled. Screaming in raw agony, she stumbled backward.

"Renee, watch out," Dana shouted.

The warning came too late. A new scream pierced the cave as Renee tumbled into the churlish sea. The sharks reacted at once. The frothing waters turned red.

Dana had to move quickly. Carefully stepping around Justin, she raced to the left side of the cave. Justin's screaming her name was the last thing she heard before plunging beneath the waves.

Salt water stung her eyes as a white trail of bubbles veiled her face. The current was fierce and powerful. Dana was slammed against the seawall. Her senses were addled; any ability to judge direction vanished. *The disc.* She blinked rapidly to clear her vision. Her feet touching the wall, she kicked off, pushing herself forward and swimming toward what she hoped was the outcrop with the computer disc.

Dana had always been a strong swimmer. Now muscles charged with fear gave her new authority in the water. When her fingers brushed against rock, she grabbed hold, pulling herself up out of the water. The disc was in a clear plastic bag. She snatched it, shoved it into her pants pocket, and looked to her right at the second outcrop.

Twenty feet away the water churned as sharks continued to feed.

Could she reach it? Again she dove into the water, swimming desperately toward the safety stones. Halfway to her prize, something moved beneath her. A shark?

Too far, too far. Everything was too far—the outcrop, the ledge. Dana was trapped.

"Dana, grab hold." An extension cord, uncoiled from beneath the monitor stand, splashed beside her. She caught the cord, and Justin began pulling her from the waves.

U.S.S. *JOHN F. KENNEDY*

The aircraft carrier *John F. Kennedy* was the technological king of the sea. Armed with Sea Sparrow missiles
and three 20mm Phalanx CIWS mounts, it had the
muscle and manpower to make sure it stayed that way.
And it was just one of the ships making up the flotilla enforcing the blockade of Vassa Island. At first glance, the
Kennedy appeared to be the grand example of govern-
mental overkill. But when tempered with the knowledge
that despite this impressive display of blatant power, one
man—a simple fisherman named Foster Merrick—had
escaped, it suddenly seemed inadequate.

The irony of the *Kennedy* enforcing a blockade was
not lost on those old enough to remember 1962 when the
man this ship was named for stood up to the Soviet
Union and blockaded the entire island of Cuba. Now the
goal was not to stand up to a military dictator or a union
of countries. Instead, it was to hold a handful of people
infected with a mysterious virus on two square miles
of land.

In many ways, the lack of a visible enemy made the
mission harder. How do you fight an adversary that's
microscopic?

Add to that the handful of people who knew the truth
about the downed aircraft and the possibility of an EMP
weapon, and the tension was supreme.

So why would the president of the United States let a
damn TV reporter board his ship? the captain wondered.

It was dangerous, bordering on recklessness, and Captain Stroud told the admiral so. But love him or hate him,
the president of the United States was the ultimate authority and the Commander in Chief wanted the reporter
there.

Now, as he stood watching the helicopter, carrying

what he couldn't help but think of as the enemy press,
Stroud was more frustrated than he had ever been.

Twenty minutes later, when he met the reporter, when
he heard the man's incredible request—no, demand!—he
realized his frustration was just beginning.

VASSA ISLAND

Leaving the sea caves, Justin and Dana hurried back
toward the dorm. The disc had worked; the program had
shut down. Dana's daughter was safe. Using his belt as a
makeshift tourniquet, Justin had stopped the bleeding.
Still, a hobbling shuffle was the best he could manage.

Although the rain had stopped, the clouds remained,
casting the island in a cold, unnatural darkness. They
smelled the fire before they saw it. A mass of dark gray
smoke rose on the horizon behind them—a lightning fire.
Moving as fast as possible, they rushed across the slop-
ing landscape, heading toward the island interior.

Justin realized his mistake as they crested a small hill.
The fire was burning in the shape of a V, and they were
caught in a pincer grip.

He paused to get his bearings, drawing on his earlier
exploration of the island for guidance. "This way," he
said leading Dana to a set of rusting railroad tracks. A
corroded mine cart lay on its side nearby. Working together they lifted it onto the tracks and Justin explained
his plan.

"Push the cart as fast as you can, then jump in and hug
the floor. If you're going fast enough, the momentum
should carry you right through the fire and out the other
side."

"No," Dana cried. "I'm not going without you."

The invisible nightmare that had chased Justin
through the darkness of his mind was suddenly there,

revealed and staring him in the face as a predator to prey. The nightmare was about failure and sacrifice.

Justin's grandfather had died a hero in World War II. Justin's father had sacrificed his life in Vietnam to save his unit. And three years ago, Justin's older brother, a cop in Cincinnati, had been killed in the line of duty, saving a group of teenagers.

Selflessness was the Rourke family watchword. Sacrifice, a tradition.

But Justin had a secret—a secret he had kept even from himself. Justin was selfish, always aware of what any given action meant for him personally. It was the reason all of his relationships were destined to die.

Put in the same position as his grandfather, father, or brother, Justin knew he wouldn't act as they had. He didn't believe he could knowingly die for another.

And that guilt, that deference to family, had haunted him throughout his life. During Operation Desert Storm he thought he would face the test, thought he would find out once and for all if he were truly a Rourke. Although he survived harrowing moments, he had never been called on to make the supreme choice.

Until now.

Here, standing on an island in the middle of the Caribbean with a woman he had known less than a week, Justin was faced with the inevitable choice of his life or hers. If he got in the cart she might be able to push it fast enough to hurl him through the flames, but not fast enough to save both of them.

It was time for Justin to choose. "I can't run, can't keep up."

"You can ride, and I'll push."

"Dana, you won't be able to get up enough speed. You have to go. Alone."

"But I . . ."

"Do it for Jenna. Go. Go!"

"What are you saying?" But she knew the answer, even without looking into his eyes. "I love you." The words were almost a shout so she could be heard over the chewing fire. Tears thicker than the smoke obscured her vision. She wiped her eyes before saying it again. "I love you."

Justin embraced her, clutching her with a strength that defied his weakened condition. "I love you, too. I always will."

He kissed her.

Tick, tick, tick . . .

The big clock was ticking, each beat pushing Dana closer to the end.

Tick, tick, tick . . .

"Do it for Jenna," Justin repeated.

With that, she slowly separated from him and firmly grasped the handle of the mine cart. She began pushing as hard and fast as she could. She pushed as she had always pushed, too stupid to know she couldn't beat the odds, too hardheaded to give up.

You do what you have to do, her father's advice sang in her head.

Less than ten feet from the fire, she jumped into the cart and squeezed herself into a ball on the wet, muddy floor.

She could hear the growl of flames, feel the heat through the thin metal as the mining cart shot through the fire. Just as the cart started to slow, when Dana was beginning to wonder if the fire would ever end, it broke free.

The brake was an aged gray timber connected to a rusted sienna shoe around the rear metal wheel. A great fantail of sparks marked her wake as Dana pulled back on the brake with all her might. A simple device, it depended solely on strength and friction to work. Her hair, still wet from the rain and the sea, fluttered like dark flags, the tattered banner of the light brigade still charging, doomed but determined.

Her fingers were white with effort. The screech of metal on metal was earsplitting. Then a new sound: the crack of breaking wood, rotting timber. The brake was snapping.

Still she pulled, ignoring the sounds and the ache and the splinters. Bit by bit the cart slowed and finally came to a standstill. As Dana caught her breath, she looked forward, seeing for the first time what had only been a blur before. The tracks ended less than five feet from where the cart came to rest.

Leaving cart and track behind, she climbed the nearest hill. She sprinted to the top, hoping to see Justin, hoping to see he had miraculously survived. Looking back over the path she had traveled, her heart was pierced by the same barbed wire of emotion that had begun squeezing it in the sea cave.

The entire hillside was ablaze.

The fire had moved faster than she would have imagined, faster than a person with two good legs and a head start could run. There was no escape.

Justin Rourke had sacrificed his life to save her.

35 CARIBBEAN SEA

A storm prevented the camera crew from going directly to the blockade, forcing them to spend the night in

Jamaica. They left at daybreak. It was a little after eight A.M. when they finally reached the ship.

Thirty minutes later Elliot Kay Simon pulled a mask up over his nose and mouth, adjusted the hat to cover as much of his head and forehead as possible, and melted into the crowd. Masks designed to filter out jet fumes were worn by many of the crew and were available throughout the ship. The uniform, actually dingy white coveralls, was stolen from the ship laundry.

He took the metal steps two at a time, moving with the confidence one would expect from a crew member.

Elliot Kay Simon did not know how he was going to get to Vassa Island, or how he was going to save God when he landed. He shouldn't have worried. Once again it was Tucker Thorne who led the way.

"You guys with that crazy reporter?" one of the seamen asked shortly after their helicopter touched down. "You're not going with him are you?"

"With him where?" asked the photographer called Brick.

The sailor pointed to a strait just visible on the horizon. "There! The damn fool wants to go to Vassa Island."

"What? With the virus? That's crazy."

"Oh, it gets worse." The crewman moved closer, dropping his voice to a conspiratorial whisper. "All the ships have been ordered to go hot, and the Sea Sparrows are being moved into their prelaunch positions."

"Hot?" Brick asked. "You mean live ammunition?"

"Yep." The sailor pointed to another ship. "Look at the *Ticonderoga*. The big guns have been moved. My guess? A few hours from now, there won't be a Vassa Island."

An official escort had come for them seconds later and the sailor fell silent, but not before Simon learned that the captain had refused Thorne's request. *No* was not an acceptable answer. God was on that island. Simon had heard Him with his own ears. The same God that had spoken to him all those months ago, the one who told him how to build the bomb and where to plant it to do the greatest damage to the research center.

If the Navy really was about to destroy the island, then Simon had to act now.

It had taken a while to find what he desired. But in the end a sailor with a trusting nature and weak threshold for pain had been more than willing to tell Simon everything he needed to know. Then Simon killed him and stuffed him in a utility closet.

Nice guy, really.

Getting away from the television crew had been as simple as walking away. It was easy to disappear on a ship of five thousand men. Finding The Thorn wasn't a problem. Word of mouth was an effective means of communication aboard any seagoing vessel. And this one was no exception.

Now for the truly inspired part of the plan.

Tucker was waiting for an answer from the president when an odd-looking seaman in a jumpsuit and face mask announced his launch was ready. Tucker was surprised. Had the president spoken directly to the captain or had the captain, fearful of Tucker's threats, relented? The sailor didn't know or care and Tucker wasn't about to give anyone a chance to intercede.

Lorrik had been given access to the ship's massive video room and was monitoring events from there. But Tucker hadn't wanted the distraction. He hadn't seen anything from Vassa Island since leaving Washington, relying instead on the stripped-down, no-frills account from the wire service to keep him updated. The pieces were coming together, logically fitting in his mind like the aberrant shapes of a puzzle.

Shortly after arriving on the ship, he had received a transmission via laptop from the news department: a single TIF file with a digitally altered photograph. Another piece snapped into place.

In its current nonsensical form, the information was not suitable for broadcast. He did, however, share it with Lorrik, who immediately sent a copy of the TIF file to Washington. But it was not enough to stop the bombing. In fact, Admiral Dougherty had argued it was all the more reason to continue with their scorched earth approach.

Tucker had to half trot to keep up with his escort. When he asked the sailor why he was wearing a mask, the man mumbled something about allergies. Climbing down the cargo net to the motorized yellow raft was like climbing down a five-story building—but with swaying and pitching. The raft, though large, felt microscopic next to the mighty carrier.

Tucker found it curious that no one was there to wish him luck or remind him that he was being a fool.

"So how do you drive this thing?" Tucker asked, trying to keep his balance on the bucking craft.

"You don't. I do."

Tucker blinked. "You know where I'm going?"

"Yes, sir." The boat was controlled by a panel built just off the outboard motor. The sailor studied it a moment, then tapped a few buttons. As far as Tucker could tell, nothing happened.

"You do know that your captain thinks this is a suicide mission?" Tucker inquired.

"Yes, sir." The sailor tapped more buttons. The motor roared to life, suddenly turning the blue-green sea into a frothy head of white.

"So why are you doing it?" Tucker pressed.

"It's God's will." The craft lunged forward, throwing Tucker from his seat. As he tried to sit up, he noticed a line of people on the deck behind them.

A little late for a good-bye party. Except they didn't appear to be wishing them luck or waving good-bye. They seemed to be angry.

VASSA ISLAND

Dana was alive. She knew this because she ached too much to be dead. Her muscles were exhausted from fighting an angry sea. Her mind wearied from trying to comprehend the impossible. This Vassa Island hell had lasted just six days, but it felt like a lifetime. She had made friends and watched them die, met adversity and beaten it, fallen in love and lost.

Tick, tick, tick.

And then there were two.

Dana and Nerine slept from exhaustion, not desire. Waking up, neither had the appetite or the will to eat. For one of them it would be her last meal.

Is this the day I die? Dana wondered.

There was little to do but watch the clock and wait, and wait, and wait.

"Someone's coming," Nerine said.

Tucker stepped onto Vassa Island and paused. It was a surreal moment. Even for someone who worked in TV, it could be disconcerting to go to a place that previously existed only in the two-dimensional world of television.

Vassa Island.

He checked the time: 10:54 A.M.—fifty-one minutes before the United States Navy turned this small island into a memory. The path from the docks to the Round

House and dorm was well worn and obvious. He ran, leaving the sailor in the tentative safety of the raft.

Tucker noticed a camera, high in a coconut tree. He waved. The camera turned and followed him. Paradoxically, now that he was here, he knew less about what was happening than the average home viewer did.

The door to the dormitory was open. He stepped inside. The world exploded into a bright bomb burst of static. At first, Tucker thought the Navy had started their assault, but as he fell to the dorm room floor, he realized this was a more localized attack.

Head ringing just as surely as a bell being pelted with a mallet, Tucker pushed himself up from the floor, turned, and screamed. Instinctively his arms went up. He noted the weapon—a two-by-four—as his attacker drew back for another assault.

"Stop, stop!" he yelled. "It's me, Tucker. Tucker Thorne."

Dana paused, board drawn back over her shoulder. "Who?" she asked as she glanced at Nerine. The veterinarian shook her head.

Tucker realized his mistake, and if he hadn't been in such dizzying pain, he would have been amused by his own stupidity. "I'm sorry. You don't know me. I've been watching you so much I feel like we're friends."

"Watching us?" Dana asked. A frown formed between her jewel green eyes. "Control."

"No, *no!*" he shouted, one arm bracing for another swing of the board. "No. Not Control. I'm a reporter with Globe Newschannel."

"A reporter? What are you doing here?" Dana demanded, still suspicious.

"Did you come to rescue us?" Nerine asked, a note of hope rising in her voice. "Have they found a cure for the virus? Is that why the Navy sent you?"

Tucker rubbed the back of his head and winced. "The

Navy didn't exactly send me. I sort of blackmailed them into letting me come."

"You what?" Nerine asked. "You idiot! Now you're contaminated just like us."

Dana tightened her grip on the board. "I'm not buying it. No one would be that stupid. I think he's the one behind all this."

"I am *not* Control," Tucker proclaimed. "But—but I know who is."

36 *KENNEDY* AIRCRAFT CARRIER

"Incredible" had been Lorrik's response when Thorne had explained his theory. The FBI concurred. A full emergency investigation had been launched. That was less than twelve hours ago, and already a half-dozen discoveries had been made, all confirming the reporter's story. But the most damning evidence was the missing person. Enigmatic was one thing, but disappearing was another.

How Thorne made that leap in logic was something Lorrik was still trying to figure out. It was as if he saw the world through a prism, splitting the white light of logic into a rainbow of possibilities.

"One of the contestants is a fraud," Thorne had said.

That someone could so successfully create a new identity—and fabricate a past so capable of fooling the show's producers, the press, and even the government—was astonishing.

An alarm—half whistle, half horn—sounded throughout the ship. An ensign appeared in the doorway of the doctor's cabin. "Dr. Lorrik? The captain wants to see you. Tucker Thorne is on the island, and he's not alone."

"Not alone?"

"No, sir. And we believe the person he's with just murdered one of our crewmen."

VASSA ISLAND

"Harlan Krest," Tucker announced, then crossed his arms and grinned like a master magician who had just completed an astonishing trick.

"Pardon?" Dana asked, confused by the reporter and now by his statement.

"Harlan Krest," Tucker repeated.

"Okay, I'll take billionaire software giants for a hundred, Alex."

Tucker smiled. Justin's face flashed through her mind. The raging beast of sadness she had corralled railed against the fencing.

"Harlan Krest is Control," Tucker said.

This guy is crazy.

Dana slowly raised the board again. Tucker's pupils grew like drops of oil in a puddle of water.

"That's ridiculous," Nerine said, sharing Dana's concern. "Harlan Krest is a billionaire, a philanthropist. His company spans the globe. It's like saying Donald Trump is Elvis. It's ludicrous."

The reporter started to stand. Dana wiggled the board. "I wouldn't do that if I were you."

He sat back down. "Hear me out. Vassa Island is under complete computer control. State-of-the-art everything. Equipment and software that in many cases are not even on the market yet. All of it produced by Krest Technologies."

"So Krest software was used to—what? Run the challenges, work the lights? It's sort of like 'guns don't kill people, people kill people,'" Dana challenged. "It's not the person who built the computer and software who's responsible; it's the person who programmed it."

"What about the helicopter and the jets?" Tucker asked.

"The ones that crashed?" Nerine asked.

"Yes. All three were top of the line. Knocked from the sky, by what the government suspects was an electromagnetic pulse."

"And you think Krest built the weapon," Dana said.

"No. I think it's nonexistent. There is no EMP weapon."

A wet breeze rushed into the room, bringing with it the scent of ozone and rain.

"Those aircraft were equipped with software built by Krest Industries," Tucker explained.

"So you're saying the software malfunctioned?" Nerine asked.

"No. I think it worked perfectly. Just as Harlan Krest intended when he designed it, complete with a hidden back door, allowing him to access and control anything using his technology."

Dana lowered the board. "So he downed the planes—"

"With a touch of the keyboard," Tucker finished. "Just like he changed the orders on the supply shipments to Vassa, and on the construction orders. That's how the fatal challenges were made."

"Why didn't someone notice?" Dana asked. "That's been bugging me since all this started. You would think someone would say, 'Hey, why do they need so many scorpions?' or 'Gee, they want us to trap the sharks in the sea cave. What's up with that?'"

"The creatures were the easy part," Tucker explained. "Just convince the insect wranglers that the scorpions were for show, nothing more. Same with the sharks."

"But the trapdoor that let the scorpions into the dorm. Shouldn't that have sounded an alarm?"

"They didn't know about it. Everyone saw slim pieces of the puzzle and nothing more. No one saw the finished product, how it all fit together. Except for those who actually created the virus. But he took care of that, too. Can I get up now? My butt's numb."

Tucker stood before getting an answer. He rubbed the back of his head then checked his fingers. No blood.

Dana regarded the intruder closely.

Tick, tick, tick. The big clock continued to mark time.

"Let's say I buy this," Dana said. "So what? It doesn't get me off the island. Doesn't cure the virus. So what if Control is a man I've never met?"

"Ah, but you have," Tucker countered. "Not only have you met him; he's still on the island."

KENNEDY AIRCRAFT CARRIER

"Who the hell is that?" the captain demanded, pointing to one of the twelve monitors on the makeshift video wall. It was from here that Lorrik had been surveying the island. "Can you get a better angle?"

Lorrik, who had memorized many of the camera numbers, punched in a different view. A mask covered the man's face. Shortly after the discovery of the murdered seaman, a member of the television crew was reported missing. Since no other bodies were discovered, it was assumed the cameraman was the person who had stolen the raft and taken Tucker Thorne to Vassa Island.

A quick check revealed the man was not who he said he was, leaving his identity and motives a mystery.

Unless . . .

"Captain, I need an immediate line to the White House," Lorrik announced.

The puzzle may be coming together, the doctor reasoned, but Tucker Thorne's life was about to fall apart.

VASSA ISLAND

Dana looked at her watch. "Okay, reporter boy, start explaining and fast."

Tucker nodded, then winced as if his brain were bouncing around his skull like a Ping-Pong ball. "Everyone knows how Harlan Krest is a mystery man."

"A bigger recluse than Howard Hughes," Dana said. "Right, we know."

"It's been years since anyone saw a decent picture of him. That's how he was able to masquerade as one of the contestants. You were right, Dana. Someone was working against you on the island, but it wasn't an accomplice. It was Control."

Nerine gasped.

Tick, tick, tick.

"Who?" Dana demanded.

Tucker reached into his back pocket and removed a folded sheet of paper. "The last known photograph of Harlan Krest was taken when he graduated from college. He was fifteen at the time. A bona fide genius. I had our computer techs back in the newsroom digitally age the photograph."

He handed the paper to Dana. Though black and white it was still recognizable. Her heart caught in her throat.

Looking over Dana's shoulder, Nerine gasped. "Cory. He looks like Cory Nestor."

A tree branch, tumbling in the wind, smashed against

the window. The report sounded like a hammer. All three jumped.

Tucker took a deep breath. "That's right. Cory Nestor is Control."

Dana looked up from the picture, half expecting the world to be as black and white as the photograph.

"With Krest's abilities and assets, it was easy for him to invent the persona of Cory Nestor. And now he's our ticket out of here—the one person who will have the cure to the virus." Tucker raked his hair with his fingertips. "One more thing, at a quarter to twelve, the Navy is going to launch a scorched earth attack on this island. We've got to find Nestor, get the cure, and get the hell out of here before that."

Dana turned and headed from the Round House. Tucker and Nerine scrambled to catch up with her.

"You know where he is?" Tucker asked.

"Yeah, I know where he is, but he's not going to tell us anything." She kept walking as the wet air licked her face. "He's dead."

"I know. I read that on the wire. In fact, I anticipated it. I don't know the details, but I'm positive he faked it. All part of the plan. Get rid of the false Cory Nestor identity, then return to the world as Harlan Krest."

"I don't think so," Dana said as they entered the Round House. "I'm no doctor but that looks like dead to me."

Cory's body still lay on the cold floor, the skin gray as a bullet, his head caved in at the side.

Tucker stumbled back. "No. It's not possible. It can't be."

"Believe me, I know how you feel. I've been living with the impossible every day for the last six days."

"You don't understand. Cory has to be Control. Has to."

Dana inhaled deeply. The air was noticeably cooler. Another storm was near. "If he was, then Control is dead."

Tucker was shaking his head, staring at the body as if witnessing the birth of an alien life-form. "But the wire, the breakdown I got on events said Renee Bellacort suffered a shock from her choker-cam, causing her to fall in with the sharks. No way a computer program would know when to do that. If Cory didn't kill Renee, then who did?"

"That would be me."

They turned as one, looking at the jungle side entrance to the Round House. Standing in the doorway, holding a gun, was Cory Nestor.

37 VASSA ISLAND

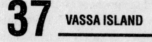

All the air was sucked from the room.

Dana watched with incredulity as Cory walked over and looked down at what appeared to be his own body. There were tears in his eyes. His body—the one that was still living—trembled.

"Zodiac!" Tucker shouted, the word so odd and out of place that it sounded like a car alarm. "Zodiac, zodiac, zodiac . . ."

The living Cory looked up from the dead Cory and smiled. "You are a fascinating creature, Mr. Thorne."

"And you are a Gemini," Tucker said.

The new Cory offered a slight bow. "Bravo."

Gemini, the sign of the—"You're a twin," Dana exclaimed.

"But raised as an only child. My mother, our mother, put us up for adoption as infants. I was adopted into the Krest family, immediately accorded wealth and status, which I ultimately tripled when I created Krest Technologies. My brother was not as fortunate. You were wrong on one point, Mr. Thorne. Cory Nestor was not a fabricated identity. He was very much a real person, but raised in less auspicious surroundings. And even though he shared my genius, he lacked my confidence."

He looked back down at the body. The sadness in his eyes seemed genuine. "I was fifteen when I found him, thanks to the Internet. It proved harder, however, to find our mother—who had gone to considerable effort to remain undetected. But with two genius-level IQs on the job, it was only a matter of time."

Thunder cracked somewhere on the unseen horizon.

"Timing is so peculiar, isn't it?" Krest said. The gun held the three in place as surely as iron chains. "You'll like this, Mr. Thorne, being the media whore that you are. Cory and I found our mother on television. Five years ago, on the eighteenth of November, to be exact."

Krest paused, as if the day and date held some special meaning.

"Oh, my God." Tucker exhaled.

Krest smiled and tilted his head to the right. "Again, I'm impressed Mr. Thorne. That was a rather famous night in the history of reality television."

Five years ago, reality television. Jenna would have just started preschool. "*True Life*?" Dana guessed. "The final broadcast."

"Oh, it wasn't meant to be final. There was still a good month to go in the program, but after what happened—well."

"Your mother was Sherine Beauvant?" Tucker said. "From *True Life*?"

"And her fame continues," Krest snarled. It looked out of place on the face Dana knew as Cory Nestor's. "You have to understand, until that show she had experienced a rather difficult life, working dozens of menial and thankless jobs. A lot like you, Miss Kirsten. So when she got a chance to be on a network television show, she jumped at it, and quickly became the star. You see, my mother was beautiful, stunning really, and despite failing at job after job there was one thing she was quite good at—sex."

Dana remembered now. Sherine—the seductress. No one, it seemed was beyond her wiles.

"Including the minister," Dana said aloud, making no attempt to hide her disgust.

Krest made a face. "Really, Miss Kirsten, coming from you isn't that a bit hypocritical?"

Dana felt the blood race to her cheeks. "Justin and I weren't married. Unlike the minister."

"Yes, he was married. But after weeks of smoldering flirtations the minister proved to be as weak as all men. It was only after making love that my mother pointed out the camera he had failed to see. And she laughed at his horror when he realized he had just committed adultery on live television."

"So the first time you saw your mother was the night she caused a man to commit suicide?" Nerine asked softly, even sympathetically.

"That's correct. And since I had found her in secret, there was no one I could share my grief with but my brother. That suicide almost ended reality television. Almost. But like a nasty virus, it came back bigger and stronger than ever. And this, *24/7*, is the worst of the worst. When the network contacted my company about the software, my brother and I saw it as the perfect opportunity for revenge."

"Revenge?" Tucker asked. "Revenge on whom? For what?"

"For murder, Mr. Thorne." Krest's eyes were dark slits. "My mother was chastised and ostracized by the very public that made her famous. Two months after the show, she killed herself with an overdose."

Dana swallowed, trying to keep the hostility out of her voice. "But why us? We had nothing to do with that show or your mother. Why seek revenge on us?"

Krest smiled again. But the gesture was not one of good humor. "You? No, you and the others are just the unfortunate victims. Fodder as it were. No, my revenge is on the audience."

Krest pointed at the main camera, holding his arm out as if trying to reach through the lens and pull the viewers through the tiny apparatus. "All of those who make voyeurism socially acceptable."

"How does this punish viewers?" Dana demanded.

Krest closed his eyes. For a second the thought of rushing him fluttered through Dana's mind. Then he opened his eyes, and the moment was gone.

"Ah, but that's the fun part," Krest explained. "Making people face the worst in themselves. You saw the numbers. Would you, would anyone have guessed that that many people would take part, would become accomplices to murder? That that many people would act to condemn a fellow human being?"

Dana was silent, his words striking home.

"By creating this scenario I created a set of circumstances where the American public was given the choice to participate or not. Effectively holding a mirror up to society. Forcing them to see the reality, see the truth about themselves." Krest fanned the air with the gun as he talked.

"But now it's over," Tucker said. "Give us the cure to the virus. Your experiment is finished. And so are you."

Krest raised the gun. "Yes and no, Mr. Thorne. The experiment is over, but I'm not. Not by a long shot. Do you know how much money I have stashed around the world? I leave behind the moiling life of Harlan Krest, never my real name anyway, and am resurrected under a new guise, a new life. Unfortunately the same cannot be said about you."

With a speed and grace that surprised even him, Tucker dashed across the room, grabbing the billionaire's gun hand and smashing him against the white stucco wall in the same gesture. Krest *oomphed* as the air was knocked from his chest. Tucker kneed him in the groin, then secured the gun.

Shaking, breathing in quick spurts, Tucker stepped back and raised the weapon. The barrel was aimed at Krest. Fear, running the length of Tucker's arm, caused the barrel to shake like wind chimes. "Okay, now you're going to tell us where it is. Where's the cure for this virus?"

Krest wheezed, his head bent, a hand on his crotch.

"Now!" Tucker screamed again. "Tell us or I swear I'll kill you—Cory or Harlan or whoever the hell you are."

A gunshot reverberated through the small Round House. For a second Tucker thought he was the cause. Then a jagging pain began cutting across his right arm. He dropped the gun. He gripped his arm. His hand quickly became soaked in blood.

"His name is God," said a voice behind him. Tucker turned. Standing in the doorway, dressed in a Navy jumpsuit, was the final piece of the puzzle. "And my name is Elliot Kay Simon."

"Merciful heavens," muttered the president of the United States. His voice transmitted thousands of miles and across the sea to the aircraft carrier—and to Dr. Lorrik. "Thorne was right."

"But he didn't expect this," Lorrik said.

"Keep me posted." The president hung up.

"Elliot Kay Simon?" the captain whispered. "The nut who blew up that research center?"

"The Krest Technologies Research Center to be exact," Lorrik added.

"But I thought he was dead."

"He was, but he got better." One more for Tucker Thorne. Lorrik would never look at a crossword puzzle the same way again.

No one had been able to figure out why Elliot Kay Simon had targeted the Krest facility, particularly since it was Harlan Krest who had paid for much of Simon's psychological care. Now Lorrik knew why.

At Tucker's suggestion, Lorrik had the FBI check out the boat Simon had been living on prior to the bombing. A series of tiny, state-of-the-art speakers, easy to miss unless you were specifically looking for them, were discovered throughout. With access to Simon's drug therapy, it would have been simple to convince the already delusional man that he was hearing the voice of God.

If he were captured, Simon's ranting would underscore his mental disability. Dying in a suicide bombing was even better. But Simon had proved more inventive than anyone, including the FBI, had anticipated, by substituting a homeless man for himself and escaping from authorities.

Once Krest left for Vassa Island the voice of God was silent. Simon thought he was dead until he heard Cory Nestor, Krest's twin, on television.

After hanging up the phone, the captain returned.

"Captain, surely now you see that we have to post-pone the bombing."

The captain, whose face Lorrik had originally thought far younger than his post would suggest, now seemed far older. "I'm sorry, Doctor. That was Admiral Dougherty. The mission is a go. We start the shelling in"—he looked at his watch—"in five minutes."

VASSA ISLAND

"Follow the stars and find your heart," Simon muttered. "The soul is nested in the signs . . ."

". . . the glory of the pureblind night, fate of the twelve so intertwined . . . ," Krest responded.

The new God. The voice Simon had heard in the hospital and on the boat. The glorious voice that led him to destroy the sinful Krest Technologies building. God was dead, or so he thought until he heard that magnificent voice coming from his own TV. And then he knew, like Zeus of old, the new God had taken human form and now walked among them. But humanity meant vulnerability. And the evil ones had taken him.

"Simon," the new God said, blessing Simon's name by passing it through his lips.

"I am here. I heard you. I knew you were calling to me and so I am here to save you."

A joy as bright as any beam to ever slip from the sun radiated from the new God. He glowed. How could the others keep their eyes open in the face of his marvelous glow?

". . . eternal circle Cerberus life, cusp and house and pure divine . . . ," Tucker said.

The Thorn knew the words. Spoke the words. How? How?

"It's a poem," The Thorn said. "And not a particularly good one. Written in the 1930s by Erikson Stronoff."

"The words?"

"Ann Frances Robbins knows the truth. You said that to me earlier. I did some checking. Ann Frances Robbins was Nancy Reagan's astrologer."

"Robbins?"

"Lao-tzu was another name you mentioned. He's another important figure in the history of astrology. Took me a while to put it together—that and the Stronoff poem. Then imagine my surprise when I'm watching 24/7 and I hear Cory Nestor quoting from the very same obscure poem."

The new God read Simon's troubled thoughts as surely as if they were typed across Simon's forehead. "Evil often speaks with a civil tongue."

Confusion gone.

"I should kill him now." Simon aimed the weapon at Tucker's head.

"No, wait," the new God commanded. "I'm not finished with him just yet."

The scorching pain in his arm kept him grounded, tethered to the present. Luckily the bullet had only grazed him. The bleeding would stop soon, but the pain screamed on. Tucker pushed it from his thoughts. Now, more than ever, he needed his wits about him.

Elliot Kay Simon had been the final piece of the puzzle—a piece Tucker had not anticipated finding its way to Vassa Island. Now he realized why the seaman had worn the mask. It was Simon who had driven the raft. Tucker sniffed the air. Scent was a powerful mnemonic. Now he recognized the faint odor of aftershave, the same aftershave he had smelled in the warehouse and in his apartment and then hotel room. It had been Simon all along. How he made it to the aircraft carrier remained a mystery.

A feisty gust of wind rushed through the open door, tossing Tucker's hair like an overeager stylist. Harlan Krest picked his gun up from the floor, then smoothed his shirt with the palm of his hand. "Tell me, Thorne. Do you really know who this is?" He pointed to Simon.

Curiosity. Krest's curiosity was all that was keeping Tucker alive.

"He's a murderer. A sick, sick man. Simon and I are well acquainted."

Elliot Kay Simon smiled, oddly pleased by the recognition. "I stuck a bomb to his hands. SuperGlue." He sang the last word. "But he didn't die. That was when I was sure he was evil."

The barrel of the gun seemed impossibly large and growing by the moment.

"Interesting, but you can't possibly know his part in all this," Krest challenged.

"To destroy the Krest Technologies Research Center and with it, any evidence of the creation of the virus. Once the game began the researchers would have recognized their own work. Your cover would have been blown."

"Blown," Krest repeated. "Interesting word choice."

The barrel of the gun was now a tunnel, a long shaft leading to the permanent darkness. Simon's wet, protruding eyes quivered in their sockets.

"Well, it's been fun," Krest began. "Kill them. Kill them all, Mr. Simon."

There was a sound, somewhere between a whistle and squeal, seconds before the first shell hit. The Round House floor, ceiling, and walls undulated madly. The ceiling bowed inward. Plaster rained down in a thick white downpour.

"Time's up," Tucker said.

The sterilization of Vassa Island had begun.

Another shell exploded nearby.

Sound was now a physical thing, a rolling avalanche consuming them all. Elliot Kay Simon, who had been standing in the open doorway, was thrown across the room, where he bounced off the Vault and tumbled to the floor. The reader board swayed in a wide arc, then fell, crashing into the Vault. The air was whitewashed with cloying plaster, dirt, and debris, making Dana's eyes as useless as her ears.

Another shell. The floor beneath her feet convulsed, knocking Dana to her hands and knees.

"Get out of here." Tucker's words were tinny and distorted, but understandable.

Dana began to crawl, hoping she was heading toward one of the two exits. Her hand touched something. Cory Nestor. She recoiled from the dead man's body. A thought occurred to her. Clenching her jaw and striving to keep her revulsion at bay, she searched the corpse until she found what she was looking for.

Another shell. Closer still. The ceiling began to crumble. Bits of wood and stone pelted her back. A whirl of dust temporarily cleared the air revealing the shattered form of what had been the Vault, now cracked and open.

Open.

Dana scrambled from the building as the north wall, where Harlan Krest had been standing, collapsed—burying brother with brother, together in death unlike in life. Something exploded fifteen feet away.

"Head for the docks," Tucker said, his words still distorted by the ringing in her ears. She saw Nerine, rattled but alive. White plaster dust covered them all.

"Simon?" Dana asked.

"Still inside, with Krest."

Another explosion, louder than the rest but farther away. "There's a motorized raft at the dock. Take it and get away from the island."

"What about you?" Dana screamed, raising her voice above the barrage.

"I've got to find the cure. I've got an idea where it may be. I'll get it, then head for the sea. Look for me in the water."

A slow, rasping screech cut through the air as buildings crumbled.

"Oh, my God," Nerine shouted. "Run, run, run . . ."

"Which way, which way?" Dana screamed, lost and confused. The place that had been their home, their prison, no longer resembled itself. Vassa Island was dying.

"This way," Nerine said, dashing down a faint trail now carpeted with rubble.

From the corner of her eye Dana saw flames racing through the forest, yellow and red clawing at the sky. Just like the fire that had claimed Justin.

A tree cracked, falling on the trail between the two.

Dana leaped, imagining the tree as a hurdle on her high school track, clearing the trunk cleanly. She hit the ground without breaking stride. Nerine turned a corner, then stopped so quickly Dana almost plowed into her.

"Look!" Nerine shouted. The dock and surrounding buildings were burning. A shell had struck the raft, igniting the fuel supply.

Stupid, stupid, stupid, was Tucker's internal mantra. He wasn't a hero. He was too smart to be a hero. At least, that had always been his excuse.

Okay, so they need the cure or the Navy would gun them down, even though Tucker was sure the virus was not contagious.

"The CDC has not determined that," Lorrik had argued.

"But I saw a mouse," Tucker explained. Amazing how seeing one little rodent in a warehouse had told him so much. "The mouse was from the research center where the virus was designed. Even if it wasn't infected, it would have been around other mice that were. If the virus were contagious, the mouse would be dead—not running around weeks later with no vaccine, no symptoms."

"Maybe he was never exposed," Lorrik had said. "There's no way to know for sure."

But Tucker knew—the same way he had known other things. He felt it. Like knowing the answer to a math ___blem without showing the work. And now that ___ ___as telling him where to find the cure.

___ ___story Radio Building was wounded. A ___ ___hole, ___ ___ enough to accommodate an ATV was ___ ___ ___. The extent of structural damage was impossible to tell. Tucker knew the entire building could collapse like a deck of cards at any moment. Ignoring the scream of shells and man-made earthquakes, he began to climb the stairs.

Stupid, stupid, stupid.

The building rumbled. The stairs swayed. He continued to climb. So far, he had been lucky, extremely lucky. But the odds were against him being right again. Still, with Krest gone, it was their only chance.

His hunch was based on numbers. Using information from the newsroom, Tucker had mapped what he called the "rolling dead spot" areas where the cameras would suddenly stop working, only to resume ten to twenty minutes later. He now knew this was how Harlan Krest masked his presence on the island. Although the dead spots varied, three locations came up repeatedly. When overlaid on a map of the island the blackouts made a perfect trail to the Radio Building.

The Radio Building, like the others, had cameras on every floor. But as with many things on the island, appearances were deceiving. Blueprints said it was four stories tall, but by measuring it in a photograph, using a doorframe as a reference point, Tucker had discovered that it was tall enough for five.

Tucker was betting this was the secret location from which Harlan Krest played Control.

Climbing the stairs as fast as he could, he passed the fourth floor and kept going until he came out—on the roof?

He went back down to the fourth, climbed up more slowly, and finally reached the roof. What was he missing? Peering down the stairwell, he did a quick count of the stairs. There were twice as many steps between the fourth floor and the roof as between the third floor and the fourth—a fact masked by the design of the stairs.

But how do you access it?

He climbed back down, counting the steps until he reached the approximate halfway point. There was no landing. The stairs continued down. Tucker banged against the wall, thumping until he heard a hollow echo. He pushed. The wall panel fell away.

Inside was an exact duplicate of the television control room, but with three times the monitors. From here Harlan Krest could see everything. Everything. Six of the monitors carried network broadcasts. A radio sat next to the main console. Whatever jamming device was blocking signals to the island, it was not at work here. Tucker had a way to communicate.

But at the moment he had nothing to report. He searched the room. Where would it be?

An explosion slapped the building, hurling everything to the right. Tapes, editing bays, and computer monitors crashed to the floor. Tucker held on to a heavy table to keep from falling. The room was too big to search inch by inch, and he was out of time. Another explosion. Again the building shook. The lights winked on and off.

The answer could be anywhere.

Something caught his eye. Hanging on the east wall was a five-by-ten poster depicting the twelve signs of the zodiac. Pens, pencils, and videocassettes crunched beneath his feet as he hurried across the room and ripped down the poster. Taped to the wall was a yellow-and-black computer disc labeled VIRUS SOLUTION.

Tucker knew squat about radios. He pressed the button marked TRANSMIT and yelled for help. "Hello? Anybody there? This is Tucker Thorne. I'm on the island. Stop the shelling. I've got the cure. Hellooo?"

The building rattled, harder this time. The lights flickered and stayed off for several seconds. If he lost power, he would lose the radio. Then the lights winked back on.

The radio sputtered. "This is Captain Stroud. Where are you, Thorne?"

"Radio Building. Captain, I've got the cure. It's on a computer disc. Stop the shelling."

Static boiled from the speakers. "Do you have access to a computer?"

A computer? There was one next to the radio. A star field screen saver filled the monitor. He tapped a key. The stars were replaced by one of the sites for 24/7. It was wired to the Internet.

"Yes, yes, I do," he shouted into the radio.

The captain gave him a Web address. The bombing would not be stopped until the cure was received and verified. Frustrated, but without a choice, Tucker did as requested. His wounded arm throbbed as his fingers played across the keys. He clicked Send, then waited.

The rumbling thunder of bomb bursts seemed to have lessened. Were they stopping or just targeting another part of the island?

From his conversations with Captain Stroud, Tucker knew if the ships opened up completely, Vassa Island would be gone by now. The captain had to be going about the attack slowly and methodically—buying them time under the guise of efficiency, doing as much as he could without directly disobeying orders.

The radio crackled. "Tucker?" It was Dr. Lorrik.

"I'm here. Have they got the cure?"

"Yes, but they're still trying to verify it. Are you in the Radio Building?"

"Yeah, I found Krest's hideaway. For God's sake, tell them to stop the bombing, Doc."

"Tucker listen to me. Elliot Kay Simon is not dead. Do you understand? Simon is alive and he's heading your way."

Simon?

* * *

At the marina, the fire reached the stored supplies of diesel fuel. The building went up in a thunderclap of flames and smoke. A spark ignited oil that darted across the water, setting the very sea on fire. The air was astringent and constricting.

Dana's eyes burned and her nostrils and throat were raw. "That's it then," she said. "We're trapped."

Something moved through the swirling black-and-gray smoke, coming from the island interior, moving out of the acidic cloud like a vision in a dream.

"Not necessarily," said Justin Rourke.

Elliot Kay Simon.

The name was a dagger in Tucker's mind.

Something detonated inside the building. The floor tilted. Lights flickered, went out, and remained out. Tucker was in the dark. He stood in place not sure what to do, where to go.

The lights blinked, revealing the room in flashing snapshots. Tucker held his breath. The lights returned.

". . . ker? Tucker? Tucker?" Lorrik's voice screamed from the radio.

He keyed the mike. "Here, Doc. How much longer?"

"Get out of there now."

"No argument here. But they've got to stop the bombing."

". . . Tucker? Simon's in the building."

Fewer than half the monitors had come back on after the last blackout. But one revealed the building stairwell and Elliot Kay Simon climbing the steps two at a time.

"Tucker, the building's on fire. The whole thing's about to go up. Get the hell out of there—now!"

Beaten, battered, burned, and hobbled, Justin stumbled from the smoke. He was covered in soot and dirt. Dried blood encrusted his right leg. Blisters dappled his hands and arms. He was the most beautiful thing Dana Kirsten had ever seen.

She ran to him, afraid to blink for fear he would vanish, disappearing into the ether like a desert mirage. But he was real, grimacing in pain at her touch, then all but falling into her arms.

"Nerine," she yelled.

The vet was already taking Justin's left side while Dana supported the right. "How? How did you escape?"

"Later." His voice was little more than a rasp. "Got to hurry."

"Where?"

"The helicopter. The satellite and radio systems were destroyed, but the rest is still intact. Or at least was."

They moved as fast as possible. Justin's head wobbled from side to side. His breath was ragged.

"Come on Justin," Nerine coaxed as they hurried down the path. "Stay with us. Don't pass out. Focus! Tell us how you survived."

"Survive. Until I saw Dana, I wasn't sure I had." He choked. His consciousness was tethered for the moment by the question. "The ground. Porous rock. Remember the warnings about sinkholes."

Dana did. "The ground is so porous that sinkholes are a problem after a big rain. And there was a big storm just before the fire."

Justin continued, "I created my own sinkhole, burrowed into the ground like a mole. Almost suffocated. Must've passed out. Don't remember much till the shells started falling."

"Amazing," Nerine said.

Dana silently agreed. Justin was alive. But could he fly in his condition?

The helicopter sat on the helipad, remarkably unscathed

while all around it the jungle burned and buildings crumbled. Rocks and earth took to the sky, launched by massive explosions.

Justin cried out in pain as they helped him into the pilot seat. His eyes fluttered, but remained open. His hands worked the helicopter controls as if operating independently of his scarred and pummeled body.

The motor coughed once, twice, then caught. The massive propeller began to turn. Faster, faster, faster. "Hang on," Justin shouted.

Smoke and dirt swirled around them, caught in the powerful vortex created by the rotors, obscuring their view. Dana felt like Dorothy in the heart of a Kansas twister. The aircraft shook, then slowly rose.

Dana looked into the swirling dust cloud, half expecting to see the Wicked Witch of the West on their trail.

Tucker needed a weapon. He grabbed something small from a workbench and continued to look. Nothing. He took a portable radio from a charger and clipped it to his belt.

With fire flooding the ground floors, hiding was not an option. There was only one way to go—up.

The metal staircase shook as Elliot Kay Simon climbed. Tucker hurried onto the roof, looking for some way to lock the door. But the only thing on the tar roof was the radio tower. Even with the door shut, he could hear Simon's approach.

Only one chance. Using the item he had taken from the workbench, Tucker moved quickly, then with a leap, he grabbed the highest rung he could reach on the tower. And he began to climb.

The door banged open. Elliot Kay Simon stepped onto the roof. Tucker continued climbing, racing up the metal struts, climbing into the smoke-filled sky.

Below him, Simon bellowed. "Killed God. You killed him—again."

Tucker kept climbing.

"God-killer," Simon screamed, rushing to the tower and grabbing the lower rungs. "You won't get away this time. Not this time."

Tucker stopped climbing, looked down at his pursuer, and smiled. "Neither will you."

Simon roared, a bestial sound with no hint of humanity. He started to climb, then stopped. His round eyes bulged larger than usual—fury changing to confusion. He couldn't move his hands.

Tucker held out the small item he had taken from the workbench. "SuperGlue," he said. "What a dilemma. Building's on fire and you're glued to the tower."

Simon screamed, "I'll die, but you'll die, too." Then he laughed, a hair-raising cackle that sounded like burning flesh.

Tucker heard a low rumbling then a *shoosh*. Suddenly the rising smoke was pushed away. A rope ladder fell from the sky. He looked up. Nerine Keleman was hanging out of the open door of the helicopter, motioning for him to climb.

The large, sliding door slammed shut. "Go, go, go," screamed Nerine.

The helicopter dipped to the right and up. As it rose, the Radio Building was revealed in full. The fire had moved more quickly than Tucker had realized. The structural integrity of the building was compromised. It began to crumble—imploding like a deflated balloon.

Elliot Kay Simon was gone.

Something whizzed past the helicopter. The machine shook in its aerial wake. Tucker saw the pilot for the first time. "Justin Rourke?"

Dana was in the copilot seat, watching the pilot more than the sky.

"Back from the dead," Justin croaked.

"Not for long," Nerine said. "If we try to escape, the Navy will shoot us down."

"Stall," Tucker shouted. "I've found the cure to the virus. As soon as it's verified the shelling stops and we go home."

"Yes," Dana shouted. Justin offered a croaking shout. Nerine grabbed Tucker by the face and kissed him full on the mouth, then pulled away and blushed with embarrassment.

"Keep us alive, Justin," Tucker said, smiling, his eyes still on Nerine. "For God's sake, keep us alive."

Part the Red Sea. Turn water into wine. Keep us alive, Justin. All three had one thing in common: they depended on a miracle.

Justin clenched his jaw as he pushed the helicopter to climb. His vision was blurred by pain. His hands felt like catcher's mitts. Twice the helicopter had dipped without his intending it to. A spasm in his good leg, muscles exhausted from overcompensating for the bad, had caused him to push on the rudder pedal.

Keep us alive, Justin.

"You can do it. I know you can." Dana Kirsten was wearing the matching headset to Justin's. Her voice, soft and amazingly confident, soothed his nerves like a balm.

"How long?" he asked the man they had saved from the building. A reporter, Dana had said. How the hell had a reporter ended up on the island? "How long?" he repeated.

"Not sure. The solution was on a computer disc. I sent it by e-mail. Any second now."

Justin nodded, blinked sweat from his eyes, and

scanned the sky. The fact that they were still alive meant the Navy was holding back. That was something anyway. If he could just find a safe cruising altitude without crossing the trajectory of any incoming shells, maybe they could wait it out. Yeah, right, and afterward Justin would make a few attempts at walking on water.

He moved the yoke forward, stabilizing the craft as he tried to get his bearings. He was flying by instinct, an instinct honed by years of experience, both war zone and barnstorming. As they rose and headed out to sea, the island fell below and behind them, shrouded in an uneven cloak of smoke and haze.

Something pinched his arm. He yelped and turned just as Dana removed the bee-sting injector. "The vaccine? How did you get it?"

"One of the bomb bursts opened up the Vault." She handed a second injector to Nerine.

"Is it twelve already?" Nerine asked.

"No. We still have eight minutes. No sense waiting till the last second, you know, in case we're busy when noon rolls around."

"Good thinking. Where's yours?"

Dana didn't answer.

"Dana, where's your vaccine?"

She waited until Nerine had used her injector. "I could only get two out of the Vault."

"You what? Why, Dana, why?"

"Without you, we're all dead. Besides, Tucker found the solution. And I still have another card up my sleeve."

Justin heard the sound of static, but the radio was ruined. Then he realized it was coming from behind him.

"Captain Stroud to Tucker Thorne, do you read me?"

"I hear you, Captain. The virus?" Tucker asked, speaking into the portable radio he had taken with him.

"It was a virus cure—"

"Yes!" Tucker cheered.

Justin didn't share his excitement. He had spent enough time in the military to recognize that a *but* was coming.

"But—" the captain continued. "It's the solution to the computer virus. A way to stop Krest's little backdoor booby trap in the software. I'm sorry son, we can't let you leave the island."

Away from the smoke Justin could see the Naval blockade. And something else. A spot on the horizon moving perpendicular to the chopper. "Oh, God."

"What is it?" Dana whispered.

"An F/A-18 Hornet, a fighter jet, and it's coming for us."

39 VASSA ISLAND

Justin pulled back the yoke, reining in the powerful machine. The craft pitched to the right, then plunged.

"Justin?" Dana screamed.

The sea, a scintillating blue in the tropical sun, filled their view as the helicopter dived for the water.

"Justin?" Dana repeated.

An F/A-18. Mother of God. Even in a military helicopter, the odds of beating a jet with thirteen thousand pounds of armament were slim.

The jet could take them out from two miles away with a single missile. In a civilian chopper, with no weapons, no antimissile systems, nothing offensive or defensive, they didn't have a prayer.

"Justinnnnn!" Dana's scream was magnified through the headsets, stabbing him like a spike through the brain. But there was no time to explain. He jerked the yoke back at the last conceivable second, the right landing strut actually dipping into the water.

Flying less than five feet above the waves, they shot forward moving with every ounce of speed the machine was capable of, hurling back to Vassa Island, hurling back to hell.

Hell was the correct analogy. What it had been emotionally and psychologically it now was physically, as hungry flames raced through the island beneath roiling clouds of black-gray smoke.

They were coming in from the east side. The island was steep here. A twenty-foot cliff separated land from sea, fifteen feet above the helicopter. Justin glanced behind him. His stomach was a pretzel. Even without sophisticated warning devices and tracking instruments, he could recognize the contrail of a missile. The F/A-18 had fired on them.

"Is that a missile?" Tucker called from the back.

"Yeah," Justin answered.

"Do something."

"I'm working on it."

The missile was moving at unimaginable speed, guided by one of the most sophisticated tracking systems ever created and capable of overcoming a dozen antimissile devices. Not that it mattered. Justin didn't have one, let alone a dozen.

"That's not just a missile; it's a heat seeker." He pulled the yoke back. The chopper rose even with the island. A pure wall of writhing flames filled their view.

"Justin!" Dana wailed again.

"Hold your breath, everybody," Justin shouted as the helicopter flew into the flames.

Hell would look like this, Dana realized. Fire everywhere. A squirming, twisting thing, alive and angry. Flames—red, yellow, orange, and every imaginable hue in between—surrounded every inch of the machine. Any second the fuel tanks would explode, just like in the movies. Soon their fight would be over.

If she went straight to hell, Dana realized she would never notice the change.

And then they were out. Smoke that had seemed so oppressive before now felt like a shower of icy spring water.

An explosion!

The helicopter lunged forward, pushed by a pressure wave. The nose dipped dangerously toward the ground. Groaning with pain and effort, Justin pulled back the yoke and worked the pedals. The helicopter wobbled then responded.

"What happened?" Dana asked.

"The new heat-seeking missiles are designed to ignore random heat signatures, but being engulfed in a forest fire can overwhelm any system." The chopper bucked, jerking them in their seats.

"Thermals," Justin shouted. "Updrafts from the fire." The craft swung violently left, then right, then left again, like a dog shaking a rag. Justin fought to keep them in the air. Each move, each bump was a jolt to his battered body, sending quakes of pain through his system. The nose dropped. The helicopter hurled toward the convulsing fire below. The collision alarm squalled. Warning lights blazed like embers.

Sweat cascaded down his forehead, pooling in his eyes. But he couldn't take his hands off the yoke. He blinked frantically, trying to clear his vision. Dana wiped his face and mopped his forehead.

Again the powerful machine responded. They were borne away from the gorging flames. Then they flew into smoke and, finally, clear sky.

"Yeah!" Tucker and Nerine cheered from the back compartment.

"We're not out of the woods yet," Justin warned, as the helicopter continued to rise: one hundred, one hundred and ten, one hundred and twenty. "Everybody, look for that jet. Find out where he is so we can go the other way."

"There are binoculars back here," Tucker said. "I'll use 'em."

The fire had reached the television transmitter tower. The base was consumed in flames. It was leaning alarmingly to the west.

"There he is," Tucker shouted. "To the south. And above us. Pretty far away. I can just make him out with the binoculars. I don't think he sees us . . . Uh-oh."

Justin looked but could see little more than specks on the horizon. "What? Another missile?"

"No. Two missiles."

Two missiles.

No weapons. Defensive or offensive. They couldn't risk the fire again. They had barely made it the first time.

"Justin?" Dana's voice registered urgency. "Shouldn't we be doing something?"

Dana. Like a pulsing light in storm fog, she was his beacon, his guide. Now, when she needed him most, he couldn't help her.

"Justin?" she repeated.

"Nothing. I'm all out of tricks."

"Bull," she said, her voice strong and confident. "You're the best damn pilot there is. They've got missiles, but we've got you."

"Dana, I can't. It's impossible."

"If we go down, we go down fighting. Come on, hotshot, show off for the girls."

"If I could put something between us and the missile,

but it's not like something is going to fall out of the sky at two hundred feet up. Unless . . ."

It was crazy. Impossible. Their only option.

"I see them," Nerine shouted. "They're coming, they're coming."

"Hang on." The helicopter dipped to the left then swung around and shot off to the north.

Timing was everything.

The tower, reaching into the smoke-scarred sky, wobbled, rocked by explosions. Then like a checkmated king it began to fall.

"They're here, they're here!" Tucker screamed.

Now.

Justin thrust the copter forward, pushing it to its maximum speed. In his peripheral vision, he could see the tower falling toward the flaming earth. The helicopter speeding on an intercept course.

The tower grew large in their vision. Dana gasped. Flying on instinct alone, Justin dropped their altitude another twenty feet, not letting up on the speed. Too fast, they would hit the tower; too slow, and the missiles would get them.

The helicopter shot beneath the falling tower, metal missing blades with less than a foot to spare. The missiles hit, ripping the tower into shards of metal.

The pressure wave was twice as strong this time, like trying to surf a tsunami with an ironing board.

U.S.S. *JOHN F. KENNEDY*

"Hawkfire One to Nest. We have detonation, both missiles."

On the bridge of the massive ship Dr. Lorrik felt his heart drop.

Dead. They were all dead.

"Roger that, Hawkfire. Can you confirm kill?"

"Hard to tell. There's a lot of debris, smoke, and fire. At least one of the missiles hit the tower but it was so close they still would have been knocked out of the sky. Turning for a second pass.

"Hawkfire One to Nest. That's a negative on the confirmation. Again, lots of debris. The ground is completely consumed in fire. If the wreckage is down there, I can't see it. Orders?"

The captain took the mike from an ensign. "One more pass, then back home, Hawkfire One."

"Roger that. Hawkfire One, out."

Can't confirm.

The doctor, the scientist, knew he was being silly. Foolish even. But he couldn't help it. The part of him that was just a man desperately clinging to hope, no matter how small.

Could this little group beat the odds? Again?

The captain looked up at the wall clock. "Noon. Even if they are alive, it's too late for the woman who didn't take her injection."

40 VASSA ISLAND

The sound was overwhelming.

The roar of the sea, and the rumble of the helicopter echoing through the hollow chamber. When the pressure wave pushed them over the side of the island, Dana had been certain they were going to hit the sea. But again

Justin had pulled them out. That was when they saw the mouth to the sea caves.

"Are those sharks?" Tucker asked, looking down at the splashing waves less than fifteen feet below them.

Though the cavern was massive, it seemed claustro-phobically small for the slashing blades of the helicopter. Entering, Dana had held her breath, bracing for the colli-sion of metal to stone. Now, as they hung hovering above the shark-filled waters, she unclenched her hands for the first time since they left the ground.

"How long can we stay like this?"

"We've got enough fuel for about twenty more min-utes," Justin said. "But we don't have that much time."

Dana rubbed the back of her neck with her hand. She remembered the cave as being cool, almost cold, but now it seemed stifling hot and getting hotter.

Tick, tick, tick.

She checked her watch: two minutes past twelve.

"Dana," Justin whispered. She read her name on his lips, the sound lost in the cacophony.

Tears filled his eyes.

Her skin began to burn. Right on time. Why couldn't she be late one more time?

"Yes, I know where the cure is," Harlan Krest had confirmed. "But you'll never find it."

Krest had jeered and the expression looked strange on a face so identical to Cory's. But then Cory was just as cruel. The sweet, shy person she had met was a fake, a fraud—worse—responsible for what was happening. No wonder he had escaped electrocution. It had all been part of the act. Everything he said and did was a lie.

The skin on her hand began to move.

"Dana," Justin said, his voice loud, fueled by panic.

She reached up to her shirt pocket and pulled out the pen, Cory's lucky pen, the one he said didn't work but he kept anyway. She had taken it from his body in the Round House.

"Safety pen," she said out loud.

"What?" Justin asked.

"That's what he called it. It was his little joke." She held out the pen, then winced in pain. The noise in the cave became part of a vast static blur that seemed to be covering the world, overwhelming her senses. She was burning from the inside out. She could barely move her fingers. She clicked the pen. Instead of a pen point, a half-inch needle protruded from the plastic.

U.S.S. *JOHN F. KENNEDY*

"Sir, we have visual confirmation on the helicopter," an ensign reported.

Captain Wesley Stroud stood with his hands behind his back. "That's it then. They're down. Let's step up the bombing and sterilize this piece of rock."

"Excuse me, sir. They—ah, they're still flying."

The captain and Lorrik exchanged a look of confusion. "Flying? How the hell? Where have they been?"

The ensign touched the earpiece of his headset, listening to another voice. "No word sir, it just sort of appeared."

Images of the legendary ghost ship, *The Flying Dutchman,* flashed through Lorrik's thoughts.

"Four people inside. All alive."

The captain checked the time: fifteen minutes after twelve. "Impossible."

"Incoming message, sir." The ensign put the message on speaker. A woman's voice filled the room.

"Hello? Hello? This is ah—Dana Kirsten. Calling the—ah—big ship." She paused. There was talking in the background. "I'm told it's the *Kennedy*?"

The captain took the mike. "This is Captain Wesley Stroud of the U.S.S. *John F. Kennedy.* What is your status?"

"Scared. Tired. But alive. And we're going to stay that way. We found the cure. For real this time."

41 JAMAICA
Naval Hospital—forty hours later

Dana shifted in her bed and thought of home and Jenna. For six days those had been forbidden topics. She had longed to go home, but she refused to allow herself to dwell on it.

Now just the freedom of thought was a wonderful thing.

She had talked to Jenna on the phone—although talk was a generous description—mostly they had cried and told each other how much they loved each other. Her parents had been much the same. Even her ever practical dad had cried with joy.

The pen had turned out to be a sophisticated device containing enough serum for three shots. Apparently after injecting themselves, Cory Nestor and Harlan Krest were going to be true to their word and cure the sole survivor. Greater still was the small slip of paper contained in the pen's lid giving the exact formula for the cure.

Vassa Island was ruined.

The sea cave had collapsed less than twelve minutes after they left it. While waiting for the cure to be verified by the CDC, they had been instructed to fly to the neighboring island of Navassa. Although similar to Vassa, it lacked fresh water, so the Navy had to drop several gallons of drinking water, along with rations and fresh radios.

From Navassa they were taken to a naval hospital and put in a quarantined ward. Even with the cure confirmed, the CDC still didn't want to take a chance. Dana could expect to stay for at least one more day.

Frustrating, but bearable.

"Hey, you!" Justin rolled into her room in his wheelchair. Tucker and Nerine followed him. They were grinning like five-year-olds on Christmas morning.

"What?" she asked. "What's happening? Are we going home? They letting us out early for good behavior?"

Their laughter was far heartier than the joke deserved, fueling Dana's suspicion. In the time they had been here, she had gotten closer to all three, but especially Justin. What they had found on the island had survived. Now she couldn't imagine a life without him.

"Have you heard the latest?" Justin asked. "They've found bones they think belonged to Harlan Krest, but we'll have to wait until everything is verified by dental records to know for sure."

"Okay," Dana said cautiously. "What else? Got to be more than that. You three are grinning like fools."

"Hey, I thought I was the investigative journalist," Tucker said. Nerine elbowed him.

Sparks between those two? Dana wondered.

"There *is* something else you may be interested in. The final vote came in while we were fighting for our lives. Since I was considered dead, that only left two people to vote on."

Dana said nothing.

"They voted to exile me," Nerine said, her smile paradoxically illuminating the room.

Dana was confused.

"You don't get it," Justin said. "She doesn't get it. Dana, you won the game."

"What? That's ah—okay, great." She shrugged, unclear what sort of response they were expecting. "Too bad the game was—"

"Canceled?" Justin finished. "No. It wasn't. The producers say that, despite the circumstances, we continued to play. And so the game continued. Besides, if they don't give you the prize, the public will lynch them."

"The prize?"

"Two million dollars and your heart's desire."

Dana was too stunned to react.

Her heart's desire! Jenna would be part of the test group in Switzerland. She had a chance to beat the insidious disease.

Tick, tick, tick . . . Immediately followed by silence.

Out of reflex, she looked at her watch. She began to laugh, her body shaking uncontrollably.

"Dana?" Justin asked with concern.

She tried to talk, tried to explain but laughter clogged her throat.

"She's delirious," Tucker said. "I'll get a nurse."

Dana shook her head and waved at him, trying to catch her breath. But she couldn't stop laughing.

Justin wheeled to her side. She motioned toward her wrist. The confusion on his face made her laugh even harder.

For the first time since Jenna was diagnosed, the clock that had been running in the back of Dana's mind was quiet. Someday, when she could speak again, she would explain the symbolism of the ticking clock. Then maybe Justin would understand why she was laughing.

She looked at her wrist again just to be sure.

It was true. Her watch had stopped.

24/7—FACT OR FICTION?
by
Jim Brown

Could something like the events depicted in 24/7 actually happen? Consider this:

> *Their kissing intensified. Was it the alcohol? Or maybe it was the naughty thrill of knowing they were being watched? Or maybe the eroticism of living in a house with hollow walls, with photographers and producers looking through two-way mirrors and cameras everywhere.*
>
> *The knife was on the counter.*
>
> *Passions grew like a storm-whipped tide. Each kiss hotter than the one before. Each touch more exciting.*
>
> *The knife was in his hand.*
>
> *Whatever the catalyst, emotions were rising. The mechanical whine of hidden technology sang a cicada chorus in the background.*
>
> *The knife was at her throat.*
>
> *He pressed the blade, pressing against her beautiful, flawless skin. His words were whispered but audible through the mandatory microphone he wore.*
>
> *"Would you get mad if I just killed you?"*

A missing scene from 24/7?
Nope. That bit of narrative is based on a real event

that occurred in the summer of 2001, several months *after* I wrote this book. The show was *Big Brother 2*, the network CBS, the contestant a twenty-six-year-old man who had passed all of the requisite psychological tests. He was subsequently kicked off the program. And the incident, although acknowledged, was never televised.

But had they been near one of the continuously *live* Internet cameras, you would have seen it all—even if the worst had occurred.

Could something like the events depicted in *24/7* actually happen?

According to many experts, it not only could happen but *will* happen. The growing number of programs and advances in technology all but guarantee it.

In many respects, the danger is the only real thing about reality TV. *Survivor* producer Mark Burnett says, without hesitation, that despite safety precautions, someone absolutely could die on his show.

And if it happens will you watch?

As a broadcast journalist, I've been exposed to the best and worst of humanity. More of the latter than the former, unfortunately. And I've become intrigued by psychological and sociological questions. It was three such questions that compelled me to write *24/7*.

First, as the situation on *Big Brother 2* proves, people are unpredictable, psychological tests unreliable, and background checks unbelievable. In the case of CBS, a background check failed to reveal that the contestant with the knife had been arrested five times for robbery and assault, the charges later dropped. So what happens when we mistakenly put a Ted Bundy or a Jeffrey Dahmer into a televised pressure cooker and say "Showtime!"?

Second, the fact that reality television will continue to become increasingly outrageous. It has to in order to stay viable. After all, how can producers shock an audience that's watched the World Trade Center crumble?

And third, the intriguing psychological and social implications of socialized voyeurism.

Take the moral dilemma in *24/7*.

Would you vote for someone to die on television? Of course not. But how about this: Would you vote for someone to die if it would save your mother? Or your brother? Or your third cousin on your father's side? How about your best friend from high school? Or that really cute coworker whose name you don't know but you pass in the hall every day?

Where's the line and when do you cross it?

Why are we so fascinated by reality TV? The truth is voyeurism is hard-wired into us. You learned to walk and talk, and many of your social skills, by watching others.

Reality TV is not a new phenomenon. It's been around for years with shows like *The Real World*, *America's Funniest Home Videos*, and *Cops*. It just didn't have a name until recently.

In 1973 PBS aired *An American Family*. For seven months cameras followed the day-to-day lives of the Loud family. No games, no voting, no million dollar prize. Just people, doing what people do. The result was a riveting documentary during which viewers saw a marriage dissolve and a son reveal his sexuality.

Some argue that reality TV actually started on radio with a program called *Candid Microphone*, which moved to TV in 1948 as *Candid Camera*.

And how about this for a reality show? Take two competing groups (sort of like tribes on *Survivor*), but instead of seeing who can eat the most disgusting thing or stand on a post the longest, we let them bash each other—really go at it. And we show the whole thing *live*.

When I made this pitch to a group of fellow journalists, they assured me such a program would never make it on network TV. I told them it already had. It's called *Monday Night Football*.

So if reality TV has been around for so long, what's the big deal?

The difference is technology.

When I starting working in broadcasting, I carried an RCA-TK 76 camera on one shoulder, a tape deck strapped to the other, powered by a three-inch wide, two-inch thick power belt, with a separate, larger belt for my light. In total, it was about seventy-five pounds of equipment.

Now cameras are small enough to take a tour of your intestinal tract.

But by far the greatest advancement (and danger) is the ability to go *live*.

In the fifties, going live from anywhere other than the studio was all but impossible. Now your local news team can go live from your living room within fifteen minutes of arriving. As an anchor and news director, I frequently took the entire five o'clock show on the road (news, sports, and weather), broadcasting the whole program from schools, festivals, the YMCA, even the cardiac wing of a local hospital. And that was with a microwave truck, which requires line of sight with the transmitter to work.

Satellites that bounce the signal off orbiting satellites allow you to broadcast live from almost anywhere in the world.

This makes news the ultimate reality show. Remember being glued to the screen, watching O. J. Simpson lead the LAPD on the world's slowest car chase? Would he kill himself or wouldn't he? Now that's reality TV.

When you watch *Survivor*, you see a program that has been shot and edited, so you see *only* what the producers want you to see.

But a live program means no censor.

Anything can happen—particularly if the program is designed to push the contestant's psychological and emotional buttons in search of their *fear factor*.

Television and computers have had a flirting relationship for years. But soon they will be married. Then along comes the Internet, making it a technological ménage à trois. Put a reality show on cable and you get nudity. Put it on the Internet with TV quality and you get—well, everything.

Even now efforts are underway to show criminal executions on the Web.

Could something like *24/7* really happen?

Television in general and cameras in particular have become such a part of our lives that they affect our language, shape our politics, and even dictate our schedules. (Just look at the empty streets on Super-Bowl Sunday.)

Early in my career I worked for News 24 in Macon, Georgia. To encourage people to remember the channel number, each newscast ended with random shots of real people in parks or schools or malls, smiling at the camera and displaying two fingers on one hand and four on the other—twenty-four. It was fun. Kids and adults alike seemed to love it. And even if you weren't in the video, you watched to see if someone you knew was.

Early one morning there was a particularly vicious murder in a quiet, residential neighborhood. A man coldly executed his in-laws, then sat on the curb to wait for the police. His eyes were distant and glassy with no apparent attachment to the real world. As he was being driven away in the back of a police car, he saw our camera. His face lit up. The glassy-eyed stare was replaced by an excited smile, and then, as if it were the most natural thing in the world, he held up his shackled hands and gave the camera a big *twenty-four*.

Cameras are everywhere.

You were on camera this morning when you went to the ATM, again when you stopped at the convenience store for a soda. There was a camera at the traffic light looking for speeders and another at work for security reasons. And let's not forget the satellites, those hurling hunks of metal that can read the brand name off running shoes, spot your dog digging up the flower bed, and even get a peek at that cute sun-bathing neighbor.

Our children grow up on camera, having their first *ta-da* moment as they slip out of the birth canal, then starring in secretive movies via the all-telling, always hidden nanny cam; all the highlights of their lives are video-taped for posterity.

Is there a camera on your computer? Is it on? How would you feel knowing that someone could turn it on from outside your house? They can.

And speaking of technology . . .

What if I told you that you were being watched right now, even as you read these words? That the moment you cracked the spine of this book you unknowingly released hundreds of thousands of nano-bots (microscopic machines) that entered your bloodstream through the pores in your hand. Even now those machines are transmitting data to orbiting satellites that feed it to a series of supercomputers, which, in turn, correlate everything—from your location and heart rate to the type of food you eat and the medicine you take. And what if some of those busy little nano-bots attached themselves to an optic nerve and began transmitting images?

Everything you see, they see; everything they see, I see. See?

Eerie, huh? Don't worry, the technology is not here—yet. But it will be, and sooner than you think.

Could something like *24/7* really happen? And if it does will you watch?

Perhaps the scarier question is the second one.

In my next novel, *The Hill*, I deal with a very different set of psychological questions. I hope you give it try.

Meanwhile, remember: nano-bots, supercomputers, and satellites. I'll be watching.

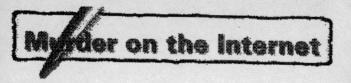